A Hypocritical Reader

Rosie Šnajdr

Dostoyevsky Wannabe Originals
An Imprint of Dostoyevsky Wannabe

First Published in 2018
by Dostoyevsky Wannabe Originals
All rights reserved
© Rosie Šnajdr

Dostoyevsky Wannabe Originals is an imprint of Dostoyevsky
Wannabe publishing.

This is a work of fiction The names, characters and incidents
portrayed in it are the work of the author's imagination. Any
resemblance to actual persons, living or dead, events or locatities is
entirely coincidental. Except for Christopher O'Rourke, though many
things that have been written about him are lies.

Cover Design by Victoria Brown
www.dostoyevskywannabe.com

ISBN-13: 978-1999924515
ISBN-10: 1999924517

Contents

A to B

I was in Tokyo and in Tokyo I would be staying. I will admit there had been some misaims. With eye screwed shut and arm correcting in shunts, by and by the card enters slot. The suck-in is slow, slow. I key in the coordinates and wait, a weight of skull propped up on greasy touch display. The machine initiates with a soothing purr. Lids flutter. Eyes roll back. Head lolls.

★★★

I wake to a solemn beep. The card slid back in disapproval. I snatch it with the teeth. In the green booth-light the saliva-arc is a lucent binary, bubbling with zeroes. Then fingertip finds crack that has formed beneath the lustrous rope of spit. Panic is exclamatory. I have no friend in Tokyo. It was that quality had impelled me. And so I find myself, adrift in an alien metropolis, six-thousand miles from the consolation of bed, somewhere on the long, long road back from drunk. I shriek then. Flail out fists at the flimsy walls.

The technological advancements that presaged the arrival of instantaneous geo-relocation spawned frenzy. Media commentators fell over themselves to get an original angle. Endless think-pieces predicted its effects: the end of the flight-age; the slow decline of geographical linguistic variation; global market equilibrium; the relaxing of state borders, accompanied by a reactionary wave of ultra-nationalistic terrorism; some ethical resistance, not to the molecular construction of the individual, but to the destruction of the atoms in the original copy.

It was the apocalyptic epidemic scenarios, or 'virus problem', that became humanity's new cold sweat. Even before the code was written, programmes of universal vaccination had been spit-balled, bankrolled and rolled-out. Legislators linked hands across datelines to insist that the machines must screen and destroy contraband—animal flesh, banned vegetable matter, weapons, drugs—and, inevitably, hot-wired machinery came to underpin a frenetic black-market. If your Italian sausage was cheap it was probably an illegal copy of an Italian sausage but there had, as yet, been no plague *sans frontier*. The pundits and politicians commended one another on their uncharacteristic percipience and a job well done. People, stupid as ever, did things like decide to spend their birthdays getting smashed in Tokyo, where there was no plan (b) if their ID cracked up in the middle of the night.

As my forehead reconnects with the illumined glass, I figure there is a chance it is a machine fault. As I consider reinsertion, I notice the lights blink. Not something they had done before. A cloud of precipitate grows and dwindles with my breath. Dimly lit beneath the fug, the words '*error... error... error...*' scroll to infinity. My sigh fogs the pane more extensively, wafting back a smell of disappointment and cheap whiskey. There were no two options. I must turn back into the dust-scented drizzle and find another pod. I get a hand around the bottle, which I unscrew and swig from, before swerving lidless into the moist Tokyo night.

***

On the walk, I set upon a plan to hack proceedings by entering the co-ordinates of a public booth in the locale of my domicile, these things putting down stronger routes, or whatever, than the cheap home-installed type. But the second machine had performed like the previous. Moreover, it had had an infelicitous urine tang that made it no place to bed down for the night. In the third pod I took a prayerful drink and tipped what was meant to be a little but turned out to be a shoe-full over the card. That's for good luck. The alcohol evaporates coolly, leaving behind an oily residue. My fingers leave greasy smears on the façade above the digitally rendered keypad. The wait is agonizing.

***

The card emerges defiant, a tongue lolling from the slot; beneath judgment is passed: '*or... error... error... error... error...*'. So, it's either I'm knocking out nodes one by one, or this whole coms-district is in nervous collapse. And there is nothing I can do but go on. For encouragement's sake, I call up the municipal network map, a constellation of improbable opportunities for redemption, as I spray my already sodden coat with an illegal copy of an expensive water retardant. I will work my way towards the Embassy building, testing the pods that I pass. It's a long walk with no metro.

★★★   ★★★   ★★★

There is a jolt when you 'arrive' that is inauspicious for the intoxicated. Space expands around with a pop. The promise of vomit tingles in my jaw, saliva accumulates but nothing untoward arises. As card slides out of the wall into my outstretched palm, a thin strip of plastic shears free. When I attempt to pick up the shard, I stumble face-first into the glass door and out into the lounge. The cat awakes to glower in disapproval from its perch on the shelf. Beneath, the couch exerts an irresistible gravitational pull. I launch myself across the corner of the coffee table and let slip the card from my grasp. It comes to nestle in the plush of the carpet. Relaxing into the comfort of domestic drunkenness, the environment undemanding enough to engender a dream of sobriety, I remember what I left behind in the pod. I also remember that I can't, this time, pop back and get it. I snarl. Then I scan through some holostreams. I picture myself on the couch, the reconfiguring shapes flickering over the restless surface of my eyeballs as lids droop, droop. I click off a holostream of Boris Karloff and fantasise about a late night snack. Then I am at rest.

I jackknife.
Having cushioned its descent from the shelf, the cat skitters off down the hall and out of the cat-flap. My viciously pumping heart begins a climb-down, gradually deescalating from threat level: imminent death. Then I feel sleep try to reclaim me, so I turn, get comfortable and let it.

As I pad towards my front door I cradle a lettuce-shedding kebab violin-like, against my clavicle. A pat down of major pockets reveals no keys. I hum a recent blues-style invention about a kebab shop man who took away my whiskey, after I let it go over the floor. I am startled by a skittling blur that I decipher as a high-speed version of exit the cat. The start initiates a series of movements that feel balletic but force me to prioritise the upright position of the kebab over my own. Leaning back against the door, I abandon my key hunt and begin to eat.

I am asleep on the couch. It takes a moment. I look down at my out-splayed fingers that have just let slip the pod door behind. I look down at the bottle falling from my noose of digits. My body convulses as a streak of cat flies past. And it isn't so much that I kneel down, but find that I am kneeling. Trouser leg takes up a little of the spilt booze. The body on the couch snorts, shuffles onto its side and emits a reedy fart.

That body is mine.

I think I might be dying.

Perhaps this is what is feels like to be the other one; the one who doesn't come back. Then I see the broken card on the carpet, next to the broken card on the carpet and it all becomes brutally clear.

—Wake up. I say it too quietly, like I'm saying it to myself.

—Wake up! The body scrambles. Its dribble-flecked face collapses into a mask of horror that I cannot help but reflect. It catches on.

'Oh fuck. Oh fuck. Oh fuck.'

It is when we hear the knock at the door that we are joined in purpose. We'd heard about what they do, the authorities, when this happens. One of us will be deleted; whichever one presents the clearest shot. My self-protective urge does not extend to my sleep-addled twin and I don't like my odds, so I do what I have to do. I go to the kitchen and grab a knife. Then, between me and the body on the couch, the front door bangs open and in we walk.

It sees the knife, for sure. But the knife is probably the least shocking thing about the situation. It has recently fed itself—a halo of orange surrounds its mouth—and the contentment appears to have made it sedate.

"Uh, hey." Closing the door slowly behind it. "We can work this out? You don't need to do anything with, with that."

It puts its hands up slowly and begins to walk towards me with what is probably murderous intent. As I'm thinking this, it makes a sudden lunge for the knife. I'm too slow to react but mid-lunge it makes a sort of crunching noise. Mouth falls open, eyes roll back and it falls to the floor. The other one is standing behind it with the heavy-based lamp raised over its shoulder. The lamp, I notice, remains lit. Some hair and flesh adhere to the brass. After a moment, it begins to spit disjointed plosives towards the pooling mess of blood. It's clearly in shock. I guess I'm in shock too. We find our knees on either side of the felled body, our improvised weapons clutched in our hands. We begin to blubber to ourselves.

Then a trademarked popping sound rebounds about the lounge and our eyes lock in wild, wet-eyed terror. The other one leaps up and scampers down the hall. After a few feet the leash of electrical cord finds its limit and, as it pauses to wrap its free hand in the wire and yank it free from the socket, I clap a brotherly hand upon its shoulder and bury the knife deep in its back. The noise is inhuman. It thrashes. I buck upon the blade's handle, whereupon the fatal damage is done. It falls forwards into the lounge. A lively arc of brilliant blood links me for a second to the simulacrum before it settles like crude graffiti over the carpet and walls. There is a fine mist over my face, over the small teeth in my mouth's rictus. This is the first thing that the third copy sees as it blinks open drunken eyes. It shrieks—as well it might—and, as there is no handle on the inside of the glass door, cowers to wrap its fingers protectively under the bottom edge. I try to clear the blood that has settled on the surface of my eyeball as I stalk towards the pod.

The fingernails are bitten like mine. Desperate grip whitens them against the glass. Both eyes screwed tight. Breath unearthly with panic. It vomits a little down itself as I scrape the rubber sole of my shoe down the glass, peeling off the fingers of one hand and pinning them to the floor. 'Please. Please.' It pleads for my life. With more difficulty I squeak my other foot down, my toe leaving a streak of gore on the glass. When I am standing on most of the fingers, I find I am too close to open the door but when I step back it just reasserts its hold. We do this dance twice then I decide to smash the glass. Nothing will come of torturing it. I get it over quickly: a mineral sample from the sideboard and a knife in the neck. Glass and blood everywhere. I drag the inert glitch out by the collar and stare into the booth wondering if more will arrive, wondering whether they will keep arriving, wondering at the nature of the problem I am faced with. I rub my chin and stand back, tripping a little on a corpse, and then grim inspiration strikes. I carefully pick up a large shard of glass and wave it in the apparition space. By easing it behind the wires of the guitar I am able to improvise hands-free suspension. I feel an unexpected surge of satisfaction and then I begin to cry.

I step in turn over the bodies and wash my arms and face in the kitchen sink. I drink two glasses of water and resign myself to picking a trail back into the lounge. The cat glares defiantly from the doormat then stoops again to lap at a pool of blood. As I lean over it to secure the locks on the door, I notice my shoes squelch with unthinkable fluids. I examine the feet of my vanquished foe to find a replacement, eventually easing the cleanest copy of my trainers from the one who fell under the lamp, somehow relieved to be taking them from a corpse that isn't one of mine.

Pop. The agonized howl that follows. The cat and I share a moment: my human eyes meeting the limpid eternity of its alert pupils. Then there's just a space where the cat was. A pet door swinging wildly. A ripple settling in the blood. With a hoarse moan, a new me walks stiffly into the frame of the hallway as a silhouette of Frankenstein's monster. The guitar neck protruding out of the torso scrapes along the wall, ringing inharmonic chords. Its mouth hole burbles up a bouquet of crimson foam. It dies on its feet, propped up on an unholy tripod of buckled legs and instrument. Then the guitar frame shudders, shrieks, and explodes into shards. It's dramatic, even after the previous scenes. I resolve two things. To creep around the body, fearing that this style of demise bodes a reanimation sequence, but mainly to find a more humane way to deal with further ghosts in the machine. And that is how I find myself sitting nervously on the edge sofa, a sharpened mop handle laid across my knees, waiting for the next apparition.

I don't know how long I've been waiting, but the sky is softening towards dawn. Sleep surprised me, overpowering the vigilance of a mortal soul readied in ambush. When I wake, I am alone. The blood has dried on the outer layers of my garments, but is still sticky where it has soaked beneath. Tired as I am, I consider cleaning the flat. I will have lugged a steaming bucket full of watered-down bleach to the middle of the floor and begun pulling a stiffening body towards the pod when it goes 'pop'.

★★★

I can barely find it in myself to tachycardia. I let go of the corpse's armpits but it stays put, as if poised mid-picnic. A foot treads cautiously out of the pod, crunching into the glass. Dead-looking eyes, wreathed in sleeplessness, take in the scene. It doesn't scream. It is surprised though, I'll bet.

'My, oh my.'

—A little help? We look at the dead. Beneath the pale face of sit-up-and-beg a gash yawns. Its coat and hair stippled with diamanté chips of glass. Then we look at the sharpened handle that has been re-screwed into the mop head. I slowly push the bucket away with my foot. Clear my throat.

—A little help? We take an armpit each and heft the dead weight into the pod. We ascertain that neither of us has a working card, but my exhausted-looking companion produces a temporary Embassy pass. We mash the key-pad and the dead meat evaporates into thin air. The memory of it doesn't.

We don't say much as we heave the other bodies one by one into the booth. It wretches as we roll over Frankenstein and eyes me reproachfully? Warily? I can't tell. When the bodies have gone it's apparent that there is still a lot of work to be done and, with it, some sharing. I try not to think about what will happen after that.

'What happened here?'

—What happened there? I am swishing a cloth in the pinking bucket of bleach between us. The blood is coming off the wall better that I had hoped.

'My card broke in Tokyo.'

—I know that. I mean, we were both… It isn't a sentence I consider ending.

'Then you know we tried it in a few pods as we made our way

towards the Embassy.'

—No. I don't think I know we went to the Embassy. I might have been here already. I don't know. I was drunk. Look, how many times did you try the card?

'I was drunk.'

—We need to know if I got them all. The son of a bitch actually winces. It could have been the murder, sure, but I think it was the plural. It drops a gory rag into the steaming slop and leans back on its haunches, tired of me.

'I tried here. I tried the public pod on the street. I tried here a couple of times more. Then I sent one to' it pauses, only to continue a half-octave lower 'our mother's.'

And then there were three. And that changed everything.

It was mid-morning by the time the flat was clean—glass swept up, blood shampooed out of the carpet, a new door delivered PodEx Express and fixed into the hinges. Then we were sat on the couch, neither of us fresh-looking, cradling steaming mugs of tea that we had been cautious enough to make for ourselves. It had its knees pulled up under its chin. There was a hole in the toe of its sock where there was not one in mine. We had come to what was the only sane conclusion: that neither of us could live. An hour or so later it's sat in the booth with a knife and I think I should give it a little privacy so I go into the kitchen and wait. I give it a good ten minutes but when I go back it's just sat there weeping. The knife balanced carefully atop its knees, catching its reflection and occasional tears. It's selfish, what it's doing, but I think I know how it feels. I pad over, watching the thin material on my sock-toe break and fray. When I take the knife it looks up. It looks broken-up: broken by Tokyo travail; broken by sleeplessness; broken by the god-awful scene it came home to; broken by the sight of me taking up the knife and plunging into its heart. And I know how it feels. I know just how it feels.

And so I find myself standing on the edge of the bridge. A chill wind blows. I drop my coat to feel it against my skin for a glorious moment: a sharp pain of air. I take a deep breath and leap clear of the vertiginous ledge destined for the cold, cold waters beyond.

***

Choose Your Own Adventure Story

Once upon a time there was a reader. Yes, the reader is you. Notwithstanding fact, the resourceful reader is invited to create a consciousness—a medium to percolate their interpretations through. Quick, dead, fabricated, intimate, animated, infamous, automated, any woman, everyman, animal, mineral, or conceptual elasmobranchii. If you have a hirsute father, you could imagine that he is telling you a bedtime story about a cow. Studies have shown that those electing to assume this perceptual frame perceive themselves to have higher than average cultural capital but are prone to bedwetting.

You could imagine that your friend is reading to you aloud in a public house and, they don't have to be, but they could be, a transformable robot. You might imagine that the writer is telling you the story but, unless you are an intimate acquaintance of said writer, this is unlikely to be a productive model. You may want to consider the possibility of imagining the reader is historical or fictional: Christabel Pankhurst, say, or Spiderman. Or else you could plunder the rich seam of crossover personalities, from Jesus Christ to Robin Hood. Maybe it is your beloved domestic pet doing the reading and only you understand, understand?

Just be aware, your mediator will be required to make a number of decisions on your behalf, so you would do well to make a careful selection. Cats are liable to prioritise intrigue over caution, dogs don't like making decisions and the tortoise is known for taking its sweet, sweet time (certainly, reports of its performance over distance have been greatly exaggerated). Lastly, unless you are a person of mystery with the ability to transverse the skyscape of urban Americana at preternatural speed, you may do well to ask yourself: can I even keep up with Spiderman? Whichever direction you come at it from, the time has come to make up your mind.

Once upon a time there was a reader and the reader was required to make a number of decisions. The decisions perform a diagnosis: "taste classifies and it classifies the classifier." I'm sorry, but that's just how it works with cultural consumption. Jesus, by now, you probably wish you had just been yourself.

If you are embarrassed by a choice of pages to turn to, stop reading. Try the radio? If the radio is something to do with the church, turn to page 102.

If you are Spiderman turn to page 76 you shameless prick.

If you are not embarrassed by a choice of pages to turn to—welcome, bold adventurer—and turn to page 31.

The Interrupted Human Remains Mr Christopher O'Rourke

It is with some pleasure that I introduce to the assembled Mr Christopher O'Rourke. Good morning, afternoon, or evening Christopher. Mr O'Rourke is twenty-six years old, having been born north of London slightly longer than twenty-five years ago. I need not mention that his speaking voice has retained little of the accent of his youth and is now a soft, low-pitched Received Pronunciation. It may please the assembled to know a little about our reader. He enjoys films, acting, and the lulling aural wash of alliterative word construction. He is a graduate of a prestigious University and is, as such, in possession of a first class degree. Mr. O'Rourke has kindly acquiesced to read for us today, as well as at any time he may do so in the future, or has done in the past. It is therefore proper and just, without deference to a particular gender polemic, that further references to the reader should prefer the pronoun 'he.' That is: he has finished reading the first paragraph and is about to commence with the second.

These buildings are glazed with sunlight. Good. The convoluted phrases of architecture cloy. Where awe once stood, crumbling ivy-smocked balustrades tear the landscape. Only the rents are real. He hesitates here, at the author's favour for consonance, and worries that such a preference for the lyrical surface of the language may prevent him from emotionally engaging with the narrative. Thomas' eyeballs roll floorwards.

— He said he liked alliteration. I had hoped this would imply a general affection for the textual surface. It was one of the reasons I asked him.

A toe has broken free from sock and the unvarnished nail blinks in the sun. The cracks between the slabs beckon. Down along the side-stacked roads the vapid horizon is a watercolour. The flat land meets the bland sky in graphic perspective. Precise lines blind like children with sticks and Tom, the sick stray dog, too weak even to whimper. He had seen them do that. The low letter slot of his father's shop permitted a silent vigil of the local children at play. His father did not. His father said to get up.

—Go play, Thomas. The plaintive utterance revealing the speaker's misconceptions about the activity urged. The command had come to signify the adult's desire for a situation wherein the child is absent, but not necessarily gaily occupied. Indeed, mere months later it was made explicit that the child should be anything other than gaily occupied during these times; a commandment that relied upon another familial semantic shift. The clammy bedspread has a red floral print. Through his fluttering eyelashes the flowers became spatters of dog's blood. Thomas whimpered. The cracks between the slabs beckoned. He equates these cracks with the paragraph breaks he teeters above. If one were to crawl into them, would one be in the story or outside the story? He wonders. Only the rents are real. Perhaps, on the first reading, he touches one and laughs. It's hard to tell.

Thomas is a hall of mirrors. Thomas is a writer of transparently autobiographical fiction. Christopher is a reader of a reader of a reader. Thomas is in love with Christopher. Don't blush Mr O'Rourke, it is too late for that. You are already implicated. It's in the fine print. A kerb survey of the road offers the mirage image of a car. He stutters on it, mispronouncing the latter in the mouth-shapes of the former. His blush blooms. It is not a palindrome but he likes it, as Thomas knew he would. His muse. His reading public: his public reading. It burns in the light between the shivers of the leaves' dappling shadows. Black and shearing white, like an old film, beloved of them both. In it, his toe is progressing towards the tarmac. Sinews whipping the hollow bones forward. Of course, living bones are full of blood and so he presumes that the prose is insinuating, in some way, that Thomas is moribund, deathly, or already dead. Predictably, Thomas the spinning top is spilling into the road. It will probably be too late for the driver to stop. Brakes squeal. The car sound roars in Thomas' skull before any nerves speak. The street swoops, he comes to rest, as a leaf in early autumn, upon the asphalt. There is no pain. No shock. There is silence. Then a sudden horn blares. Tom let his lids slide shut. The membranous awnings offer no respite from the noon sun. Cocooned in glistering pink where motes swim. A scuffle registers like a report of conflict in a distant land. It is sad to think of, but insubstantial.

—You fucking little sod. The distant voice is muted. The anger is parodic, perhaps of a Dickensian villain's vituperative rasp. He thinks he finds this self-consciously inter-textual reference excessive. Of course, it is just clumsy and forced. Thomas never said he was a good writer of transparently autobiographical fiction. What writer of transparently autobiographical fiction is? I can think of two. Shut Up! Okay, okay.

Thomas is a gingerbread man crossing the Lethe on fox-back. The stream of unconsciousness deepens and Thomas inches closer to savage-toothed snout. A crafty style threatens to gobble him up. Shifting shoe soles whisper on the softening tarmac. The bitumen is warmer than a longed-for embrace. Some seconds pass. His eyelids flutter. He thinks of the flies that laid their eggs in the pink sores of the dead dog. Alone, his stick had probed the corpse for science. Uncovered plump maggots under the matted flesh folds. His stick had tested the durability of the composting flesh each day, his bold work amply fulfilling the requirements of play. The furtive experiments ended suddenly when, with really very little pressure, his stick punched through into the abdomen and released a hellish stench. He had run home retching and clutching his purply stick, flinging the evidence behind the privet hedge. He sunk to his knees and was sick over his father's vegetable patch. An investigative toe in his back. His lament is a low groan, and with a shudder, he lies back. Dreams of him.

Yes he who is forefront in his mind in every sleeping moment has let him lie on his tongue and though a wholly unsuitable muse to live on through him is reason enough for him to offer his frame to the mastication of traffic yes?

—Are you, … are you…? The text indicates a [long pause] in editorial parenthesis. He puzzles at the length of long. Questions his conception of the passing of time. His heart rate is apt to make him hurry. Will he never get it right? His considerations and the interlude resulting from his conclusion make the pause uncomfortably long. There is some foot shuffling in the cheap seats.

—Look, get up. Get up! He is manhandled. His torso twisted up off the road by his shirt. His limbs hang loosely, his head lolls like a puppet unstrung. Thomas the rag-doll. The driver drops him, heavily. Shouts echo in the distance. A car starts, reverses in shunts to circumnavigate Thomas' prone figure.

—I didn't do it. I didn't hit him. The driver shouts through the window over his shoulder to the footfalls smacking the street in hot pursuit. He is sceptical. You said it. We're all sceptical, Christopher. We know what we heard.

The part wherein Mr. O'Rourke has a drink of water too close to the microphone when his gullet gulps the last. The assembled look to their laps. Thomas groans. The assembled are a silhouette against the sun and plunge Thomas into darkness. One is medical to an undisclosed degree and, feeling his panting breath on her cheek, searches for the carotid pulse. He appears to be alive but may, upon examination, be broken into two thousand, nine hundred and three bits. Assesses consciousness. The situation is grave.

—The patient is fictional and, as such, unconscious

The assembled gasp. Thomas opens one eye. Glowers. Opens his mouth.

—I am not. I am an autobiographical fiction. At my historical inception was my consciousness and he was conscious of all that befell me at this moment, if it happened, and… I don't need to explain myself to you. You never existed. I can make you into anyone. I remember you, Stetson. We became friends. Thomas sniggers. Well I never! And they never did.

The medical accepts Thomas' second opinion on account of the nauseating déjà vu that at once grips the assembled. Christopher admits that this could be a second reading, a third, he just doesn't know. That was in the contract. The medical insists Thomas be still at once. The medical insists Thomas be still at twice. Remaining still is easy for Thomas. It is his aim. The hubbub is at once lost amongst the clamour of his brain, however fictional. As the assembled babble, Christopher presses his right ear—which can be either—to the skull. Christopher hears all. As ambassador of Thomas, we ask him to narrate. He gurns. He gulps.

Thomas is thinking that... We did not say dictate. Show a little flair. A popular artist has devoted much of his recent career to constructing bronze simulacra of himself and placing them strategically across the island. They glower at London from rooftops, line the beaches, and in winged form tower over the unruly north. These simulacra have clockwork gizzards. As my ear pressed to his skull, an ear to any figure announces the countdown to the coming apocalypse. An avant-grrrrrr. Iron men all, these robots, in time, will clatter to salute and tear their heavy feet from masonry to do his bidding. To take London, Gateshead, Birmingham, and Crosby Beach for art. But Christopher is a slow compositor and Thomas' mind sharp.

In this digital age academics at a prestigious University make a socialistic pact and relinquish their intellectual property. Their web-of-minds converge in ultimate hypertext. Press a reference, receive full text, link to above, until: in glorious, vainglorious palimpsest the world-equation is unearthed. His dangling ankle, recently having become entwined with the microphone wire, pulls his own plug. He continues unabashed. Thomas sits up, spot-lit. Less Bottom, more ass. He hadn't planned on this song and dance.

—STOP! He is not miming. This is not performance art. Pssst, it's the hanging wire—there! With a squeal Christopher is brought to life. In unholy accord Thomas regains unconsciousness and Christopher stoops once more to listen.

Ubiquitous commercialism becomes the new religion. Read All About It. Forget Newspeak, doublethink, any manner of arduous reprogramming. In this pinnacle year of the digital age—an undisclosed year in the not too distant future— loosening morals and tongues can be pinned with the most unexceptional of devices. Introducing the government-issue spell-checking software that will revolutionise the world. Of course certain compromises needed to be made to secure the necessary sponsorship for design, development, deliverance. But, hey, just take a look at the transformation! If it pleases, an autoerotic reverie to demonstrate. Thomas strokes his expanding purple Coke. How it had responded to Christopher's first hesitant acknowledgements. Christopher's fingers are awkward as he attempts hurriedly to unbutton Thomas' shirt and reveal inch after inch of perspiring Flash Bathroom Cleaner. His fingers stroking his responsive Visit Naples! He looks so beautiful with his clothes open revealing his nubile young body. He can't hold it; it is too much. Glaxowellcomes over his own rippling Chess – the musical!

Christopher totters back. Thomas, having anticipated the possibility of some discomfort on the part of the reader, had assiduously typed and then cut his rebuff. Some profane exclamations gather notional dust on a notional clip-board on a lap-top, since lost.

Act II, Scene V

It is a temperate evening in late August. The pair sit in a pub garden, surrounded by empty glasses and a miasma of cigarette smoke. It is clear they have been there for some time.

THE VOICE OF CONCERN   Precisely: I've no idea.
CHRIS O'ROURKE   It leaves off with Christopher feeling violated by Thomas' thoughts…
THE VOICE OF CONCERN   …so, if the reader is annoyed with the writer he would probably stop reading. Wouldn't he?
CHRIS O'ROURKE   I would.

The pair take considerable draughts. Chris taps his cigarette against the ashtray.

CHRIS O'ROURKE (*sotto voce*)   He could lie down?

Their eyes meet for a second. An expectant hush descends upon the beer garden.

THE VOICE OF CONCERN   That's it! That's perfect. He could just lie down. Thomas will be furious! Perhaps it is The Voice of Concern who tells him to do it.

CHRIS O'ROURKE   I think Christopher would probably think of it on his own.

THE VOICE OF CONCERN   No. It is just the kind of thing that The Voice of Concern would come up with. It would be all like: "That Thomas is a hell of a piece of work. I wouldn't take that standing up." It's perfect. He will just lie down.

Taps cigarette on the ashtray triumphantly. Has a draft. A Spotlight picks out Thomas in the corner the beer garden, with his hand clasped about his right ear. He clutches a notebook. He looks angry.

That Thomas is a hell of a piece of work. I wouldn't take that standing up. Ashen faced, Christopher lay down. ~~Christopher got up.~~ The sun sets abruptly, as a ground level window blind slides down. Ah, if I'm not mistaken that window is Christopher's. A bin across the street begins to whirr, slewing light across the street. Thomas is revealed by the beam, represented by chalk outline. A Bony arm snakes from the left aperture of the bin and disappears into the front. The light focuses, over-focuses, focuses.

THE NIGHT CAME ON AS THOMAS'S BODY LAY ABANDONED ON THE TARMAC. AN UNSEEN NIGHTINGALE BEGINS A LAMENTFUL NOCTURNE. HEADLIGHTS CURVE AROUND THE CORNER AT THE TOP OF THE STREET AND A CAR APPROACHES FAST.

The acetate is replaced by another. Upside down. The bin swears. The words are righted.

IT SKIDS. STOPS BARE INCHES FROM THOMAS' PRONE OUTLINE. IT INDICATES AND MAKES AN ILLEGAL TURN INTO THE ADJACENT ONE WAY STREET. THOMAS IS COLD, SO COLD. PERHAPS HE IS ACTUTALLY DYING.

~~Christopher is overcome with guilt and slowly rises from the stage.~~
Christopher is smoking supine. He is humming the nocturne between puffs. He looks jolly. Thomas doesn't.

[Time passes.[†]]

—Before we recommence, I shall admit that a reasonable amount of money has now changed hands. At one point Thomas was crying. The voice of concern was not overly concerned; Thomas cries a lot. —

The sun rose over the cold form. Heroic cheekbones glistered in the growing light. He had died for love, he had died for art, he had died for the art of love and for his love of art. *O pai Dios!* Truly we are lamentable. The silence and the morn's mist are indivisible. Their aesthetic use is one. A single drop of dew has amassed in the hollow between wasted youth's nose and eye. No charnel house had he to keep his bones warm. No trail of mourners wailing. No casket. No shroud.
—Nothing in *The Times.* Shut Up! Shut Up! Shut Up!
   The corpse is off-mark. His new position makes the chalk line an echo. In the new composition, he appears to dangle from the interrupted white line. Thomas is a puppet on a string. This card is the hanged man. Fear death by author.
   It is around eight o'clock. A latch rattles behind a door across the road, betraying a brain, still befuddled with sleep, seeking egress. A yawn. Then the happy slapping of Converse on stone steps. The footfall takes pavement, drawing closer. A smoke signal—the comforting smell of their shared brand. The footfall has stopped. Something is occurring.
—Oh my fucking God. What the…
   Here comes the end. Shut Up! Running.
—Thomas. Shit.
   Shit.

---

† *No major characters were harmed in the making of this editorial parenthesis.*

His beautiful hands grasp the cold body. The backs of his knuckles flutter inches from his cheek.

—O, Thomas.

It's hard to tell how long exactly before it happens, but Christopher notices a manuscript pinned to the dear dead boy's chest. A few pages of a bold type. Their detachment is painstaking. Hands are shaking.

I told you I love you. I told you I love you. I told you I love you.

I could go on. Thomas did.

The pages whisper to the ground. There is a moment of still silence. Clenching his eyes against the spectacle, Christopher slowly heaves the ashen remains of Thomas into the cradle of his lap. The dew-drop slithers down Thomas' wan chin, cleaving a pink trench in his make-up.

—O, Thomas. What have you done? What have you done? O, Thomas.

His eyes slide open.

—A-and, I told you you loved me too, a-and I think you'll find this proves it.

[long pause]

—Unequivocally.

Without opening his eyes, Christopher gathers the pages from the road. Released, Thomas slides prone. The manuscript becomes a weapon. The blows it delivers decompose it. Thomas has wrapped his arms about his eyes. He's protesting. Christopher is swearing. Thomas gets up. Christopher is leaving. Thomas watches Christopher leave. Reaches into his pocket and taps out a cigarette. Lights it, as he turns and walks. Hollers over his shoulder.

—Hey! … Hey! The dog, yeah, he really was dead. Honest.

leans down to wipe the toe-cap of his old-school high-top trainers. Pulls golf sock to full tension on downy calf & smears other below ankle

His legs, so attired, embody nonchalance. Scans across a paragraph of popular book. Words, yeah? —the book is a talisman. It's shit really.

It fits, just so, into the back pocket of his summer shorts. The cover faces inwards, to illustrate his insouciance about its display there.

He flexes the spine and yawns loudly, glancing out across the quadrangle. Cliques mingle. Rests novel on knee and opens new leather satchel.

Last night in the yard, he had removed it from the plastic. He checked the overlooking windows for lights. They were all out drinking, yeah?

Holding it by the strap, he had thrashed it soundly against the concrete steps. So now, it exudes that functional #thriftshopvintagechicshit

It contains a half-pint of full-fat milk. This he unscrews and swigs from. Most people never drink milk in public #Fauxletariat #DrinkinMilk

Milk flecks the shoulder of his artfully dishevelled high-street chain-store uniform. Its out-size is a happy accident of charity shop rail.

Shoulder milk is the perfect expression of indifference to the public gaze. After checking that nobody's looking, he slops a little more on.

For Bolshevik-chic, students may prefer to roll their own? Is the wrong answer, chum. The answer is a pipe, which a philosopher might smoke.

This is the answer because nobody who reads this book could be a philosopher. He checks his socks positions, but they're still wrong, right?

Milk dries scratchy on polyester. He chews pipe, imaging the smell of the exotic tobacco at home in the dustbin. He'd been sick in the sink.

If you want to tell everyone that delusions of exceptionality are unavoidable go to p. 60

If you want to tell everyone that you don't think you're exceptional, it's 94.

Möbius Strip

5

Everything ends. You draw on a cigarette and shorten it. You hear the compact disc die and fold me closer, peppering the sheets with ash: the seasoning of our season. For years we smoked hungrily, burning much in common until life became as yellow as our frequent pubs. Earth-moving coughs testify that we would have killed each other eventually. Maybe. Now, in the frame of the open window, wine dark clouds wrack the horizon. I watch the sky haemorrhage into darkness. Above us, the coils of smoke unfurl.

Tomorrow is raining. Too much is broken without the additional sacrifices of an omelette, so we will go out for breakfast.

—Will we go out for breakfast? I have to ask.

Bathroom, formerly a temple of gratuitous intimacy, is awkward for two. I retire to the kitchen and sieve the debris for a thinning packet of cigarettes. I open the back door to the gin-clear rain. I am unwashed and in clothes from the floor. I feel like I'm sickening. Then you, blushing with shower-heat, appear to make a cigarette sparkle.

—Let's.

We have dressed like angels of conscience, in black clothes and in white. On the front doorstep, we conspire a dialogue with the rain. It whips me and whispers around you. You hum you are in sudden lip-sync with the downpour. It is only after we are steaming up the windows of the café that the rain shudders to a stop outside. It's like this: home is in bits, the bits are in boxes, the boxes are named and independently directed. It's nobody's birthday.

—It was nice, you will say slowly, to have a last night. Not to forget how good it was is important to me. I don't offer any words back. I alternate final glances of your face with the tabletop, trying to avoid the kind of stare that could be misinterpreted as recriminating. As the coffee cools, sip will follow sip, until your empty cup rests in the orbit of its debut stain. The chair opposite is stark with your loss.

4

"It was nice"—I hesitate in pursuit of equanimous phrasing—"to have a last night." You give me your hallmark statuesque glaze. In the excruciating minutes that follow, your eyes follow my mug from table to mouth until it becomes like a game to me. Like those last brave hours, your purpose is concentrated in my movements. There are several moments of imminent dialogue, first personal pronouns strangled at articulation, but in the end there are no new ways to skin this cat. I rise wordlessly from my chair. You give my empty coffee cup your full attention. You don't see my wave retract into the safety of a fist.

Outside, the fluorescent fuzz of the café signage is muted by the growing light of a brightening day. Sterile with cloud the sky is without comment. Something has dissolved like a vapour trail, like skywriting. No longer will I be sorry to love you.

At the house, my key unlocks the latch of our old door. The hall is catacomb for bric-a-brac. I walk between the boxes, looking down. My outdoor shoes treading grime into the pile.

3

One child is whooping round the roundabout, dragging the squeaking cage of metal behind it. Another child is squealing and trying to get off. Zipped up in my jacket, I begin to walk the path around the park. Killing time until I collect my boxes: singularity, gift-wrapped and autographed. Marker-pens that smelt sharp as glass. London breathes traffic as I twist a ring on my finger until it is warm. It will be embarrassing for both of us when we meet by accident years later and I am still wearing it.

A walk in the park was a Sunday ritual. It is Sunday and I am just here. The children have finished their game. They kick through leaves as they cross the park, leaving the playground I now draw level with empty. In a daring hiatus in my circuit, I will stop here. A headache will not forget me. Lying back on the roundabout I look at the blank, irresponsible skies. Whiteness stuns me. This gasping expanse maps out London, widening like something sticky spilt in my mind. Blocks of houses construct themselves at preternatural speed, like weeds growing under the watchful eye of a stuttering time-release shutter. London becomes England, becomes Europe, becomes a shrinking globe and I am falling and falling away from it with increasing speed, closing my eyes to infinite possibility and the distances I am liable to fall back to earth. The thud I hear is just my crescendoing heart. My feet, hanging off the edge of the damp merry-go-round, scrape against the earth and I murmur your name in thanks.

2

The first box is a box of feathers. I hitch it certainly, like a familiar child, into my arms. It is a nothing walk to the door with this, the closest box. Latched, the lid of our former lives offers little resistance. My car awakens me with a forgotten alarm yowling. The neighbour's curtains twitch. I try to look penitent as I banish the suburban keening. I place the box atop the levelled back seats and return to the hall of the dead. The second box is a box of rice. Others follow like eager rats, effortless but evil smelling. The ninth box is a box of anvils. In the walk from the far end of the hall I am forced to rest twice. Pavement to car pulls a muscle in my back. It is nothing, though, compared to the last. The tenth box is a box of dark matter. It has to be dragged out of the orbit of the house. It is so heavy that, upon its removal, the house bobs a full foot upwards. It flattens the back tyres of my car into the tarmac.

I don't know why I return to the house. Your boxes leer and trip. A final survey of the rooms is kaleidoscopic. The days are plaster slapped upon the walls. They threaten. They proffer doubts. I hack up something nasty. I crush my cigarette into the wall: an exclamation point curling on impact. I feel dizzy. I close the front door behind me and lean back against it. Once, I pressed you against the inside of this door and the post arrived. We rolled around the floor, laughing and laughing.

1

It is o so dark in this black street. The lamps leading away from the junction attract wildlife: children with old eyes and hands thrust deeply into the pockets of their hoodies. They appear to mutter. I can hear my footfalls echo around their whispers. A distant siren warps a curve of audibility. Further down the street it will re-emerge, louder and longer: a patrol car looking for trouble. Our house, when the corner I turn reveals it, is black in every window. My key in the lock opens a cavernous mouth. Heavy and hungry it slaps behind me. I flick the lights and perch on a box looking at the floor meeting the wall opposite. They will never know the one without the other. A floor is not a floor anymore without wall. It is just ground.

A van growls to a halt outside. The siren wraps past and disappears. I heft up two small boxes and clamber out, tipping my head to the driver who disappears into the hallway for more of all my baggage. It's just a building when my stuff is gone and every room reeks of impersonality, so my attempts to say goodbye are abandoned. No more is this wall and this floor a home, no more. I ask if the driver will take me to the address of a friend who is putting me up. Wendy will crack a consolatory bottle and attempt to throttle the melancholies out of me. Wendy puts a record on. Wendy makes coffee. Wendy yawns precociously at ten-thirty and silently remembers that I am bad company. I light up the last in the packet at twelve o'clock, long since alone. I climb up other stairs, pausing in contemplation of the punishment that lies in wait between the fresh guest sheets, in the lilac room. Accepting. Accepting and burning. Shot through with fever. It's o so dark.

1

I search for a space. Manoeuvring is difficult with the boot so full of boxes. My head is a dead weight and throbbing. On the motorway, I had to open the windows to stay awake. I flipped on the stereo. I guess I'll post you back the tape. Sorry. I disposed of all your tokens when the decision was reached and now I am sorry. Perhaps I'll keep it. Just another thing I owe you. It's all displacement—the CDs that worked their ways between collections—symphonic osmosis. We probably break even all things considered. Reversing in inquisitive shunts, waiting for a blind impact, a sudden nothing crush of soft car corners, but I make the space intact. An awful sky heaves overhead. The water cycle is a circle like a rainbow is a circle, but time is straight. The alien key-set baffles me. I shuffle through their indistinguishable shapes until, finally admitted, I climb three flights to the top of the building. Flat 1. The notion of taking all these steps with dark matter fatigues, so I resolve to spend the night with only the box of feathers, a double duvet smudged with ash, and I realise I haven't wanted a cigarette for hours. I elect to sleep diagonally, in the enormity of cover and think of tomorrow, tomorrow, of only tomorrow. I will dream of yesterdays.

2

Whilst you are moving your boxes out, I am in the Sunday pub holding the curve of the tabletop. My knuckles whiten when I contemplate falling. I wash my mouth with beer mechanically. I drain three this way. The alcohol is innocuous after our solemn fourth-pint vows. Fifth-pint oaths. I fume. I smoke. I drag. I suck. I am this way for hours, until I grant impermanent amnesty to the very last. I will not burn you, little heretic, with your carcinogenic doctrine. Not yet. I play with it in yellowed fingers for another quarter of an hour before putting it back into the pack. Solitary confinement. I place the beer mug and its dregs in the centre of the table, the universe of my vision. Now tomorrow has finally come and everything is wrong.

I'm shivering and sweating and pounding. It's the fourth, isn't it Tom? Tweaking the taps backwards in thoughtful repose Tom will nod and I look rough and why don't I go home for a bit and should he call my better-half, or a taxi, or something? No. The fourth. The fourth means time for Sunday curry: two madras, two lagers, naan in the restaurant where the once new scarlet wallpaper has faded and begun to peel. We never did try that new place. The new-places-to-try list ballooned beyond capacity and burst messily. It is all over this pub, all over our lives, all over the idea of Sunday curry. So, I won't go. You shan't stand me up three times today. I leave to walk home the dangerous way, the way you used to forbid, on weak legs.

3

The rain is nothing now. I walk alone along the streets you led me down twenty minutes before. Tracing my way back to the flat, I take a wrong street on purpose, to lose your scent. We'd be in the park now. Christ, you probably are in the park! I am lost this way for an easy hour. I will think about you a total of thirty seven times but I won't cry. I find a street I recognise: Black Street. The kind of place you'd only be seen dead in at night. I always scolded you for walking it back from the pub without me. Tuesdays. You could've been killed. You'd say it was easier that way. I nearly walk right past the house. Inside, I'll do the grown-up stuff, which I know you will forget. I check the windows are shut, that the water and gas are off. I find last night's music quarantined in the airing cupboard. I put it in one of your boxes, smiling a placid, bovine you-smile.

4

We leave and I become "unresponsive", despondent. Shuffling through the rain, with comic suffering, is your sweetheart. Unlivewithable darling. We find a café and I order our coffees. You won't want breakfast, so I don't ask. Then I won't talk and you don't talk and eventually we part.

5

You flap about in the bathroom and it feels like an invasion, despite last night's intimacies.

"You look awful."

You tell me you feel awful. You make a breakfast plan and pause. Staring around me into the mirror. Witnessing your shock register as you realise that I am at liberty to refuse. The last night has ended. This is injury time. When you leave, I drop my gown and shower with ends of bottles. It takes three old shampoos to soap me. At least there'll be less to pack, I said, when you refused point blank to divvy out the toiletries and I told you that, with a week to go, there was no point buying new and they'd have to last. And both of us fools for scratching and biting all week, making memories we'll hate to remember. When I enter the kitchen, you're smoking at the rain.

We ate a last supper early. You made a show of seducing me although it was all agreed by prior arrangement. I loved you for that. We held hands as we walked home and I wanted our skins to fuse. I wanted, at that moment, to banish time and walk next to you for unmetered eternity. Wet stuff, not just the snivelling rain beginning to stir again. The crying night. You opened wine at home and we drank and smoked and talked like the movies, our eyes fondly glazing at all the right moments. You would never believe that I wanted to be yours for the night. You took my hand and led me to bed. Lovers anointed with sweat. As the disc ends, I hold you like a trophy. I almost burn you with my cigarette but you don't notice and just keep talking and talking about smoke and ash and I think you are beginning to run a fever. Your breathing softens. Your eyes, trained upon the window, close. West. The sun sets its circle in the West. I smooth your hair until my lids grow heavy. The old television is winking off. On the last night, last thoughts include the thought that it is my sleep which ends everything.

Cut out your eyes: you have to watch the film of what you've lost.

The red balloon that rose into the sky, unimpeded by your screeched entreaties and the hammering of hot empty fists and a galosh on the zoo floor.

A latchkey that was not returned in a game of catch with an older but no wiser sky, which sent it back wide into the neighbour's hedge. The furtive search was fruitless, asserting your immaturity with an irrepressibility of tears and, later, parental recrimination about your apparent unreadiness for unaided domestic entry and egress.

One day the cat went out the cat-flap. He did not come back.

Four years of co-impression went to Scotland in the back of a Mazda. Matthew's parents kept him in touch for a few months, but the voice in the telephone was incapable of jumping kerbs, or grinding snail-shells into fairy dust.
When your grandpa passed, your parents had a party. You cried alone in your room, writing poems that demonstrated the exceptional nature of your compassionate depths.

Your dreams of love—exquisitely sharp—disappeared with the arrival of boyfriend #1. He had none of the chivalric impulses you had been led to expect and would not take direction. He laughed at your poetry and, a short while later, made like the cat.

You lost a portion of your heart to 'boyfriend' #2, whose exuberant charm was found to be neither chivalric nor exclusively directed towards your person.

When a Wellington stuck in the festival mire, you abandoned the other and continued unshod, to the Levellers and trench foot. Husband #1 cradled you for a week when all was lost, but a respectful year later he made his excuses before quitting the house for good.

Your wallet.

Your wallet.

Where is your wallet?

'I'm lost.' Then turn to page 94.

'I've lost.' Turn to page 102.

'You've lost me.' Page 76.

The Cake Woman

She could be asleep. A soft sound reverberates. Smith is breathing through his small teeth. She is perfect. Forty-two photographs testify to her perfection. His cake wife is asleep. Her marzipan flesh is marble white. The blade gleams in the carefully angled spotlights, as his hand lingers above the final correction. He is giddied by her beauty. For the first time in twelve hot hours, he sits. He shares a glass of water with the bristles of a new brush. It is a bloodless communion. In a small fridge the food colours gradate by tincture. They are delightful. The middle shelf is a blood bank of crimson nuances, thick from chilling and bright. Yet, in all of them, not a colour is 'right' and Smith must now begin to mix the every colour of her living flesh. Her skin has dried under the hot lights. Papery flesh sucks up the dye, ensuring that the proper process of painting must, for the colour not to bleed, be completed in a million little licks. It is painstaking but he remains frugal in his application.

Each shade of dye he mixes demands an examination of the photographs. The whorled flour fingerprints that adhere here from the earliest stage—those clever sponges and their freshly baked jigsaw—crust into sores of yellow and red. Tongues of flame begin to devour her, growing from her joints where he began with her first purple blushes. There is no denying that from an inch she is little but a careful pointillism but Smith, barely three away, is mesmerised by her sensual tonality. He sucks his breath. Giggles. His muse may have been a diminutive woman of five foot two but, in cake terms, she is a giant loosed. He has made the most of her. He drafts the small blue veins of her eyelids. He gives her a bright red smile. It's all over.

Click. How careful he was not to wake her, but the pose had to be right. It was an hour at least until each heavy limb—how unlike her cake self—was manipulated into position. The dim electric light made documentation substandard but flash was impossible, given the circumstances. As it was, he eased down the shutter and watched her lids for a wakeful twitch. Click. Click. It never came. Smith developed them, hung them, and thumbed them above a corpse of Victoria sponge. There is no greater honour that a man may bestow upon a wife than to cook her. After a lengthy and scrupulous surveillance, he exits. He turns out the light. *Click*.

She was forged in a furnace. The kitchen range was fed and roared all day. Sponge after sponge slab tiled each surface and began to pave the floor. The siamese caterwauled at the window but Smith remained impervious to her whining and her paws on the glass. Little-night-time-toe-biting-man-hating-cat. Her blue eyes stalk him as he performs his labours in the heat of blazing hell. She who has a tongue but can never tell. Hssss. Smith huffs the flour from the face of his watch. He has two hours as the last cake is cooling from the oven. Swinging open the top half of the back door and leaning over the edge his wet face dries quickly in the chill air. A unfamiliar twitch squares his mouth. Perhaps, he is anxious. She had better not arrive home early and ruin the surprise. His dusty hands folded like prayer over the bottom door. The cakes are removed to the basement. The last lifted as a scuffling results in the appearance of nose and claws over the edge of the bottom door. An ungainly struggle later and she wins the ledge, from which she hops down easily and sits to lick a paw with practised nonchalance. Her eyes trained on Smith's boots in cautious defiance. With tired legs his aim is off and the cat skirts past him into the lounge.

'You didn't cook again, I see. It's like a fucking morgue in here. Why did you leave the door open?'

Tom cups his balls with both hands and shuffles a stockinged foot into a small spot of flour on the linoleum. Tangerine lozenges from sweetshops of his youth.

'I wasn't hungry, love.'

His martryed stomach growls.

'Huh. Well, I'm famished.' She sags onto a kitchen chair and, sliding off a shoe, begins to palpate her foot.

'It's Monday. Did you sign on?'

Tom gurns at his error, releases himself, turns toward the basement. He pushes the door closed behind him against the hiss of her exasperation. A missile rattles against the other side. Her shoe. He waits on the third stair. The kitchen tap makes an old pipe beside him whine and judder. Within three minutes a whistle signifies the kettle has come to the boil. Only when the maddening chatter of the television erupts does Smith emerge. His reaching fingertips fumble the counter in the dark, until they find the knife block. With practiced stealth he draws the largest. For a moment he electrifies the blade in the emerging shaft of telly light, then retreats to the sanctuary of his, the lowest, floor.

He picked her purse steadily for months to buy the necessary equipment. Each unnoticed note was another lapse to her. She doesn't know where it goes. Smith does. In mute satisfaction he flips a switch and bathes his cave in stadium light. The blade sparkles. He eases it into a cake. Begins the sculpture he could carve in his sleep. Her head, her breasts, her thighs, her hands. The delicate curve of her throat. When each piece is cut and laid out of the table he has the bones of her. Slicing each block horizontally, then approaching the industrial vat of strawberry jam. A vital gluey marrow. His breath is dry ice. A mad scientist from a Hammer horror. He closes and opens his eyes, each time unveiling a magnificent body of work. He has documented the stages of creation with the camera, like an autopsy in reverse. When finally the bones are laid and the jam circulates it is time for her to recuperate, for him to sleep. He shrouds her in muslin. Ample protection against the spiders, the flies, their maggots, all manner of senseless corruption.

He washes the knife carfully in the dark, the obsidian blade surrenders flesh crumbs. Wiping it dry, he slips it back into the block. The fridge drowns him in a cold blue light. Exsanguinated by a wicked transfusion. His eyeballs are glazed with exhaustion. He caps a beer on the worktop, chipping it. His pained face looks left and right for a solution. Hopeless. Settles against the cooling range for its remaining warmth. He smiles between draughts, sets the empty bottle down and rests his eyes. Fate conspires and within moments Smith sleeps fast.

A sharp blow on the top of his skull awakens him to a bitter smell. He can see her knees. He compares their familiar edges. She is dressed for work and brandishing a teaspoon. Today it is her weapon of choice.

'Coffee. Beside you. No, the other side of you, stupid.'

She waits for him to find and sip before she begins. He knows what is coming and he daren't look up. He can feel the burn of her eyes, her terrible disapproval. She is asking him why he didn't come to bed. Why he prefers the kitchen floor. This goes on for some minutes but Tom switches off. Just wait, he thinks. He begins to substitue the noise with dialogue from a duet they sung at a pub karoke. Twenty pairs of eyes admire them through a cigarette haze.

'Tom? Tom? Oh, for fuck's sake.'

Evidently, she had stopped. The ruffle of her skirt as she moves towards the door. The cat slinks through her legs and ambles into the living room, stopping once to eyeball her recumbent foe.

'Goodbye Tom.'

There is a silence crisp and thick. Smith breaks off a piece to dip in his coffee and savour. Visualises her knees and realises he has noticed a small scar he had forgotten and can now include. Lovers find perfection in imperfections. The old coffee table had caught her there. She had stopped shouting at him and he had washed the wound, dressed it, and made tea.

In fifteen minutes, with paper, kindling, and coals, Smith has invented fire. He sets down the stairs to resume creation with a pain in his side from a night on the tiles. He unpacks and piles the blocks of marzipan on the bench, unwraps one and rolls it out on a length of marble worktop, purpose bought. He cuts the cloth to a pattern and slowly the cake woman's bones grow meat. He is aware of the details. They will need fleshing out.

Oh, Tom, remember Scarborough.

Tom remembers Scarborough.

I looked like a princess in my little red dress. I wore the earrings you bought me for our first aniversary. We were kids then. They were little faux gold dolphins with crystal eyes. I loved them, didn't I? Your fingers smoothed the blonde curling-iron ringlets behind my ears. We danced. You were awkward but I didn't mind. We will take lessons! The hotel was a ruin so we had another cocktail and another. You carried me back in a fireman's lift, me kicking and squealing in false protest. Two kids in love.

The cake wife had begun to talk sweetly the moment he laid down those plump marzipan lips.

I love you Tom, I love you so much. Kiss me like Scarborough, they said. Tom bent in aquiescence to his supine bride. His touch the softest, his dry lips taking a little sugar. Rising he licks them. His stomach gurgles. He hasn't eaten since yesterday morning and his stomach gurgles. His excitement at her sweet words have made him a little sick. He can't eat. He feels the giddy rush of fresh love. The lover has no need for sustinence but their lover's lips, breasts, hips. His distraction makes her run to fat. That's okay, princess. I will be your surgeon. This bobbled, hardening corpse imprisons the princess that only he can free. Once a liberal marzipan sarcophogus is moulded around the cake bones he stalks the stairs. Returns momentarily with a tray masked by a tea towel which he sets down next to the patient. Swishing the cloth free, his magic show reveals an array of blades. And for my next trick. Smith hovers his hand above each, feeling for the warmth of the right descision. She is understandably nervous. Repeats old words.

I want you to. Her flushed face opening like a flower. Will it hurt, Tom?

He bends over her carefully, the vegetable paring knife in his calloused palm and begins an expert nose job. He cannals out the nostrils with a skewer, careful to maintain the integrity of the fragile septum. He imagines her anaethetised. The flesh above is shaved off to within a hairs-breadth of sponge bone. Next comes the skin of her teeth—exactly three and a half of these poke through the gap in her smile. The spare flesh on her cheek-bones is finely honed to brute perfection. The sloughed skin beginning to pile on the concrete floor.

Her sweet face is his own. Without body work she is museum Egyptiana. He imagines gilding her in gold leaf. Her kohled eyes under the blue sickles of shadow, like she used to wear. He imagines taking the knife and slicing into her, pouring cream over each of the pieces. A milk bath. Her grinning lips sweetened by him. How fine her lipped chin will look encircled by a bowl rim of the anniversary crockery. This is all for her, all her, but he has a right to claim a small part for himself. He has a right to something. The thought makes him bend and steal a second, more urgent, sugary kiss. Gurgles.

Something more business is needed for the hips. He has to be careful with this one, he knows, to flatter. Of course it never mattered to him and, like her, his frame holds a little more flesh than those first years. Too much and she will think he considers her additional pounds as surplus. Some few millimetres than actual is the recipe for satisfaction. The first cut is grievous with intent. He planes the left flank, the right, heaves the knife up across her belly and up over the breasts. Gulley between them. Slabs of meat from the side peel slowly off under their own weight and slap onto the floor. The top pieces are peeled away. Butcher, baker. A potato peeler carves out sloping thighs. The marzipan here is drier—the site of inaugaral application—and shaves easily. He collects each curl in a pile on the tray. They will transplant as hair. Soon knees, and elbows are unpicked and only lumps of hands and feet remain. As his labours near their completion Smith shrinks in shy admiration, averts his eyes. Her marzipan flesh is marble white. The blade gleams in the carefully angled spotlights, as his hand lingers above the final correction.

His leprous hands hover over the wardrobe handles. He gurns. Fatigue has begun to undermine problem solving skills. She calls to him through the layers.

—I feel safe with you. You always know what to do. You'll look after me forever, won't you Tom?

—Sweetness, I will.

The hot tap should be called the hot-and-cold tap. Cold before it begins to warm, a few seconds hot until it scolds. He faces his refelction. His eye-lids are purple and puffy. His loose cheeks rashed with stubble. A splash of dye has made a beauty mark. The irony is not pretty. He stoppers the basin and turns the tap. Lets inconsistent temperature pour a temperate bath as he begins to scrub. He needs to remove every trace. The red dyes are not easily vanquished. I look like a killer. He smirks as he addresses himself in the mirror, recognising a creator. Fifteen minutes and it has become difficult to distinguish the stains from the raw skin between. It will do. He picks the last from under his nails. Erases the mark from his face. He gets into the suit. Just to see. It doesn't quite fit. The mirror is a cruel mistress. It cannot but be. He will suck it all in, when he meets her at the door. When he carries her down the stairs. There are some spare hours between which he will lose in sleep. Folding the suit carefully over the chair he clambers between the sweetly musty sheets. The alarm clock colon blinks. A silent warning of his error.

'Who the fuck is she, you bastard?'

Her silhouette appears collosal against the square light of the distant door. There is a suitcase on the bed into which she is throwing clothes. The shock has made little dint in the fug of desperate sleep. His tongue is thick.

'I see you wash and shave for her. Does she like you in that suit? How could you? How could you? It's our fucking anniversary, or had you forgotten? Jesus, Tom. Seriously, this is it. This—is—it.'

She slaps the suitcase closed. The fastners snap. Tom hefts himself onto his elbows as she dissapears out into the light of the hall. No. Tom tries to shake the dream from his head. It won't budge. Smith's stomach gurgles.

His intentions were obvious when he alighted the bottom-most step with the cream jug. She screamed. When he returned blank eyed with the carving knife she was sobbing softly.

'You better believe it will hurt.'

He turned to the worktop and planted his hands either side of the kitchenware. He breathed in deeply. Gathering himself. Choking a sob. Exhaled heavily. When he turned to her he held the jug in a whitening grip. As he advanced she refused and pleaded in turn. Attempted to rouse him with his name, mouthing it plaintively. As the jug began to tip above her she hushed. The cream began to descend. When the first drop hit her cheek she screamed again. Smith's mouth became long and thin. He upended the jug, throwing its remaining contents forth like a bucket of paint. The cream flowed down her face, down the bench and onto the floor. His bare feet printing dance steps on the floor as he fetches the knife.

In darkness still ripe with the smell of birth the blind cubs suck and wriggle. Mother is asleep. Footfalls advancing on the den arouse her. Familiar yellow eyes appear in the entrance. Vulpes vulpes. He has a hand by the wrist in his teeth. He has been to the shallow hollow to get her food. Mother begins to gnaw at the plundered limb. The food is sweet and plentiful. The cubs suck and wriggle. The foxes will be fat this winter.

Epistles

Dear Tom,

The news I have to tell you warrants the epistolary form. Our child has passed.

Sincerely,
R.

---T.Smith@mail.com---
Rosie,
I've been calling and calling you. Please call me back. We need to talk about this.

Tom

ROSIE-EX
15:32

Understatedly, I've been preoccupied!

ROSIE-EX
15:34

UNDERSTANDABLY! Call me.

This is...Rosie's...answerphone, leave a message after the tone. [Bleep]
...Rosie. ...It's Tom. [Weeping. Fumbling.] Call me, please.

Status Update: CHRISTABEL SMITH has passed.

Hey, this is Chrissy. I'm probably on a date with Justin B, I expect. Leave a message and I'll call you back.

Hey, this is Chrissy. I'm probably on a date with Justin B, I expect. Leave a message[…].

Hey, this is Chri[…].

Hey, […].

Pessimists should turn to page 83.

Optimists should turn to page 44

Nativity Play

Felicity absented in the autumn. More coat than woman, she comes to rest on the bench. In spring she had been abashed by a child's exclamation at her slippered feet and the growing forgetfulness they implied. Once a little light snow fell but didn't settle and the sky is no longer so blue. Her tinny ears rouse a string section. Someone's painting the leaves all wrong this year. Her fingers rattle against the plastic of her handbag; she is taking tea in a bright corner of her youth. Wish you were here. Her mouth twitches; an echo of a smile circa '52. Roger cracks a wry joke. Wish you were here. Wish you were here. Won't you take another cup, my dear?

One, two, three, eyelashes glimmer between craftily parted fingers. Why do you cheat, James? He is his mother's, eight, nine, ten, spit. Well. I was my dead father's ringer by twenty-three, twenty-four. At thirty-nine, I sigh. It's all hopelessly genetic. Cushions to be replaced by sods, etc. Forty-nine. Fifty. Squeal. Coming Daddy, ready or not!

Gertrude slips on her coat. Inside the den, Jim is a mass of cushions. Her son disassembles the pyramid, revealing first arm, then leg. The mountain groans as she creeps past. When her keys rattle, the dog shivers and knocks over a wellington. She whispers, 'Please Marigold, Jim will take you later.' Outside everything is crisp. Naked trees brace the snow-fat skies. To traverse the garden she has to weave through a congregation of snails. Tells them: you should be asleep, my friends. At night, the blink of the alarm clock colon betrays the passing of seconds. The total absence of sleep.

'I ordered us the dressed crab.'
The baked potato steams. The lettuce wilts.
'Don't.'
The man plants his chin between cupped palms, his elbows

ranging well across the mid-line of the table.

'So you're serious, then?'

Her fingers drag a garland of keys, back and forth. The keys stop.

'Cromer was a mistake.' Her voice is flat.

The keys and they resume their shuttle.

'Three days is a long time to be mistaken, G.' A pause. 'I want to tell her.'

'Tom.' She hisses the word, but her small finger steals out to stroke the fabric of his shirtsleeve.

Outside, his phone rings. He pulls at the tips of his leathered fingers with his teeth. Inhales. Exhales slowly, breathalysing for guilt.

'Tom are you there? Hello?'

'Bloody Fucking Christ!'

'Tom?'

He lifts his foot to assess the damage

'Sorry love! I've only gone and trod in a puddle.'

'Oh.' She abandons that theme. 'I wanted to remind you about Daisy's play tonight. You'd forgotten, hadn't you?'

'I had not.'

Tom limps on his sodden shoe, his mouth an incompatible rictus of contentment.

'Some milk too, on the way? Right-o.'

'Yes. Right. Bye then.'

A date-night picture of June, which attends her calls, fades into a sunset screensaver.

Houseplants sag in the fug of the kitchen. Outside, a light snow has settled on the sill. Kneeling in the adjoining lounge space, June tries to attach wire and paper wings to the mobile shoulders of her daughter. Daisy glowers at the fey winged lady atop the twinkling pine. Being a tomboy is difficult at Christmas. She plucks and pulls at the unfamiliar constraint of blobby woollen tights. With her eyes thus pinched in quiet scepticism, she has never looked more like her father. June squashes the child's plump cheeks between her palms.

'We're all done here, fish face.'
Daisy explodes in a sudden, high-pitched peal of mirth.
Then the house phone rings.
Tom will be late. He will meet her at the hall. Or not.
The phone rings off.

Susie scratches at the rash brought on by her tinsel collar. Against expressed orders, Simone waves shyly to her cousin. James chews nervously on his watchstrap, until a ribbon of saliva oozes towards the stage. Rudy and Mo attempt to push each other over. Farouk sees them and says 'umm' but doesn't properly tell. Meanwhile, Ryan's hand makes a forbidden journey down the front of his trousers. A phone trills. Now at full gnaw, James stares out into the small audience of grandparents, parents, and siblings. A phone trills.

In the audience, Gertrude is tapping her wrist aloft, attempting to manoeuvre it into James' eye-line. A phone trills. Jim nudges June.
'You were told to turn that off.'
A phone trills.
'It'll be bloody Tom. Wanting to explain why he'll be late this time.'
Gertrude draws her arm in.
June balances her purse on her bump and, popping the over-sized clasp, rifles within. "You have ten messages from Tom Mobile," her robot voice half-sneer as she presses the button that to scroll through.

In the empty cloakroom there are some loose face-paints, an avalanche of forsaken shoes, a little girl. The child balances on her back foot, wobbling, acclimatising to the gloom. Then her toes crush a blue face crayon. She leaves a stutter of prints behind her, marking her progress. As she pulls on a first red galosh a commotion rises behind the heavy doors of the hall. She heaves a theatrical, like-Daddy-does sigh. Then she pushes the fire bar. The door swings out into the night. Her fingers twitch at the mischief of it. The playground is illuminated by a sudden flare of security light. There is somebody else out there. There is strange music on the wind.

They're not shining the stars as bright. They've stolen the joy from the night. The lady is old. Wrinkles wobble around the babble of her mouth. She is not talking to Daisy, but around Daisy, like a hug made of incomplete thoughts. Wish you were here. Her eyes are puffy and wet and kind. Most of the talking is too quiet to listen, but there are some loud words.

'Roger was my Granddaddy's name.'

Felicity wraps her arms tightly around the child, like she can't ever let go. The smell is of must. Nearby an idling car crunches its gears and speeds away, in communion with the cold, cold night.

Sometimes miracles happen and Emily had nearly finished packing. She was checking the contents of the open case against a mental inventory, spelling out the process in the air upon randomly assigned fingers. The doorbell interrupted. A short first ring gave way to a second more insistent blast. Through the open sash window giggles seemed to emanate up from the street below. By necessity, her packing had been conducted around the curved instep of her husband's foot. The foot, which had sought a cooler climate, now protruded some length into the room. From beneath the duvet, small snores attested that Philip was, on this occasion, not the source of this most characteristic expression of mirth. She paused, zipped the case, and moved towards the window. Her visitor was hidden beneath the small porch. The taxi driver must be having a good morning, she thought. The bell rang again. Three abrupt bursts. The husband, unmoved by the shrill music, continued to sleep fast. From outside an electronic sound, like a false chord, was met with a second splutter of laughter and a cross whisper. Piqued by curiosity, Emily abandoned her case and skipped quickly down the stairs. In the hall, the frosted glass betrayed a monstrous silhouette. Some devilish trick of the morning light was casting her caller's shadow in epic proportions. After a second, during which the caution occasioned by this surprise was checked by a resurgence in her spirit of inquiry, Emily reached for the latch and pulled the door open wide.

An angel was on the doorstep. Against the reasons why this was impossible, Emily balanced the pressing evidence to the contrary. Two sandaled feet, the white capacious robe that extended some eleven feet from neck to hem, and the bearded face above with its with broad, beneficent smile. Wings. It had fucking wings. Her thoughts had begun to loop and flutter about this fact when the angel's robe undulated and emitted a beatific chord. As if on cue, the angel proffered her a gift, lifting a small black object towards her, balanced upon its open palms. As she reached out to take the object, she recognised it as the wallet she had lost the night before. The angel turned with incongruous difficulty and stepped down heavily from the doorstep. It began to make slow progress up the street. As her eyes adjusted to the morning light, the wire skeleton of the glittered paper wings betrayed themselves. Then, the silhouette of the two bodies stacked beneath the sheet. As Emily studied the outline of the humped lower figure and the smaller person perched carefully atop, the angel turned and gave a final wave, as a final blast of the glorious chord rang from the lower-angel's electronic keyboard.

Did this happen? 54;
Didn't this happen? 31;
This didn't happen. 44;
What does 'happen' mean? 83.

Future Perfect/Nothing Arizona

I will be slack-mouthed before the refrigerator, straining to satisfy an incompatible kind of hunger, when I realize that the time has come to meet my universal twin. I will not have had this feeling before, but it will be unmistakable and immutable. By the time the temperature of the open chiller will have equalized with the ambient room about, my airline ticket to Phoenix Sky Harbor will be booked. In a distant galaxy, on a planet that differs from ours principally by the astronomical rate of their technological progress, other Rosie will have put on her space helmet. It's a futuristic affair, I imagine.

I am making another list of all the things I am good for.

Panic hits the psyche like strychnine. I can get up. This will help nothing. I don't get up. I could flee the close walls. This will help nothing. I will feel the same but I will be outside. I could walk in tight circles. I have done this before. Had hoped that activity would distract from the overwhelming tide of adrenaline. The frantic need to do something that nothing is. I long to be drugged into sweet amnesiac slumber & would kill to stop this. Another wave of adrenaline hits and I realise. It's too late. It's impossible. It's. It. I. It. It's just another panic attack.

I am making another list of all the things I am good for.

Having disembarked in Phoenix, I will have driven my rental north through Encanto, Glendale, and thence wide-eyed into Surprise. At Wickenberg, I will continue up the Route 93 to Nothing. From there it will be but a short trek to nowhere where I figured it would all go down. Nowhere being no place close to Nothing: a set of co-ordinates some distance into the desert. My ambient absorption of televisual survivalism will have equipped me for the landscape, I might have mouthed, somewhat hubristically. As for Rosie, I can help Rosie out. All the while my copy of *The Ego and His Own* will have lain where it had dropped, a crumpled bird on the kitchen floor, lit nightly by a shard of refrigerator light. Lit until the bulb burns out.

★★★

There is a moment between sleep and dreaming—coming back from/going to—where the motes can be seen to transition into dream-shapes. In Classical Latin: *Muscae*, flies (pl.); *volitantes,* flying (pl.). The flying flies. The retinal shadows engage the brain's visionary faculties and make sense. No, it isn't narrative, as we remember when we wake; but it's not not narrative, so we feel when we sleep.

Welcome to the desert of the real. I acknowledge the pressing need to exist but there is nothing can peel me from this kerb. Books have no music. Music no taste. Food is only an abstract noun. I can't pick myself up. I can't put myself down. The inescapable expanse of existence disemboguing like something sticky spilt in my mind.

I holiday in my happy place, my toes rearrange patterns in the screen of sand on the peeling boards. The sea insists upon approach and retreat. The round moon highlights exalted phrases and, above, the fronds of a buckled coconut tree hush. I bring to my lips a blushing glass. A cigarette drills smoke into the air, up-lit by candlelight. My ineluctable lungs insist on inspire and emanate. Within lies a full-bellied calm. As if from the sea, a figure approaches. Our shipwreck couture a dead spit, though she is older than I am. She seats herself lightly in a chair beside me. She takes up my drink.
'Hello you.' Says one of us.
'Hello me.'
And that's just it.

Truly, there I will have been, in nowhere, awaiting my self from a distant galaxy. It was inevitable that Rosie would be identical to me, barring slight changes wrought upon her by her civilisation's recent discovery of rapid, long-distance space travel. Won't we will have a lot to talk about. I will have supposed there was nothing stopping a whole raft of mes arriving. Intergalactic mes that would have experienced other slight differences: left-handedness, halitosis, quixotism. None who had found what they were looking for that day in the fridge, or wherever they searched for relief from their incoherent urges. After a certain point, the mes would be—for better or worse—less me-like and unaware of the pressing need to come together in nothing. But if a congregation did turn up, we would probably just have a party. And I will have packed a bottle of mescal to that end.

A shark swims by its dead eye a reflection of my own.

I sat on my hands from Cambridge to Stiffkey, gripped by the terror I would snatch the wheel and careen us into the traffic. I stood upon the beach drowning in impossible horizons. I pretended an interest in the marine life because you had always liked it that Rosie was interested in marine life. I posed for a photograph in front of the rape, the yellow sea unravelling my yellow hoodie. Later, I lay rigid in the tent, paroxysmal against the fear that I was going to strangle you whilst you slept.

A
A
Once
Reader
There
Time
Upon
Was
You make it up.

[★★★]

Knowing me, I will have started early on the mescal. Jesus, but the desert will have been hot. The slight wind forming a screed in the hot sand, like Sanskrit for the piece that passes. For peace. There will have been cacti in true form, promising bitter water in respite of fire and I will have hacked off some chunks before I settled down behind this rock. Come into the shadow, Rosie. I won't have figured out what really to do with it, save for drinking the drips of sap pouring off the edge of my prickly paw which, anyway, would have been opaque and, I'd be telling myself as I drank it, bad drinking. I will have been thinking about how displeasing I would seem to me, a drunken host alone in the desert. Above, there will have been vultures in a holding pattern.

The oneirocritic is the critic of your dreams. She dissects and catalogues your hypnogogic visions, your stupors, revisions, your prophecies and loss. Her paradigms frame and canonise choice nightmares, trances, desires, scratching the broken record of failed romances, linking fever to a genealogy of succubi.

What are your core beliefs? You don't just know them, you don't magik them up from the fathomless depths of your unconscious mind, you can't ask someone the answer. There is a process. There are leaves to this book. Find the apex of your fright and concentrate it. Put it into words. Palpate the dimensions of your jaw for the locus of tension. Scrape it out and daub the clotted mass onto a page, like language. I am crawling out of my skin because I am in a valley of desperation. Crawl back into your skin. The valley of desperation has edges to trace, dimensions to find. The rocks close in with every blink. I am desperate because I feel like I have no power to progress. Repeat process. I am desperate because I feel I have no power. Synthesise. I am addicted to progress. I am addicted to me in the future. Self-prescribe. Belong, somehow, to now.

I will have sat in the heat of the day. No leopards. The insentient sun punishing my body, unconscious of the capsule plummeting through the universe towards nothing. There will have been no gleam, yet, in the massive sky. No signs of imminent arrival. So I take another pull on the mescal. I scratch at the twitch in my jaw.

Note to self: they will know if you quote from Under the Volcano.
Note from self: they will not know if you just quote 'the'.

The Prisoner's Cinema appears, a psychedelia on the unstimulated inmate's walls. It plays montages of slasher movies, bank heists, hit jobs. It plays a technicolour brain-blow of intrusive thought; of impulses pullulating with the horror of loss. It plays matinees, dinner shows, late nights, early birds. Do you think the prisoner's cinema is a game? There are no pages to turn to.

★★★

Curiosity is only a kind of hunger, of which there are several kinds. I'd have toasted the vultures for their optimism and checked my in-focusing out-focusing watch. She will have counted down to blast off days ago. It could be any minute now and I feel over-prepared.

The next exercise will be a meditation in compassion for the benefactor. Snatched minutes of post-orgasmic bliss: like flesh in full sunlight, a post-alveolar rrr, or a cat's trill. But the mechanism by which cats purr is speculative. Not a language. And, if I'm not mistaken, this cat is being skinned. The trill morphing to shrill screaming in the ear canal. A gushing in of norepinephrine in the locus ceruleus. The ribs constricting around sticky lungs. The throat closing in on itself like an anemone. A desperate itch deep, deep beneath the skin. Escalating atmospheres of hydrostatic pressure. The plunging stomach flips and catches. I tell myself that there has been an inscrutable tilting the axes of reason. That the ceiling is not lowering to crush. I think about breathing. The automatic becomes the aim of my focus. Inviting the jaw to soften, soothing the crushing pain of the jaw's grip, allowing the squealing cat in the jaw.

Thomas lay in bed, his peeled eyes drying, his knuckles sharp and white, sweat twinkling on his cold flesh like morning dew. Perhaps he is actually dying. The marker-pen slashes that measure out inches and feet on the white wall provide conclusive proof. The ceiling has descended eleven inches in the first hour of what promises to be a long night.

***

There is an essay by Barthes on the piano. Tomorrow will have been raining. A pyramid of boxes: missing.

The flies that laid their eggs in the sores of this dead dog contend that it is in their nature, as it was in the dog's nature to follow the children with the dog biscuits into the alley and to die there. Long before it's legs skittered in mortal throes, the children had already lost interest. Had already complained about the smell of the garbage that summoned the congregation of flies. You must sleep soon, friends. Then, the total absence of sleep: the clock colon blinking in silent error.

On the horizon, which is milky either because the desperate glare has ossified my eyes into pearlescent globes or because the horizon is milky, is a lone desert fox. Its leanness, its obvious hunger, is undercut by the insouciance of its movements, of it sniffing the morning air, apparently for meaning. And possibly for not.

Thomas is walking somewhere, presumably to a destination. His Converse conversing with the asphalt in deadening whispers. Each step raises a small plume of dust. When his brisk pace slows he is looking at the ground beneath him. The sudden hollowing warrants the clank of boats on the bottom of a vanishéd marina. There they would have lain like dead birds, their sails spasming pathetically against the dry stone. Scrape. Scrape. Landed anchors rolling point to point, conjuring the death throes of a spun coin. The sudden vanishing of desire for destination; the sudden vanishing of desire for the departure: these facts manifest as an irresistible pull towards the ground.

***

There is a deep impulse in me to make the text the agent of horror and, so, I sit on my hands.

I can't read the newspaper. I don't want to read the newspaper. I am reading the newspaper. As I flick between social media platforms constructed selves jostle to become spirit guides, to render intelligible my emotional reaction to global terror, domestic villainy, misogynistic tyranny, and this cat video. The cat is wearing a hat, which creates conflict. My smart phone could reach out to those crouched in hope on the possession-littered beaches of Lesbos. It doesn't, of course, but we are potentially connectable. That, my friend, is progress.

Reader expectations bleed between the lines.

Once upon a come-down-day, I bent too quickly and accepted as reality an ebullition of fireflies. I swatted as I remarked upon their unlikeliness. But they were only white blood cells elongated in passage through my retinal capillaries. It was only an entopic phenomenon. It was only a shame. My sweated palm rotating uselessly around the screw-top lid. The total absence of mescal.

Thomas is knitting his twitchy fingers together in front of the dizzying swirl of television. His eyes are bald and vulnerable. Cherries ready to be plucked.

Zap. The cold white-tiled surround sweats steam. Zap. The mesmeric blue light. Zap. The electrified grill. Zap. Zap.

Thomas is dizzying his fingers together. His obvious head inviting hands to snap it from the neck beneath, like a parent re-orientating a child's shoulders away from a busy road, away from the clamour of danger.

Each ten metres of water adds an atmosphere of pressure. There are pressing dangers. Failure to equalise your cavities—nasal, ear canal, the clustered mass of alveoli—will sunder tissue. Unmanaged ascent will pop your cells like grapes. There is a depth at which a diver will experience intoxication-like symptoms, which subside only upon measured ascent. The mechanism is unknown. The depth varies. Take only rubbish, leave only bubbles.

Every time it rains I decide whether it is a good or a bad thing, which determines entirely my experience of it.

An empty coffee cup swings from his crooked index finger as he walks through the halls of the institution. The mug's easy movement is enviable and at odds with the clamorous buzz beneath Thomas' hot skin. His vision of the ceramic cracking satisfyingly upon his temple, the dimming circle of consciousness is both a terror and a comfort.

Here comes the end.

There, perhaps, she will have found me, dead in the desert beside an empty bottle of mescal, the vultures picking at the sinew of my bones.

There, perhaps, she will have found me, lotus-like, in the desert, offering an oasis of warm mescal, toasting the vultures, circling so high they looked like fire-flies against the benevolent sun.

Nativity Play

In Gloucestershire Roger was losing his life. Wife, Mabel Godrest'ersoul, had, some twelvemonth prior, taken communion with the cold, cold earth. Children, June and Jim, were a grandchild apiece. The squalling wretches had been brought in favour but had manifestly destroyed his peace. As his fingertips let slip the vestiges of mortal life—beating, breathing, and the like—he knew he had been robbed of the cataclysm the event should imply. It was expected that he die. But he had not expected it. In a final act, gravid with discontent, he clawed the spectacles off the hovering clock of a doctor before crumpling back into bed with an almighty grunt. Then, there was nothing more could be done.

Queer one, her. The ladder creaks as he over-leans to paw another frosty clump of detritus from the gutter. A heap of thawing slop has accumulated on the pavement below. He watches her cross the road to avoid his mess. Emma? Gemma? Geraldine? In all truth, he had been watching her for months. From the cramped attic window. From the gloomy porch where he suckles the smoke from his pipe. All hours, it is, she's to be found passing back and forth in the wide eye of the kitchen window, or else silhouetted on the lemon conservatory blinds. The shadow fretting its hands. Last week she had been talking to herself at the bottom of the garden in the pearlescent fog of twilight. He strained to hear but she was speaking too softly and the still night permitted no approach. It takes all sorts, he had guessed.

Wide eyes on wide road. Woman crossing up ahead. Easing up the foot. Tap the leathered sheaf of the wheel as the radio plays jazz. A piece of rhythm jerks at the spine. I am not dancing. It is involuntary motion; my volitive act is the stillness that succeeds it. The air is ripe with the stench of cheap upholstery shampoo. Get in the car Jenny. You're Mummy is looking for you. She's so cross. She sent me to take you home. The car boot was like a coffin: hot, airless, and its lid immovable. Jenny was not thinking about Edgar Allan Poe or The Waste Land. Little Jenny was six—and-a-quarter. Head so thick with fear no thoughts squeeze through. Barely aware of the cooling touch of her wet dress; the smell of pee. I suck the air between my small teeth as I glimpse into the rear-view mirror. There is some psychic discomposure that I turn the music up against.

The plasma television rumbles rolling news. Jenny Hookham's mother has made a second plea for information. Jake sits at the bar, his resting hands frame a three-quarter-empty pint glass. It won't be long before the office will swallow him up. Jenny Hookham's emblematic last picture wallpapers his hungry mind. The police have no new leads. Old Mother Hookham pale and haggard on the screen, hardened by grief. Her voice, granular: if anyone knows anything that might help me find my daughter. Her manner has become more business-like; brief. Could that be an angle? What a monster! And everybody knows she did it. Tell us where Jenny is! Mrs Hookham, over here! Over here! Snap. A fine story that would be. Something meaty to sink his teeth into, something to get him off roundabout farms, fetes and school sports days. He drains his glass, his own face the monstrous fish looming up from the bottom.

The lunch hubbub is in full swing. Clinking glasses. Cutlery squeaking against plates. The congenial roar of fifty conversations. I float. Autopiloting the lunchtime service: compiling an orderly list of functions. When a sudden barrel-change catches me off-guard, the buzz threatens to spiral down, down into chaos. Yet, the woman on table thirteen can wait another few minutes for her meal, which will not cool in the heated lift. Punters amass at the bar, holding out notes, rolling their eyes in pursuance of mine. Passing cattle. They too can wait. The cellar is quiet, dark, cool. I press the ball of my thumb into my spasming eyelid and take some deep breaths. By the time the hose has been clipped to a new barrel, the light at the end of the tunnel has grown unbearably bright. It takes a marathon of will to alight the steps. The pub I emerge into is rammed. I cough, or choke. Pint of mild and a Pinot Grigio, mate? As I force a smile, I notice my shoelace, which has come untied, is browning in the beer slop.

At the back of the saloon bar, Theodora is dining alone. When the crossword becomes a too obvious veil for her lonesomeness— inspiration and proper investment having departed several minutes hence—she carefully folds the paper and places it in her bag. Her movements are measured, stretching the activity to barely plausible length, unsure of what activity, if any, can succeed it. It is Theodora steepling her hands under her chin. It is Theodora watching the barman tending the taps, leaping to slap forgotten levers, as he alternates brisk customer transactions with private moments cautiously probing the keys of the till. He had overcharged her by accident? But she hadn't been of a mind to make a fuss. The wall of customers at the bar retire in pairs, holding their amber tinted beacons aloft and alighting at empty tables all about. When all are occupied, a man approaches to hover his hands above the vacant seats at Theodora's table. His raised-brow smirk, she interprets generously as 'May we join you, please?' To which she nods briskly. In their train, the barman unceremoniously delivers her plate.

"I ordered us the dressed crab."

"Don't."

Theodora tries and tries and tries not to listen. She coughs politely, to indicate that the barman has arrived with their crabs. Then, apparently feeling the spell broken, they eat in the near silence of too polite conversation. It almost comes to feel like they are eating together. Theodora very nearly contributes to their clipped discussion about the forecast for snow. She will not have finished her potato before the lady rises to leave, offering the gentleman no parting embrace.

He strips the suds from the pane in a series of quick swipes. The rubber wiper squeaking against the glass as it reveals it. A silhouette appears in the frosted glass, slowly crisping into a pleasing shape as the woman inside approaches. He is minded to help her with the heavy door but stops himself in the act, too humbled by his marigolds. His eyes followed her passage up the street.

"It's too cold for bareback, son." He mumbles, chafing together his rubberized palms.

A car passes close to the kerb, cracking ice on a puddle that has collected over a clogged drain. Muted strains of saxophones trail behind it. The water in the bucket steams in the cold air. Sometimes he treats his cold hands to a short bath in the warm soap. After which he can de-glove and roll a cigarette with a near full range of movement. He takes that moment now, the low winter sun blaring on the freshly clean windows, his revived hands rolling the paper closed. After a lustful drag, he bends to upend the bucket into the road. The water collects above the drain, ice pieces fizzing in the warm suds. Then some dickhead talking on his phone splashes right through it, cursing and waggling the water from his soggy shoe as he crosses the road.

"Twat."

—Give it up. Give it up, mate.

Tom feels a sudden rush of confusion. The speaker is skinny. Within his yellow cowl a nervous face swims between child and adult. The locus of Tom's consciousness has shifted five feet northwest, to a safe distance behind his left shoulder. A shining blade protrudes from a sleeve pulled low for secrecy. It slits a loose figure of eight in the cold air, implying a casual attitude but encouraging haste. This kid doesn't have a casual face. The problem is: Tom doesn't have a pattern for this transaction. Warily, he offers up his phone on an open palm. He fed a horse that way once and wasn't bitten. Thin, nicotined fingers peck him as the phone vanishes. The knife flicks back and forth, indicating Tom's other pockets, inquiring after their possible treasures. Tom stutters, 'I've got twenty-five quid in my wallet. But there's other stuff in there and I need it.'

The youth makes a strange sucking noise.

—Man, I got no use for your cards and shit. Just give me the cash.

The boy's pulls the edge of his hood forward, shuffles on his feet. Tom is trembling as he removes the wallet from his pocket and, as he tries to undo it, it drops at the youth's feet. His assailant sighs theatrically and stoops to pick it up. Removing the notes, the mugger turns and begins to walk away, discarding the wallet over his shoulder. It lands in the slush like a dead bird.

—There's thirty-five here, you lying fuck. I should do you for that. He says, turning back to wag the knife, pausing as if caught in indecision.

Then his shoulders slacken and he folds back the small penknife blade and departs. The relief leaves Tom unmanageably unsteady and he slides to his knees on the cold, wet pavement. Feels a chilling damp seep up his woollen trousers as he scoops together the cards and receipts that have splayed forth. A single snowflake falls. Then another. A light snow begins to fall on the wet ground.

—You'll end up inside if you keep on.

The phone is an old model with scuffing that suggests it has been dropped more than once. I try to give it back, but Frank is already preoccupied. He is hunched over my coffee table, his tongue jutting out over a painstaking attempt to conjoin some cigarette papers. I put the phone on the table instead. He doesn't yet look up.

—No good, is it?

—No good.

—No fucking good… Huh. I have the cash monies.

He holds the unlit joint in his mouth, freeing his hands up to pull a clump of notes from his damp jumper pocket and to fish through his frayed jeans pockets for change. The total is just shy of enough. He sparks the joint and inhales deeply, settling into the sofa to exhale a veil of smoke. After a few deep drags his wet eyes find mine across the haze. I don't like you anymore Frank, I think, and it is almost true. At school his attentions had been limited to corridor assaults, but once, in the privacy of my Mum's two-bed, we had listened to his father tearing into his mother through the thin dividing wall. I held him for an hour that night whilst he cried bitterly. Since then, he's been more or less hollowed out. When he passes the final third of the joint across the table, an arcing rope of saliva binds it to him. I bring my hands up warily, repulsed by the thought of the sogged roach. Hoping the joint will find its way back before the string of spittle bursts. My naked toes curl up against that thought. As he repositions it on the ledge of his lower lip the spit-line slackens into him, soaking a thin, dark trench on his grubby top. As he's pulling at the last dregs, his thumbs flick idly over the buttons of the stolen phone. He startles.

—Daddy been a bad boy, hey?

—What?

He shows me the screen.

—What?

—Uh, there's texts to the wife and a load of moist stuff to some other skank!

—So what? I ask, but Frank, his eyes red from the skunk, sighs out the smoke from his final toke. He crushes the roach into an ashtray that I had earlier slid beneath his trembling column of ash and begins to rattle at the keys. His determination akin to a total dematerialisation from the now.

People are ants. You are Spiderperson. As you turn your red palm towards the uncommonly warm April sunlight a glorious spray of silk glistens, arcing towards the mast of a distant building. Spidercome. Heh. The mast beckons invitingly, as you test it with your weight. A safe hit with good tension. You respond by leaping clear of the vertiginous ledge. A chip of old stone clatters on the pavement below, loosened by your stockinged foot. The ants chirrup and stare aloft. Good that they are looking up. The short free fall onto the tension of the silk rope ends with a small bump and you swing forwards, tensing foot arch, knee, thigh, buttock into a graceful poise. Spiderperson! The lack of a theme tune has begun lately to grate. You begin to compose one as you swing but it sounds a bit like Batprick's so you stop. Fuck Batprick. An impulsive Tarzan cry echoes around the skyscrapers. The ants chirrup.

Closing in on the glazed face of the masted edifice you curl your fingers and toes for a graceful impact. P—p—p—punk. The silk won't quit your palm, so you release your other hand to wipe them. An error. You paddle the air like amateur funambulist until you can re-establish your fingertips on the pane. It is un-elegant. The ants chirrup and you have to give them the finger. Within, the office has begun to stir. You're heading up, but pause briefly to glower at the guy reading about that fat chick you dropped last week. He can't see your lips move, but he pales and clicks off the monitor anyway. Spiderperson. Dum de dahh dahh. De da deee din. Dinnah dinnah dinnah dinn—Batprick.

At the top of the building you look down. An error. There is no venom can cure vertigo. Hugging against the pane you fish into your tights, coveting Batprick's utility belt and the clean lines it grants his spandex suit. Sufficiently recovered you pump the nozzle that connects to the canisters on your back. A spray of suds glistens in the noon sun. A rainbow forms briefly in the precipitate. When you return the nozzle to the back of your tights, a chamber of soapy water dribbles down the crack of your Spiderarse. Occupational hazard. Wadding some web into a ball in your palm, you indolently push the grubbying slosh around the pane. Consoling yourself with the knowledge that in some Bat place, at the same Bat time, Batprick is doing his community service. And Batprick will be repaying his debt to society with a black Bat eye.

THE END.

Summer Camp

The lacquer emerging from beneath the swooning bristles was a babyish sort of pink. The technician had been stealthily shaping her nails for weeks now. Gone were the delicate almonds she had nurtured since puberty. In their place, sweeping talons advertised their impracticability. They tapped impatiently beside unopened cans of tonic water. They obliged her to wait for the bathroom to empty, to slap at the taps with her palms like a cat.

When the colour simpered on each finger the technician rose, sweeping up the cushion that had been balanced on his knee. Retracting, it seemed, a proposal.

"There you are, Delores. I will return this afternoon for your pedicure and then you will be beautiful."

But Delores could not see that there was anything wrong with the varnish he had applied there yesterday. 'Thank you. I simply can't wait. Incredible work. As always.' The technician, who had already turned in progress to the next sunlounger, shied away her compliments with a trailing hand; his plump hairy fingers rough, manly, bitten to the quick.

"Fish lady."

She had not begged his pardon; fearful she had heard correctly, fearful that his agglutinated consonants might not be unmated from the startling imputation they had formed in her ear. She felt the vanilla-scented lotion stinging in the recesses where the exfoliation had been most painstaking. But by the third week, the ritual had begun to enliven her to his idiosyncratic adieu.

"Be Shh Reedy."

Hearing this, she remained quiet. Glad to be thought of as thin. And her skin glowed. It was many months later—time in which she had made steady gains in overall lustre—before she was able to appreciate his valediction for what it had become.

"Beach Ready."

Helen was most devastating. When she had first appeared beside the pool, the body of women moaned. When her plump lips were squeezed together in an infantile pout she ached with beauty. There was a satisfaction to be had in observing her mouth open to impart, with a lilt and a lisp, grotesquely snaggled teeth. It was no great accident when the long chiffon robe, which dripped like milk from her alabaster collarbones, got caught beneath the kitten heel of her feathery slipper. Those are pearls that were her teeth. Look! When she reappeared, her mouth was haloed with yellowing bruises, it was dazzlingly clear that the implants had been a great success. Her jaw hung now, comely and slack, offering up their unreal brightness to the other women. Speech had become an impediment, so she didn't. Speak, that is.

Oh yes, we were the lucky ones. The natural beauties. Populating the other sunbeds were women who simply could not be seen, their voluminous bandages moistening with perspiration beneath the burning noon sun. A rising stir preceded any unmasking. The surgeon always dismissed the women's chatter as foundationless gossip but we just knew, like we had once known when a chicken was roasted by the clarity of its juices. We didn't eat that way anymore. And we certainly didn't slave over ovens. One fiendishly hot afternoon a group of us spontaneously began to claw at the linen sheets of a mummy— the one with the impossible proportions. The trussed hourglass bucked and wriggled like a worm beneath a pin, emitting an unearthly moan. We were eventually separated from our quarry by a man who ran out shrieking from the salon block, swinging a dirty mop. Broken nails studded the chrysalis like a Christmas orange. It was just hysterical.

Then there were the others. They only came out at night, their wobbling forms up-lit by the venous pool light. We were kept separate, as if they were another kind of animal. So we had to spy on them. Our bloody celery poked glory holes in the foliage that screened the cocktail balcony. A night safari. Their doughty forms were an inspiration to us. As inspiration to them, our shrieks of mirth.

It was early one morning when I spotted the first emaciated gazelle treading cautiously out into the light. Scars where the loose skin had been taken up were caked over in a body paint that, though expertly applied, could not entirely disguise their raw contours.

"H-h-hi." She said breathily, still sounding like a fat girl.

I wanted to respect the sisterhood but I also wanted to avoid any confusion about pecking order, so I just patted the back of her hand and said 'Yes, that's much, much better.' With that, she toddled away cheerfully, still walking like a fat girl.

There was such a thing as an exeat, or, as we heralded it, the 'beautiful enough' form. It was a telltale sign of the second-week sister to carry it about, hopefully presenting it to the men. They would slowly scan the form, then the sister, then briskly shake their heads and walk away. Longer-term residents had their forms pinned above their cots in the dormitory. The small blank signature box appeared to them in their dreams, where it yawned to infinity. Only Helen had tried to sign her own form. Her initials daubed in the copper brown clots she had spat in the weeks following her tooth job. This hadn't worked either. We wondered whether it was because she had lied.

Quite often there was crying. I was leafing through a glossy between treatments when it all became too much. The sobbing had been going on for ages. Somebody had to do something about it. When I raised my arm to summon an assistant, I saw that all the other women were pointing their thin reproachful eyes at me.

I tried Helen first. Watched her picking over a fruit salad for an hour, receiving approving glances from the waiter, until I saw her vertebrae align and the globes of her bottom peel from the vinyl seat. Outside I made my way to the lounger next to hers. 'Good morning.'—.' Emboldened, I continued, 'So, Helen, I was thinking—

The music that had tinkled in the background was increased in volume. I tried to speak again. So, Helen, I was thinking—But another sudden increment in volume meant I was speaking to myself. The thumping bass shook the palm leaves above. Helen peered over her sunglasses, giving me a look that I had to interpret as admonishing despite the botulinum toxin in her forehead. I pretended not to understand, to casually sip at my cocktail. But the noise shook my jaw until pretty soon I had chewed my straw flat.

The gazelle was next in my sights. It had grown no less timid. At lunch it was sole occupant of a corner table. A man stood behind, slapping its hooves whenever they extended towards the food. Clearly, she had caught an infection from one of her wounds. A negative pressure drain gurgled mournfully beneath the table as I sat down. Its wild eyes rolled in terror but it couldn't escape, so I ate my peas. Having made a near full rotation of my steamed vegetable portions, I glanced up. Its fist was clamped around a fork, white in the knuckles. The man was keeping an uncompromising grip on its wrist. This was my chance. I teased out a locket from my hair and, slowly, defiantly, began to saw at it with my table knife. The guards sprang me from every angle. I fought and fought, putting my claws to their one good use. As they carried me from the restaurant, I used my unrestrained foot to motion between the gazelle and her plate. 'Eat,' it said. And eat she did.

I was told in no uncertain terms that the new length did little for me, on account of my heavy jaw. Tomorrow perhaps there could be extensions, but today not. He couldn't work magic, lady. It was my own fault. Having suffered the indignation of the hairdresser, I was loosed into the yard. I hid the shattered nails from the technician as I passed, but he didn't look up from his work in progress. The gazelle I traced to a distant bench, where she was snoring softly in time with the grunt of the suction machine. Her hands rested upon a small postprandial pot. As the clip of my heels closed in, she startled into wakefulness. It was too late by then. I was upon her. I sat beside her and peeled apart the mouth of my clutch. I fumbled under the make-up, moisturisers, scent, and tissues for my crumpled exeat form. 'You have to sign this. It's payment for the meal. You have to sign.' She shrugged, her rounded gesture allowing for flesh that wasn't there anymore. I pointed a lipstick into her face and twisted it up, staring deeply into her soft-lashed brown eyes. When she took it,

I began to wriggle my shoes off. The lipstick trailing off the page as I ripped it out of her hands and ran. My feet slapping heavily on the flagstones, unaccustomed now to flatness.

Breathless and bedraggled, I offered up my form to a man who stood next to the door on the only exterior wall of the compound. He took the paper, turning it up, down and over but found no purpose there. He handed it back, shaking his head.

"Look lady, I don't know what you think you've got here, but you can leave any time. You only stay here if you want to be beautiful."

And with that he swung open the door. Held it there like a true gent.

That is a dream from which s/he wakes sweating.

Thomas is led by the hand across the busy market street and to the house. The door is open. She has been babysitting for her friend.

The woman leading him is a neighbour who knows the house well.

Go into the back garden.

The father is there. They discuss his wife, who has been suffering from depression and agitation.

You talk to him and eventually see the man's wife lying crumpled on the ground near to a shallow hollow.

He explains something. Leads them back through the house. There are noises coming from the floor. The bottom door, he bolts and says is stuck. Climbs over the top of the door. Says he will walk round and let the woman out the other way.

She watches him cross the street towards a pub. Shouting. A commotion ensues. [He was asking for help, because someone had broken into his house.]

They climb out of the window. S/he runs out of the house shouting in panic. [It may have dawned on the woman that the man's wife was dead.] They find a policeman.

The News Report is a man killed his wife. Apparently, mentally unstable. Risked revealing the secret of the child in their basement.

Use that horrible 1.29 seconds of not knowing whether the story is true. Dream begins to prompt further memories of adoption into family.

Adoptive m/other takes teenaged Thomas to visit his father in prison.

He is old & weak and his face is deformed by scar tissue. He is barely human. It is his birthday. You hug him and say happy birthday. He is scared of going to a lower security prison because he could be killed. You are scared because it means he is less secure.

Leaving the institution, you think of your disabled brother who you have never met. He is somewhere in an institution.

If you would like to give the stranger a lift turn to page 94.

The Lost Property

The plan proceeds from within to without; the exterior the result of the interior.

Le Corbusier, *Towards a New Architecture*

Thom Smith is missing. Neighbours heard the cat mewling; had seen claws skittering beneath the door, prying back needles of timber from the threshold. It wasn't any of their business. The cadaver would decompose beneath a pencil sketch of the Chrysler building; beneath a blueprint of the flats, his flats, in which the dead cat stank; beneath an empty frame, itself a geometric delight awaiting Thom's divine inspiration to fill it up. When the smell slunk around the jamb, the larded hindquarters of the neighbours' dog began to quiver and its nostrils twitched. A petition of querulous whines as prelude, then the bitch began to bark. The sputum-strung gallery of her throat wheeled from bejewelled fingers that bargained for peace with chocolate. Days later, when the owner began to detect a faint peculiar odour— the sweet and rotten stench of loss—then, something had to be done. She located the factotum, who carefully wiped his loaded brush back into the paint tin and laid it carefully atop where it was fated to dry and spoil.

In the removal of the decayed cat—amidst a profusion of profane condemnation, amidst the certitude that this Smith guy was some kind of animal, amidst the scrape of a shovel and a hurtle to vomit from the kitchen window—the post-it note is found. Fluttering on the refrigerator, the once blue ink bleached to a barely decipherable lilac, 'Gone to find myself. T. S.'.

Here, then, the architect's flat but whither our architect?

Before the West Face

I double in the white heat of the day, the hot black glass doors of the West Entrance close behind me. This is the end. I imagine the steps I have taken outlined in chalk: soleless haloes sketch my circuit of the West face, dim marks leading along the wall and into the elevator, more livid the recent steps emerging from the opposite elevator. Here, on the threshold, they double: a son's faltering bid to mimic his father's prints in the sand.

In the descent of the lift, it was my own ghost that I saw in the mirror. Attacking myself with a fury that dissipates into the biological scrutiny that preceded it. I am pulling my face. I am prodding my face. I am touching my face. My fingers hover above father's cheekbones. And I know now I will not know him. My trail on the floor above can be followed back to the office, between the close walls of the corridor. My heart threatening to shatter as the door closed behind me with a polite but final snick.

We had talked briefly. Then he had pushed out his palms. This apparent offer of an embrace resolving into resignation, as his fingers splayed, shoulders hunched, and head tipped. There was nothing he could do for me.

When I had rapped the door of the West Office, my stiff spine and swirling brain had reminded me of a spinning top and, by extension, the other childish things I had put away. I hesitate in the open lift mouth, easing my shoulders in slow circles. On the way down I force myself into a state of agitation. I whisper incantations in the mirror until I can hardly talk around the rapidity of my breaths, can hardly hear myself over the blood in my ears.

It is time. Three-eleven: palms flat against the wall, my breath pumping out of me and condensing on the marble frieze. In the foyer, I had killed time. Acute anxiety deconstructing itself, pulling high tension wiring steel by steel out of my vertebrae.

In the preceding minutes I relax, moving through a variety of postures; the quarters of my body pivoting into composure like a Rubik's solution. Three-three: I lose all sense of awareness of my body and the foyer is so silent I can hear my watch ticking, in tune with the distant clop of an old man's shoes. For some seconds I stand in the doorway, guiding the heavy door to a gentle close with a trailing hand. The bright sunlight outside but inside, this cold darkness. I stood before the building as the bell-tower chimed for three.

Enveloped in the reflected fluorescence, I grin. Today is the day my life will begin again. Today is the day my search ends. I can feel it in my bones. My lips swallow a word—Father. Then I back into the west of the city, into a feverous year of searching. So white. The building a sensuous echo, the heat of the day ebbing as I recede.

Before the North Face

3:00 p.m.
The bell tolled but you just went inside. You went inside. Yes, of course you looked at it first: the doors were black slabs and the building was a white slab chequered with windows. The uniformity resolved your purpose. This was no time to be romantic. You had come for your wife.

3:01 p.m.
Inside was a slightly different matter. The walls curved inward towards the ceiling and the division was difficult to be precise about. The walls were endowed with a mural. A crude community project, possibly. In lurid colours, people with uneven numbers of spidery fingers and a spirited curve of red that looked like a rent in the paint, as if the building was cut and bled of it. The violence of the smile was a happy, definite force. You understood the need to put a brave face on it. It is a picture of a Mummy who is very like your wife. Although this is a garish, childish rendering, its qualities tessellate in your minds eye because memory has been fickle. Alcohol leaching the colour from the still-life of your high-spirited moments. The bride is spider-fingered and her smile wounds you in sleep. You did. Nowadays the photograph in your wallet curls at the edges, the finish thumbed from gloss to matt. You turn away from the mural and walk. Summoning the lift, you put a brave face on. You try to be reasonable about this. In the ascent, you pause to straighten the knot of your tie. It is time.

3:13 p.m.
The door numbers indicate a short walk will suffice to bring you to the North Office. No tricks there. Your watch indicates your earnestness —one minute early. An automatic hand returns to confirm the lie of your tie, the other raps crisply upon the door.

3.15 p.m.
Look, I am trying to be reasonable about this! How can you tell me you cannot tell me? Does that mean you know, or not? I

came here because you told me you could help me. I came here because I have to find my wife.

3:22 p.m.

During the descent, you admit that you lost your temper. In such situations, can this be considered unreasonable? No. Spots of blood prickling on your grazed knuckles. What you didn't get was the result, Sir. Unconsciously you begin to chew a thumbnail. The mirror betrays this flicker of humanity and you whip your hand from your face. You flatten your arms to your side, an un-indulgent enclosure of the bodily self. Pitching a mantra. I can count on me.

Before the East Face

One hundred walks in the park in stop-motion. The process was almost organic. Around the stumps of walls the steels appeared. They grew like ambitious ivy, always a little higher than their host, as she sat cross-legged in East Park. It is the building of a building, building her hopes. This is immense. Colossal. Striping out the cards on the grass in the ancient pattern she hankers for fate's fingers, but the cards are a magic trick and the building foils them. They read nothing like the promise of the building. Perhaps the cards are jealous. A breeze scatters the pack. You recover and count them. The lost card an invisible talisman.

Approaching from the East impacts upon her. She is too much in her head, she thinks. She thinks. She thinks the sun is exciting. It makes the building foster the Sanskrit shadows of pigeons alarmed by her steps. Imagine her daughter. She sits on the edge of a fountain, imagining her daughter. When the building fixes on her and she cannot escape the fire of it. Closes them. Her eyelids offer no respite from the reflected glare. Opens them. To look directly at the building is irreverent and it causes her eyes to burn with guilt. Closes them. It is too early to go into the building but it is so hard not to want to move towards warm light, then to be swallowed into the shadows within. In the pink glare her neck is blessed by stray droplets.

She thinks inside the building. She shall put palm to the black glass, it will not be cold like it promises. The heat of the glass will infuse the meeting of her palm and its reflected other. The door will give in. There will be no confusion in the building. The building will be temple-empty and her path will be clear. With such clarity she can trace the square her passage through the building will make. She will circulate the peripheries of the East face.

The foyer will compose her, for she will be nervous though her faith may never waver. In the foyer energy streams will trail in every direction. There is love in this building and it is love will return her daughter. The lift will be called and she will await it, a blessed gift from the higher-planes of mortar consciousness. It will taste her between its four mirrors on the journey. It will want to keep her because she is so full of love. It will treasure her from four angles; in minutiae, in a way just small enough that she is able to comprehend it, the lift reflects the way the building will have owned her. Each side an eye.

Then there shall be the corridor and the office in the middle. The fifth of eleven square tinted widows and the only one ajar. The other doors are but false prospects. They file away to nothing in the distance and behind them, who can tell? Behind her door is he who can find her daughter. She waits again to feel the love of the building, to let the lines cool her awkwardness. They do. She begins the ceremony, observing every ritual politeness. She will not rush this. She is desperate to hear. She must not rush this. Opens them. The pigeons have resettled.

Before the South Face

I am looking for my brother. What I have found: a plane, a train, a taxi, a building. I have some minutes before my appointment. I stand at the foot of the South face; a little girl facing a chalk cliff I have set upon to climb. The town clock chimes in the distance and I count the chimes because I know how many are coming. It is time.

It is a short walk through the black glass doors. Their mystique is brief because I do not hesitate. There are people in the foyer. An old man makes a little progress along the far wall before stopping to examine a painting there. I am a little afraid of him, his nervous hands fluttering over the picture. His erect spine has a common tension with the building. He looks like he might work here but his interest in the mural betrays him. Perhaps he is a tourist? Perhaps he is lost? Lost in this building! The other man is younger. I am aware of myself, watching him. I lean back against the cool wall and allow myself to watch him only from the corner of one eye. He slumps towards the wall and I watch his fists grinding. Motes swim — the debris of humour. Perhaps he is ill. He slides along the wall as if martyred by vertigo. His progress, slow, ends in full crumple. His hands and forehead pressed there, as if it were the level ground at long last. A minute or more he is like this. I move a foot. I wonder should I help him. Suddenly he is away from the wall and the lift swallows him up. The old man too has gone.

Entrance an ageing woman in bright, loose clothing. Her raised hands itch through the dust in the beams of light thrown down by the small high windows. She appears to be coming straight for me. Is she waving? By now she is close enough to me that I am almost sure I do not know her. Indeed, her eyes are closed? In trepidation of the embarrassment of her harassment—and because it is time—I turn and hurry to take the far lift. It arrives and it is empty and I am glad. I compose myself within it. The possibilities of my meeting, the certain replies to my questions.

In the office the official is cordial. I want to strike him. He has no right to give me bad news with ease. My supplications to his better nature fix his frog grin. Of course, he is sorry. But it is a big world. People have their privacy. Perhaps, Miss, your brother is not lost. Perhaps, Miss, your brother does not wish to be found.

1. This train terminates at Ponders End.

2.

3.

4.

5.

6.

7.

8.

9.

I would like to die:
(a) peacefully, in my sleep—turn to page 94.
(b) in the heat of battle—turn to page 76;
(c) saving a child—turn to page 54.

Document

It is supposed to have begun in the borough of H_____ on a bitter winter's evening, yet the first I heard of the matter was as late as last Wednesday. Having found myself obliged to visit a district library to consult an obscure text; and having found a dusty gap on the shelf where that missing book was supposed to sit; I sought a productive means by which to spend the evening of my vain stay in the margins.

I sent a line to a business acquaintance who kept premises nearby and was able to arrange to meet him in the bar of an imposing Gothic-revival hotel, which impended over one of the less reputable passages that opened from the main drag.

It was our custom to meet whenever his procurement of stock brought him to the monthly antiquary market in my district. It was his custom to bring to our meetings either a new and tempting manuscript, or else a manuscript that he felt I had neglected to see the temptation of at one of our previous encounters. He was persistent with good reason because he had the curious talent of being able to read my tastes before my tastes had become fully legible to me.

Thus was I lost in thought, when the proposed hour of our meeting struck.

As the final chime rebounded amid the miscellany of hotel patrons, the distant door slid open. The brash lobby lights made the figure on the threshold a sinister silhouette, but the shadow's dimensions and disarray divulged its source to be an emaciated ragged woman. The beggar made slow progress through the lamp-lit hall, flitting between the shadows cast by its columns. Returning to my thoughts and my ale, the wench was quickly forgotten by me. I was luxuriating in one of those exquisite moments where one has ones thoughts to oneself and likes it, when the beggar impertinently scraped back the chair opposite my own. It was then that I realised I had been much mistaken.

The figure now seating himself was that of my business acquaintance. It was little wonder that I had not recognised his black shape from across the room, so changed was he since our last meeting. In the place of a man who had always been meticulous in his habits of dress, stood a hunched, wraith-like being, whose clothes hung about him, crumpled and spoiled. His pink eyes rolled between black lids. It was evident that he had been gravely ill.

Ashamed of the grimace of revulsion with which I had met him, I looked down at the table and determined to make no immediate comment on his appearance. Perhaps I would be able to make inquiries later in the evening, if there arose a moment in which my lurid fascination might be mistaken for natural and sympathetic concern.

I should explain that my acquaintance—let us call him 'Thomas'—is far from a close friend. He is not charming. Those accustomed to the observance of social graces would describe his manner as abrupt. Sympathetic gentlemen might have excused his behaviour on the grounds that he was a man possessed by his work. In truth, I think it went further than that.

Thomas's passion for books was equalled only by his distaste for the emotional oscillations and illogical demands of his fellow man. Those who had the misfortune of piquing his interest were likely to expend a good dealt of energy ensuring that they never again drifted into the rolling orb of tarry smoke that emanated, apparently unceasingly, from the bowl of his cheap clay pipe.

Yet, despite his objectionable nature, I have done a great deal of business with Thomas for the simple reason that he is scrupulously, almost pathologically, honest. Indeed, this trait, which might have been a virtue in a better man, had been responsible for ensuring that none he met had ever left his company without knowing precisely Thomas's opinion of their life and work. He was humanity's greatest critic: ruthless, remorseless, operating with fatal precision.

With pained insouciance, I looked up to take in the spectre that Thomas had become. Indifferent to the kindness of my gesture, he fished about in his various pockets. Then, having wordlessly packed and lit his pipe, he exuded a great lung-full of smog across the table. It was literally an assault upon my senses. Unmindful of the choking he had occasioned, Thomas turned his attention to business. Yet, as he placed a sheaf of papers between us, it became apparent that his hand was in the grip of a most uncharacteristic tremor. This was, in all probability, a lingering symptom of his recent illness.

Placing the pages face down upon the table, he paused, apparently wearied by this small activity. Yet, when I reached for them, he was able to plant his palm quickly and firmly atop. His rheumy stare was unnervingly stern. After a tense moment in which he seemed to weigh my very soul, his chapped lips and began to twitch and gibber. There followed speech.

"The provenance of these papers will shock you. It is likely that you will have trouble believing all that I must tell you of them. Yet, believe you must and you shall."

His knuckles whitened and an involuntary spasm caused him to crinkle the paper. He smoothed the pages out fitfully; almost, it seemed, fearfully. The document looked cheap and modern. It was not at all the kind of thing I would usually be interested in and I rather suspect that it was their unlikely aspect, rather than Thomas's dramatic prologue, that had begun to intrigue me.

Thomas dragged lengthily upon his pipe, then, still holding down the papers, he leant forward to continue his speech. I felt his breath, ragged and foul, on my face. Several droplets of sweat began to emerge on his temples. Covering the lower half of my face in a barely plausible mimicry of thoughtful interest, I hoped that his illness was not contagious.

"You do not know Rosemarie," he whispered, as though daring me to draw closer.

I did not.

"I knew her as a mischievous little girl, as a bashful adolescent and, finally, as a the fine young woman she then became. You know that I am not" and here his foxed skin crumpled around a knowing sneer, "indulgent by nature, but she was one who seemed to fall outside of the grosser lot of humanity."

For Thomas, this was fond talk and I was taken aback; his irritation at my speechlessness writ large in the glinting of small teeth between snarling, rotten-looking lips. He reset his heading.

"She was terribly afraid of me all her life and the better for it. She would never dare have lied to me."

Apparently troubled by a twinge of pain, he screwed up his

eyes. A glob of rheum teetered on his lashes and splashed down in his ale. I do not think he saw my own lip curl in disgust because he did not look up for some time. Indeed, when the pause had become uncomfortably long, I hesitantly raised my hand and reached towards his thin shoulder, thinking he might require assistance.

Before my fingers made contact, his eyes snapped open. Each of them was red as a harvest moon. As he opened his mouth to speak, he released a moan that appeared to emanate from deep inside him. The whole performance was so deeply unnerving, that I did not know whether I should try to help, or try to run.

—Ah, but you are not well, my friend. I gasped, crouched over my seat.

"No." He snapped, his sore eyes fixing me in their full horror, "I am not myself, but that is not your concern."

As I re-seated myself, Thomas flexed his free hand over the table. His fingers worked themselves open and closed spasmodically. Still clutching at the air, he continued his story.

"When I saw Rosemarie last, she had much to tell me. A week earlier, she had paid a visit to an old friend, just as you are doing now. You do not mind if I call you my friend?"

His bloody eyes were for a moment so wild with desperation and I did not dare do else but nod. My action seemed to salve him a little.

"It is good to have had a friend, perhaps."

Bony fingers clawing at the air between us.

"Oh, but Rosemarie was forever with such people as she called her friends. The friend she visited that night lived locally; but a stone's throw from here, had I only had one."

His laughter was barely a wheeze. I tried to smile with him but my goodwill was too weak to propel my mouth.

"This friend, you see, was a client of mine, so I knew that he was a nasty piece of work. Well, despite my forbiddance, she had arranged to meet him at his house. She described the building to me. Yes, I remember her exact words, for they were quite vivid. 'It was,' she said, 'a building of such astonishing blankness, that it almost sucked at the eye.' When she was able to tear her attention from the façade, she followed the black-tiled path to the front door and rang the bell once, twice, thrice. It was none answered. When finally she knocked, the door swung inwards on its hinges.

"As her eyes adjusted to the gloom inside, she saw that winter had been encroaching there for some time. The hall tiles glistered with frost; a view that she described as 'almost unearthly.' Rosemarie, as foolishly brave as the day she was born, stepped over the small pile of sodden post that littered the threshold and walked towards the staircase, leaving a trail of footprints in the ice.

"The creak of the lowest step startled her, but she ascended all the same, driven, no doubt, by her insatiable curiosity. 'Curiosity killed the cat,' I used to tell her this when, as a youth, I would catch her creeping about her father's garden. I even demonstrated it to her once, leading her to a barn in which a calico kitten had been curious about a rat-trap. I suppose I am sorry that I did not manage to cultivate the kind of relationship that would have given my advice more import.

"At the top of the four short flights, the door to her friend's flat stood open. Inside was pitch-black. The light-switch click echoed through the empty rooms but procured no light, the power, she reasoned, being out from the storm.

"She did not turn back. O, that she had turned. Instead, she took a box of matches from her pocket and lit one. The small circle of light it provided was barely enough to guide her into the sitting-room. Her friend was nowhere to be seen, but a shelf of his bric-a-brac—bird-skulls, instruments, geodes, and bones—threw ghastly shadows on the near wall.

"Amongst the hellish trinkets, she found the nub of a candle, which she lit. Its guttering light revealed a clutch of papers on the small floor, which she dutifully gathered up. Rising, then, to her knee she saw it. Her shriek pierced the darkness. She had come face to face with his latest acquisition. Where the wicker chair had been was now a statue. A creeping mess of branch-like protuberances, arachnoid and grasping.

"Embarrassed by her over-reaction, but unable to shake away the waves of fear that seemed to pulse from the beastly artwork, she hurried down the stairs and into the street. She would not have called upon me under any other circumstances, I think, but my shop was near and nothing else was. She arrived on my doorstep pink-cheeked, distressed and still clutching the document. This document."

His claw, finally loosed from its convulsion, clattered down upon the page.

Now he had stopped, his story seemingly at an end, he smiled broadly and laughed. The source of the laughter apparently private, I waited uncomfortably for it to end.

Relieving his hold upon the document for the first time since he had set it down, he flexed the newly freed fingers in an experimental manner before placing the hand in his pocket, evidently unconcerned with, or resigned to, the result of the exercise.

—How much do you sell it for?

The smile returned, but the laughter sputtered, the laughter guttered, the laughter was swallowed down, down.

"Oh, no. For you, my…" his wizened hand hanging between us like twigs "friend, this is a document without a price in pence and pounds."

No detail of his outlandish tale that evening surprised me so much as that! My own hand crept into the space that his had occupied atop the papers, lest he change his mind.

I felt I had to offer to accompany him back to his lodgings given his frail state but was relieved when he sharply refused.

He slowly pulled himself into an approximation of standing, seemingly unable to untangle his disease-ridden bones into the full upright.

"I shall not see you again. Consider the document a parting gift."

After the shocks of the evening, I was glad enough of his promise not to seek the explanation for its assertion. He shuffled away, his eyes swivelling in their sockets, his fingers crabbed into accusatory poise. It seemed as if his body was attempting to reject him.

I did not attempt to read the document immediately. I gathered up the pages and, protected them between leaves of a sturdy book, then stowed them safely in my bag. I left the bar, glad to be rid of the unnerving companionship of my business acquaintance and eager to return to my lodgings. I was tired, even a little stiff, as a result of having sat for so long in tense expectation of his words.

However, there was to be one more twist in the evening's tale, for as I stepped out into the cold, cold night, I fairly brained myself on a statue in the same mould as that which Thomas had described. Its flowing branches, though seemingly hostile to pattern or verisimilitude of any kind, were vital. It was a beastly, inhuman, and human thing all at once. How could that be? How I could have missed it when I entered the building? I hurried around it, into the night.

At home I eagerly undressed, climbed beneath the bedclothes and slept the sleep of the damned. You will hardly believe me, friend, but I quite forgot the document until this very day. Until I read it to you now.

was bright and uncommonly warm. An omnibus passed before the high noon sun and cast her, for a moment, in shadow. When it returned, the light irradiated her fashionably pale summer dress. She strode towards the free library, but her thoughts were elsewhere. He had visited her earlier in the previous week, imposing with the excuse that he would benefit from her opinion on an excerpt from a new novel he had been asked to review for the magazine. As a sensible young woman, he wondered, did she feel that, was it a bit, well, a bit too near to the knuckle? As she walked, she blushed. He had, perhaps, wanted to see her as well. The young couple had been forced to spend the night alone, in a cave. She was an innocent young thing and didn't understand that there would be repercussions. There was a was bright and uncommonly warm. An omnibus passed before the high noon sun and cast her, for a moment, in shadow. When it returned, the light irradiated her fashionably pale summer dress. She strode towards the free library, but her thoughts were elsewhere. He had visited her earlier in the previous week, imposing with the excuse that he would benefit from her opinion on an excerpt from a new novel he had been asked to review for the magazine. As a sensible young woman, he wondered, did she feel that, was it a bit, well, a bit too near to the knuckle? As she walked, she blushed. He had, perhaps, wanted to see her as well. The young couple had been forced to spend the night alone, in a cave. She was an innocent young thing and didn't understand that there would be repercussions. There was a duel for her honour. It was set in the south of France, which she was careful to mention she intended to visit one day. Her answer had been meticulous. She said she thought it was not too near the knuckle, but that it seemed to her to be awful tosh.

'It is awful tosh, isn't it? I will say as much in the magazine, but with care that those who worship Auntie Ethel are not able to intuit it. I am glad you do not like it. I shouldn't have wanted you to like it. Or to think it too near the knuckle.'
His eyes traced the ridges that seemed to him impossibly elegant. She smiled across the silence and fanned away the uncommonly warm spring air with a painfully casual hand.

'It is rather warm in here, isn't it John.'
He examined his fingernails minutely, but his face betrayed the glimmer of a smile. She sipped her tea and determined that she must further review this problem of caves, by thoroughly examining the extract in context.

The thoroughfare was popular and crossing it was not without its perils. Nevertheless, she proceeded across to the library, deciding that it would most likely be worth risking the stream of automobile. She passed safely through the open door and into the quiet and cool inner sanctum. As she moved to browse the recently acquired novels she noticed a familiar form at the news table. She coloured slightly. It was him. All began to blur before her. He saw her and, smiling and expectant, he motioned that they might meet, in a moment, when her business was complete. All books now seemed to her surrounded by a circle of invisible censors. The inane chatter of the plain women, who browsed the ranks of battered Corellis, aroused within her a burning need to make a judicious selection.

Will you select the contemporary popular novel that was the purpose of your visit? If so, turn to page 31.

If you think you would do better to select something impressive and improving—possibly even scientific—turn to page 44.

Postlewd

★Total Sensory Depravation★ the letters raised this, nothing more. The white flyer had been vacuum moulded, bore no trace of ink. R. had found it behind T.'s ear that afternoon in bed. She often found things there. Something of the freaky magician about her. Coins and gum and grams of varying potency. T. took the card between his finger and thumb like a piece of glass. Turned it three ways: back, front, back. There was no address. Sometimes R. told you and sometimes she didn't. She told T.. T. was quietly sceptical. Used it to edge together a line on the table next to the bed. Inhaled deeply through a rolled flyer. Pinched his nose. Sat carefully. Nobody will be able to hear the music. Nobody will know if anyone is there. No fun. R. snickered. Her studded tongue shuddered in her open mouth. She rose slowly from the bed and stretched before the window. This only light source made her a lithe silhouette as she dressed with efficiency. T. the faithless. She turned to look over her shoulder, her eyeball glassy where the light bent around. You needn't come. She smiled but he couldn't see it. Left.

T. spent Tuesday smoking. Downloading a playlist onto his digital music player. He still wasn't going, but in case he changed his mind. R. hadn't been around again since she left. It didn't indicate. R. was just like that. T. was cool. He didn't mention it. Downloading was tedious work and his eyes were pink from the thick smoke. The room sticky with the smell of the skunk. The Internet distracted him frequently. He trawled through porn sites seeking a girlish rush from the graphic images. Every act repeated. Men like clones. Wet skin so tightened by silicone, it looked like it would squeak under caress. It wasn't working. Frustrated, he switched his hunt to text. He sighed, felt predictable, loosened his belt. At the shopping list of genres T. paused to survey his mood. Hovered over 'Man Friendly', laughed and hammered the button over 'Rough Sex'. T. was not a romantic. T. was an old hand. He had to skip three screens of titles to find the untapped material.

Red was six foot five, strong but not handsome. She had a paunch and her checked shirt was tight round it. She was called Red on account of her red hair which was long and tied in a ponytail. Her hair was dirty and it fell in her eyes. The red haired Texan sat in her pick-up outside the motel and chain-smoked. She hated waiting. It made her mad.

T. hated waiting. It made him skip text. Skimmed words tumbled into his brain. Prostitutes. Brother turning tricks. Teach him a lesson. T.'s fingers slipped under his clothes. He parted himself with a deft finger. He hadn't expected to be wet already. Perhaps the thirty smiling, blonde cocksuckers had done something for him after all. They had grinned blithely in the short free videos as they rolled pools of ejaculate across their conspicuously talented tongues. Bodies shaved closely in all the right places. The foregrounded organs convulsing lightly as they began to sag. Perhaps it was just anticipation of the act. He stroked each cunt lip, plump with blood. Lowered a single finger against the warm wet hole, delicately hushing it. He pushed just the tip of his finger in, his clitoris hungered by the intrusion. Another fingertip, forced in alongside, stretched him to satisfaction. He shuffled forward on the chair and tilted his hips. In one smooth thrust T. had forced both fingers up to the hand, with an almost inaudibly low moan, and held them there enjoying the sensation of being full. He returned his attention to the monitor as he began to fuck himself slowly. His clitoris grazed by the shifting material of his trousers. The fucking brought forth come in excited dribbles. They rolled down the tilted cheeks of his ass and soaked through onto the chair beneath.

Red had put the tape over his mouth before he had noticed her in the dark motel room. His first scream was only air out of his nose; a noise stuck in his throat.
"Do you know what Mom would say, bitch? She'd say you were a dirty little bitch who needed to be taught a lesson."
Red loosened her belt and opened her fly. She didn't wear shorts. Her huge purple dick thrust out of her pants like a weapon. The small boy gagged in fear. She enjoyed her brother's eyes on her,

despite she was only doing it to teach him. She flexed her circled fingers up and down the rigid shaft, flicking the foreskin up and down inches away from his blinking face.

"Momma told that this aint no life for you. Whores get what they get and what whores get is fucked."

She took the hand from her dick and grabbed a fistful of his hair. She dragged him up and onto the bed forcing his face into the dirty sheets. She used more tape to fix she wrists behind his back, being careful that his face was sideways so as he wouldn't suffocate. She pulled up his legs and though he resisted he was soon on his knees because of Red was so strong. His denim skirt was really short and it rode up to reveal some red lacy panties which barely contained his bald pussy.

T. slowly pulled out, his cunt awash from the long deep thrusts. He felt a sensation on the cusp of pain. An openness. His vagina seizing with longing. His clitoris electrified under his first touches, thirsting for a rhythm.

The panties crumpled against the wall and slid onto the floor in the corner. Red spread his brother's legs widely and stared at his prize. She watched his little asshole clench. She pulled his vagina lips apart with her thick, tobacco stained fingers and jabbed at the opening roughly. The boy's yelp was muted by the tape.

"What? You got none wet for your own sister?"

Actually she was a little disappointed.

"You get fucked for money but your own sister's dick aint welcome? You scared it's too big? No dick is too big for no little bitch whore."

Without warning Red pushed her finger deep into his tight, dry vagina making him buck violently. He was crying. Red felt a little pity and made a snap decision to make it easier on him. So she lashed her thick tongue into him and wriggled it a little. Then she began to lap at him like an ice cream, slathering his dry hole with spit. Next she spat in her hand and rubbed the length of her cock. It was solid. She mounted the bed on her knees and positioned herself between his spread legs. She pushed the head of her dick against his hole and rubbed it against him, enjoying the tease.

"Now you're gonna find out how a whore gets fucked, not like those pussy frat girls pay you to do it."

She punched into him. His cunt was still quite dry and the resistance gave good friction. She looked down at his cunt hole stretched taught around the fat stem of her huge cock. She paused, deep inside him and took a deep breath and laughed as she began to thrust slowly in an out. She began to thrust harder and faster ramming it into him. To her surprise his cunt slickened.

"You whore assed bitch, you like big dicks. You like your sister fucking you. You little slut.'

She was mad. She was mad twice. Once because her little brother was a slut and twice because his wetness had lessened her pleasure. She slipped in and out of she with relative ease now. She pulled out, her unsatisfied dick running with cunt juice.

"Your whoring pussy has had too much dick, I reckon. You know what that means bitch. You did this to yourself."

She rubbed her fingers in the cum and pushed a wet finger against his tiny asshole. It was clenched hard but was no match for a little force and her finger soon wiggled inwards. He was trying to shout but only whimpers were audible. She pulled out and pushed two fingers into him, stretching the hole. Her fingers were big and it obviously hurt him and his face was red with pain and shame. She finger fucked him slowly.

"You better relax bitch. This is medicine. It'll taste all the worst if you don't let it happen."

Her fingers were in him past the second knuckle before she pulled them out. She jabbed her dick into his cunt to get it nice and wet before pushing the massive head against the tight hole above. She pushed in with an even pressure and, as he roared into the tape, he yielded to her inch by inch. As she began to fuck him the little muscles caressed her swollen dick and made her balls ache. As her ecstasy grew she had almost forgotten altogether the purpose of the act. She reached round and began to stroke his clitoris. She hardly noticed her thrusts being tentatively met. As he shuddered beneath her she drove into him her deepest thrust. Her orgasm rushed through her and she squirted load upon load of cream into the bitch's ass.

T. focused on the array of gross images as his hand clipped backwards and forwards. He was close. He ached for resolution. His mind poised on the act of forced entry, the penile tip penetrating the first inches of his forbidden cunt. His ass. He came violently in silence.; His body, wracked by orgasm, spilled from the sticky chair as its weak leg gave way. T. spent some minutes recovering on the floor. Made a decision. Detached the music player. Hit the shower. The cool water dribbled across his clitoris, still itching with the heat of orgasm. Submerging his head in the streaming water, his ears filled with noise, his open mouth filling like a basin, running over his breasts and feet.

T. in the mirror: clean, dry, sweet smelling. Selecting a sweet scent to dab about his wrists and neck. His hair curling slightly as it dries off. Standing in the gaping maw of his wardrobe. Would it matter what he wore? Nobody would see him. He pulled an old skirt, a tee and tied his hair back. Rubbing some powder into his gums to allay the effects of the dope, T. checked off the possessions in his handbag and shuffled into a coat. Out the door. Down the street. Into a cab.

The driver wasn't sure a pretty boy like him would want to get out in this part of town. The driver was a redhead. T. smiled sweetly, told her to go fuck herself, and skipped the fare.

—Oi! Oi ... you fucking little bitch.

He ran down a side street and heard the tyres squealing as the cabbie pulled away. Collecting himself briefly he began to trace his way to the address. He was nearly, very nearly there.

—The password is...?

You have got to be kidding? No. Some fat cunt on the door. Well this is new. I've got a quarter of a gram that, will that do? No? Okay, okay I have an invite. Not a password but these cards must have cost a lot and she could only have made a few. Here, I've got this card. He waits for a slanging match but the bouncer loses her suspicious edge, smirks and waves him through. The knuckles of her hand somehow graze his ass as he passes, but T.

can't be bothered to debate it. In the cloakroom a girl and a boy, possibly; conscientiously androgynous. At first T. thinks them partygoers but they motion to take his coat. They roll some earplugs at him. He plugs an ear-bud into each ear and they check the volume and acquiesce, wrapping the touchpad round with tape. Fine. Bind the eyes.

Nothing much now. The cold air from the door on his bare arms. Hands on his shoulder pushing him through. He fumbles at a pocket and quarries a pill. Hesitates at waist height. Is it safe here? He can't see anything. Then nobody will, so take it. Dry. The chill breeze culled by a wall of hot air. Brushes past warm arms. It is packed in here. It could be a thousand, could be twelve. His hand finds the wall. He edges past the bodies and tries to make the square. Find the dimensions. It is slow progress. He stops saying 'sorry' only some minutes in, knowing long before that nobody can hear. With a sudden hip-wrench he realises he has bumped against a drinks table. Fingers a capped bottle and expertly ledges the top off with the help of the table edge and a pop of his palm. The beer is sweet. The chemical taste that was dogging him drowns. His skirt twitches with someone passing along behind. He jumps. A warm hand on his left thigh. R.? How did she know? The bastard can see? He raises a hand towards his blindfold. A hand firmly takes his wrist, returns it to his side. Okay. R. has it her way. Hardly a surprise.

She is unusually scented. Delicate in skin, R. eschews scent on all but important occasions. She must stoop to drag her uneven smile across his neck. Her sharp tongue traces a circle. A pattern she has made him familiar with. He melts a little. Self-conscious of the crowd. Another brushes past and T. smacks the back of R.'s hand. She ignores this, moving it upwards, pushing his skirt up against his buttock. T. muses the possibility of others seeing what he isn't able to. Not if he knows R…. Suddenly the premise reveals itself.

R. has the edge. Hers are the only eyes at this party. The pill begins to break over him. His stomach churns. His jaw quakes as he thinks, for only a moment, he may be blissfully, blissfully sick over the floor. Skin is electric and R.'s fingertips edge up the tight skirt towards his… wait. He mustn't, he mustn't. Not here.

Fingertips quake along the inside of his thigh. Then the presence at his back fades like a dream in sunshine. He sways, his cunt bared, alone.

His mind is beautiful and versatile. It doesn't know what to do. R. has left him, sensations heightened, fingers on the tops of his thighs, wild with lust. His right hand inches across onto his exposed mons. Caresses it like R. ought. His finger filters down through the strip of hair and make fatal contact. His clitoris dances. His mind dances. His fingers begins their own waltz. Is he really, truly doing this? Here? Someone says 'yes.' He almost hears it. Come begins to streak a lightening trail towards the floor. His left hand jacking up the skirt, his right hand jacking for all it's worth. Suddenly her fingers are hot, wet and under a familiar pressure. He is not forsaken. R. is kneeling before him, his lover, her tongue tracing the backs of his stalled fingers. He parts them and with them himself. The tongue laps tentatively, expertly, teasingly.

The brush of an ignorant stranger against his left arm announces the danger, the dangerous high of publicity. R.'s skull ruffles up his skirt as her tongue dips into him. He nearly falls away with the depth of sensation. Her tongue probes and pushes and takes. The tongue dips deeper, the thick root of it opening him up. Tongue's tip fluttering deeply inside him. Little teeth glancing against his labia. Giving up the grip it had on him, the tongue slides upwards. Some kind of reach around is happening. The tongue continues to work him, but a finger—no thicker— two fingers push against him from behind and gaining a little advantage in the slough of his juices. Their tips pop inside and cautiously begin to stroke. He wishes for the reach of R.'s long dick. R.'s fingers are also long, though, and arc a rigid curve up into him. The tongue keeps a different stroke, a compliment. It is about to go one of two ways. He wobbles as if about to faint and then comes hard and fast. Forgets not to shout. Hopes it doesn't matter. He can't hear himself, a beat blares in his flushed ears. The fingers shift out still clamped by his spasming muscles. The tongue work becomes wispy, flushing out the vestiges of his orgasm. His right leg stutters.

The chemicals refuse a post-orgasm come down. Synapses spit

and crackle in ecstasy. She doesn't give him long. A hand presses urgently atop his shoulder. In obedience to the pressure he kneels. A velvet pressure against his lips. He traces out his tongue and gathers up wetness. Before he can open his lips for her, she pushes inward. His lips pop around her penis which glides across his wet tongue and hits his throat. Sickness resurfaces. I can do this. Her penis is racing with blood. R. is rougher than usual. Fucks at his face until his nose is full of sweat from her hair. She needs this. Her urgency reawakens him. He sucks, slightly redundantly, at the passing flesh. Settles for sealing his mouth around it in the knowledge she is taking more than he can give. The drugs bubble. It takes a minute at most for a rumbling cascade of hot ejaculate to spray his throat. She pulls out a half-inch and the second wave coats the back of his tongue. He sucks down the salt tang, drawing his mouth tight around the faltering erection. She pushes back his forehead roughly with the butt of her palm and pulls out. Another pop.

R. can recover fast, but T. wants her already. Inside him. All over him. And, somehow, she delivers. Circumnavigating his trembling body, using her rare vision, she grasps his waist and pushes him forward. His hips clatter against the drinks table. She pushes him down. He lets her. Bent like a bracket, he feels cool air wash over his wet exposed cunt. Her tongue is back that quickly, Surprised, T. slumps against the table, hoping it won't collapse. It is solid and he contentedly shifts some weight from his unsteady legs. The tongue rolls thickly around his loosing cunt. He feels his own wetness transfer from his thighs onto the woman's twitching jaw. When she reapplies herself the come returns cooler and stickier. The tongue flicks away, flicks back against his sphincter. Without ceremony the lubricated tongue heaves into his arse. He bucks and, remembering his afternoon, nervously laughs. The feeling is beyond discomfort but not painful. The tongue bucks back and forth, lunging into his steadily relaxing anus. It exits and he waits, gaping.

It doesn't take long. A thick head bumbles against his rim, slips up and down gathering his come. A firm arm wraps around his waist and a splay-fingered hand grasps his mound. An accidental index on the clitoris is a blessing. The head forces into him with little mercy. The eager shaft is slimmer and easily follows the bursting head. In a moment she is waist deep in him. Hold herself there. Enjoying him. Pauses. Begins to pump long even strokes. As the ferocity builds, T. lays a hand across the hand on his cunt, encouraging it. The hand feels big, perhaps because the thick dick in his arse feels big and makes him feel small. The fingers poke downwards teasing the entrance of his vagina. As the index brings his sticky come up to his hard clitoris, the fucking becomes intense. She pumps him. The music in his ears is off beat. It works. As the dick pumps, the hand pumps, the silence then the beat. As something beautiful, a firework, explodes inside, wash after wash after wash of rapture pales out to a gentle euphoria in T.. The wilting penis withdraws and he feels his empty anus blink.

Begins to right himself but a hand is on his back. It is surely impossible, but her erection has revived. As his sphincter shrinks in phases, like a camera shutter, a head wipes itself against his vagina. He has forgotten the room. He is warm. He is wet. So content. The head pumps into his opening. Only the very end penetrates, a fluctuation at the very edge. He wants that familiar pull of it sinking deeply inwards. Suddenly, a feeling, something like a wad of spit lands. Running down his leg. Another spatter on his lower back. More and more and more like thick spring rain as the dick rams home with a violence that begins to shift the blindfold. The women: unfamiliar, glassy eyed, pumping their army of dicks as they jostle to finish in his eyes and hair.

Poor Tom's a-cold.

Edgar

Printed in Great Britain
by Amazon

Churchill's Secret Weapons

CHURCHILL'S SECRET WEAPONS

THE STORY OF HOBART'S FUNNIES

PATRICK DELAFORCE

ROBERT HALE · LONDON

© *Patrick Delaforce 1998*
First published in Great Britain 1998

ISBN 0 7090 6237 0

Robert Hale Limited
Clerkenwell House
Clerkenwell Green
London EC1R 0HT

The right of Patrick Delaforce to be identified as
author of this work has been asserted by him
in accordance with the Copyright, Designs and
Patents Act 1988.

2 4 6 8 10 9 7 5 3 1

Typeset in Garamond by
Derek Doyle & Associates, Mold, Flintshire.
Printed in Great Britain by
St Edmundsbury Press Limited, Bury St Edmunds
and bound by
WBC Book Manufacturers Limited, Bridgend.

Contents

Acknowledgements

Special thanks go to Major Roland Ward RE for his great sapper network of 'Funnies' and to Major W.R. Birt for allowing me to use extracts from his *History of the 22nd Dragoons*, Ian Hammerton for extracts from his *Achtung Minen*, Andrew Wilson for extracts from *Flame Thrower*, to John Smith for extracts from *In at the Finish*. Many thanks to Cassell PLC for permission to use extracts from *The Second World War* by Winston Churchill. My thanks also go to Geoffrey Flint for painting the cover to this book, to Birkin Howard OBE for permission to use his dramatic sketches of AVREs in action, and to the Imperial War Museum Photographic Department for their excellent photographs. Superb regimental histories were written by the late Captain Harry Bailey of the Playboys, by Major G. Storrar of 'A' Squadron, 141 RAC and by R.J.B. Sellar's of the Fife and Forfar Yeomanry. David Sclater, Ted Cheetham and Tom Bishop also lent me vital books. Thanks too to Richard Bullock for his *D-Day Memories of the Westminster Dragoons*, L.A. Wells for his journal *Projectors to Petards* and Andrew S. Gardiner for his personal journal.

Many others were of considerable help, including Frank Armitage, Charles Baldwin, Frank Barber, John R. Bull, Monty Clay, R.F. Collins, Travers Cosway, Bernard Cuttiford, Philip Vaughan Davies, Geoff Dewing, Alan Duncan, Raymond Ellis, Cyril Gloyn, H.R. Hill, E.R. Hunt, Brian Hutchinson, Ian Isley, E. Kitson, John M. Leytham, Ken V. Mee, I.D. Moran, Martin Reagan, J. Robinson, Syd Sadler, Charles Salt, Colonel David Squirrel OBE, Major John Stirling, F. Williams, T.W. Wood, Major General J.C. Woollett CBE MC, W.A. Woolward and Major General A.E. Younger, DSO, OBE.

To all of them, very many thanks for your help in the making of *Churchill's Secret Weapons*.

Glossary

AA & QMG	Assistant Adjutant & Quarter Master General
AFV	Armoured fighting vehicle
AG	Army Group
AP	Armour-piercing shell
APC	Armoured personnel carrier
APCR	Armoured Personnel Carrier Regiment
ARE	Assault Regiment Royal Engineers
Ark	Turretless tank with ramps, diminutive of Ark Royal
ARV	Armoured recovery vehicle
ATEA	Amphibious tank escape apparatus
AVRE	Armoured Vehicle Royal Engineers, a Churchill tank with a Petard mortar
Baron	Early minesweeping flail tank
BARV	Beach armoured recovery vehicle (Sherman)
'bash on'	(slang) to advance briskly
Besa	British small arms machine gun
Bobbin	Carpet-roll attachment for tanks, carried on AVRE
'brewed (up)'	(slang) destroyed and burnt out by enemy fire
Buffalo	British nickname for an American LVT, carrying thirty infantry or small vehicles
Bullshorn	Minesweeping plough attachment
CAC	Canadian Armoured Carrier Regiment
CARC	Canadian Armoured Car Regiment
CDL	Canal defence Light M3 Grant tank with blinding searchlight
Centaur	Bulldozer turretless tank with large clearing blade
CIGS	Chief of the Imperial General Staff

CIRD	Canadian indestructible roller device
CLY	County of London Yeomanry
CO	Commanding Officer
Conger	Rocket-launched minesweeping device
Crab	Sherman tank with minesweeping flail, with chains on a revolving drum
CRE	Commander Royal Engineers
Crocodile	Flame-throwing apparatus on a Churchill VII gun tank, with oil carried in a trailer
D.D.	Duplex-drive Sherman amphibious tank
DUKW	American duplex-driven amphibious vehicle
'Element C'	German beach obstacle
'to empouch'	to load infantry into AFV
ENIGMA	Code-breaking machines at Bletchley Park
Fascine	Bundle of sticks carried on an AVRE, used for filling ditches and craters
FFI	French resistance movement
Flying Dustbin	High-explosive demolition charge for a Petard
FOO	Forward Observation Officer
'Funnies'	British generic term for the specialized armour of the 79th Armoured Division
General Wade	Explosive charge carried in an AVRE
Goat	Mechanical demolition placer
GOC	General Officer Commanding
Great Eastern	Rocket-launched ramp on a Churchill tank
GSO	General Staff Officer
HE	High explosive
HLI	Highland Light Infantry
Honey	American fast light reconnaissance tank (General Stuart)
Kangaroo	Turretless tank for transporting infantry, usually a Canadian Ram
KOSB	King's Own Scottish Borderers
KOYLI	King's Own Yorkshire Light Infantry
KRRC	King's Royal Rifle Corps

LCA	Landing craft artillery
LCI	Landing craft infantry
LCT	Landing craft tank
LO	Liaison Officer
Lobster	Tank-mounted flail device
LSI	Landing ship infantry
LST	Landing ship tank
LVT	Landing vehicle tracked
Marquis	Early tank-mounted flail device
MG	Machine gun
MOD	Ministry of Defence
Monitor	Shallow-draught heavy-gun naval vessel
OAC	Obstacle assault centre
OP	Observation point
OR	Other rank
Panther	German Mk V tank
Panzerfaust	German hand-held infantry anti-tank weapon
Pepperpot	Concentrated all-arms fire plan with short duration
Petard	Large-calibre demolition gun mounted on an AVRE
Porpoise	Amphibious sledge
RAC	Royal Armoured Corps
RAP	Regiment aid post
RASC	Royal Army Service Corps
RDG	Royal Dragoon Guards
RE	Royal Engineers
REME	Royal Electrical and Mechanical Engineers
RHA	Royal Horse Artillery
Rhino	Self-propelled pontoon ferry
RHQ	Regimental Headquarters
RNR	Royal Naval Reserve
Rodent	Lightweight minesweeping device on a Weasel
RTC	Royal Tank Corps
RTR	Royal Tank Regiment
SBG	Small box girder, a mounted bridge on an AVRE
Scorpion	Early minesweeping flail device

Skid Bailey	Assembled Bailey bridge mounted on skids or tracked bogies, pushed or pulled by AVREs
Snake	Tubular explosive device for clearing mines
SP	Self-propelled
Spandau	German MG34 or MG42 machine gun
SQMS	Squadron Quarter Master Sergeant
SRY	Sherwood Rangers Yeomanry
SSM	Staff Sergeant Major
SWB	South Wales Borderers
TAC	Tactical (HQ)
Tapeworm	Safer development of Conger
Terrapin	British amphibious truck with eight wheels, carrying eight to ten infantry
Tetrahedron	German beach obstacle
TSM	Troop Sergeant Major
Wasp	Small flame-thrower mounted on a Universal carrier
Weasel	Small tracked amphibious Jeep

Illustrations

IWM = Imperial War Museum

Maps

1 Churchill's Secret Weapons

A year to the day after the outbreak of the Second World War the Prime Minister, Winston Churchill, wrote a memorandum to his Cabinet. Britain was alone: France had fallen, U-boats were rampant, the Blitz was under way.

> This war is not however a war of masses of men hurling masses of shells at each other. It is by devising *new* weapons and above all by *scientific* leadership that we shall best cope with the enemy's superior strength.

Arthur Bryant in *Triumph in the West* wrote:

> What Alanbrooke [the Chief of the General Staff] shows in his diary in the mingled exasperation and admiration of his day-by-day entries, is the real Churchill – the man who rallied a defeated nation in storm and disaster, passionate, impetuous, daring, indomitable, terrible in anger, pursuing every expedient – sometimes brilliant, sometimes, for he was prepared to try almost everything, *fantastic* – that could bring about victory.

This then is the story of how the great man – soldier, journalist, war leader, painter, author and bricklayer – with the particular help of three relatively unknown men, created, devised, tested and finally brought into decisive action a whole range of dreadful, secret weapons. Many of these were brought together for the great invasion of Europe 'Operation Overlord' in June 1944. It was, in the event, a huge sprawling armoured formation that by sea and land smashed open Adolf Hitler's Atlantic Wall. Then came the battering open of the Channel ports – Le Havre, Brest (with the Americans), Calais and Boulogne – followed by the icy cold winter campaign at Walcheren to free the port of Antwerp.

On the borders of the Third Reich, in Operation Plunder, this composite force of secret weapons, forced the crossing of the river Rhine on their way to beat, flame and blast their way to Bremen and Bremerhaven, across canals, dykes and rivers. A photograph shows the indomitable Prime Minister aboard a secret 'weapon' accompanied by his generals, smoking a cigar, halfway across the Rhine.

Churchill had a reputation for pushing his military commanders to the limit, and then firing them if they appeared to be dilatory or inefficient. Apart from the Chief of the Imperial General Staff (CIGS), Alan Brooke (later to become Viscount Alanbrooke) and perhaps General Alexander and Lord Louis Mountbatten, he appeared to have no favourites. But there is no doubt that he had three protégés, whose unorthodox talents he had identified at an early stage in the war.

The first was Frederick Lindermann, Professor of Experimental Philosophy at Oxford University, known as 'the Prof' and later to become Lord Cherwell, was undoubtedly Churchill's *éminence grise*. General 'Pug' Ismay, Chief of Staff to the Prime Minister, a member of the Chief of Staff Committee and head of the office of the Minister of Defence, wrote:

> Churchill used to say that the Prof's brain was a beautiful piece of mechanism and the Prof did not dissent from that judgment. In his appointment as Personal Assistant to the PM, no field of activity was closed to him. He was as obstinate as a mule and unwilling to admit that there was any problem under the sun which he was not qualified to solve. He would write a memorandum on high strategy on one day and a thesis on egg production on the next. He hated Hitler and all his works and his contribution to Hitler's downfall in all sorts of *odd ways* was considerable.

In one of his roles the Prof was responsible for the second of Churchill's protégés, a certain Millis Jefferis, who at the outbreak of war was a major in the Royal Engineers and a rather dangerous genius. War, amongst other things, is all about making large, dangerous noises and explosions in the enemy's ranks. Jefferis was *the* explosives expert who devised awful weaponry for the Army, the Royal Navy and the Royal Air Force. At the outbreak of war he was, in effect, on Churchill's payroll, in charge of a small highly secret establishment. As it grew in importance and size this 'research and development' unit , known as MD1, was known by other traditional development agencies as 'Churchill's Toy Shop' or 'Churchill's Toy Factory'. At that stage, to keep the other jealous departments relatively happy, Churchill made the Prof, who could be challenged by nobody, titular boss of Jefferis's secret establishment. Churchill protected him, encouraged him in every possible way and caused him to be promoted to Lieutenant Colonel, then to Brigadier and then to Major General, and also, had him knighted.

The third protégé was an extraordinary man. Percy Hobart was hated by every other general – particularly the 'cavalry' generals. He was feared by every officer and man he encountered. He was irascible, in many ways a bully, but in various other ways a genius. A sapper by training, he became Britain's foremost armoured fighting-vehicle expert between the wars. Uniquely he formed three of Britain's few armoured divisions: the Desert Rats (in which the author was a troop commander), the Black Bull (in which the author fought as a troop leader and FOO) and finally the Bull's Head division. On two occasions, in 1940 and 1942, Churchill rescued this abrasive difficult general from obscurity, even oblivion and ensured that he would lead – third time lucky – the sprawling formation which later became known as 'Hobart's Funnies', a force of 21,000 men and several thousand tracked weapons that surged irresistibly across north-western Europe.

Winston Churchill had a magnificent, far-ranging imagination, and was the original 'inventor' of many of the new technologically brilliant weapons used during the Second World War. On 17 July 1917, as Minister of Munitions in Lloyd George's government, he prepared a scheme for the capture of the two Friesian islands, Borkum and Sylt, to be used as valuable naval and airforce bases. The invading troops would be loaded into a hundred bullet-proof lighters and fifty tank-loading lighters, each carrying a tank or tanks and fitted up in the bow for wirecutting. By means of a drawbridge or shelving bow, the tanks would land under their own power and thus prevent infantry being held up by wire when attacking forts and batteries. This was undoubtedly the concept behind the landing craft tanks (LCTs) and landing ship tanks (LSTs) which stormed the beaches in the European theatres of war in 1943 and 1944. A few prototypes were employed and lost in the short Norwegian campaign at Narvik in 1940. Nothing daunted serious trials of LCTs continued in October 1940 and thirty more were built. Improved designs followed and in the summer of the next year they were used in the

Middle East. Churchill gave directions for a larger craft called an Atlantic LCT, then LST. The first was named the Winette after Churchill, and others were ordered in the USA and Canada. In February 1942 production in the USA was on a vast scale.

The young Churchill's second idea, also developed in July 1917, was for a torpedo- and weather-proof harbour, like an atoll, made of flat-bottomed barges or caissons, fabricated not of steel but of concrete. They would float when empty and would be towed to their destination. On arrival, sea-cocks would be opened, they would fill with water and they would settle on the sea bottom, then would later be filled with sand by suction dredgers. Although General F.E. Morgan, Chief of Staff Supreme Allied Command (COSSAC) in his book *Prelude to Overlord* gives Commodore Hughes-Hallett the credit for originating the idea, there is little doubt that Churchill's concept resulted in the famous Mulberry harbours that were towed across to the Normandy coast in 1944. Indeed in 1942 Churchill gave directions to Admiral Louis Mountbatten that floating piers should be designed which would go up and down with the tide. The minute ended with: 'Don't argue the matter. The difficulties will argue for themselves.' And Churchill kept on nagging to ensure that the project was completed.

From his early youth Churchill had been a student of military history. He wrote many books on military subjects including *The River War, Marlborough* and *The World Crisis*. His knowledge of world-wide military strategy was immense. In his bold plans for the British and French navies to seize Constantinople through the Dardanelles, the brave, flawed naval and military operations ended in disaster; but the concept of Gallipoli was, in itself, characteristically audacious. During the Second World War the CIGS, Alan Brooke, spent much time damping down his master's desire to launch distracting invasions. The campaign in Greece was a case in point. Churchill was adamant. The mainland campaign was a fiasco and the taking of Crete another heroic disaster. Nevertheless once agreed, the main overall strategic priorities were adhered to.

His years in and out of the British Army, skirmishing in India, the Sudan and 'fighting' journalism in the Boer War, plus the command of a Guards battalion on the Western Front, had had a profound effect. He knew the vital importance of reducing potential manpower losses by the use of effective weapons, particularly tanks. He was always conscious that a relatively small number of men at the 'sharp end' fought and died, whilst the tail of staff, administration and back-up services grew longer and longer. He knew that the German Wehrmacht was a lean, efficient fighting organization with half the 'tail' of the British Army.

In June 1938 with Lord Chatfield, the First Sea Lord, he went to sea in destroyers on exercise in submarine detection by the use of Asdic apparatus. He had spent four years working on the Air Defence Research Committee which had given him access to the most modern developments in Radar which affected the Royal Navy. In August 1939 he talked frequently to Professor Lindemann about Atomic Energy, and sent a paper on the subject to Kingsley Wood, Secretary of State for Air, which later became codenamed 'Tube Alloys'. In September 1939 Churchill joined the War Cabinet and became First Lord of the Admiralty. Immediately he originated discussion and the development of small anti-submarine and anti-air vessels which were called 'cheap and nasties' – cheap to us, nasty to the U-boats, of catapulted aircraft for use in the open oceans, of more powerful radio direction finding (RDF) stations, of the anti-torpedo, 'Actaeon' nets, of shields for infantry, of an antidote to magnetic sea mines (degaussing), of unrotated projectiles (UP) and for rocket propulsion for use against low-flying enemy aircraft.

When he became Prime Minister in May 1940, retaining the office of Minister of Defence, his ingenious mind explored even more ideas: 'Operation Royal Marine' for mining the river Rhine with fluvial mines; radar-directed multiple projectors and rockets; small circular pill boxes sunk in the centre of RAF aerodromes which could rise to ward off parachute attacks; and the firing of small aerial mines from ships' guns (later known as 'hedgehogs' these became a successful U-boat deterrent). In May 1940 he was stressing to General Ismay the urgency of the provision of proximity fuses to be fitted to rocket projectors to defend aircraft factories; the necessity for a self-stabilizing aircraft bomb sight; and the desirability of smokescreens for protecting key factories and industrial targets. In July after Dunkirk, the threat of invasion was very real. He wrote, 'It may well be Hitler has some gas designs upon us.' The Randle factory had been producing chemical warfare gases but no projectiles or containers for air or artillery to discharge them had been made. Churchill wrote: 'The highest priority must be given. I regard the danger as very great. The possibility of our having to retaliate on the German civil population must be studied and on the largest scale possible. We should never begin, but we must be able to reply. Speed is vital here.' Two thousand tons of mustard gas had been ordered in

October 1938 but by 9 December 1940 only 1,485 tons had been produced. Ironically the three chemical warfare regiments were virtually redundant by 1943 and were converted into armoured engineers of 79th Armoured Division.

At the end of August the Prime Minister strengthened his control of the war machine. In a minute to the Secretary of State for War, he said: 'I have found it necessary to have *direct* access to and *control* of the Joint Planning Staffs because after a year of war I cannot recall a single plan initiated by the existing machinery' and 'to help me in giving a vigorous and positive direction to the conduct of the war, and in overcoming the dead weight of inertia and delay which has so far led us to being forestalled on *every occasion* by the enemy.'

The lack of weapons for the newly formed Home Guard was a great source of worry but Churchill's own secret research and development establishment soon produced appropriate anti-tank weapons both quickly and cheaply. General 'Pug' Ismay recommended the setting up of a Petroleum Warfare Executive to produce tank-born flame-throwers. Churchill thought they would not be needed as the threat of invasion had receded. By D-Day four years later only one regiment of Crocodile flame-throwers had been trained and landed as back-up troops in Normandy. They were so successful that two more regiments were hastily trained and arrived to fight in the Low Countries and Germany. Churchill was lukewarm about setting up a Petroleum Warfare Executive to develop flame-throwing weapons. Eventually on D-Day one full regiment shortly followed by two more joined the 79th Armoured Division in action.

Churchill called the period after the Battle of Britain in the summer and autumn of 1940 the 'Wizard War', 'a secret war whose battles were lost or won unknown to the public and only with difficulty comprehended even now'. Here Professor Lindemann, the Prof, was of immense value; he kept Churchill informed of every new scientific weaponry developed by the enemy and of all the steps being taken to counter them. Indiscriminate night bombing of London and other ports and cities, and the mauling of the RAF, threatened by mass attacks to cripple the country. The Prime Minister ordered the highest priority for radar applications through the Air Defence Research Committee. 'I took special interest and used my authority.' Parachute and cable (PAC) rockets were a good interim defence against low-flying attack and 5,000 a month were produced. Secret developments were carried out of the mass discharge of rocket batteries (unrotated projectiles). By May forty rocket batteries of ninety-six projectors were ready for action, to reinforce the 1,687 heavy and 790 light anti-aircraft (AA) guns, operated by nearly 300,000 men and women. The search and development of photo-electric (PE) proximity AA shell fuses, however, was only completed after the main threat had come and gone.

The Luftwaffe navigated originally by radio beacons. The British countered with 'meacons', which picked up the German signals, amplified them and then diverted them. But the Prof reported in June that the enemy was developing a radio beam like an invisible searchlight which would guide the Luftwaffe bombs by day *or night* with considerable accuracy to their target. The codeword was Knickebein. Churchill chaired an urgent meeting with Lindemann, various scientists and the RAF commanders. Dr R.V. Jones, Deputy Director of Intelligence Research at the Air Ministry, devised a counter-device to distort, jam and divert Knickebein. Churchill said, 'Being master and not having to argue too much, once I was convinced about the principles of this queer and deadly game I gave orders for all counter-measures to receive absolute priority.' For the next three months the Knickebein stations near Dieppe and Cherbourg had their beams deflected or jammed. The Luftwaffe still bombed, but by guesswork.

On 15 October 1940 the Prime Minister had issued a strongly worded document on 'priorities'. First was the radio sphere, in which scientists, wireless experts and highly skilled labour devoted themselves with appropriate resources to winning the 'Wizard War' and protecting factories, warships, harbours and crucial targets. The priority was the GL sets, radar sets for anti-aircraft gun control. Aircraft production was the second priority and tank armoured divisions third.

But the 'Wizard War' continued. Herman Goering's Kampfgruppe 100 used a special radio beam called the X apparatus with which Luftwaffe bombers with pathfinder groups caused havoc with the 'Baedecker' raids, starting with Coventry. Decoy fires codenamed 'Starfish' led some of the main attacks astray and by early 1941 the X apparatus was mastered, but, then along came the new Y apparatus, a radio beam with a radio rangefinder which 'told' the aircraft commander when he had reached the correct distance to his target. New counter-measures were introduced and Churchill wondered whether the bombing of Dublin on 30 May 1941 was a diverted Y apparatus attack! Soon the new airborne radar called A.I.

was installed in Blenheims and Beaufighters. Churchill called it the 'Smeller', and it eventually helped to defeat General Martini's Luftwaffe bombers in the 'Wizard War'.

The quest for new weaponry continued. Early in January 1941, immediate action was demanded for the development of the proximity fuse against high-altitude enemy aircraft flying at over 10,000 feet 'to burst salvoes of eight in close proximity to the enemy aircraft with fatal results'. And the AD fuse, a rocket and parachute device which fired aerial mines at very high altitudes, was being tested by General Loch's research training department. The AD fuse rocket was then hung from small balloons for the defence of factories and key river estuaries, and by March 1941 the 'Wizard War' had been won – until 1944!

By Christmas 1940 Churchill discovered that the Ministry of Supply had got their sums wrong with regard to the supply of weapons and ammunition. The fear of a German invasion was still prevalent. Deliveries of gas shells to the RAF and Army chemical-warfare units had fallen to 500 per month from the 1500 ordered. 'Who is responsible? At any moment this peril may be upon us,' wrote Churchill. Fortunately the German gas invasion never came. Conversely there was a massive over-production of 2-inch and 3-inch mortars and the inefficient Boyes anti-tank rifle. And of course abysmally low stocks of mortar bombs and standard .303 rifle ammunition. The Prime Minister wrote to the CIGS: 'The failure to marry the ammunition and the AT rifle is one of the worst blots on our present munitions programme.'

Churchill kept control of all the developments of the new weaponry. Trials of the Whittle jet engines had started. 'The present turbine blades are working. Every nerve should be strained to get these aircraft into squadrons next summer.' But the jet plane code-named 'Squirt', was not demonstrated until May 1943. At the same time research via the Prof, now Lord Cherwell, and Sir John Anderson into the atom bomb 'Tube Alloys' was to be stepped up. Mr W.A. Akers of ICI was I/C Directorate of 'Tube Alloys'.

In December the Prime Minister saw a demonstration at Shoeburyness of the test firing of the secret Type K (anti-aircraft) rocket, two Apparatus L and J rockets for the defence of aerodromes against low-flying aircraft, and Rocket U (5-inch and 3-inch) to produce an AA barrage. They were all UP (unrotated projectiles), and highly secret.

Late in 1942 a splendid scheme was mooted by a Mr Pyke who

was on Earl Mountbatten's staff, called 'Operation Habbakuk'. The idea was to use artificial icebergs as Atlantic staging points for aircraft. Churchill wrote a long detailed memorandum for the Chief of Staffs on 7 December and well into 1943 had weekly reports of progress: 'How are the snowploughs, force and equipment getting on?'

'Operation Husky' was the name of the thirty-eight day campaign to capture Sicily after the 8th Army and 1st Army had linked up to secure the end of the Afrika Korps. Montgomery had kept up the pressure and by May 1943 nearly a third of a million Axis forces had surrendered. Mussolini gave up on 25 July and for a few days it seemed as though Italy would fall to the Allies.

Many other unusual inventions and ideas were in the pipeline. Besides 'Habbakuk' the floating seadrome made of ice, which was being developed in Canada, there were Bombardon, a steel outer breakwater used for artificial harbours, Gooseberry and Lilo, artificial breakwaters, Whale a floating pier, Tentacle, a concrete floating airfield, Phoenix, a concrete caisson and eventually Mulberry, a complete artificial harbour. The tide of war had changed. All these possibilities were directed towards offensive amphibious landings on European coasts. Churchill wrote: 'The whole project was majestic. Now the structures I had thought of in the First World War to create artificial harbours in the Heligoland Bight [are] to form a principal part of the great plan.'

Jet-propelled aircraft development was still very slow indeed: 'There are numerous reports of German jet-propelled aircraft and we cannot afford to be left behind.' The CIGS, Alanbrooke noted in his diary: '19 April we were shown at Hatfield latest aircraft without propellers, driven by air sucked in, in front and squirted out behind. Apparently likely to be the fighter of the future.' Churchill wrote to Sir Stafford Cripps: 'I am particularly interested in jet propelled type of aircraft of which you showed me a model.' But the British development work lagged behind the Germans.

The Navy were also not forgotten. In September the First Lord of the Admiralty was being tackled on an acoustic torpedo for the defence of submarines when submerged and attacked by hostile submarines. The Prof was summoned to give the Prime Minister a lecture on acoustic homing torpedoes. He also had to produce a paper on the relative efficiency of the high explosives used by the German and British forces. A change to aluminized explosives was then agreed.

On 23 April the Prime Minister wrote to Sir Edward Bridges and the Defence Committee (Supplies) on 'Tank Policy'. One paragraph read: 'What has happened to the amphibious tank? Surely a float or galosh can be made to take a tank of the largest size across the Channel under good conditions once a beach landing has been secured.' Just over a year later several hundred Sherman dual-duplex (D.D.) tanks, whose conception was credited to Mr Nicholas Straussler, swam ashore in support mainly of British and Canadian forces, but also on the American sectors. Eventually 600 production Valentine tanks were converted and completed in 1944. But it was Churchill who first conceived the idea then pushed and prodded this secret weapon through to fruition. The swimming tanks – *schwim panzer* – totally deceived the German defenders at dawn on D-Day the next year.

Churchill's advisers had warned him in the autumn of 1943 of the impending attack on mainland Britain by pilotless aircraft or rockets. 'We must expect the terrible foe we are smiting so heavily will make frenzied efforts to retaliate. The speeches of the German leaders from Hitler downwards on certain mysterious allusions to new methods and new weapons which will presently be tried against us . . . a new type of bomb, a sort of rocket-assisted glider, guided to its target by the parent aircraft.' Already new British 'gadgets' were in operation. 'Gee' was a new radar position-finder for the RAF bombers; 'Oboe' was a radar blind-bombing device used by Mosquito pathfinders; and 'Window' comprised tinfoil strips dropped to confuse German radar. Peenemunde on the Baltic coast was identified as the main German research centre for their rockets and pilotless weapons, Hitler's 'secret weapons'. On 17 August RAF Bomber Command struck and were sufficiently successful to force construction of the future V-1 and V-2 rockets further inland to the Hartz mountains.

With Generals Eisenhower and Montgomery back from Sicily and Italy to mastermind the invasion of Europe Churchill set up a weekly committee of which he was the President, to keep all the preparations for 'Overlord' under constant review. On 24 January 1944 a major conference agreed on the plans for the 'Mulberry' harbour. The Admiralty needed 8,000 yards of block ships and so about seventy merchant ships and four obsolete warships were allocated. Five Gooseberry breakwaters would be needed for each divisional assault area, with two being absorbed into the Mulberries. The block ships would move under their own power and be sunk in the right place. Phoenix concrete caissons would be towed across the Channel in instalments and twenty-three floating pier units called Whales would be deployed. So would the outer breakwaters, the steel Bombardons and Pluto, the submarine petrol pipelines then under construction to run from the Isle of Wight to the Normandy coast and later from Dungeness to Calais.

Well might the PM say to the House of Commons on the night of D-Day: 'Nothing that equipment science or forethought could do has been neglected.' To Josef Stalin he sent a message: 'Everything has started well. The mines, obstacles and land batteries have been largely overcome. The air landings were very successful. Infantry landings are proceeding rapidly and many tanks and self propelled guns are already ashore.' And '*Most especially secret*. We are planning to construct very quickly two large synthetic harbours on the beaches.'

2 Churchill, Tank Warfare and His 'Tank Parliament'

Despite having served as a cavalryman in the 4th Hussars, Winston Churchill showed a deep and expert knowledge of tank (and anti-tank) weapons throughout the Second World War. One of the first things he did in office was to investigate tank production and design. The devastating success of Guderian's and Rommel's panzers sweeping through the Low Countries, brushing aside puny French and British tanks in the process, had demonstrated that war on land would be dominated by armoured vehicles. Churchill wrote to Professor Lindemann on 24 May 1940:

> Let me have on one sheet of paper a statement about the tanks. How many have we got with the army? How many of each kind are being made each month? How many are there with the manufacturers? What are the forecasts? What are the plans for heavier tanks? The present form of warfare and the proof that tanks can over-run fortifications will affect plans for the 'Cultivator'.

A weekly tank production report was now produced for him.

After the realization in mid-1940 that massive trench warfare was unlikely, a secret machine 'Cultivator No. 6' a trench-cutting machine for attacking fortified lines, had its production halved, and shortly afterwards reduced to a quarter. The Prime Minister wrote to the CIGS: 'The spare available capacity could be turned over to tanks. If the Germans can make tanks in nine months, surely we can do so.' He demanded proposals to produce an additional 1,000 tanks capable of tackling the German models which were likely to be in the field during 1941. By November 1940 he was castigating General 'Pug' Ismay and the Ministry of Supply.

26

We have completely failed to make cruiser tanks. We must therefore equip our armoured divisions in the best possible way open to us in *these melancholy circumstances*. At this stage in tank production, *numbers count above everything else*. It is better to have any service-able tank than none at all. The 'I' [Infantry] tank should not be disdained because of its slow speed, and in default of cruisers, must be looked upon as our staple for fighting. We must adapt our tactics for the time being to this weapon *as we have no other*. Meanwhile the production of cruiser tanks and of A22 [a new model] must be driven forward to the utmost limit.

Just before Christmas he was pressing for the new 2nd Armoured Division to land at Suez and get into action in the Western Desert. Then he described the mechanization of the Cavalry Division in Palestine as 'a distressing story' – 8,500 fine troops never received their armoured vehicles because the priority was North Africa and the defence of Britain. Churchill was angry and suggested that they should be allocated captured Italian equipment or a supply of 200 Bren-gun carriers.

At the end of February he wrote: 'I am very much inclined to a greater development of armoured divisions than we have now. Tanks and tank guns, not personnel, are the bottle-neck.' And a month later the pressure was directed on the Admiralty. 'Give me a report on the progress of the ships to carry and disgorge tanks. How many are there? What is their tonnage? How many tanks can they take in a flight? When will each one be ready? Where are they being built? What mark of tank can they carry?' In the spring of 1941, there were, 1,169 heavy tanks in Britain and monthly production was 200. He was incensed to find out that 238 cruiser tanks had been allocated to one division and only 38 to another. This was the newly formed 11th Armoured Division, under Churchill's protégé General Hobart. Churchill was not convinced that each armoured division should be 'entirely homogenous. A judicious mixture of weapons, albeit of various speeds should be possible. Some of these armoured vehicles ought to carry field artillery and even one or two large guns or mortars. Let me have a report on what the Germans do.'

As a result quite soon all armoured divisions had their own self-propelled field guns on tank chassis. Later Hobart's third command, 79th Armoured, had twelve squadrons of Churchill tanks with large spigot mortars which threw a Flying Dustbin – a high explosive demolition charge – at enemy strongpoints. Churchill was undoubtedly the architect of the modern armoured division.

In April the Prime Minister discovered that the famous 7th Armoured Division, after much good hard service was sent back over 400 miles to Cairo to refit, wearing out the tracks of many of the tanks. 'It was an act of improvidence to send the whole division all this way back in view of the fact that *German* elements [i.e. not Italian] were already reported in Tripoli. Workshops should have been improvised at the front for lighter repairs and servicing personnel sent forward.' Eventually LAD detachments (Armoured Troops Workshops) of the REME were sent up almost into the scene of battle. The Germans always sent their REME equivalent sometimes with transporters onto the field of battle at night to retrieve their damaged tanks. Sometimes they hauled away damaged British tanks, or destroyed them! 'There seems to be a degree of slackness and mismanagement about this repair work which is serious,' was Churchill's view. On 20 April some captured tanks were to be examined 'by a skilful designer of British tanks or some other suitable engineering expert'.

This led to the first urgent sitting of Churchill's 'Tank Parliament' which was held at Downing Street on Monday, 5 May with the CIGS, the Assistant Chief of General Staff (ACIGS), General Pope and General Martel (commanders with considerable tank experience) and Martel's armoured divisional commanders. From the Ministry of Supply came Mr Burton, Admiral Brown and General Crawford. The CIGS tried to ensure that all the tank generals kept to the party line. Usually they did, except for Major General Hobart, who always spoke his mind. The Prime Minister wanted tank training to be divided into two parts and to minimize excess track usage 'model tanks must be provided' and tactical training carried out with Bren-gun carriers at the same speed as a tank. The Jefferis bombard (the sticky Puffballs) was 'now distinctly hopeful' and 2,000 had been ordered with 300,000 anti-tank projectiles and 600,000 anti-personnel projectiles.

Rumours had now reached Churchill that the Germans were constructing tanks with armour between 4 and 6 inches thick. The next month he quizzed the CIGS about the tank composition of a British armoured division. The German panzer division had two light and one heavy brigade (270 and 135) compared with the 7th Armoured Division in North Africa with 400 heavy tanks (including the cumbersome 'I' tanks). 'What is the additional outfit of our armoured brigades in light tanks or armoured cars?'

In June the nomenclature of the British tanks was discussed. Churchill wanted names (Matilda, Valentine and then Churchill), rather than code numbers or letters like 'I' and A22. The Prime Minster discovered that a new Russian tank of over 70 tons was now impervious to the German A/T 6-pounder gun. In July he noted that the Germans were making 'a good deal of use of flame-throwers. How does this matter stand?' Three years later British 'Crocodiles' and 'Wasps' flame-throwing tanks and bren carriers were in action. President Roosevelt was sending a 'windfall' of 200 American light cruiser tanks to North Africa which Churchill hoped would be allocated to the Cavalry Division (about to become the 10th Armoured Division). The Prime Minister discovered at the end of August that more than 50 per cent of the 408 cruiser tanks in Britain were unfit for service, and the situation was getting worse every week! There was a disastrous operation when two of the new Churchill tanks were shipped to the Middle East theatre for trials. The tanks were loaded on an open deck on board ship and were rusty and waterlogged on arrival; the tank fitters in charge were flown ahead by air, and the Port Ordnance Officer noticed that they were not properly 'greased up' but could not be bothered to report the fact.

General Ismay was under fire in November. 'Let me have your full report about 1st Armoured Division [who had just arrived in North Africa]. When did their tanks arrive? And what is their condition? How far are they desert worthy? What about their axles? How far are they trained? Could anything be done to speed up their unloading?'

At the end of the year Churchill recommended that a 'special corps of mechanised engineers' be formed. A year later the 1st Assault Brigade Royal Engineer was formed, the cutting edge of the 79th Armoured Division.

To the Lord Privy Seal, Stafford Cripps, Churchill wrote:

I held last year a number of 'Tank Parliaments' at which all the Divisional Commanders were present. They seemed a very fine lot. But of course the experiences we have gained at the front should make continual changes. I am not sure that speed is the supreme requirement of tanks, certainly not of all tanks. Armour and gun power decide the matter whenever tank meets tank. Anti-tank weapons are advancing fast in power and thin-skinned animals will run ever increasing risks.

After General Auchinleck's defeat in North Africa by the newly arrived General Rommel, Churchill was faced by some unpalatable facts. The British cruiser tanks were mechanically inferior under battle conditions. The British 2-pounder anti-tank gun with its short range and inferior performance gave little protection to the Allied forces. Auchinleck (the 'Auk') wrote: 'To meet German armoured forces with any reasonable hope of decisive success our armoured forces as at present equipped, organised and led must have at least two to one superiority . . . . There are signs that the Royal Armoured Corps are losing confidence in their equipment.' The well-trained but newly arrived 1st Armoured Division lost over a hundred tanks in its first battle. Churchill must have had moments of despair but he certainly did not show them.

In April he was confronted with a problem with the new Churchill tank and its 2-pounder gun. Nearly a thousand had been supplied to the tank forces in the UK. In the last six months of 1942 it was decided that either 1,000 new tanks (MKII with improvements) could be produced mounting a 6-pounder gun or 500 new ones could be made and 500 of the existing thousand could be reworked. But what does one do with 1,000 outdated, unused 2-pounder tanks which would be massacred in action? Churchill proposed several ideas. Some could be used for training, and some for the Canadian A/Tk Brigade, who spoke well of them. Two or three hundred could be used for the defence of aerodromes. He wrote, 'I am going to inquire myself into the possible uses of the thousand (unwanted) Churchill tanks.' In due course several hundred Churchill tanks had their gun turrets removed and replaced with the secret new Jefferis spigot mortar developed from Jefferis's shoulder gun, the PIAT (see chapter 3). These so-called armoured vehicles royal engineers (AVREs) were specially allocated to the 79th Armoured Division which was yet to be formed.

By July 1942 Churchill considered that an invasion of the UK was now unlikely and the 8th Armoured Division was sent out to Cairo to reinforce General Auchinleck's forces. The surrender of Tobruk with its garrison of 33,000 men was a major disaster and President Roosevelt made an immediate decision and despatched 300 brand new Sherman tanks in six fast ships off to the Suez Canal. The ship with all the engines for the tanks was sunk, however, and the President at once sent replacements.

A vote of censure in Parliament was now called for after the long succession of military misfortunes and defeats. Sir Stafford Cripps drafted a report for the Prime Minister. Item 4 dealt with weapons. 'After nearly three years of war we still find ourselves inferior in vital weapons such as tanks and anti-tank guns. This inferiority has been largely responsible for the debacle.' And under Item 5, Research and Invention, he said, 'We have somehow failed to make good use of the abilities of the very skilled research workers, scientists and inventors in this country.' General 'Pug' Ismay proposed the creation of a South African armoured division to fight in North Africa.

By now Churchill had imposed his views on his generals. An armoured division now had a tank brigade of about 200 tanks plus a motorized (infantry) brigade instead of the original unwieldy 350-tank division. At the end of July tank and anti-tank gun production was outstripping 'demand'. Supplies to Russia during the summer months of long daylight had been suspended and with the American Grant and Sherman tank in use in North Africa, UK supplies were out of balance. But about 20,000 2.4-pounder tank and anti-tank guns were in existence, and were about to be joined by yet another 20,000. Mr Hore Belisha had criticized the failures and inferiority of British armour in the House of Commons. On 27 July Churchill wrote to the Minister of Production, the Secretary of State for War, the CIGS and Sir Edward Bridges, Secretary to the War Cabinet. 'This weapon [2.4-pounder tank and anti-tank gun] is already out of date. We shall be justly censured if we commit ourselves to a further enormous production of it. It [the anti-tank gun] cannot stop a tank except under the most favourable of conditions. Even the 6-pounder is now falling behind.'

'Operation Rutter', which aimed to employ a combined service force for an attack, or rather raid, on the port of Dieppe was renamed 'Operation Jupiter'. After unfavourable weather the attack was postponed and General Montgomery, just before he flew out to take command in North Africa, recommended cancellation. For a variety of reasons the raid went ahead with quite disastrous results, and the Canadian forces lost 2,500 men. Dwelling on the lessons to be learned the Prime Minister wrote: 'It was a costly but not unfruitful reconnaissance in force. Tactically it was a mine of experience. It taught us to build in good time various *new types of craft and appliances* for later use. Team work was the secret of success. This could only be provided by trained and organized *amphibious* formations. All these lessons were taken to heart.' During the Dieppe raid three prototypes of the Churchill flame-thrower tank took part. Designed by a Major J.M. Oke all three were captured or destroyed. The new

Mark IV Churchill infantry tank, slow 39-ton machines with heavy armour and small guns went into the action. All twenty-eight were knocked out or captured.

Churchill did not trust his tank generals to give him a true and unbiased picture at all times. On 18 September 1942 he wrote to Brigadier Hollis, Secretary to the Chiefs of Staff Committee: 'I shall be glad to receive a report on the Churchill tanks from the two or three divisions which have most of them. Do *not* let it be known that the report is for *me*, as I simply want to know how the tank is viewed by the *troops*.'

The Select Committee on National Expenditure had just produced an impartial report about the Army's tanks and guns. Churchill said of it: 'It is a masterly indictment which reflects on all who have been concerned at the War Office and the Ministry of Supply. It also reflects upon me as head of the Government and upon the whole organization ... The Committee have certainly rendered a high service in bringing this tangle of inefficiency and incompetence to my notice.' His Chiefs of Staff were proposing to send the newly formed 11th Armoured Division to North Africa with 2-pounder Crusader tanks. 'Pray let me have a plan to replace the 2 pounder by 6 pounders,' he wrote. General Anderson's 1st Army in Tunisia now complained bitterly of their ineffective 2-pounder tank guns. On 26 December Churchill pressed for the brand new secret 17-pounder anti-tank guns to be issued to 11th Armoured to combat the newly arrived German 'Tiger' tanks. He wrote to the CIGS: 'We cannot go on with these Gazala defeat outfits without exposing ourselves to very grave Parliamentary censure.' The various tank battles in North Africa around Gazala (the Battle of the Cauldron) had caused enormous losses to the undergunned British armour. However, Montgomery's splendid attritional victory of El Alamein on 23 October followed by 'Operation Supercharge' had transformed morale as the 8th Army moved closer to Tripoli and then Tunis.

In the spring of 1943 the quest for a British heavy tank of 60, 70 or even 80 tons was resumed and codenamed 'Stern' and also the search for the elusive amphibious tank with 'float or galosh' underneath to make it float. Furthermore, a debate ensued about the merits of the 75 mm gun (mounted in the new Shermans), a 76 mm high-velocity gun and a 95 mm tank howitzer.

Preparations now began on a large scale for the Second Front, codenamed 'Overlord'. The immense build-up for the invasion of the French mainland preyed on Churchill's mind. In *Closing the Ring* he wrote:

> Memories of the Somme and Passchendaele were graven in my mind, and were not to be blotted out by time or reflection. It still seemed to me after a quarter of a century that fortifications of concrete and steel, armed with modern fire-power and fully manned by trained resolute men could only be overcome by surprise in time or place by turning their flanks *or by some new and mechanical device like the tank.* Space forbids description of the many contrivances devised to overcome the formidable obstacles and minefields guarding the beaches. Some were fitted to our tanks to protect their crews, others served the landing craft. All these matters *aroused my personal interest and, when it seemed necessary, my intervention.*

In January 1944 he was writing.

> 'D.D. tanks which could swim ashore had already been successfully used in the Mediterranean and would certainly be wanted again.'

There was also a process of 'waterproofing' ordinary tracked and wheeled vehicles to enable them to drive ashore under their own power through several feet of water. He was chasing the Minister of Production and Minister of Supply. 'Pray let me have the report about the production of 300 D.D. tanks by the end of April.'

A few weeks before D-Day General O'Connor, one of Montgomery's corps commanders, issued a memo about the armour protection and escape arrangements of the new fast cruiser tank, the Cromwell, and the Prime Minister asked Duncan Sandys to investigate. Crew members would find it difficult to escape if cordite or petrol in the compartment above them caught fire. Nevertheless, the 7th Armoured Division were allocated these tanks for the Normandy campaign and suffered heavy losses.

Once General Rommel was known to be in command of the coastal defences of Normandy, Churchill wrote, 'Great additions and refinements began to appear. In particular we had to discover any new types of obstacle that might be installed and *contrive the antidote.*' And immediately after D-Day he wrote:

> There was no doubt that we had achieved a tactical surprise. Landing and support craft with infantry, with tanks, with self-propelled

artillery and *a great variety of weapons and engineer demolition teams* to deal with the beach obstacles, all formed up into groups and moved towards the beaches. Among them were the D.D. (swimming tanks) which made their first large scale appearance in battle.

Churchill's secret weapons were a vital part of the successful 'Overlord' D-Day landings.

Prime Minister Winston Churchill inspecting Recce Regiment Cromwell Tank at Malton Harrogate, 31 March 1944

3 Churchill's Toy Shop

Lieutenant Colonel Joe Holland, a sapper officer, was tasked in 1939 with forming a department at the War Office to be called Military Intelligence Research (MIR). He was General Staff Officer 1 (GSO1) and recruited his old friend Major Millis Jefferis as GSO2, to head a division known as MIR(C) to design and produce special weapons for irregular warfare. In June 1939 Jefferis was working on a 'product' that needed special magnets and almost by chance recruited Stuart Macrae, the editor of *Armchair Science* magazine as *his* number two. 'After lunch, brandy and deep thought I offered to design such a mine (magnetic to stick to the side of a ship) for him free of charge.'

Millis Jefferis, a short dynamic man with sandy hair, a leathery-looking face (he had soldiered on the North West frontier, and earned an MC) and a barrel-like torso. As a Royal Engineer he had commanded 1st Field Squadron RE at Aldershot. He was an explosives and sabotage expert who had a habit of walking about with his pockets crammed with detonators, small batteries and pieces of wire. He was a genius: given a problem that required death and destruction of a certain kind he would quickly and personally devise a solution that could be developed, engineered and put into production – efficiently and cheaply. But he had no ambition, despite being a regular soldier. He did not have the skill or tact to deal with the predatory War Office departments which were longing to stage a 'take-over'. By the end of the War, as Major General Sir Millis Jefferis, KBE, MC, he owed his fame to his genius, but his rank and honours to Winston Churchill (and his *éminence grise* Professor Frederick Lindemann), his two 'protectors'. He also owed them to Stuart Macrae who was a capable inventor but also a brilliant 'empire builder', who kept the jealous War Office departments at bay – hence their nickname 'Churchills toy shop' for MIR(C).

Starting with a staff of two, with Macrae pushing from below and Churchill and Lindemann pulling from above MIR(C), became

MD1. The development from a very small amateur R & D unit to an official part of the huge Ministry of Defence signified a great step forward for Jefferis and Macrae, in recognition of their work and ideas. By the end of the war their secret establishment in Whitchurch, near Aylesbury (and Chequers) had a staff of 250. It had designed no less than twenty-six weapons which had been accepted by the armed services and were in quantity production. These ranged from small booby traps to heavy artillery, aircraft bombs and naval mines. Many of these highly specialized weapons were devised for the equally secret 79th Armoured Division whose first major task was to breach Adolf Hitler's Atlantic Wall.

The first Macrae-Jefferis 'product' was the naval limpet mine, which was tested in the Bedford Public Baths. Macrae was responsible for the magnet and Jefferis for the idea, design and explosives. Over half a million limpets were made and 'Cloak and Dagger' units sank hundreds of thousands of tons of enemy shipping. The Italians captured a small supply and in turn sank Royal Navy vessels in the Mediterranean. Two years later, on 18 June 1942 Churchill wrote to General Ismay:

> Please report what is being done to emulate the exploits of the Italians [frogmen divers] in Alexandria harbour and similar methods of this kind. At the beginning of the war Colonel Jefferis had a number of bright ideas on this subject which received very little encouragement. Is there any reason why we should be incapable of the same kind of scientific aggressive action that the Italians have shown?

This suggests that he may not have known of the successful British limpet mine.

Jefferis had a portfolio of secret projects. His work on explosive booby traps for blowing up railway lines took him briefly to the ill-fated Norwegian campaign, where he blew up bridges. His 'product' was called a TV switch and was used in conjunction with a Camouflet Set, heavy metal piping which could force a 3 inch diameter hole 5 feet deep into the earth under railway track or bridges. By November 1939 Macrae sent Holland a report that eleven devices were in production and five more in the experimental stage.

MIR(C) in the early days was allocated Room 173 at the War Office and two months after war was declared, Winston Churchill became enthusiastic about 'Royal Marine'. This was a rather ambitious and daring scheme to immobilize the River Rhine using special mines and bombs. Professor Lindemann was installed at the Admiralty with half a dozen statisticians and economists whom 'we could trust to pay no attention to anything but realities'. They also *'pursued all the enquiries which I wished to make myself'*. Lieutenant Colonel Holland and Major Jefferis had a face-to-face briefing by Churchill. After a week's work on 24 November Jefferis produced rough models at the Admiralty. The mine, no bigger than a football, would be dropped from an aircraft and had to sink to the river bed and remain dormant for a predetermined period. It would then rise to near the surface and float down the river and detonate any vessel encountered with sufficient force to cause a wreck. MIR(C) called it the 'W' bomb (W for water); it would carry 10 lb of explosive with chemical pellets controlling its progress. Despite some amusing and dangerous moments, Captain Macrae demonstrated some prototypes to a group of VIPs.

Churchill sold the idea of 'Royal Marine' to the War Cabinet and, taking the Prof, Jefferis and Macrae, also sold it to the French. At the height of the 'Phoney War' the French did not want to upset the Germans who might retaliate by bombing Paris to pieces, but after the Blitzkrieg of May 1940 1,700 fluvial mines were streamed into the Rhine and all river traffic between Karlsruhe and Mainz was suspended; extensive damage was done to the bridges, barrages and pontoon bridges on the Rhine. In all over 20,000 'W' Bombs designed by 'Churchill's Toy Shop' were made and issued. It was a great success for MIR(C).

Macrae devised a universal switch, a booby-trap gadget of which 30,000 were made at a cost of ¾d each and then an anti-personnel switch, nicknamed 'The Castrator', of which 1½ million were made at 2s. each, plus 1s. for the cartridge. He wrote: 'It was becoming clear that the Ministry of Supply strongly disapproved of this pirate design section [MIR(C)] which had sprung up from nowhere without its co-operation and was rapidly making a name for itself.' But with a little help from the Prof, the Ministry was kept at bay. In June 1940 Churchill wrote, 'There was no time to proceed by ordinary channels in devising expedients [for the defence of the realm]. In order to secure quick action, free from departmental processes, upon any bright idea or gadget, *I decided to keep under my own hand* as Minister of Defence the experimental establishment formed by Major Jefferis at Whitchurch.' The ambitious Captain Macrae secured excellent offices and a workshop at Radio Normandie's building at 35 Portland Place. When their store of incendiary devices and bombs was destroyed at Hendon, the resourceful Macrae succeeded in requisitioning a large property at Whitchurch, 5 miles north of Aylesbury and 10 miles from Chequers for MIR(C). Known as The Firs, and owned by a very patriotic Major Arthur Abrahams, it was a large house which provided both offices and sleeping accommodation as well as extensive stables which were soon converted into workshops. There were also fields that could be used as firing ranges and where experimental demolition work could be carried out.

The next product was the Sticky Bomb, a grenade which could be thrown at a tank and would stick for five seconds and then blow a hole in it! But early developments were not successful. 'While engaged upon the fluvial mines in 1939,' Churchill wrote in June 1940, 'I had had useful contacts with this brilliant officer [Jefferis] whose ingenious inventive mind proved fruitful during the whole war. Major Jefferis and others connected with him were at work upon a bomb which could be thrown at a tank perhaps from a window and would stick upon it.' Churchill was present at a demonstration at Hangmore ranges, near Farnborough for the first testing of the Sticky Bomb. They caught alight well enough but failed to damage the tanks, so it was back to the drawing board.

Macrae and others continued their attempts to get the Sticky Bomb right. In his diary he wrote, '28 July 1940. Successful trial of ST [Sticky] Bombs at Farnborough. PM very satisfied'. In a chalk quarry near Chequers, the spectacular show started with an impressive noise as the glass container filled with nitro-glycerine exploded on the target. Churchill was delighted, borrowed a tommy-gun and sprayed a derelict army lorry with bullets. His daughter, Mary Churchill joined in too. The Prime Minister wrote a note instructing MIR(C) to go ahead; dated 2 October, under the heading 'Sticky Bomb', it said, 'Make one Million', and was signed 'WSC'. In fact 1½ million ST or No. 74 Grenades were eventually produced, another significant victory for MIR(C). Churchill wrote: 'in the end the "sticky" bomb was accepted as one of our best emergency weapons. In Syria where primitive conditions prevailed, it proved its worth.'

In Cabinet papers 120/379 of 27 August 1940 headed 'Most Secret', General Dill informed General Ismay that among the devices by MIR (before it came MD1) were the light Camouflet Set, pull switches, pressure switches, striker pattern delays and limpets. Among the 'work in hand' were scatter bombs, an untouchable device, a clam, an anti-tank mortar and a new design for an easily produced machine gun.

In the same month, also in Cabinet papers 120/379, Churchill

Churchill firing a Thompson (tommy-gun) at Shoeburyness, 13 June 1941

wrote to General Ismay; 'Report to me on the position of Major Jefferis. By whom is he employed? Who is he under? I regard this officer as a singularly capable and forceful man who should be brought forward to a higher position. He ought certainly to be promoted Lieutenant Colonel as it will give him more authority.' The Army predictably resisted as Jefferis was only 150th on the list of Royal Engineers Majors. But Churchill kept at it and in a personal minute dated 8 September (C70/1) wrote to General Dill, 'Surely it is important to bring forward able men in war time, instead of deferring entirely to seniority.'

Macrae had been working hard on what was originally called the Blacker Bombard. Major L.V. Blacker, a very smart Irish officer, complete with eyeglass, leggings and unlimited charm had thought up an anti-tank weapon which would fire a bomb containing a 10 or 20 lb charge against a tank. The actual gun barrel was attached to the charge; it had a shaped head containing the charge and a tall tube with stabilizing fins. The tube would serve as the gun barrel and would be fired off as a spigot. Millis was thrilled because the War Office Ordnance Board had consistently turned it down. On Sunday, 18

August 1940, Macrae's diary read: 'Gave demonstration of Blacker Bombard at Chequers. Used 23lb bomb. PM most impressed and gave the all clear to go ahead with this project. As First Lord of the Treasury, authorised us to spend £5,000 for a start.' The threat of invasion was causing Churchill much alarm. Neither the Home Forces (armed with a few miserable Boyes A/Tk rifles) nor the Home Guard had any weapon to deter the Nazi panzers if they arrived in the UK.

At the Chequers 'shoot' were General de Gaulle and Field Marshal Smuts. The first test missile almost wiped out the French general. Macrae wrote, 'Some unkind people afterwards suggested that the PM had in some way bribed Norman Angier [who fired the Bombard at Chequers] to have a go at this!' The bombard was then put into production as the 29 mm spigot mortar and 1¾ million were produced. Churchill himself ordered the first quarter million on 26 March 1941. He wrote to the Secretary of State for War on 23 April about rumours of new German tanks with between 4 and 6 inches of armour 'impervious to any existing anti-tank gun or indeed any mobile gun. Tests have shown that plastic explosive applied to armour plate in the bombard developed by Col Blacker and Col Jefferis has very great cutting power. This may be a solution to the problem. We must not be caught napping.'

Churchill watches Smith gun 'demo' at Shoeburyness, 13 June 1941. In the background there is a 6-Pdr A/Tk gun

In September 1941 Churchill wanted experimental bombard batteries or regiments to be set up at once to develop the use of the weapon. In a memo to Colonel Leslie Hollis, General Ismay's principal officer in the Ministry of Defence, he said: 'Many are now being delivered. What has been done about their tactical employment?'

So 'Churchill's Toy Shop' had four great successes to date: the fluvial mine or 'W' bomb, the limpet mine, the Sticky Bomb and the Blacker Bombard.

The move to The Firs made a great difference. Captain Macrae transformed the house into offices, a large drawing office, a mess with a large lounge, a dining room and bar plus many bedrooms. He also fended off more determined takeover bids from the Ministry of Supply. He then persuaded the Prof that the Prime Minister's favourite, Jefferis, was being badly treated. General Ismay wrote in his memoirs: 'Another of my foster children was one of Churchill's pet creations. I was instructed to take Major Jefferis [and his charges] "under my protection" lest the Ordnance Board and the Ministry of Supply who were unlikely to approve of freelances should make things difficult for him. Jefferis with continuous support and encouragement from "The Prof" and the Prime Minister himself did valuable work.' The Prof made his first visit to The Firs on 17 December 1940 and was duly impressed. He made weekly calls thereafter to see work in progress and brief the Prime Minister.

The Puff Ball was another of Jefferis's 'products'. It was a poultice charge designed for aerial attack on tanks. The Prof introduced Group Captain Pendril to MIR(C), but he was unfortunately killed when testing this 9 lb soft-nosed bomb. He flew his Hurricane too low over the target tank, straddling it with a string of bombs. One detonated against the tank, starting a chain reaction until the last bomb went off close to the Hurricane. Nevertheless the RAF accepted 50,000 Puff Balls for low-flying strafing of tanks and trains. But later, on 6 May 1942, Churchill wrote to General Ismay on the subject of bombing policies.

This is very unsatisfactory. The whole object was to give the Middle East a supply of puff balls (aerial anti-tank bombs invented by Colonel Jefferis) in time for any battle they might fight. Now we have just enough in both places not to be an important feature in any operations that may occur. I made some efforts to get these out to the Middle East before the November battle. Even so it has not been possible to bring them into action in any appreciable numbers.

MIR(C)'s transformation into a special department under the Prime Minister came into effect on 1 November 1940. Control was exercised through the Prof, and the department became known as Ministry of Defence 1 (MD1). The Ministry of Supply was now responsible for the administration of the unit but the control rested with the War Cabinet. Transport and drivers appeared on the strength and MD1 could place supply contracts direct with subcontractors, which were paid for by the Ministry of Supply. The new establishment was finally approved on 4 April 1941 and Captain Macrae ensured that everyone was promoted, Jefferis (finally) to Lieutenant Colonel and Macrae to Major.

In January 1941 three booby-trap mechanisms, the pull, pressure and release switches were approved and listed in the official Ordnance *Vocabulary*, but with MD1 inspectors travelling the country to ensure quality control. Direct phone lines from The Firs to 35 Portland Place, with scramblers for secrecy, ensured swift communication with Whitehall and the War Cabinet. Four design teams beavered away in a converted loft above the workshops at The Firs. In a summerhouse in the grounds a Mr Bridle carried out all the explosive filling, in bottles, shells or canisters – an illicit filling station which upset the Ordnance and Ministry of Supply. A year later less dangerous high explosive (HE) and incendiary filling sheds had been built. Two large swimming pools were constructed for underwater explosive tests.

Macrae started up an MD1 factory, with young Welsh girl labour under Leslie Gouldstone, acquiring a dozen automatic machines for weapon production. The first product was an ingenious delayed-action fuse thought up by Jefferis; because no contractor was capable of handling this tricky job, MD1 simply did it themselves. A detachment of Military Police now guarded The Firs, which was surrounded by barbed wire and sentries. This certainly impressed the high-ranking officers of all three services who visited. A large canteen, a theatre to give cinema shows and *The Firs* newsletter appeared, all pioneered by the indomitable Major Macrae. 'The Royal Navy invaded us in a big way but the RAF were close runners up. This was all good for trade,' he wrote.

The 'Clam' was the name for Macrae's pocket version of the limpet, a small magnetic explosive device with 8 oz of ICI explosive. 'For the Cloak and Dagger boys it was God's Gift from Heaven,' Macrae wrote. It could put any motor vehicle or aero engine out of action and give a tank a nasty surprise. MD1 supervised production of over 2½ million including a million which were sent to the Russian armies.

Jefferis wanted to keep MD1 as a small research and development unit, but the rest of his team knew that unless they expanded with a flow of new weaponry, they would eventually be absorbed or shut down. Brigadier Oliver Lucas of the Ministry of Supply was determined to close it down. So Jefferis and Macrae arranged a major 'toy' exhibition at Princes Risborough attended by the Prime Minister, Lord Beaverbrook (Minister of Supply), Lord Cherwell, (as the Prof had become), General Richard Paget (Commander in Chief of the Home Forces), General Alan Brooke (CIGS), and General Clarke (Director of Artillery).

The Bombard, the MKI and MKII (Sticky Bombs), and the new highly secret Jefferis shoulder gun were all demonstrated very successfully. Then the spigot mortar was demonstrated at Bisley to a vast array of Army VIPs, again successfully. And some ultra-secret new hollow charge weapons were also shown. Major Raymond Birt of the 22nd Dragoons watched a demonstration at Helmsley of devices to discourage would-be invaders of Britain. 'Certainly the toys behaved with perfect efficiency and with devastating effect,' he wrote. They consisted principally of large barrels filled with mixtures whose base was tar and petrol and which were either rolled, or lobbed by an explosive charge from the hedgerows into the midst of an armoured column. The procedure was described with enthusiasm by the demonstrating officer as his audience watched the barrels consumed by flames of colossal heat and fury. 'You see, gentlemen that this mixture not only *sticks* to an AFV but burns for *at least* five minutes. Inside it is all roast duck.'

But the arguement about the 'political' ownership of MDI rumbled on, with Jefferis wanting to be merged and the rest wanting independence. Lord Meltchett of ICI was a powerful ally against a Ministry of Supply takeover.

Jefferis had suggested to Commander Charles Goodeve who was in charge of the Navy's own weapon development team that the Bombard could be developed for anti U-boat work. He then produced a design for the spigot mortar to fire a whole ring of bombs either ahead or astern from a moving ship, and this was eventually developed as the Hedgehog. The Prime Minister was persuaded to visit Whitchurch to see a very successful demonstration. Twenty-four rounds were fired rapidly, two at a time, so quickly that all twenty-four were in the air simultaneously.

Churchill was enthralled and asked for repeat salvoes. The Hedgehogs, firing 60 lb bombs went into service with the Royal Navy, and were credited with thirty-seven confirmed submarine killings.

Lieutenant Colonel A.C. Brinsmead was then based at Whitchurch to help develop other products, including a 'wreck dispersal pistol', which caused the rapid disintegration of any concrete-filled obstructions and was used in wreck-dispersal and the destruction of coastal defences. An acoustic decoy 'Squawker' was another of Brinsmead's inventions, a gadget which persuaded enemy mines, and even torpedoes, to explode! Secret trials took place of bombs which jumped about on the ground (Kangaroo), bombs that leapt in *and* out of the sea and rockets which fired bridges over rivers. Professor Lindemann was once chased by a large homing bomb fitted with air fins and propelled by a monster rocket! On one occasion a workshop filled with mortar bombs and carboys filled with lethal liquid caught fire and destroyed a whole corner of one of the buildings at The Firs.

Sergeant, later Sergeant Major, Tilsley, was the senior NCO and supervised much of the filling of projectiles, detonators and fuses. A special electronic apparatus was available for measuring velocity.

Major Macrae presented Lord Cherwell with a plan to upgrade MDI to become a directorate and eventually, on 27 April 1942, it became a Directorate Grade B under Cherwell's control. Jefferis became a Brigadier and Macrae a Lieutenant Colonel and Assistant Director.

Another major product development occurred. The new Jefferis shoulder anti-tank gun, which had been demonstrated at Princes Risborough, was a vast improvement on an earlier Blacker invention. After much thought and several prototypes Jefferis used the Newmann effect of shaped or hollow charges. HE placed behind a metal cone with the concave part of the cone facing forwards, produced great penetration over a small area, and would bore a small hole through a tank's thick armour plate. Eventually the projector infantry anti-tank (or PIAT) was developed and became the Army's most effective anti-tank weapon for the infantryman. A special nose fuse Code 425 (then later 426) was needed to detonate the round and The Firs factory turned them out in the thousands. The main snags were the 60 lb weight and the comparatively short range of up to 200 yards. Victoria Crosses were awarded to the brave infantrymen of the Lancashire Fusiliers, the Canadian

Westminster Regiment, the Green Howards and the 7th Gurkha Rifles who engaged and destroyed enemy tanks with PIAT.

Despite Churchill's constant pressure on the War Office to produce better tanks and anti-tank guns, it was well-known at the 'sharp end' that the Allied weapons were always a year or two behind those of the Germans in battle effectiveness. On 27 July 1942 the Prime Minister minuted the Secretary of State for War, the CIGS and the Minister of Supply that the 2.4-pounder tank and anti-tank gun, 40,000 of them altogether, were already out of date. He wrote: 'The Bombard or the Jefferis rifle rocket give better results and are much easier to make. Even the 6 pounder is now falling behind.' It was no use – the British and American tanks and anti-tank guns only 'caught up' in the last three months of the war! And on 13 November 1942 he wrote: 'I saw the Jefferis gun last week. It appears to be a powerful weapon which would enable infantry to face tank attack. How many have been ordered? When will they be delivered? How is it proposed to distribute them? I should hope that the Middle East and India would receive their quota at a very early date.'

Jefferis had another success with an up-graded small delayed-action fuse for demolition work and booby traps. The original Time Pencil was a rather dodgy and dangerous device, but after an immense amount of work the LD (Lead Delay), later called Switch No. 9, was developed. Over 5 million devices were made at Whitchurch for use around the world; it was a very reliable little 'banger' which caused confusion to the enemy. Another device for saboteurs was the Aero Switch, which was inserted by hand into an enemy plane (on the ground!) and which exploded initially at 10,000 feet and later at 5,000 feet (MK2). Thousands were then manufactured at Whitchurch. There was also a little anti-personnel mine which cost 5 s. called the Macrae mine, later the 'M' mine. Some were used for protecting overseas camps and airfields with a firework instead of HE to give a bright alarm flash, and so MDI made millions of them.

Lieutenant Colonel Macrae met Churchill on many occasions. Every fact in every speech which involved secret weaponry had to be carefully checked and that meant a visit to Chequers. Moreover many 'product' demonstrations at Princes Risborough were attended by the Prime Minister. 'He would be like a small boy on holiday. The faithful Commander Thompson would be in attendance carrying a Sten gun and when there was any lull in the proceedings Winston would lower himself to the ground and bang away at the nearest target. He could be very troublesome on these occasions through his reluctance to take shelter when necessary.' When his daughter Mary, or the Prof persuaded him to visit The Firs, it made the day for MDI and the Welsh factory girls nearly burst themselves with cheering.

The discovery of the hollow charge for the PIAT was dramatic. MD1 designed a whole range of them, called Beehives. The smallest weighed only 6 lb but would drill a hole through 2 inches of armour plate or a yard of concrete. Larger sizes were ideal for demolishing pillboxes and coastal defences. Jefferis looked round for suitable guns to fire his hollow rounds. The Ordnance Board predictably went berserk, but two guns were developed at Whitchurch; a 4.5-inch naval gun for use by MTBs against trawlers, and the 7.5-inch AVRE which, mounted on a tank, fired a larger plastic round at low velocity of about 800 feet per second. The spigot bombard with a hollow charge was refined for many usages.

By 1943 Jefferis and MD1 were Churchill's military 'gurus'. In January and April he wrote to the Secretary of State for War about the new PIAT. 'The principle of absorbing recoil dynamically is of course not new but Brigadier Jefferis was the first man to make a workable weapon with which a 3 pound projectile could be fired from the shoulder to anything like the distance now achieved. Moreover the design of the ammunition which has a far greater penetration than any previous type was entirely his work.' Churchill wanted his protégé's work to be recognized as the Jefferis shoulder gun. 'Everyone speaks of Mills grenades, Stokes guns, Hawkins mines, Kerrison predictors, Northover projectors.' The War Office won. The name remained the PIAT.

Before 'Operation Husky' to recapture Sicily the Prime Minister was chasing the COS Committee and Chief of Combined Operations about artificial piers for use on flat beaches. 'It is nearly six months since I urged the construction of several miles of piers. Was Brigadier Jefferis consulted? I was hoping to reduce the strain on landing craft [of which there was a distinct shortage] by the rapid building of these piers; let me now [10 March 1943] have plans for four miles of piers before "Husky".' The next month he wrote to General Ismay. 'I was shown a sketch the other day of a ship with a landing bridge which Brigadier Jefferis suggested could be used for landing tanks on low cliffs apt to be weakly defended. This proposal seems very attractive and I hope it is being followed up energetically.'

Colonel Macrae had developed the first Kangaroo ('K') bomb, which was designed to pop up and plaster itself on the belly of a tank and then explode it. A first order was placed for a million to be made by MDI. In August 1944 MD1 put three design teams onto what was called the 'K' delay bomb, which could lie dormant for a predetermined period and then come to life and (jump up) to explode. The fuses were made at Whitchurch but the bomb was finalized and in production shortly before the end of the war.

The spin-off by Jefferis of the Beehive series of hollow-charge bombs into the AVRE 7.5-inch Petard spigot mortar to be fired from Churchill tanks which was named the Flying Dustbin was crucial for the 79th Armoured Division. Their 1st Asssault Brigade RE had twelve assault squadrons, but their new deadly weapons only arrived in April 1944.

Jack Robinson was a REME Staff Sergeant with the 33rd Armoured Work Shop in the 79th Armoured Division. He was seconded to REME HQ as a trouble-shooter for the special new equipment. He and two fitters made the first plough to dig up mines, which was attached to the front of a Churchill tank and was called the Bullshorn. It had to lift tank mines from sand on the seashore without exploding them. If a mine exploded on a beach it could make a hole filled with water and clay, in which following vehicles would be bogged down. Sergeant Robinson and two fitters took the prototype plough by transporter to The Firs for final testing and modifications under Captain Rosling. After Christmas 1943 an order for twenty-four was placed with G.A. Harvey Limited of Greenwich. When Robinson went there to supervise production, to his surprise General Montgomery arrived to give the workforce a 'pep' talk. He then inspected the Bullshorn and asked how it would be disconnected from the front of the tank when its job was completed. Robinson produced a large spanner to undo the nut on the shaft that held the plough to the tank. The general was unhappy about the tank crew getting out to unfasten the plough, possibly under fire, so the nut was discarded and a pin fitted that could be blown out by an explosive charge – MD1 believed in explosives! The MD1 staff gave Robinson a 'beautiful' fighting knife they had made – 'They must have thought I was going to get close to the Germans' – and Brigadier Jefferis sent him and his fitters back to their unit in his staff car.

Captain C.V. 'Nobby' Clarke of MD1 had an idea for a rocket-operated tank bridge and Lieutenant Colonel Macrae obtained two

Churchill tanks complete with drivers. Sketches were produced for the 'Great Eastern' and masses of girderwork appeared from G.A. Harvey of Greenwich. Eventually a Bailey bridge was carried on the back of a Churchill tank in a folded up position. On reaching a canal or narrow river, rockets would fire the folded part to form a bridge over which tanks could run. Clarke's choice of a large number of 3-inch rockets almost took the 40-ton Churchill tank with them over the 'obstacle'. Eventually ten Great Easterns were produced and used by the 79th Armoured Division in Holland early in 1945.

Some AVREs carried General Wade explosive charges devised by MD1 which were eventually placed by hand to blow up concrete beach walls and pillboxes. But without Churchill's Toy Shop 'magic' PIAT, the Beehives and the 'Flying Dustbin' AVRE tank, 79th Armoured Division would have had no major weapon for the D-Day beach landings.

During 1943 much thought was given to the planning of 'Operation Overlord' and the 79th Armoured Division was primarily formed for the purpose of beaching numerous specialized armoured weapons and then breaching the Atlantic Wall. Major General Hobart, their commander, was not quite in the same league as an arms inventor as Millis Jefferis, but as another dedicated sapper officer he was determined that he, and *anybody* in his division who had a useful idea, should be given the opportunity to investigate and develop it.

4   Percy Hobart – Churchill's Protégé

Percy Cleghorn Stanley Hobart was born in 1885, and was called Patrick by his family, and Hobo by the Army. After Clifton College he went in 1902 to the Royal Military Academy, Woolwich, and thence to the School of Military Engineering with the Indian Army. He was commissioned two years later into the Royal Engineers and during the First World War served with the Indian Corps, initially with the 1st Sappers and Miners. He won the MC at Neuve Chapelle in 1915 and fought at Festubert, and in the September offensive. He joined the General Staff with the 3rd Lahore Division, and went to the Mesopotamian theatre of war where, as Brigade Major from 1916 to 1918, he won the DSO, was wounded and taken prisoner by the Turks. He was rescued by a Rolls Royce armoured car unit and by the end of 1918 had been mentioned six times in despatches and earned an OBE. From Palestine he joined the Waziristan Force and was promoted to Lieutenant Colonel in 1921. Staff College at Quetta followed, after active service with Borrett's Wana column against the tribesmen. Although by training and experience a sapper, in 1923 he made a major change and joined the Royal Tank Corps, convinced that the future of the Army lay with armoured forces. As the tank representative at the Staff College in the UK he became a brilliant teacher of tank tactics and made an intensive study of the new Vickers medium tank. Four years later he went to the Tank Corps Centre at Bovington and became a very senior second in command with the 4th Battalion Royal Tank Corps (RTC). At that stage there were only four regular RTC battalions in the British Army.

Major General Sir Percy Hobart, KBE, CB DSO, MC – 'Hobo'
GOC 79th Armoured Division

He married Dorothea Field in 1928 and his sister, Betty, married
Lieutenant Colonel Bernard Montgomery, an instructor at the Staff

College, Camberley. Then for a short time in 1930 he went back to India to command the Southern Armoured Car Group before returning to become commanding officer of the 2nd Battalion RTC at Farnborough, then part of the 1st Brigade RTC. In 1933 he was appointed Inspector of the RTC and also Commanded the 1st Tank Brigade, where he formed a strong friendship with *the* tank expert, Liddell Hart.

Liddell Hart wrote in his book *The Other Side of the Hill:*

The Command of this tank brigade – the Experimental Armoured Force of 1927/28 – was given to an expert in handling tanks, Brigadier R.C.S. Hobart, who had both vision and a dynamic sense of mobility. He did much to develop the tactical methods and wireless control required for fast moving operations. He also seized the opportunity to try out, in practice, the theory of deep strategic penetration by an armoured force operating independently. The CIGS Montgomery-Massingbird put a curb [on this]. The enlargement of this first tank brigade into an armoured division was deferred for a further three years.

General Guderian the great German expert on panzer tactics wrote, 'It is the old school. I put my faith in Hobart, the new man.'

Hobart commanded the Tank Brigade for over three years and in the summer of 1936, Michael Carver (subsequently to command 1st RTC in the North African campaign, and later still to become a field marshal) wrote, 'That summer on Salisbury Plain we exercised under the eagle eye of the fierce brigade commander, the great 'Hobo' Percy Hobart. He was a merciless trainer who drove us all hard and overlooked no detail, his intensity matched by his keen interest in all ranks under his command. He was universally respected, admired and served with enthusiasm.' But Carver also thought that 'Hobo' was a bully! Hobart's first meeting with Winston Churchill was at an RTC dinner in 1935.

He next spent two years at the War Office as Deputy Director Staff Duties and Director of Military Training. Leslie Hore-Belisha, the War Minister then created Britain's first Armoured Division to replace the Cavalry division training in Egypt. So Hobart flew on a flying boat to Alexandria on 27 September 1938 and from more or less scratch raised the 7th Armoured Division, later to become known as the famous Desert Rats after their black jerboa desert rat emblem. He found the 7th Hussars equipped with light tanks, the

8th Hussars with Ford trucks, and 11th Hussars in First World War Rolls Royce armoured cars. The tank group consisted of the 1st and 6th Battalions Royal Tank Corps (RTC) in light tanks and some Vickers medium tanks. The Pivot Group consisted of the 60th Rifles and 3 RHA with 3.7-inch howitzers. The conversion from cavalry to armour was a bitter blow to the proud Hussar regiments and the Commmander-in-Chief, Gordon Finlayson, known as Copper, was most unreceptive to any new ideas. Hobart wrote to his wife shortly after his arrival:

> I had the Cavalry CO's in and laid my cards on the table. They are such nice chaps, socially. That's what makes it so difficult. But they're so conservative of their spurs and swords and regimental tradition etc., and so certain that the good old Umpteenth will be all right on the night, so easily satisfied with an excuse if things aren't right, so prone to blame the machine or machinery.
>
> And unless one upsets all their polo etc. – for which they have paid heavily – its so hard to get anything more into them or any more work out of them. Three days a week they come in 6 miles to Gezirah Club for polo. At 5 p.m. it's getting dark: they are sweaty and tired. Not fit for much and most of them full up of socials in Cairo. Take their clothes and change at Club. Don't return to Abbassia till 2 a.m. or 3 a.m. Non-polo days it's tennis or something.
>
> Well, well. But I am trying not to be impatient and to lead gradually, not drive. The result is I get depressed by how little is happening: and impatient with myself.

When Gordon Finlayson returned to the UK to become Adjutant General he wrote a damning report about Hobart.

> Wide technical knowledge Royal Armoured Corps. Unduly optimistic about its capacities. Marked reluctance to listen to others' opinions and is too impatient with staff officers too jealous with regard for his own formation. Gives impression not placing much value on other arms: has caused misgivings and shaken his position as a Commander, result is he does not get the willing best from his subordinates and has not welded them into a happy and contented body.
>
> General Hobart's methods of managing officers and men do not give the best results. I cannot regard him a suitable commander in the field nor for promotion. Credit due for much hard peacetime work

here both to the Mobile Division and Administrative Area.

Better scope for undoubted energy, peculiar temperament and particular abilities in such spheres as that of Technical Adviser AFV or in administrative capacity on staff. Not likely to qualify for the highest command and appointments.

Difficult to serve with or understand. Active in body and mind. Very hard worker. Brain quick and full of ideas. Considerable drive. Impetuous in judgments which are not as consistent and confidence-bearing as a Commander's should be. Manner and temperament not usually sympathetic, personality average. Interested in welfare and carries out well his administrative responsibilities.

Hobart carried out training, with many exercises in the desert, using his own experience gained in Mesopotamia. He insisted on three roles for his motley collection – dispersion, flexibility and mobility. He stressed too the importance of integrating the supporting arms (field, anti-tank and AA artillery and the infantry battalions of the Pivot Group) with his tank battalions. Desert navigation, constant vehicle maintenance, the study of repair facilities by base workshops – all these lessons were learned and by the outbreak of war, the 7th Armoured Division was a capable fighting formation. Four new medium tanks were arriving each month equipped with the new 3-pounder gun.

However the new Commander-in-Chief, Lieutenant General Maitland Wilson (who had known Hobart at Staff College), arrived and quickly found fault with him. In November he wrote to General Archibald Wavell recommending that he be replaced. Wavell agreed and Hobart's biographer, Kenneth Macksey, notes; 'Neither General Wavell or General Wilson come out of this transaction with credit.' Wavell did however, write: 'I hope that it will be found possible to use General Hobart's great knowledge and experience of Armoured Fighting Vehicles in some capacity.' When 'Hobo' left, all the men of his division lined the route to the airstrip to cheer their General on his way. Another famous General, Richard O'Conner, who commanded the 8th Infantry Division at Matruh, wrote of the Mobile Division: 'It is the best trained division I have ever seen.' Six months later, 7th Armoured, using Hobart's methods, won a famous victory over the Italian Army at Beda Fomm.

The return home must have been a bitter moment. An appeal to the King for reinstatement failed. The War Office was unhelpful and on 9 March 1940 the Major General, now on retired pay, became a Lance Corporal in the Chipping Campden Home Guard!

On 11 August 1940 Liddell Hart wrote an article in the *Sunday Pictorial* headed 'We have wasted brains' about the generals of great experience – Martel, Pile, Fuller, Lindsay and Hobart – whose considerable talents were not being utilized. General Pile, who was commanding the AA defences of London, wrote to Churchill. 'I told him we had a superb trainer of tanks in Hobart,' he recalled, 'but he had just been sacked.' But Hobart, difficult and proud, at first refused to meet the Prime Minister, 'unless he was reinstated and his honour satisfied'. Liddell Hart and Pile together persuaded the reluctant 'Hobo' to visit Churchill at Chequers. He asked for advice. 'Do I come dressed as a civilian, as a Major General of the British Army or as a Corporal in the Home Guard?' On 13 October he was interviewed by the Prime Minister and Clement Attlee, lunched at Chequers and was asked to talk about tanks and the number of divisions and tanks needed to win the war. The next week Churchill wrote to General John Dill, the CIGS:

> I was very much pleased last week when you told me you proposed to give an armoured division to Major General Hobart. I think very highly of this officer, and I am not at all impressed by the prejudices against him in certain quarters. Such prejudices attach frequently to persons of strong personality and original views. In this case General Hobart's original views have been only too tragically borne out. The neglect by the General Staff even to devise proper patterns of tanks before the war has robbed us of all the fruits of this invention. These fruits have been reaped by the enemy, with terrible consequences. We should therefore remember that this was an officer who had the root of the matter in him, and also vision. In my minute last week to you I said I hoped you would propose to me the appointment that day, i.e. Tuesday, but at the latest this week. Will you very kindly make sure that the appointment is made at the earliest moment.
>
> Since making this minute I have carefully read your note to me and the summary of the case for and against General Hobart. We are now at war, fighting for our lives, and we cannot afford to confine Army appointments to persons who have excited no hostile comment in their career. The catalogue of General Hobart's qualities and defects might almost exactly have been attributed to most of the great commanders of British history. Marlborough was very much the conventional soldier, carrying with him the goodwill of the service.

Cromwell, Wolfe, Clive, Gordon, and in a different sphere, Lawrence, all had very close resemblance to the characteristics set down as defects. They had other qualities as well, and so I am led to believe has General Hobart. This is a time to try men of force and vision and not to be exclusively confined to those who are judged thoroughly safe by conventional standards. I hope therefore you will not recoil from your proposal to me of a week ago, for I think your instinct in this matter was sound and true.

And John Colville, private secretary to Churchill, noted in his diary that Churchill said to General Dill: 'Remember it isn't only the good boys who help to win wars. It is the sneaks and stinkers as well!'

On 4 November Hobart had another interview with the Prime Minister, still demanding action in response to his appeal to the King and refusing a new appointment! Two days later Churchill wrote:

Dear General Hobart,
The matter is one for you to settle and personally I could not attempt to sway your decision. I should have thought however that in times like these the Command of an Armoured Division about to be formed gave high opportunities for useful service. Pray let the CIGS know what you are doing as other arrangements must be made.
Yours etc
Winston S. Churchill.

Two days later Hobart wrote back: 'I greatly appreciate that you should have found time to see me and to write. I am most anxious to be of any service I can to the country – or to you. I will undertake the work you mention or any other to which I am appointed. I will do my best. I am informing the CIGS.' Hobart wrote a detailed paper on the system and priorities for creating the new armoured formations which he discussed with the Prime Minister over lunch at Chequers on 23 November.

So at long last Hobart obtained his third major command in the newly formed 11th Armoured Division (the 1st Tank Brigade, and the 7th Armoured Division being the first two). In December 1940 there were two armoured brigades: the 29th with the 23rd Hussars, the 24th Lancers and the 2nd Fife and Forfar Yeomanry, plus the 8th Battalion Rifle Brigade; and the 30th, consisting of the 22nd Dragoons, the 2nd Lothians and Border Yeomanry, the Westminster Dragoons, the 12th Battalion King's Royal Rifle Corps (KRRC) and the 13th Regiment Royal Horse Artillery. The official birthday for the new division was 11 March 1941, when Divisional HQ was formed and took control. On the Yorkshire moors Hobart now trained this undergunned (they only had 2-pounder's), lightly armoured and slow (18 m.p.h.) tanks into a cohesive formation. Captain Edgar Palamountain, in *Taurus Pursuant* wrote: 'No formation ever trained more intensively. All the General's relentless energy and determination were concentrated on the task. Up hill and down dale, both literally and figuratively, he chased his men, from Brigadiers downwards. Yet all respected his remarkable talents and the single-mindedness with which he used them. General Hobart was a hard taskmaster.' The 29th Brigade was concentrated in Whitby, the 30th at Helmsley and the 11th Support Group around Malton with Divisional HQ near Scarborough.

In his history of the 22nd Dragoons, who were originally part of the newly formed 11th Armoured Division (before transferring to the 79th Armoured Division for the north-western European campaign), Major Raymond Birt wrote of Hobart:

He was indeed, the divisional Commander, and as such on all official occasions a Jehovah-like figure to the regimental soldier, but he was also 'Hobo' – a familiar name in conversation, a driving force of immense energy whose momentum transmitted itself to every individual in his command, and was something of a legend as the creator of the famous 7th Armoured Division and one of the army's best tankmen. We knew him well, and the claim is one that soldiers of an earlier generation may find strange . . . The troop leader out on exercise, or the instructor demonstrating in his hut the intricacies of an injector-pump, could never be sure that there would not suddenly appear the hurrying figure of the GOC who would listen courteously for a while before leaving without a word, but having conveyed that he had never passed a more instructive five minutes in his life, and that troop training and injector-pumps were as much the instruments of the destruction of the enemy as a high explosive bomb. With whatever thunders the GOC could shake his senior officers (and echoes of such storms were sometimes heard or rumoured), he was to most soldiers of the regiment one of those leaders whose bearing inspired an instant confidence, an awareness of one's own worth provided (and the threat was plainly to be seen in the firm mouth, the direct eyes beneath their heavy sweep of eyebrows and the long aggressive line of the nose) one was learning to live at a prodigious and nonmathematical rate of minutes to the hour, days to the week, and weeks to the defeat of the King's enemies.

Hobart also stamped his mark literally on his new division. The flash or emblem was his family crest of the Bickling Hobarts: 'A bull sable, passant, regardant', which translated into a ferocious black bull with red horns and hooves, pawing the ground on a bright yellow background. Lt John Borthwick, Hobart's ADC recalls: 'When I first heard Hobo speak it was in short staccato bursts but gloriously articulate. He was not an inspired orator but he did inspire curiosity and even admiration.'

Hobart was of course now part of Churchill's 'Tank Parliament' to consider tank and anti-tank questions. The first was held on 5 May at 10 Downing Street. Much drama ensued. Martel, known as 'Q', thought that Hobart was corresponding directly and secretly with the Prime Minister on 'Tank Parliament' matters. He wrote in his autobiography:

> I held periodical conferences with the Commanders of formations, so as to be sure that we were *all* thinking on the *same* lines. There was almost unanimous agreement on nearly every point but General Hobart often held views which differed materially from all the others, imbued with the all-armoured idea, he wanted Armoured Divisions to be composed mainly of tank units.

Hobart wanted to move his armoured formations side by side at speed to seize vital ground, forcing the enemy to counter-attack against a box with an anti-tank screen and defensive minefields.

In his opening address to a newly joined Royal Armoured Corps (RAC) draft Hobart told them: 'There are no short cuts to good tank maintenance. It depends on the knowledge and skill of every man in the crew.' And to his wife Dorrie, he wrote: 'This is the third new Armoured formation I have formed and built up. No one else in the world has done this. Ever. Three times lucky. This Division has been built literally from zero: from a bucketful of men pulled out of civilian life. Here I deal almost entirely with men under my command: 99% of my time. Only about 1% with those above me. Now, I'm damned bad with my superiors.' He remained scathing about the cavalry officers: 'Most charming fellows and they are really working quite hard, but their standards are low, they are easily pleased. They always want to run before they can walk – or even stand. It is very dangerous. The fact is that this is a professional fight and they are incurable amateurs.' Nothing changes. Wellington used to say the same thing about his cavalry – rash, impetuous, difficult to control and always charging ahead of their support troops!

Major Birt of the 22nd Dragoons described the end of 'Operation Percy' on 6 November 1941 on Rievaulx moors.

> Shortly we heard a roar of cheering and saw – with unbelief and delight – the most famous hat and the most famous cigar in the world. Trudging along at the briskest possible speed at the head of his company of high ranking officers, was Winston Churchill. The now familiar, almost impudent, V-sign was flourished at us. With immense satisfaction we cheered down the line the man who embodied so splendidly the pugnacity and determination with which the nation had faced the hard times and who was himself the inspirer of much of our new-found courage and respect.

The Prime Minister sent a message to all ranks of the 11th Armoured Division: 'I am glad to have seen this grand Division which General Hobart has trained so well. I hope a chance will come for it to play a glorious part in the destruction of a hateful enemy. Friday will be a whole holiday. Winston S. Churchill.'

In the spring of 1942 the 30th Armoured Brigade left to join the new 42nd Armoured Division and 159 Infantry Brigade from the 53rd Welsh Division took their place. The Crusader tank took the place of the Valentine – a fast, good-looking tank with a similar gun to the Valentine but a thinner skin. By August 1942 new 6-pounder guns appeared in the Crusader turrets. General Montgomery ran a fourteen-day exercise in Sussex, Surrey and Kent called 'Tiger', to try out the new divisional organization with a second 25-pounder artillery regiment and an armoured car regiment – a copy of the current German equivalent. The Prime Minister now earmarked the 11th Armoured Division for the North African theatre of war and they moved to East Anglia to mobilize for overseas. Hobart was excited at the thought of returning in triumph and leading his Black Bulls into their first action. It was not to be, aged fifty-seven, he was not able to persuade a medical board that he was fit to go on active service. His patron, Winston Churchill once again intervened on his behalf. On 4 September 1942, he wrote to the Secretary of State for War:

I see nothing in these reports [of the Medical Board report on General Hobart] which would justify removing this officer from the command of his division on its proceeding on active service.

General Hobart bears a very high reputation, not only in the Service, but in wide circles outside. He is a man of quite exceptional mental attainments, with great strength of character, and although he does not work easily with others it is a great pity we have not more of his like in the Service. I have been shocked at the persecution to which he has been subjected.

I am quite sure that if, when I had him transferred from a corporal in the Home Guard to the command of one of the new armoured divisions, I had instead insisted upon his controlling the whole of the tank developments, with a seat on the Army Council, many of the grievous errors from which we have suffered would not have been committed. The High Commands of the Army are not a club. It is my duty and that of His Majesty's Government to make sure that exceptionally able men, even though not popular with their military contemporaries, should not be prevented from giving their services to the Crown.

Nevertheless on 15 October Hobart had to hand the 11th Armoured Division to Major General Brocas Burrows and was given a great send off. 'The reason for the Divisional Commander's [Hobart] departure was one of those mysterious wartime "top secrets" which encourage the mildest speculation in the closed world of the army,' wrote Major Birt. 'There was an impression that he was to develop something in the nature of a secret weapon.'

5 Hobart and His Third Division

Churchill managed to steer his difficult protégé through the minefields of his foes at the War Office into a new, vital and very secret appointment. One clause in Hobart's new brief read: 'Your formation will be trained primarily in their *special* roles and secondly as normal tank formations. Your Headquarters must be capable of functioning operationally.' In the battles to come the new division never fought as a division, or by brigade or regiment. It was to be widely dispersed, supporting at one stage or another every formation in the British and Canadian Armies and many of the American formations as well. The newly formed 79th Armoured Division became known as the 'Zoo' or 'Menagerie', composed of strange, dangerous beasts whose primary task was the breaching of Hitler's defensive barriers along the French coast. Here General Rommel had sowed 4 million mines and constructed hundreds of concrete pill-boxes. Half a million troops and conscript workers had been working flat out to strengthen the Atlantic Wall. The beaches were strewn with steel and concrete wrecking devices, usually with mines firmly attached to the top. Every accessible landing place was covered by enfilading fire from the fortified houses, bunkers or pill-boxes. The sand dunes and lateral roads were now huge minefields with their sinister *'Achtung Minen'* signposts. General Montgomery, on his return from the Sicilian and Southern Italian campaigns, was under no illusion. 'Armoured columns must penetrate deep inland and quickly on D-Day. We must gain space rapidly and peg claims well inland.' Churchill was acutely concerned lest the slaughter of the Canadian troops on the Dieppe beaches would be repeated on a far larger scale on the beaches of Normandy.

Dieppe had shown that no preliminary bombardment from the seas would totally wipe out the enemy's defences; so covering fire was essential before and during the landing from guns, mortars and rockets mounted *in* the assault craft and special support craft. But by the summer of 1942 only bridging tanks, minesweepers and a special searchlight mounted on a tank, known as the Canal Defence Light (CDL) were available.

Early in April 1943 Hobart took command of the 79th Armoured Division with the HQ at Hurts Hall, Saxmundham. It had originally been formed in October 1942 and comprised the 27th Armoured Brigade (4/7 Royal Dragoon Guards, 13/18 Hussars and the East Riding Yeomanry) plus 185 Infantry Brigade (which subsequently transferred to the 3rd British Division).

The CIGS, Alan Brooke, wrote in his diary on 25 March: 'Then to see Hobart on questions of organisation of his division which was to handle various specialised forms of armoured vehicles such as amphibious tanks, searchlight tanks, mine destroying tanks, flame throwers, etc. It was a very happy brainwave to have selected Hobo to control and command all the supplementary tank equipment. With his fertile brain and untiring drive all these various forms of tank made unbounded strides and contributed greatly to the successes in Normandy. He had found a job completely to his heart's liking and he put everything into it.'

He might be aged fifty-eight and deemed unfit to take a division overseas, but Hobart's energy was phenomenal. The Division was quickly reorganised with three brigades of armour (the 35th Tank Brigade, later replaced by the 1st Tank Brigade, the 27th Armoured Brigade, which remained under command until March 1944; the 30th Armoured Brigade and a brand new concept, the 1st Assault Brigade R.E.). A specialist unit, the 43rd Royal Tank Regiment (RTR) was the divisional experimental unit, and left the Division in March 1944.

Simultaneously the War Office, MD1 and various factories were bombarded with requests and demands for the new armoured equipment he wanted. He turned the division into a 'think tank' for new ideas for armoured weaponry. Sergeant Jack Robinson of REME recalled:

> We were experimenting with a radio receiver that we had fitted into a Churchill tank. The RAF had a transmitter that sent out dots and dashes which went into a beam. It was used to guide planes to small airfields. It could be used to target a building, then the tank could pick up the beam. General Hobart came to see a demonstration. He

used a portable receiver we had, said 'good show' and went. I don't think the thing was used in action.

John Woollett, later to become a major general, recalls, 'One evening the CE Lieutenant Colonel Willott was talking to General Hobart about a mine clearing device he was having made (the Mighty Wurlitzer) [A device whereby 16 pipes were hung on to the outside of a tank and fired forwards about 20 yards into a minefield]. First thing next morning 'Hobo' was in the training area asking to see it. On being told that work had only just started, he replied, "What have you been doing all night?" '

> On another occasion the GOC attended an indoor exercise on the breaching of beach obstacles and listened to the answers, to the problems of devices to use, and the loading of loading craft, depending on the type of obstacles known to exist at the assigned landing place. The CRE asked the GOC if he wished to comment at the end. He said, 'I have heard a lot about how you deal with the obstacles you expect, but what you must be ready for is to get through *whatever* you encounter. You may be landed *anywhere* because those in charge of landing craft are even more amateur sailors than you are amateur soldiers' and with that he swept out! I recall too being told at 0700 hrs to have a demonstration of an assault bridge and a fascine [a large roll of wood paling] ready at the Orford battle area, 10 miles away, by mid-day! By surviving 'Hobo's training we acquired great confidence. By 3–4 months from arriving in Aldeburgh the squadron was fully capable of carrying out its operational tasks.

Sir Miles Thomas of the Nuffield organization was briefed by Hobart on a 'jumping' tank or transport vehicle with a rocket pointing downwards at each corner and then touched off simultaneously the vehicle would jump and if the rockets were mounted on swivels, the vehicle *could* be steered!

One advantage Hobart inherited with his new divisional HQ was that the Aldeburgh–Saxmundham area was the battle training area of the 54th Division. 'In March 1943 exercise "Kruschen" took place to develop techiniques for assaulting strongly defended positions similar to those that would be encountered in Europe,' wrote Geoff Dewing in *Aldeburgh 1939–45*. 'Kruschen' showed that sappers working in the open and under fire would stand little chance of surviving long enough to do their job. The 43rd RTR, however, had an unusual blend of 'early' flame-throwers. Soon they were joined by AVREs, Congers, Crocodiles and many other devices. Lieutenant Ian Hammerton wrote:

> The 43rd Bn were in a double tented camp – bell tents inside marquees because of winter weather. I was there to learn about minesweeping. There were two kinds of flail tanks – the Baron, a turretless Matilda fitted with two outboard mounted engines driving a rotor mounted on a jib in front of the tank, the rotor drum having many chains attached which flailed the ground, thus setting off mines. And the Scorpion which was a turretless Valentine equipped in similar fashion [which had been used with moderate success at Alamein and subsequent battles]. Soon however the new American Sherman tank was being prepared as an improvement on the Matildas and Valentines.

The 43rd RTR arranged courses for the Division on flails, AVREs, Congers, Crocodiles and other devices.

On 8 June the CIGS, Alan Brooke, flew to Northumberland 'to inspect more 79 A/Div tanks that swam under their own power, tanks that scaled sea-walls, tanks that pounded concrete fortifications and explosives or spanned ditches with bridges, tanks with searchlights, tanks that emitted flames or acted as ramps for other tanks'. And five weeks later he flew on a bumpy flight to the Norfolk Broads with Hobart and enjoyed his first trip in an amphibious tank, the new Dual Duplex, which Churchill had thought up: 'Most interesting and inspiring. I was delighted to see old Hobo so happy and so well employed.' A few days later, after consultation with the Prime Minister the CIGS gave orders for '900 tanks to be converted despite the view of the Admiralty and Ministry of Supply that such unnatural hybrids could *never* be made seaworthy'.

Charles Salt of the 43rd RTR, who worked on the Crocodile, wrote:

> We were based in the grounds of Sudbourne hall and village. One room was most Secret and a 24 hour guard was placed on it – the home of the CDL apparatus. During my service life I had never seen so much 'Red' there were Generals, Staff Officers., foreign as well as Commonwealth top brass. 43 RTR were classed as an experimental regiment within the 79th Armoured Division. On the beach at

Orford one 'Funny' was being demonstrated, like a huge Catherine Wheel, a framework fitted with explosive charges, alternately on either side, the intention being that it would propel itself through a minefield and clearing a path. Some of the charges failed on one side. The whole contraption went out of balance, turned in a circle and headed back towards the top brass. No need to sound the 'retreat'. You saw all these weirdos trundling around, Crabs, Crocs, Fascines, Petard, CDL, Carpet layers, Bridging tanks, Bangalore Torpedo (Snakes), and you thought 'what the hell is that' but seeing them in action made you realise the ingenuity that had gone into the design of such vehicles.

6 Hobart's 'Zoo'

The D.D. Tank – Schwim-panzer

Some experimental amphibious tanks in prototype form were tried out towards the end of the First World War, with permanent flotation chambers and marine propellers. A light tank T880 MKII with a pair of pontoons strapped to the side and an outboard motor on the back was a Heath Robinson effort. An *émigré* Hungarian engineer, Nicholas Staussler, produced a number of prototypes with a Crusader MKI, then a Tetrarch light tank and then a Valentine infantry tank.

In 1940, however, the War Office were initially unimpressed by his first design which comprised a canvas screen around the heavy (16-tons) tank hull which displaced enough water to allow it to float like a boat. A single duplex drive could be attached to the tank, which would drive it through the water at up to 4 knots. The steerable propellers were driven off the tank's gearbox. Certainly Churchill's idea of a 'galosh' and his constant pressure for the development of a swimming tank was successful. Later a secret trial which took place on Hendon Reservoir impressed both Churchill and the CIGS. As a result 600 Valentine tanks were converted and when completed used by the 36th Tank Brigade.

General Hobart made two decisions shortly after taking over his command. The 'swimming tank' ought to lead the amphibious craft for the invasion in Sherman tanks. They should be manned by the 27th Tank Brigade, which was very well known to him. To them he said, 'Confronting us is the problem of getting ashore on a defended coastline. The success of the operation depends on the element of surprise caused by new equipment. Suggestions from all ranks for improvements in equipment are to be encouraged. To assist secrecy it is preferable for all ranks to have *direct* access to their CO for putting forward their ideas.'

Major John Stirling of the 4/7th Royal Dragoon Guards reported:

> On 6 April 1943 the Regt attended a lecture by the Divisional Commander [Hobart] in the cinema at Keighley. He told us that we were to begin training as part of the assault force that was to attack the Western Wall. *We were to be equipped with one of the most secret and startling devices that the war had yet produced.* This was a tremendous day. Up to now we had been pushing forward blindly not knowing for what we were working or for what we were intended. Life appeared to have no particular object. We hoped that one day the war would end but it was difficult when one looked at the map or read the newspapers, to see how this was going to happen. Now in a flash, our eyes were opened. At once, life took on a new meaning and everyone cheered up tremendously. Our morale rose by leaps and bounds. The new device of which the General had spoken was the D.D. tank.

On the same day, when Hobo briefed the East Riding Yeomanry in Keighley's largest cinema about their new role in D.D. tanks Charles Whiting described him as 'a lean elderly looking General with big ears, a white close-cropped moustache and black horn-rimmed spectacles, this rather eccentric General who had commanded the First British Tank Brigade when it acquired its official status in 1934. The man who had conducted some far-reaching experiments in tank warfare which in fact laid the foundations for much of what the German Panzer divisions were then currently practising.' Security was intense. 'Scores of red-capped, white-belted military policemen were stamping around the area.'

Fritton Decoy, a secluded inland lake was chosen by Hobart to train the D.D. units. The admiral who owned it gave permission for the Army to use it. The D.D. school set up there included dummy loading craft ramps and cisterns in which crews learned escape drills from submerged tanks. Amphibious tank escape apparatus (ATEA) was developed from the Davis escape apparatus used by submarine crews. Initially the rate of exit from LCTs was considered far too slow by General Hobart who 'persuaded' Brigadier Duncan to do better. Eventually with due co-operation from the Royal Navy, D.D. tanks were leaving their LCT at a rate of every fifteen seconds (not, of course, under gunfire in a heavy sea, however). On 15 July 1943 the CIGS spent a day watching D.D. trials; indeed he 'sailed' in one and then gave permission for 500 new Sherman tanks to be converted to D.D., overriding the Deputy CIGS who was very dubious about the whole business. Major John Stirling describes some of 4/7 Royal Dragoon Guards problems on their first sea voyage in December 1943.

> As was to be expected, we found that there were a great many complications; we now had not only ourselves to consider, but the Navy who had always to think of winds and tides and currents. They too had big problems to master in launching several Squadrons from numerous craft in such a way that they could all link up together and arrive on the beach simultaneously. This was no easy matter with clumsy vessels like D.D. tanks, which were little better than rectangular blocks in shape, only capable of four knots and therefore unable to catch up if once they got left behind; and in fact, if it was against a current, they had to go flat out in order not to go backwards; and both we and the Naval craft commanders had much to learn before we became proficient.

Linney Head in Pembrokeshire, an existing tank range with sea on two sides was an ideal place for testing D.D. tanks at sea. Hobart had to fight the RAF tooth and nail to wrest control, since they had a small radar station there. Eventually it was made available from August to October 1943. After that sea launchings were made at Stokes Bay off the Isle of Wight, where most of the D.D. instructors were Canadian. In the very first test with expendable Valentine D.D.s only one out of the first five launches was successful, but Hobart remained cheerful and optimistic. Once General Montgomery saw the D.D. tanks swimming in Studland Bay, he held a conference in his train and decided that the D.D. regiments *would* lead the assault on D-Day.

Eventually over 30,000 launches were made, with 'only' seven casualties (mainly to 4/7 Royal Dragoon Guards). When in the water the D.D. tanks looked like harmless rubber boats, with only the top part of the canvas screen visible when they were launched about 4,000 yards offshore. On D-Day this was a great surprise to the German defenders. In the event 122 D.D. tanks were actually launched at sea (many more had a dry landing), 83 landed in great style, but 39 sank (mainly from 741 US Tank Battalion, which launched 6,000 yards out in a rougher sea) – Force 4 on the Beaufort Scale was the official safety level of 'rough' sea.

General Hobart had organized the training of no less than ten regiments equipped with Sherman D.D.s by D-Day – 4/7 Royal Dragoon Guards, 13/18 Hussars, the Nottinghamshire Yeomanry, the East Riding Yeomanry, 15/19 Hussars plus the Canadian 1st Hussars and Fort Garry Horse and the 70th, 741 and 743 US Tank Battalions. However, on 15 October, after seven months of extensive training on D.D.s the 27th Tank Brigade was taken from Hobart's command and came under command of the 1st Corps as an independent assault brigade.

The CDLs

One of the strangest weapons in the Army was the CDL tank, code for Canal Defence Light (a name which deceived both friend and foe). Invented just before the outbreak of war by a Professor Mitzakis, the CDL was a tank-mounted night-fighting searchlight. The War Office was so impressed by it that 300 specially designed tank turrets were ordered for the 35th Tank Brigade (49th Royal Tank Regiment (RTR), 152 RAC and 155 RAC) based in Penrith. Two other regiments (11th RTR and 42nd RTR) sailed in 1942 for the Middle East for eighteen months of tactical training in the Sinai Desert. The CIGS noted in his diary: '5th May 1942 caught train for Penrith, went to Lowther Castle to watch demonstrations of tanks employing searchlights to blind the enemy in attack and defence (CDL).' It was a highly secret weapon, and immense trouble was taken to keep it so. From Matildas the CDL was upgraded to the General Grant tank, which retained its hull-mounted 75mm gun, a Browning MG and the special arc lamp with 13 million candle power. The beam of light projected through a slot 2 inches wide by 24 inches long, and was generated by a very powerful carbon arc lamp. At 1,000 yards' range it could cover a front of 350 yards. CDL could blind the enemy with a flicker by an automatic movement of a shutter across the light aperture.

Major E.R. Hunt of the 49th RTR was detailed late in 1943 to lay on a special demonstration of CDLs for the Prime Minister, the CIGS and other top brass. 'I was detailed to lay on a demo with 6 CDL tanks for him. A stand was erected on a bleak hillside in the training area at Penrith and in due course the great man arrived accompanied by Alan Brooke and others. I controlled the various manoeuvres of the tanks by wireless from the stands ending the demo with the CDLs advancing towards the spectators with their lights on and halting just 50 yards in front of them. The lights were switched off and I awaited further instructions. After a brief interval, the Brigadier (Lipscomb of the 35th Tank Brigade) rushed up to me and ordered me to switch on the lights as Mr Churchill was just leaving. I immediately ordered the 6 CDL tanks to switch on: 6 beams each of 13 *million* candlepower came on to illuminate the great man quietly relieving himself against a bush! I immediately had the lights extinguished! And Mr Churchill departed by torchlight.'

CDL training continued at a great pace, first in the Lake District and then at Linney Head in South Wales. By the time of the invasion 60 CDLs in Grant tanks were ready for the fray, but it never came. Despite the fact that General Montgomery's main battles were commenced at night, the CDLs were never used in their main role in action. Trooper L.D. Moran of the 11th RTR recalls:

> In action the tanks were supposed to advance in line and the CDL beam from each tank (a parabolic beam parallel from top to bottom and widening from side to side) would coincide with the beams from the tanks on either side giving a triangle of darkness in which the infantry could advance unseen by the enemy. The light was supposed to blind and confuse enemy gunners and make their range finding inaccurate. The enemy were supposed to contract severe headaches, and their eyesight become temporarily useless. A colossal waste of money and time.

Two famous tank experts, Generals Martel and Fuller, plus Lord Louis Mountbatten, were great admirers of the CDL. Fuller wrote, 'I regard the failure to use this tank as the greatest blunder of the whole war', and Martell said, 'In North Africa we could have cleaned up with them. And against the German defences in Normandy we could have broken through with a tenth of the casualties that we suffered at Caen.' Professor Mitzakis the Greek inventor thought that it was not used 'because secrecy about the tank was carried to such absurd lengths that even the generals who should have used it, didn't know what the tank could do'! Certainly Alan Brooke was very familiar with CDL, but perhaps he failed to pass on his views to Montgomery. Another reason may have been that the CDL tanks stood out clearly from the flanks and were vulnerable to accurate anti-tank fire. The dust and smoke of battle also reduced their effecteness and it was difficult to find a wide, very flat terrain suitable for CDL, apart from a desert battlefield. For a variety of reasons the CDL were not used in action in their true role.

The Flame-throwers

At a small farm called Moody Dawn, near Winchester, the Army, with technical assistance from the Anglo-Indian Oil Company, and with the petroleum warfare team, developed a large flame-thrower. The most effective model was produced in 1940 by the Lagonda Car Company. It fired a mixture of diesel oil and tar, with a range of about 100 yards. It had a flame 30 feet in diameter and used 8 gallons of fuel a second. Later models, made by other companies pushed the range up to 200 yards, with a corresponding increase in fuel consumption. Lieutenant Jack Cooke of the Royal Naval Reserve (RNR) then produced the Cockatrice, a formidable vehicle weighing over 17 tons, which took a lot of stopping. The flame gun was mounted on a 2½-ton Bedford lorry with a tank holding 2 tons of fuel. A gunner within the turret mounted behind the cab operated the flame gun. Initially the Cockatrice was designed for airfield defence against enemy airborne troops. Some were mounted in coasters plying between the Rivers Thames and Forth to deter low-flying enemy bombing aircraft. Three units of the prototype flame-throwing tanks codenamed OKE were deployed on the Dieppe raid but did not survive.

In 1941 the 7th Buffs were converted from infantry into 141 Regiment Royal Armoured Corps. As three fighting squadrons were formed from four companies, 200 men had to leave. In September 1942 they, with their Churchill tanks, became part of 31st Armoured Brigade, together with the 7th and 9th RTR. From Ashford, they took part in exercises 'Harlequin', 'Hammer', and 'Canute'. Lieutenant Andrew Wilson, author of *Flame Thrower*, recalls the arrival of the new equipment (fuel container for the Churchill Crocodile) at night. 'There in the hard clear light on the training area stood a curious object with two enormous rubber tyres, shaped like the blunt prow of a boat with a big steel pipe cased in armour plating. This was meant to be coupled to the back of the MK VII Churchill Tank.' Later 'a demonstration crew manipulated a system of valves and gauges. Instead of the co-driver's machine gun there was now an ugly little nozzle with two metal tongues above it like the points of a sparking plug. There was a continuous hissing and ticking from the trailer.' Later still:

A little burst of fire, like a struck match above the nozzle tested the spark and the tank began to move forward. It went towards the first target, a concrete pill-box. Suddenly there was rushing in the air, a vicious hiss. From the front of the tank a burning yellow rod shot out. Out and out it went, up and up with a noise like the slapping of a thick leather strap. The rod curved and started to drop, throwing off burning particles. It struck the concrete with a violent smack. A dozen yellow fingers leapt out from the point of impact searching for cracks and apertures. All at once the pillbox was engulfed in fire – belching, twisting red-roaring fire. And clouds of queer-smelling grey-black smoke. Then another rushing. This time the rod went clean through an embrasure, smacking, belching, roaring. The flame shot out through the back of the pillbox, fanning like a blow-torch.

Andrew Wilson watched the fearsome Crocodile chasing its flame round corners into zigzag trenches and destroying houses by a 'wet' shoot; the rod from about 100 yards away drenched the target with a stream of colourless liquid and later on sent a shot of flame. 'It rose into a fierce red cyclone. Beneath the creaking metal the ground was black and smoking!'

The makers sent down trailers to the Buffs 'like Meccano, with a conversion kit for the tank, a heavy towing link, the armoured fuel pipe which ran to the flame gun, the electrical equipment and air lines.'

Driver mechanic R.F. Collins was initially posted to 'D' Squadron the Buffs, a training unit under Captain William Douglas-Home, but in Normandy he became a driver in 'A' Squadron of 1 Troop's 'Baker' tank. He found the Churchill tanks too heavy, too slow, too hot, too cold, heavy on fuel and miserably armed. But the Mark VII, towing its 8 tons of trailer, would go anywhere up hill or down dale as long as there was grip for the tracks and maintenance was tip-top.

Not until 1943 when Hobart saw a Crocodile at Orford and personally buttonholed Sir Graham Cunningham at the M of S was a development plan agreed. The CIGS, Alan Brooke then included flame-throwers in the official brief for Hobart's 79th Armoured Division. One of Hobart's assistants, Brigadier Yeo, helped put pressure on for the final production of the gun, trailer and satisfactory fuel. It was a close-run thing since 141 Regiment RAC, the Buffs, had their sixty Crocodiles ready only a few days before D-Day.

The Churchill MKVII tank had a flame nozzle which replaced the hull-mounted MG, so its main gun could still be used. The trailer carried 400 gallons and fuel consumption was 4 gallons per second. The duration of a flame shot was usually one to one and a half seconds. In the armoured, two-wheeled trailer, in addition to the fuel, were bottles of nitrogen for pressurizing the fuel, which passed through a pipe fitted under the hull of the tank. The pipe was protected by an armoured shield. The most effective flame range was 90 yards and the maximum 120 yards. It took a minimum of one and a half hours to refuel and usually fifteen minutes to 'pressure up', less in a real emergency. The equipment (trailer, nozzle, piping and controls) was manufactured in kit form for REME workshops to convert in the field. Eight hundred kits were manufactured, and by the end of the war three crocodile regiments (the Buffs, the 2nd Fife and Forfars and the 7th RTR) were in action. Two hundred and fifty kits were reserved for a possible campaign against the Japanese. Crocodile training and casualties in the field took up the balance.

The Crocodiles were an unknown factor before Normandy, and most infantry commanders were unfamiliar with their strengths and weaknesses. At close range they were lethal on enemy pill-boxes, strongpoints, occupied houses, Spandau positions and trenches. They could fire most woods (but not those with thick foliage), and the flame fuel could burn on water, and across most canals. Their appearance was extremely good for the morale of the British, Canadian and American infantry and conversely induced panic and terror amongst the defenders. Their weakness of course was the necessity to use them in close-quarter action, where it was essential for the infantry being supported to assault the enemy positions as quickly as possible after flaming to obtain the maximum demoralizing effect. Because of the high pressure of the pumped up oil, the optimum time lag before action was within thirty minutes of the flame attack.

The Flail Tanks

The clearance of huge minefields under fire was a major problem for any army. Casualties to sappers clearing laboriously by mine detectors and 'potato-picking', were unacceptably high. Experiments had been made by a Major du Toit of various rollers – spiked, jagged or plain, but a mine hidden in an indentation in the ground would escape detection. And Rommel had laid 4 million mines on the coastline of Normandy.

Various early tank minesweepers had been tried, but not particularly successfully. The Baron, the Marquis, the Scorpion and the Lobster were the earlier models. At the battle of El Alamein the 42nd RTR was a Scorpion regiment. The Scorpion was a Matilda tank hull with a flail device, comprising a series of heavy metal balls connected by chain to a roller, mounted between two substantial arms. These were rotated by a Ford motor housed and mounted in an armoured box on the side of the tank. Not only was it unreliable (the auxiliary motor to drive the rotor was under-powered and soon became overheated) but its speed was only ½ m.p.h. The machines, without guns, were used singly to clear a 9-foot track. If the motor failed or the vehicle was knocked out, the lane was blocked.

The Engineer-in-Chief, in conjunction with the Department of Tank Design in the Ministry of Supply had been devising and testing tank mine sweepers for many years. When Major General Hobart took command in spring 1943, there were two candidates for development: the official version, which was complicated, with chains, cogs and wheels all over the place; and a version of a Sherman gun tank with the flail rotor projecting on a pair of arms from the front, which was called the Crab. Hobart approved the latter, and perhaps with some help from the Tank Parliament or CIGS got his way. The decision to use them was taken in June 1943, but practice and exercises were initially carried out with elderly Barons and Scorpions.

When the new Sherman 75 mm gun tank Crab flails were available, each troop was allocated five. One tank would start flailing a suspected minefield at 1½ m.p.h. Tanks could not fire as they flailed because when the drum rotated and 'flogged' the fifty chains against the ground, a huge cloud of dust, mud, grass and sand arose, through which visibility was poor, even nil. Sometimes the other two Crabs flailed in parallel to create a triple lane a minimum of 24 feet wide. Sometimes the other pair acted for a time as protective sheepdog gun tanks. Station keeping was difficult. Wire cutters were fitted to the ends of the rotor drum, tearing up hostile wire entanglements.

On level ground the flails ploughed up the ground to a depth of

3 or 4 inches and detonated every mine that they struck, but a deeply laid mine or one planted in a hollow in the ground, might escape. A Teller mine could be detonated to a depth of 4–5 inches, each mine accounting for one chain. Provided the Crab was tackling the mine-field at the 'right' angle of approach up to twelve or fourteen mines could be exploded before the roller needed new chains. Wear and tear was even heavier if a metal track or road had to be cleared.

A normal Sherman MK V weighed 32.6 tons and the additional flailing weight took this up to 36 tons. All movement other than in action was preferably made by transporter. Each squadron had four troops, plus an HQ troop of three Sherman gun tanks.

The Canadians also developed something called the Canadian Indestructible Roller Device (CIRD), mighty rollers on booms ahead of the tanks, which could advance at normal speed and detect mines without endangering its crew, but this ideal weapon was apparently not used in action.

In November 1943 the 30th Armoured Brigade (the 22nd Dragoons, the 1st Lothians and Border Yeomanry and the Westminster Dragoons) came under Hobart's command as his flail brigade. Under Brigadier Nigel Duncan they were at once equipped with the new Crabs. The 22nd Dragoons were not at all enthusiastic as Major Raymond Birt writes: 'The better informed talked corner-wise from their mouths of secret weapons and fantastical machines. On the gravelled forecourt of Maughersbury Manor, the regiment listened to the crisp invigorating voice of a familiar figure (Hobart) in whom we saw no alteration except for an increase of colour above the left flank of his battledress blouse.' The Dragoons were told they were being converted to flails, 'nor were we at all delighted that instead of going into battle in the pride of a cruiser tank formation, we were to crawl into action in what appeared to be the menial task of scavengers and road sweepers, creeping along at a mile per hour.'

When Captain David Squirrel, Technical Adjutant, Westminster Dragoons went to collect five Shermans from the Milner Safe Company in Liverpool, who had converted them to flails, 'we were amused to see them being tested by factory staff in full view of several hundred other workers in the Trading Estate.' They were still on the War Office secret list!

The 1st Lothians and Border Yeomanry had fought with the British Expeditionary Force and suffered with the 51st Highland Division at St Valery. Only eighty survived, under Lieutenant Colonel C.J.Y. Dallmeyer. Initially they joined the 42nd Armoured

Division, then the 11th Armoured Division and finally the 79th. Their Lothians pipe band of thirteen pipers and seven drummers was a great source of pride. Andrew Gardiner played a side drum.

> Our tanks were given names after characters in Sir Walter Scott's novels. 2nd Troop were allocated a number from *The Talisman*, as follows: 'Talisman', 'Coeur de Lion', 'Knight of the Leopard', 'Sir Kenneth' and 'Saladin'. I spent some time painting the names on both sides plus the Crusader motif copied from the header of the *Daily Express*. Ammunition, emergency packed rations, small personal items were carefully stowed away in bins and any free spaces in the tanks.

He dismantled his side drum and packed that too! The lucky Lothians were to be the reserve regiment of the Brigade on D-Day.

Ian Hammerton, recently commissioned joined the 22nd Dragoons, recalls:

> Hobo as he was known to all and sundry called upon us all to gather round. He started his talk by reminding us about the Lord Mayor's Show. 'You all know that before the show some chaps come along and clean up the road and make sure all is ship-shape,' he began. 'That's what you're going to do when we cross the Channel into France. You have been chosen to sweep away all the mines in front of the advancing army.' There was a silence as we pondered unenthusiastically the role of the minesweepers. 'Some of you are going away to learn about some new secret equipment. You must not, under any circumstances, repeat a word of what I have said to anyone. Your lives may depend on it.' Hobo left behind him a sad and disillusioned collection of men. No sweeping across the fields of France at cavalry speed in our Cruiser tanks – just sweeping mines.

Major Birt writes: 'Men returning from Saxmundham brought back extraordinary and fearsome tales of 79th Armoured Divisions "Zoo" of machines, concealed behind such names as "Crab", "Centipede", "Scorpion" and "Crocodile". Some of the machines seemed to belong to the fantasies of the dreamers of war with Mars.' He described the new divisional emblem. 'Significantly it was the head of a fighting bull, whose angry eyes stared steadily and directly [and fiercely] into the faces of its beholders.'

On 31 January 1944 the tank strength of the Westminster Dragoons was a motley collection – nineteen Sherman MK V's, seventeen Centaur P's, four Cromwells, six Valentine Scorpions and three Sherman Crabs, a total of forty-nine. On joining the 79th Armoured Division they exchanged their Covenanter tanks capable of 40 m.p.h. for the flails, capable of 1½ m.p.h. Major Birt wrote about their flail:

> The principal problems in the use of the flail tank were these. Firstly, to maintain a straight and accurate path to the objective when the tank driver was completely blinded by the swirling chains, and when the crew commander's vision – at best – was like that of a man peering into a rich and smutty fog late on a November afternoon. Secondly, to direct three tanks together through a minefield so that the path cleared of mines should be wide enough for the follow-up infantry and tanks, and yet maintaining so accurate a direction on the line set by the leading tank that the finished lane should be entirely clear of mines and of three tanks' width all the way through. Thirdly, to protect the flailing tanks during the fifteen or twenty minutes when they were committed to crawling their slow, undeviating way in the face of enemy gunners and where – except to a flank or to the rear – their own gunners were blind.

On the heathland west of Orford, exercises were carried out frequently: 'Elk II' on 22 January, 'Bullshead' on 19, 20, and (full scale) 22 March, followed by 'Smash I', 'II', 'III' and 'IV'. 'Fabius' was a marshalling exercise in May. Waterproofing took place in late spring across the division to ensure that vehicles did not 'drown' in a few feet of sea water. His Majesty King George VI inspected all the flail tanks of the Brigade on 22 April at Petworth where live mine fields had to be flailed. The King turned to Major Brian Wallace of 'A' Squadron, Westminster Dragoons, and stuttering slightly said, 'If it [a flail] has been fed and watered could I see it working?' Lieutenant W.S. Hall noted: 'We mounted and gave the flail a bit of a whirl which Brian assured me pleased H.M.' The next month 'C' Squadron had a Crab drowned in front of General Eisenhower when he came to inspect them.

The AVREs

Winston Churchill was particularly involved in the concept of the AVRE (Armoured Vehicle Royal Engineers). He had foreseen the need for engineers to be mounted in tanks for the breaching of sea defences; he had identified the need to utilize surplus Churchill tanks and his protégé Millis Jefferis, by developing the Petard hollow-charge bombard, had produced the ideal weapon. A Canadian officer, Leiutenant J.J. Donovan had, after the débacle at Dieppe put forward various ideas for protecting the sappers in the front line of fire. The Churchill tank, although slow and ponderous, was roomy, had tough defensive armour and side-access hatches in the track frames. Through these a demolition NCO from the crew of five could exit with General Wade charges, and place them in position against sea walls or whatever the object that needed to be demolished. The bombard was fitted to Churchill Mark III or IV types. On the back of the tank could be placed either a huge brush-wood paling fascine for filling in ditches, a Bobbin log 'carpet' for treacherous muddy ground or a small box girder bridge (SBG). Other variants duly followed: a skid Bailey pulled or towed to span a 60-foot length; a mobile Bailey (pushed forward, disengaged and mounted by the AVRE, allowing the front half of the bridging to fall into place); and an armoured sledge to be towed behind an Ark (a turretless tank with a ramp), various mine-clearing devices, and many other useful or dangerous 'extras'.

The main weapon, the Petard, carried a 26 lb charge within the outer casing (the Flying Dustbin) giving a gross weight of 40 lb. This could be fired up to a range of 230 yards but the most effective range was about 80. Practically any target of steel, brick or concrete could be destroyed. Later the long-range gun batteries at Cap Gris, in their huge bunkers, withstood a Petard attack. With its usual impeccable logic the Army decided that two Chemical Warfare Group (CWG) RE regiments should now be 'translated' into assault regiments RE. No. 5 CWG consisted of 77, 79 and 80 companies and No. 6 CWG of 81, 82 and 87 companies. Later in November 1943 they were joined by the 42nd Regiment, deriving from the disbanded 42nd Armoured Division producing 16, 222 and 617 Assault Squadrons RE. Lance Corporal Geoffrey Flint who joined 79 Assault Squadron RE was posted to No. 5 CWG. 'In those days laying a war gas was exactly the same as it had been done on the Western Front in the Great War, he recalls: 'The gases were mainly chlorine and mustard. The latter saturated the ground and could remain active for up to six months. Part of one's training was running through some gases *without* respirators!' Five-inch rockets and then 4.2-inch mortars were the main gas projectors.

Early in May each of the six new RE squadrons received six decrepit Churchill gun tanks, an officer and about fifty other ranks of the RAC to give preliminary instruction in the driving and maintenance of Churchills. Lieutenant Colonel G.I. 'Ginger' Watkinson became Commander Assault, Royal Engineers (CARE) during July and a training area was openend up at Linney Head in South Wales where many trials and exercises took place. Many failed ignominiously. Hobart was not amused at this 'trial and error', particularly if in front of senior VIPs. Lieutenant John Leytham of 82 Assault Squadron recalls one demonstration:

> All went well until an AVRE managed the impossible feat of remaining on top of the concrete wall [of a coastal defence emplacement], unable to move back or forward but gently see-sawing up and down in the breeze. The ex-commando officer giving a graphic description of the exercise over the tannoy then said 'Now see what the silly bugger has done.' Obviously Hobart was present because the unfortunate officer was posted with uncanny speed!

Lieutenant Colonel Stuart Macrae, Jefferis's deputy at MD1 recalled:

> Hobart was a great martinet. I was present at his base at Orfordness on several occasions when he was about to make an inspection. The tension was terrific. Officers would stand around restlessly. Then about four outriders on motorcycles would appear followed by a fleet of cars. When they stopped the General would descend from one of them with his Chief of Staff on his right and some other high ranking officer on his left. They would march forward in line in a most aggressive manner and the inspection would begin.

When Hobart visited Whitchurch to inspect the 'Funnies' he was a stickler for protocol and bawled out the hapless Brigadier Jefferis for not paying him enough respect.

Some of the newcomers to the assault squadron came from the Royal Armoured Corps. According to Trooper Bill Wood, on joining 617 Assault Squadron RE, 'we had to give up our black berets and red and yellow lanyards, so we became almost mutinous, in favour of the disgusting khaki beret type hats made of some coarse material.'

Driver/Mechanic Ian Isley joined 16 Assault Squadron RE at Woodbridge. One of his first tasks was to drive a highly secret Churchill Ark to Chilwell, wrapped in tarpaulins. He recalls: 'Our training on the battle area at Orford was very intensive with inter-troop and inter-squadron competitions, everyone trying their best to shave off seconds from getting in and out of the Churchill tank side hatches, dummy loading and firing Petards, crossing and climbing obstacles, etc.' When 16 Assault Squadron joined, they were billeted in a street of Victorian houses in Aldeburgh. On arrival they split up for training with the troop officers, corporals and selected sappers going on a Churchill tank driving and maintenance course at Catterick, the troop sergeants to a course at the Assault regiment Royal Engineers (ARE) school where the Commander Royal Engineers (CRE) trained them in the construction of the special ARE equipment whilst Major J.C. Woollett, the Staff Sergeant Major and remaining lance corporals went through a refresher course on basic sapper training. The Churchill tanks were not easy to drive well with their crash gearboxes, great weight and danger of bogging if the tracks were made to slip. Major Woollett's main problem was the amount of training needed to produce radio operators: 'Taciturn north country sappers did not take to this easily so we had to import the more voluble southerners.' Woollett went on a two-week course on the Churchill tank at the Vauxhall factory in Luton, where they were constructed.

John Leytham was dealing with paper work in the 82 Squadron RE office one afternoon in May 1943 in a Nissen hutted camp at Wantisden when an elegant young staff officer entered and enquired for the OC, Major Fred Landy.

I explained he was out training. 'In that case *you* had better come and meet the General yourself.' A most unexpected visitor and a bit of a shock to the old constitution as I went out to meet my doom – Sir Percy. Outside the marquee in their somewhat deserted camp stood this man of formidable reputation, dressed in an OR's great coat and cluthing a bunch of bluebells behind his back. After the formal introduction and explanation I faced a barrage of questions which I answered with equal rapidity whether right or wrong until there came a pause. Now Sir Percy had a reputation of always looking at a unit's cookhouse and their messing arrangements. I was rather proud of what we had achieved in our primitive conditions, so I asked 'Would you like to see our cookhouse, Sir?' After a cold and calculating stare came the answer. 'I don't think that will be necessary, Leytham – good afternoon.' And off he went. 'Well' I thought 'you're either in or you're out' and the next twenty-four hours would give the verdict. When Fred Landy got back and heard of the visitation, he paled and said 'Thank God, I was out' such was Hobo's reputation.

Sapper Sidney Blaskett of 81 Assault Squadron recalls:

Our first experience of the Churchill tank was an early model with fixed turrets and 3.7 inch naval guns. Before long we received Mark IV tanks which had no gun in the turret mounting. We began rudimentary training with the Petard mortar, the making and use of fascines, the assault bridge and skid Bailey bridging equipment. Also the obstacle and mine clearing explosive charge known as the Snake, a bren-gun carrier converted into a tank to hold liquid nitro-glycerine which was pumped into 100 feet of 3 inch hoses after it had been played out by a rocket attached to it. At Fairley we had the Petard mortar fitted into our tanks. Despite the good work the Petard did in the Normandy campaign we never fired them before D-Day.

Altogether the 1st Assault Brigade RE had 312 Churchill AVREs under command. The sapper Assault Squadrons were divided into two groups – one to push lanes through the beach defences, the other to clear the beach of underwater obstacles.

Sapper Ian Isley of 16 Assault Squadron RE described his life and times with the AVREs.

Sitting in a tin box for most of the time one doesn't have much idea of what is going on around one. Certainly officers who attend the 'O Groups' are well informed of what is going to happen, or should happen. They in turn tell their tank commanders what will be their part of the action and some tank commanders tell their crew – but not all tank commanders bother to impart this information to their crews. The wireless operator is reasonably well informed being on net to the outside world but the remainder of the crew are in complete ignorance. The driver is told to advance and to steer left or right as required, the turret gunner and the front gunner wait to be told when to load and fire and the poor old demolition NCO sitting on the tool box behind the driver just has to sit there patiently listening to all the commander's instructions over the intercom.

A few words on the life of an AVRE crew. It was very crowded inside that tin box – instead of a normal Churchill crew of five we carried six men – the demolition NCO already mentioned, the men in the turret, the commander, wireless operator and gunner, who had seats the size of dinner plates to sit on and as hard. The front gunner in the hull had a lightly padded seat with a canvas sling type of backrest to support him and enable him to open his sliding hatch and lift up the 40 lb Flying Dustbin and load it. The driver had a conventional seat but the position of the backrest was critical inasmuch as the clutch stop beneath the clutch pedal had to be hit 'just so' in order that a gear in the gear box could be slowed enough to enable him to change gear with the crash gear box. The gear box had four forward speeds and one reverse. One normally started in second gear and changed gear at exactly 1,500 revolutions – any other reading would result in a missed gear, a terrible noise from the gearbox and instant loss of steering – the tank had to constantly be in gear to be steered. The noise in the tank, even with the headsets being worn, was indescribable. Unlike conventional tanks we had no track top rollers and the track was noisily dragged along channels each side of the hull.

Contrary to popular belief the interior of the tank was bitterly cold most of the time and it leaked like a sieve through the various hatches whenever it rained. The two large air intakes for the engine were located in the turret compartment and sucked in large quantities of air through every open orifice. Every grain of dust and every raindrop within yards of the tank suddenly defied gravity and was drawn into the interior. In action, the driver had a thick armoured glass block to see through but when this was not in use the driver had an open rectangular porthole to see the way ahead. All the dust from the vehicle ahead and all the dust from the rotating tracks in front of the driver were sucked through this opening and no matter how good the goggles were, if the driver fell asleep without washing his eyes out, his eyelids and lashes were glued together on awakening.

My overriding memory of those days was the feeling of tremendous fatigue. At the end of a day we had to maintain the vehicle and carry out routine servicing tasks. When this was done we had to build whatever devices were needed for the next day. It could be putting a fascine together or building a short box girder bridge and winching it up or some task that was always in addition to the normal duties of a tank crew. Sufficient sleep was our main concern and every opportunity was taken to catch up on our much-needed rest. It was not unusual to bed down in the early hours of the morning and be awakened four hours later to prepare for the events of the day ahead. If one was saddled with guard duty the hours of rest were even more curtailed.

In February 1944 87 Assault Squadron RE was equipped with a dozen Centaur tank dozers with turret and gun removed and a bulldozer blade fitted to the front for clearing away debris and filling craters. In April, AVREs with Petards already fitted arrived, but even more came without Petards which Divisional REME had to install. Lance Sergeant L.A. Wells of 80 Assault Squadron RE recalls: 'Our battle tanks began to arrive. We were at Milford-on-Sea, proper AVREs at last but without MGs or Petards. These arrived in dribs and drabs later on, only a few days before D-Day.'

7   Countdown to 'Overlord'

The plan for D-Day was that the D.D. Sherman tanks would lead in and then each of the invasion beaches would have eight composite teams of selected 'Funnies' – AVREs (plus back-up specialities, General Wade charges, SBG bridges, fascines or Bobbin mats) and Crab flails alternately mixed. The commanding officers for each team would alternate between RE and RAC/RTR. The loading tables to get these teams to the right port, the right ship and the right beach – and on time – would tax the war planners.

Hobart not only kept up the intense rate of training with frequent exercises but kept up the same amount of pressure to ensure that supplies of the special weapons appeared on time!

Lieutenant Ian Hammerton of the 22nd Dragoons recalled: 'What an immense undertaking was being prepared. Every wood held its quota of huts or tents, piles of ammunition and other stores. Troops of all kinds were everywhere, tanks, lorries, carriers, guns of all calibre and much other equipment lined roads under the trees hidden, we hoped, from enemy planes. Everything combined to give us a gigantic boost of confidence.' Syd Sadler was posted to REME workshops near Yoxford to service Churchill and later Sherman tanks; by September 1943 he was in Lowestoft working on D.D. Sherman tank experiments, then to Bury St Edmunds to experiment on steel and wooden structures for bridging tanks. REME carried out flail-tank modifications with welding fabrications. Eventually he went to Eastbourne in May 1944 to weld extra turret protection to tanks with attached track links.

But it was a close-run thing getting the Division fully equipped before 'Overlord' began. Trooper Bill Wood reported:

> The equipment began arriving in dribs and drabs, the work and train-ing became progressively harder, all sorts of impossibly heavy iron-mongery, great bundles of chestnut paling, explosive charges in their

various forms, all with fancy codenames, the cock-ups were many, the humour caustic. Modifications were many, the electric welder was striking an arc every day. Trials and schemes before disbelieving senior officers.

Sapper Ken Mee joined 79 Assault Squadron RE and subsequently wrote an eighty-page journal describing his experiences. Qualified a skilled welder, his first job was to correct a small fault in 2,000 sten guns in three weeks. A delicate weld was needed to secure the barrel, which when fired would slowly unscrew from the breech mechanism and fall out. He then worked on 7.2-inch field guns and armour plate shields for Bofors AA guns. At Linney Head, near Pembroke, he learned how to drive a Churchill tank and fire .5 Besa MGs. Then he had a spell at Fort George near Inverness as a member of a high-priority experimental team, consisting of an officer, a blacksmith, a carpenter, an electrician, an MT fitter, a painter and himself as the welder. They experimented on tank landing craft beach landings, and only sank one tank in the process. Next they tested waterproofing kits of sealants, balloon fabric and sheet metal ducts developed by the Bostik company. The composition of beaches, sand, shingle and the dreaded blue clay were studied: many experiments were done to get Bangalore torpedoes (two 20-foot lengths of 3-inch bore steel pipe) loaded with explosive into sand hills and dunes. These were later christened 'Snakes' for obvious reasons. Somerfeld track was then assembled from surplus railway lines to make shingle rail mats for stabilizing beaches. Later carpet-layers or Bobbins were developed and tested on the shores of the Moray Firth. Mee helped make minefield markers from empty 4-gallon petrol tins, and metal supports and cradles for the deadly Beehives, which were carried in a few AVREs to be positioned by hand against the side of concrete pill-boxes and then blown from a safe distance. Then he went down south to Orford in East Anglia to work on the fascines, SBGs and finally, just before D-Day, the secret Petards.

Major A.F. Younger, the officer commanding 26 Assault Squadron RE, recalls:

Sometime in April, I was summoned to HQ Canadian Division for my first briefing about Operation Overlord. We would be landed ahead of 7 Canadian Infantry Bde on each side of the River Seulles in Normandy. 26 A/Sqn would create two exits from the beach to the west of the river leading to Courseulles-sur-Mer. Of course all this was top secret, not to be discussed with anyone. There was still no indication of the landing date. I was issued with good maps of the actual area but American or British names substituted for the French names. I worked with the Canadians to develop their plans.

The final movement order for D-Day was thirty pages long and contained hundreds of entries. Serial 1 on Page 1 was 'H-Hour, 26 Assault Sqn Royal Engineers'. At Gosport, 26 and 80 Assault Squadron laboriously waterproofed all their AVREs for their assault landings. Opposite them were the friendly and hospitable 1st Hussars of Canada with their D.D. tanks who would lead the way in.

Lt Ian Hammerton of the 22nd Dragoons recalled:

> Our 'B' Echelon 3 tonners arrived with tank ammunition. There were armour-piercing, high explosive and smoke shells for the 75mm gun boxes of .3 and .5 Browning MG ammunition, smoke bombs for the 2-inch bomb-thrower, Mills grenades and phosphorous instant smoke grenades, Sten gun and personal revolver ammunition . . . we could expect at least two thirds casualties. At least 16 of the troop might be wiped out. Nor were we to stop to care for any wounded. Not very cheering.

Captain John Leytham; who was second in command of 82 Assault Squadron RE took over a partly bombed hotel on Canford Cliffs in Spring 1944 overlooking Brownsea Island and Poole Harbour used as a practice area by the D.D. tanks. Flotilla No. 28 of RN LCTs now were allocated to 82 Assault Squadron.

> Pink gin and cigarettes were plentiful at minimum cost. Our first major dress rehearsal was on Studland Bay and the final dress rehearsal took place on Hayling Island on which occasion the enemy took [terrible] toll of our unfortunate allies in arms off Slapton Sands. I had a pass issued by 50 Div . . . Our interest lay with 'Jig' beach protected by fortified buildings dominated by a fortified sanatorium and pillboxes with the usual array of mortars, MGs, A/Tk guns and a field gun housed in a concrete bunker. The beaches were backed by sand-dunes, heavily mined and screened with barbed wire. Behind the dunes was a lateral coast road in an area of soggy grassland with dunes. Our task was to create six lanes on 'Jig' beach [east of the

village of Le Hamel. Models of the objective and aerial photographs were available but only code names for the objectives]. For this we were to be given six minutes before the first wave of the Hampshires of 231 Brigade were to land. The first three lanes (Jig Green West) under Major HGA Elphinstone my OC and Capt Taylor, Westminster Dragoons Flails as his 2 i/c. The next three lanes (Jig Green East) under command Capt Stannion, OC 'B' Sqn Westminster Dragoons, with myself as his 2 i/c.

General Hobart's intense energy encompassed choice, testing and development of the awesome weaponry available. Many AVREs were only delivered a month or so before D-Day, and their Bombards were not test fired. And only 60 Crocodiles were in fact ready for action by D-Day.

He had to chase up government departments and visit factories to encourage quicker production. He had to carry out enormously detailed training programmes in East Anglia and in Wales and then, at the appropriate moment invite key VIPs such as General Morgan of Cossac (the Overlord planners), the CIGS General Alan Brooke, his key supporter, General Paget the C-in-C Home forces, and Lord Louis Mountbatten i/c amphibious forces.

One key exercise was carried out in front of VIPs early in 1944 as General Alan Brooke's diary records.

January 26th. Have just dined and am now off in my train for a day with 'Hobo' and his swimming tanks and wire-destroyers.

January 27th. Eisenhower met me at the station last night and we travelled up by special train through the night. Hobart collected us at 9 a.m. and took us first to his HQ where he showed us his models and his proposed assault organisation. We then went on to see various exhibits such as the Sherman tank for destroying tank mines with chains on a drum driven by the engine, various methods of climbing walls with tanks, blowing up of mine fields and walls, flame-throwing Churchill tanks, wall destroying engineer parties, floating tanks, teaching men how to escape from sunken tanks, etc. A most interesting day, and one which Eisenhower seemed to enjoy thoroughly. Hobart has been doing wonders in his present job and I am delighted that we put him into it.

The AVREs were shown off by 617 Assault Squadron RE. Bill Wood in No. 2 Troop 'dropped a fascine in a ditch, took it [AVRE 2 Fox] in my stride, like a Grand National runner, swung round to a pill box and as the demolition NCO opened the pannier door to place a Wade charge, I saw to my surprise, one of the observers was General Eisenhower. I wonder if that's why we weren't used on Utah Beach?'

Major Roland Ward of 82 Assault Squadron relates: 'Dick Stafford's AVRE fell over upside down off an Assault bridge in trying to climb over a wall in the Orford battle area. Eisenhower ran forward quite concerned for the crew, but 'Hobo' said "Don't worry – they do it every day".' Although Eisenhower was impressed with 'Funnies' and Montgomery offered them to the American forces for use on D-Day, General Bradley turned the offer down. Their casualties on Omaha beach were very heavy and despite the steep slopes and determined defenders, the landings would have been more quickly established if Hobart's 'Funnies' had been deployed.

Eisenhower was however delighted with the D.D. tanks and actually 'drove' one of them. The 70th, 741st and 743rd US Tank Battalions started training on Valentines at Fritton a week after the visit. The two Canadian armoured regiments, the Fort Garry Horse and 1st Hussars already had two months of training in D.D. 'swimming'.

It is probable that not enough time was spent convincing General Montgomery of the merits of *all* Hobart's 'Funnies', for although CDL made a great impression on all nocturnal exercise visitors, they were never used in battle actions. And if Montgomery had been more convinced of the merits of the Crocodiles more than one regiment would have been equipped with them before D-Day.

The ideas to which Montgomery eventually yielded were that CDLs (if it was to be a night attack on the beach), AVREs and flails, although waterproofed, would be brought ashore in LCTs to tackle the first of the beach obstacles – following closely behind the D.D. swimming tanks. Each beach team was composed of all the devices (including armoured bulldozer, AVREs with fascines, Bobbins or bridges) deemed essential to breach each selected gap in the beach defences. Timetables were planned and revised after exercises had proved or disproved various elements. Apart from the D.D. and flail tanks all the other AVREs and AFVs were highly vulnerable to anti-tank guns from the fortified houses and pill-boxes lining the coastal road and beaches.

Hobart sifted through his staff and disposed of many of them. Between mid-summer 1943 and the end of the war he had five GSO1s (Operations) each lasting about six months. He had three GSO1s (Technical) and three GSO2s (Operations). His Assistant Adjutant (AA) and Quartermaster-General (AQMG) Lieutenant Colonel Kitchiner, served with the Division from October 1943 onwards, but seven of his deputies (DAQMGs) arrived and fairly quickly departed. His two key brigade commanders were Brigadier N.W. Duncan, of the 30th Armoured Brigade and Brigadier G.L. Watkinson of the 1st Assault Brigade RE, who both joined him in 1943 and stayed firmly in command until the end of hostilities, but the three assault regiments of the Royal Engineers had a total of nine commanders from 1943 until the end of the war.

The Chief of Staff to General Montgomery was Major General Francis de Guingand, who wrote: 'Some of the staff under me would become terrified when they knew General Hobo was about. He was such a go-getter that they never really knew until he had left what new commitment they had been persuaded to accept. I found his visits acted as a tonic, for his enthusiastic and confident nature would never consider failure. An answer *would* be found – and it usually was.'

At a fairly late stage a small naval scouting submarine brought back geological samples of the landing beaches in which traces of soft blue clay were found (which would bog down all armoured fighting vehicles (AFVs). Immediately Hobart deployed MD1 (who produced a huge rocket-driven carpet-layer device for a tank) and REME workshops. So the Roly Poly (a prototype mine-detonating device of massive iron rollers pushed ahead of the tank), the Bobbin and the log carpets were quickly devised. Tests were carried out at Brancaster, Norfolk, where the soft blue clay was found.

Operation Fabius, the final full-scale loading exercise for the invading forces, was on 3 May. In March units were being detached to integrate with the assaulting divisions. The 3rd British Division on the eastern Sword beach west of Ouistreham would have the Crab flail tanks of 'A' Squadron 22nd Dragoons and 77 and 79 Assault Squadrons RE (of the 5th Assault Regiment RE). The 3rd Canadian Division on the central Juno beach opposing Courseulles and St Aubin would be backed by 'B' Squadron 22nd Dragoons plus twelve Crabs of 'A' Squadron Westminster Dragoons and 26 and 80 Assault Squadrons (of the 5th Assault Regiment RE). The 50th Northumbrian Division on the western Gold beach tackling la

Rivière and Le Hamel would be supported by 'C' Squadron and 'B' Squadron Westminster Dragoons plus 81 and 82 Assault Squadron (of the 6th Assault Regiment RE).

Those of Churchill's secret weapons which were deployed on D-Day were the armoured RE troops, the D.D. swimming tanks, the 'surplus' Churchill tanks fitted with Jefferis's Bombard, his other 'Toy Factory' products and his original ideas for Mulberry harbours. There were no CDL or flame-thrower tanks in the main assault. Finally, his tough, difficult protégé General Percy Hobart put most of the complicated beach assault landing programme together.

John Leytham took the last sacrament before embarking, 'hedging ones bets, you might say', and noted that the detailed loading orders included a number of wooden crosses. Leytham was issued with a beautiful silk map of Europe, a file, a small compass, a concentrated ration pack, a limited supply of Benzedrine and RAF photographs of Gold beach. Most of the D-Day forces read or heard messages from General Dwight Eisenhower, General B.L. Montgomery and General Douglas Graham (for Gold beach attacking forces).

When Sapper Ken Mee went to war in the AVRE recovery tank, 'I was fortunate that I only sat (as co-driver) between an oxygen and an acetylene cylinder plus hoses and cutter, also a box of gun-cotton slabs, primers, detonators and cordite fuse together with Wheatstone bridge and electric detonating devices.'

Major W.R. Birt of the 22nd Dragoons recounts the last stage of their journey towards the Portsmouth dock basins on 3 June.

0215 hours. The wait has prolonged itself. We are eight hours behind programme. Heavy with rum-laced tea we doze in the back of the car. Under the green balconies a group of soldiers have been singing for hours to the tinkle of an RAF man's ukulele. A strong tenor leads a drowsy, bee-contented hum. They sing over and over again 'Roll me over, Love'. Then the mood changes with notes long drawn they turn to 'Home, Sweet Home' and 'Love's Old Sweet Song'. From the balconies close above us, in the darkness, girls' voices joining sweetly, strongly. There is a sudden move ahead of us. Above the growl of the lorries we hear the lilt of 'Goodbye, ladies'. There is a thin and fading answer from the balconies of 'We'll smile as we wave you goodbye'.

What a marvellous way to go to war!

ORDER OF BATTLE – 79th Armoured Division

DIV. HQ.

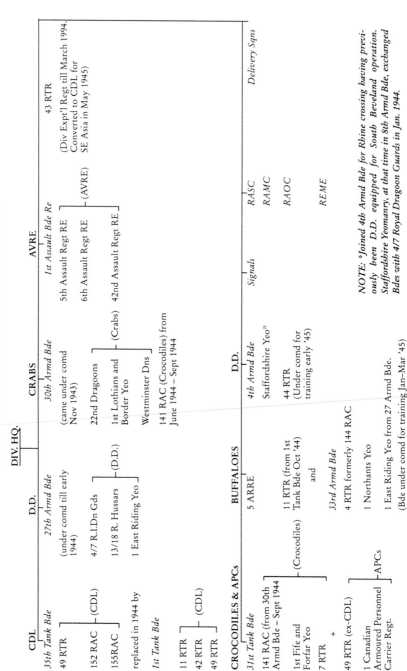

CDL

35th Tank Bde

49 RTR — (CDL)

152 RAC — (CDL)
155 RAC

replaced in 1944 by

1st Tank Bde

11 RTR
42 RTR — (CDL)
49 RTR

CROCODILES & APCs

31st Tank Bde

141 RAC (from 30th Armd Bde – Sept 1944)

1st Fife and Forfar Yeo — (Crocodiles)

7 RTR

+

49 RTR (ex-CDL)

1 Canadian Armoured Personnel Carrier Regt. — APCs

D.D.

27th Armd Bde
(under comd till early 1944)

4/7 R.I.Dn Gds

13/18 R. Hussars — (D.D.)

1 East Riding Yeo

33rd Armd Bde

4 RTR formerly 144 RAC

1 Northants Yeo

1 East Riding Yeo from 27 Armd Bde.
(Bde under comd for training Jan–Mar '45)

CRABS

30th Armd Bde
(came under comd Nov 1943)

22nd Dragoons

1st Lothians and Border Yeo — (Crabs)

Westminster Dns

141 RAC (Crocodiles) from June 1944 – Sept 1944

D.D.

4th Armd Bde

Staffordshire Yeo*

44 RTR
(Under comd for training early '45)

BUFFALOES

5 ARRE

11 RTR (from 1st Tank Bde Oct '44)
and

AVRE

1st Assault Bde Re

5th Assault Regt RE
6th Assault Regt RE — (AVRE)
42nd Assault Regt RE

Signals

Delivery Sqns

RASC
RAMC
RAOC

REME

43 RTR

(Div Expt'l Regt till March 1994. Converted to CDL for SE Asia in May 1945)

NOTE: *Joined 4th Armd Bde for Rhine crossing having previously been D.D. equipped for South Beveland operation. Staffordshire Yeomanry, at that time in 8th Armd Bde, exchanged Bdes with 4/7 Royal Dragoon Guards in Jan. 1944.

8 Across the Channel and on to the Beaches

The account that follows of D-Day concentrates mainly on the activities of the 'Funnies'. Space does not permit me to recount the bravery and resourcefulness of the D.D. tank crews once ashore, of the brave Royal Marine Commandos, the intrepid infantry (and only they can hold down 'won' territory), the gunners who were in action continuously and the intrepid airborne troops dropping, landing and fending-off the German counter-attacks inland. My book *Monty's Ironsides* describes how the 3rd British Division fought their way ashore and inland on Sword beach on D-Day.

General Eisenhower took the brave decision to defer D-Day by 24 hours because of the unusual high westerly gales and seas running at Force 4 to 5. The huge expeditions of Americans, British and Canadians were already at sea – many of them being seasick despite pills. Five divisions – two American, two British and one Canadian – were to be landed on a 40-mile strip between Ouistreham to the east and Varreville to the west. Airborne divisions would drop inland to seize vital communications, the 6th Airborne over the Caen canals and River Orne. For months the young leaders had pored over maps and air photographs of their beaching points – no real names, just codes.

The beaches carried mines on steel bench obstacles called 'Element C', gate-like structures invented by a Belgian, curved steel rails, metal hedgehogs and tetrahedra. Even landing at low tide needed dedicated RE beach-clearance teams, or the use of Petard or HE to shatter the obstacles. Crabs would then flail their way up the beach through minefields onto lateral roads. All the gun tanks, D.D.s, Crabs that were not flailing and AVRE Petards would bombard the concrete pill-boxes or 'post' HE through their gun slits. The RAF and the Royal Navy put down huge bombardments and barrages but the defences on most of the eleven British and Canadian beaches were still capable of fierce resistance.

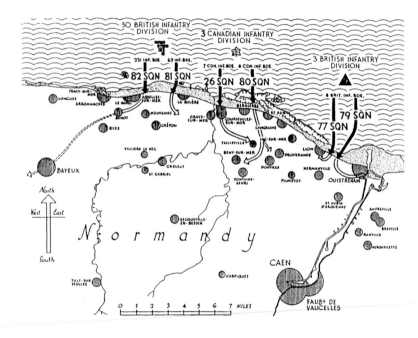

Fig. 1   Landings on D-Day – 6 June 1944

Sword Beach

The D.D. tanks of 13/18 Royal Hussars led the AVREs of 5 Assault Squadron RE ahead of the 8th Infantry Brigade (the 3rd British Division) towards Sword beach. The small resorts of Riva Bella, La Brèche and Lion-sur-Mer had been turned into fortresses, guarded by troops of 716 Infantry Division. The casino at Riva Bella and strongpoints inland, codenamed 'Hillman', 'Sole' and 'Daimler', were particularly difficult to storm. 'A' Squadron 22nd Dragoons were to flail through the beach minefields.

A wind was blowing Force 5 from the west as the LCTs of 'A' and 'B' Squadrons 13/18 Royal Hussars came into line and dropped anchor, 5,000 yards out just after 6.15 a.m. on 6 June. Under a heavy bombardment by the RAF and Royal Navy, of the forty D.D. tanks embarked, thirty-four entered the water. Three sank (one rammed by a friendly AVRE/LCT) and the rest touched down, but five were swamped by the breakers and the rapidly rising tide. On the right (Queen White beach) the 1st and 3rd Troops of 'A' Squadron 22nd Dragoons with AVREs of the 77th Squadron provided four beaching teams directed on the holiday villas of Lion-sur-Mer. As the assault craft raced for the shore they were met with heavy and accurate gunfire. Queen sector guarded the entrance to the heavily fortified Caen canal under observation from the long-range guns of Le Havre to the east. Three troops of 77 Assault Squadron RE beached at H-hour but the LCT with the fourth troop came under heavy anti-tank fire, which killed Lieutenant Colonel Cocks, commanding officer of the 5th Assault Regiment RE. The badly damaged LCT had to return to the UK without discharging its load.

Captain A. Low of No. 2 Troop, 77 Assault Squadron RE recounts:

About 1200 yards out, the house known to us all as 'Sad Sack Villa' was spotted and the LCT commander set course to land ten yards to port of the house. We were ahead of the D.D.s due to touch down before us. All craft were ordered to stop to allow them through. Approximately 1000 yards off shore the LCT (R) opened up. Rockets collided in mid-air and rained down on craft waiting to go in. One landed immediately under our staboard bow showering the bridge with pieces of casing. LCT were then ordered to beach at full speed. Our gaps were hidden by dust showered by the barrage on the beach, but at 300 yards the building was again visible a bit to port. Twenty yards from the beach, the craft was attacked by four planes with *British* markings, two bombs landing very close to our doorway. We climbed on to my tank as the ramp dropped. Ahead of us was a gun apparently concentrating on the troop on our left. One flail flailed straight for the gun. I followed out with the Boase carpet. Another Crab flailed a second path up to the sand dunes and this I used to push the Boase Bangalore into a sand dune about six feet high. I had trouble cutting the receptacle on the Boase which had pushed easily into the dunes, as snipers kept up a steady hail of lead wherever I appeared.

Grenades were now being fired or thrown at Low's AVRE. The Bangalore made a good gap in the dunes but he could not lay the carpet on it as both flails had gone forward. 'The infantry who had landed right behind us were now pushing forward.'

On 'Sword' Beach Churchill AVREs (*left*) bombard fortified sanitorium. Flails in action (*right*) (Birkin Haward)

Sergeant T.R. Kilvert commanded an AVRE in No. 1 Troop, 77 Assault Squadron.

Almost in, 400 yards to go when my AVRE had a violent shake, we had been hit. Damage not known because the LCT had also sustained damage a bit forward and we had to get off at once. The LCT stopped: again, my AVRE was hit going down the ramp now and the water was almost up to our cupola. Again we were hit but on our Bobbin, it being at a crazy angle. Coming out of the water, hit again and at last dry land and following the Troop Leader's AVRE up the sand. Hit a mine, one bogey gone, and following in the leading AVRE's track, we were ordered to put up a windsock to mark the route. Struck a second mine, two bogies gone and left track gone. Two of crew jumped out to put up a windsock, one blown up by a mine as he came round the tank. Take out all the arms, and jumped out myself, destroying Slidex and code papers. We were all out now, petrol was pouring out of the AVRE and filling the mine crater.

Sergeant Kilvert and the survivors helped clear mines and obstacles. At 10.30 five lanes had been cleared but traffic was held up on the laterals. The Squadron rallied on No. 1 and 4 Troop lanes. Later Sergeant Kilvert led sappers into Hermanville-sur-Mer with Petard and Besa machine gun fire. Then 80th Assault Squadron RE followed in to help with the capture of Lion-sur-Mer and Sergeant Barclay's unit disarmed sixty-four Teller mines and thirty-seven shells before last light. Sapper Glancy climbed to the top of the 10-foot stakes on the beach to disarm many of them.

Casualties were heavy and by 9 June out of a total of 17 AVREs originally embarked only three were fit for action. During D-Day 'Bullshorn' ploughs, SBG bridges, Bobbins and Porpoises (towed waterproofed sledges) were used to good effect.

Lieutenant Knapp and Corporal Applin of the 22nd Dragoons flailed their lane under heavy fire. Sergeant Smyth and Corporal Nash of No. 3 Troop landed to the west, and Smyth made straight for a 75 mm gun firing from the right flank and ran over it at a good cavalry gallop. But Sergeant Turner and Corporal Aird, after making an excellent lane, were killed an hour later by sniper fire.

Major W.R. Birt, described Queen Red beach, which was even tougher still, involving the clearance of La Brèche and Ouistreham by 79 Assault Squadron RE and the 22nd Dragoons Crabs.

> Stretches of Fortress Europe were held by garrison troops with little stomach for fighting. Renegades, some of them from Russian POW camps, or mean-spirited men of 'punishment' battalions, stiffened with a sprinkling of tough Nazi officers and NCOs. But on Queen beach the defence was grim and fanatical. The Germans fought the irresistible wave of tanks and men that was flung upon them until it was seen to be engulfing them. Then firing their useless rifles and shouting perhaps their final salute to the Fuehrer who had willed their deaths they ran out into the fire of the tank guns – men thirsty for the privilege of destruction in battle.

Five minutes *before* H-Hour, 79 Assault Squadron RE landed on Queen Red, but fortunately the naval smokescreen provided some cover. Many Crabs and AVREs were knocked out by anti-tank fire and many mines had to be lifted by hand in the open. It took five hours before eight lanes were cleared from the beach to the lateral road. Three assault bridges were dropped and three Bobbin log carpets laid to form roadways.

Ernest 'Doc' Kitson, who was with 79 Assault Squadron RE recalls:

> At about 7 a.m. the *Warspite* 600 yards to our rear nearly blew us out of the water with broadsides from its 14 inch guns. For twenty-five minutes the shore line fairly danced with the shelling. The LCTs touched down about 80 yards apart and two flails led us off; we were next. Behind us was a bridge tank and two more AVREs. We carried a log carpet (logs lashed together 2 feet 6 inches apart, thirty in number) to lay on patches of clay. We also had a Boase Bangalore which I had armed half an hour before touchdown. The weather was dull and gusty. Later arrivals coming ashore were commandos and D.D. tanks. We laid the bridge against the cliffs and two flails mounted and started flailing the gardens of the houses which were mined. Both were shot up before the mines were cleared. A D.D. tank got athwart the bridge and had to be moved. Luckily the bulldozer mounted and taking a huge bite had slithered down making another ramp ... After 10 a.m. the armour reached the hilltop of Colleville and fired down into the trenches. An indelible scene of Beachmasters marshalling incoming troops: barrage balloons, some held by two-man teams, some blowing in the wind, the teams had become casualties, the speed with which the tide rolled in, the thick smoke of tanks brewing up and the wounded and the dead floating face down. Later self-heating oxtail soup tins worked wonders, put new life into us.

At about 2.30 p.m. Kitson took part in what his officer described as 'a jolly tea party' helping the commandos clear up Ouistreham, so that they could go forward and link up with the Airborne at Pegasus. 'Ten tanks went in to the lighthouse area on the other side of a two-arch stone bridge across the canal. We had twenty machine guns firing at once and fire was coming from the enemy.' Kitson's officer was wounded near his eye. As Kitson was applying a field dressing, Robinson, the driver said, 'They are coming out with a white flag.' Kitson persuaded his young officer not to 'shoot the bastards'.

Sapper Ken Mee was a crew member of a Churchill recovery tank with 79 Assault Squadron. The turret had been removed and armour-plated flaps inside a sheet metal box mounted to waterproof the vehicle. On board were two motorcycles and a jeep. Their LST towed Rhinos – large pontoons with two stern drives as propulsion – behind it. Vehicles left through the bow doors onto the Rhino operated by RASC drivers. When Mee's recovery tank appeared in the sixth wave on Red section of Queen beach, the Beachmaster 'was in naval uniform, gold braid and brass buttons, no steel helmet or camouflage for him. He had a pylon with four large tannoy speakers mounted on top each covering a quadrant.' One of the Rhino stern drives broke down and the Rhino went round in circles! 'The Beachmaster called out "Get off that bloody merry-go-round, and come and fight this war" La Brèche, our landing point, was a small seaside town but no one was building sand castles or sun bathing at the time.' Through their viewpoint in battle condition – 5 inches by 1 inch – Trooper Boxall, the driver, suddenly saw a column of Germans advancing 'six wide and stretching back to the turn off'. Luckily Ken Mee decided not to Besa them as they were all prisoners of war being neatly marched back to captivity.

Lance Corporal Geoffrey Flint recalls:

The night crossing had been very rough and most men had been badly seasick. My AVRE was I think the first to land on Queen Red Beach, at La Brèche as it was the command tank. I saw 5 German soldiers on the beach shot down by supervising SS men. Our immediate task was to clear beach defences (hedgehogs) and neutralise mines and shells on poles (afterwards to secure an exit from the beach). The beach was rapidly filling with disembarking troops with active shelling, mortaring and MG fire. Casualties started to accrue. Then the tank was hit – immobilised by an 88 mm shot from a pill box. We baled out and sheltered on the incoming seaside of the AVRE. A D.D. Sherman bravely placed itself between us and the pill box, fired one shot into its aperture and silenced it ... We assembled at a small exit road between houses. The final task was to clear mines in the road verges with bayonets and one mine detector rescued from the disabled AVRE. I tossed a coin with a corporal to see who would use the mine detector. He won and approached the metal inspection cover. There was a tremendous explosion and the lower half of his body rose high in the air, hit the side of a house, leaving a large stain and fell into the garden.

During the afternoon, 79 Assault Squadron under Major J.H. Hanson sent ten AVREs to help 4th Commando retake the key lock gates and bridge at Ouistreham. The west bank was taken and intense Petard and Besa fire from the AVREs so demoralized the enemy that 4.30 p.m. fifty-seven prisoners had been taken and the bridge had been secured for the 3rd Infantry Division to take over on D+1.

No. 2 breaching team landed on time and Crabs began their work but were soon knocked out. As a result of a tragic explosion that took place at Gosport on 2 June when a twin Bangalore was detonated by mistake, causing many casualties, there had been insufficient time before embarkation to replace it. The high sand dunes were now tackled by dropping an SBG bridge to allow tanks to climb over and more or less slide down on the far side. The SBG bridge fell prematurely when the bomb release was hit. Captain Geoff Desanges, with sappers Price and Darrington, placed General Wade charges against the dune. An enemy MG killed Desanges but Lieutenant Tony Nicholson lit the fuse successfully before he was wounded by the same MG. By this time all the AVREs had been put out of action and the gap was completed by an armoured bulldozer.

The story of No. 3 beach clearance team is quite remarkable. Two Dragoons Crabs were knocked out and the lane was completed by hand by the dismounted assault sappers. An SBG bridge was launched but was soon blocked by a D.D. tank which fell off to the side of it. A second gap was made by the armoured bulldozer. A log carpet was laid but another D.D. tank struck a mine and the sapper Squadron Leader (Major Hanson) and Lieutenant W.H. Hutchinson cleared another track round it by hand. Another sapper officer, Captain D. Ayres was killed whilst clearing the beach as was Captain G.C. Desanges by small-arms fire.

'C' Squadron 22nd Dragoons had five tanks destroyed out of twenty-six and by the end of the day another ten more or less seriously damaged. Seventeen men were killed or wounded and another twenty-five unaccounted for. Corporal Agnew's tank was hit three or four times by an armour-piercing shell (AP) and burst into flames. Sergeant Cochrane's tank turret was hit by an 88 mm shell, causing three casualties. Lieutenant Allen's tank was hit three times and he and three of his crew were killed. Sergeant 'Timber' Wood took on a pill-box, laying down mortar fire and silencing it. Major Birt reports: 'This was fierce shooting at close range; like so much of the fighting on this beach, tanks ran for the gun emplacements in a grim race to put their shells almost point-blank through the mouths of the concrete "boxes" before they themselves were put out of action.' All eight lanes on the beaches were through by eight o'clock and the Dragoons Crabs started clearing the beaches and opening up the lateral roads, thick with mines and wire. Snipers from the villas of Lion and La Brèche were a deadly hazard and inland strongpoints were laying down concentrations of heavy mortar and artillery fire on the beach exits. Captain Wheway rallied his surviving tanks between two large villas and flushed out a score of Germans in the trenches. Sergeant Turner, Corporal Aird and Trooper Hogg were killed by incoming fire in this second stage. At 10.30 the Squadron Leader, Major Clifford, and his second in command, Captain Barraclough, arrived with the 27th Armoured Brigade plus the troops of Westminster Dragoons flails. By the end of the day fierce fighting was going on in Hermanville and a strongpoint in Lion-sur-Mer was still holding out.

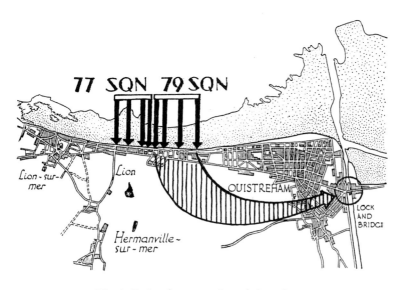

Fig. 2 Ouistreham – 79 Assault Squadron

Lieutenant Richard Bullock, the 2nd Troop Leader, 'A' Squadron Westminster Dragoons, landed three hours after H-Hour in support of the Staffordshire Yeomanry Shermans attached to the 3rd British Division. From Sword beach near Lion-sur-Mer through Hermanville, his troop made their rendezvous with Major Brian Wallace and the rest of the half-squadron. Quite soon three neighbouring tanks went up in flames. 'I belatedly realized that someone was shooting at the great array of vehicles spread over the plain – at least a hundred sitting targets.' Bullock's tank was hit by an AP shell – 'an enormous clang as the shell went through the flailing gear'. The damage was done by a two-man anti-tank gun team who had been left behind in the German retreat. Later the Dragoons moved beyond a crest and saw ahead the first tank battle with a counter-attacking force from the 21st Panzer Division.

Juno Beach

The 3rd Canadian Division's task was to force a landing between Gold and Sword, taking from west to east the small resort towns of St Aubin-sur-Mer, Bernières (Nan beach), Courseulles (Mike beach) and Graye-sur-Mer. On the left flank was the 8th brigade and on the right the 7th Brigade. The beaches were coded from west to east, Mike Green, Mike Red, Nan Green, Nan White and, at St Aubin, Nan Red.

The assault at Bernières in the left sector was delayed by rough seas with a strong cross-current so that the D.D.s of the Fort Garry Horse were brought in close to the beach. The LCTs carrying 80 Assault Squadron RE and 'B' Squadron 22nd Dragoons touched down well to the east of their target breaches. The first craft to land at 7.45 carried the CARE Brigadier Gerry Watkinson and Major R.T. Wiltshire, OC 80 Assault Squadron RE. A sea wall over 10 feet high was the most immediate problem on Nan beach. The brave Canadian infantry had landed ahead of all their support so AVRE Petard fire could not be used to breach the wall. Two assault bridges were laid against it, making reasonable exits for tracked vehicles. The defence by 716 Infantry Division was surprisingly light but two 50 mm guns caused AVRE casualties. No. 1 Team lost an AVRE to a mine which was bulldozed aside and the lane cleared by hand. Then the bulldozer was blown up and its driver killed. Two Crabs cleared a path through the half-broken sea wall up to the first lateral, where AVREs dropped two fascines into an anti-tank ditch. There were plenty of mines, Teller and AP on and around the road. No. 2 Team beached 300 yards east of target. A bridge AVRE was hit by a 50 mm anti-tank gun which was in turn demolished by a Petard. Eventually AVREs and flails alternately bombed and swept their way up and over. No. 3 Team had an easier time and a bridge tank allowed Crabs to pass over and up and keep flailing, bypassing Bernières. No. 4 Team touched down 150 yards east of target. An

LCT collided with a bridge AVRE and their crew were sniped and attacked by grenades. A Bobbin carpet was laid over the soft sand. Lieutenant J.W. Hornby was killed when directing traffic. The Canadian D.D. tanks arrived an hour *after* their infantry had stormed Nan beach.

Sergeant Frank Weightman commanded an AVRE tank with the 2nd Troop of 80 Assault Squadron in No. 4 team. In his LCT were AVREs, four flails and a bulldozer. On the crossing, 'we all groaned with sheer misery, sickness and the cold. There was only the AVRE for shelter packed as it was with equipment, ammunition, explosives, rations for weeks and the five of us. Myself, Claud Raynes (Driver, a staunch-hearted Jewish lad from Manchester with poor eyesight), R.G. Swabey (Wireless Operator, a good one, always keeping his nervousness under firm control), George Raines (Gunner or Mortarman, a cheery young Geordie) and H.A. Meads as co-driver (exchanged a few days later for Arthur Turner, from Staffs). But no corporal to squeeze in as 2 i/c and Demolition NCO.' After a mug of rum, 'we were feeling better now and were so hungry that we were munching ration biscuits as we drove clearly off into about four feet of water.' The turret had jammed and visibility through the periscope was very limited.

> The tide was early, high and choppy with the following wind. Only 60 yards of beach from the water's edge to the solid masonry at the foot of the sea wall, crowded with various ruined steel obstacles, reached through a mass of beached and washed up landing craft, stranded, wrecked or smashed. Captain [Sir Francis] Grant and [Troop Sergeant] Bill Reed preceded by two flails dropped off well and tried to blast an exit with Petard bombs. No success, they were impeded by the Canadian infantry who were taking cover. Jock Martin (fascine) and Sam King (SBG Bridge) both met deep trouble.

Lieutenant Ian Hammerton of the 1st Troop 'B' Squadron, 22nd Dragoons wrote in *Achtung Minen* that after an appalling journey in their LCT it was 'the nearest thing to purgatory we will ever experience. The Skipper "Dutch" Holland was the only man who was not ill. All we wanted to do was to get on to firm dry land. Never mind the German army.' The Dragoons watched a Spitfire attacking the beach defences destroyed by an LCR Hedgehog rocket-launcher. A few minutes after landing, 'Paddy Addis my gunner fires HE at a corner of a railway steel gate called "Element C" until it is a wreck.'

The tide was soon coming in fast and flooded their Crab. 'Digger' Butler, the co-driver, Collinge, the driver, and Lieutenant Hammerton abandoned 'ship'. 'There were some bodies of Chaudières Canadian Infantry floating amongst the debris and flotsam bumping against us.'

Nevertheless by 9 a.m. the four lanes were clear and after a quick stop for self-heating soup, No. 8 Beach Group HQ ordered the Dragoons to keep sweeping the beaches until midnight. On the left of Nan beach, Lieutenant Burbidge's 4th Troop had cleared their lanes west of St Aubin by 8.30. By midday the Dragoons Crabs were setting off with the 2nd Canadian Armoured Brigade along the road to Caen and harboured two miles inland.

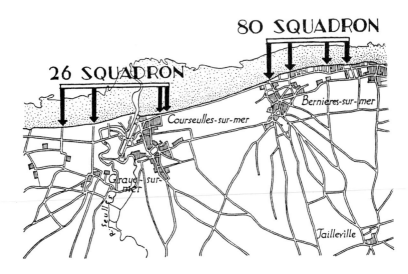

Fig. 3 Courseulles-sur-Mer – 26 Assault Squadron

On the right sector, Mike beach, the 7th Canadian Infantry Brigade were given the task of capturing Courseulles-sur-Mer and Graye-sur-Mer. Eight Canadian 1st Hussar D.D. tanks managed to land and silenced three large enfilading guns. Then 26 Assault Squadron RE, under Major A.E. Younger, with Lieutenant Barraclough's 2nd Troop 'B' Squadron 22nd Dragoons found themselves at H-hour still looking for their landing marks. Finally they were put down in the wrong sector among a fantastic jumble of LCTs on the beach below Graye-sur-Mer. Four armoured bulldozers of 149 Assault Park

Squadron landed with the first wave at 8.25, some 35 minutes late.

Two teams, No. 3 and No. 4, landed on the east side of the river Seulles estuary. The obstacles were sand dunes, a 10-foot sea wall and 'Element C' beach mines defending the main objective of Courseulles-sur-Mer. No. 3 Team declared their lane open by 9 a.m. An anti-tank ditch was filled with a fascine and improved by an armoured bulldozer.

One AVRE carrying a fascine fell into a huge bomb crater over 12 feet deep, so an assault bridge was laid over the submerged Churchill tank and fascine! Armoured bulldozers filled in the sides and thus was christened 'Le Pont AVRE'. Corporal H.R. Hill commanded a Bobbin tank on Mike Green sector and was responsible for fixing a green windsock to mark the beach for the second wave of assault troops who arrived at midday. Captain C.J. Henry went inland with his crew and opened a weir to allow a demolished culvert to drain and his party took thirty prisoners. Major A.E. Younger reconnoitred the route into Courseulles, removed mines and charges from one bridge and with French assistance swung back another. He then declared the Mike to Nan sectors linked up at midday. When the tide went out six AVREs and 2 bulldozers assisted in the salvage of 'drowned' D.D. tanks and obstacle clearance.

By the end of D-Day the Canadians were firmly ensconced and in control of their bridgehead. 'B' Squadron 22nd Dragoons had lost only one trooper wounded, two flails wrecked and another five tanks more or less seriously damaged – incredible figures after a hard day's fighting.

Gold Beach

The 50th Northumbrian (Tyne Tees) Division and the 8th Armoured Brigade (Red Fox's Mask) were two experienced formations from General Montgomery's desert legions. Gold was a 4-mile stretch of beach between Le Hamel and Cabane (Jig) western sector and La Rivière (King) eastern sector. Two key objectives for D-Day were the capture of the elegant inland town of Bayeux and of Arromanches. The latter, just to the west of Le Hamel, was destined to become the home for the famous Mulberry man-made harbour. The plan was that 23 (Malta) Brigade would assault Le Hamel with six breaching teams over 2,000 yards of mined beach defence, and the 60th Brigade would capture La Rivière with six breaching teams concentrated in a half-mile stretch.

Two additional problems on Jig sector were the known patches of soft blue clay on the foreshore for which Bobbin carpet rolls were needed, and inland beyond the lateral road a huge swampy marsh, le Marais. Sherwood Rangers Yeomanry D.D. tanks led with breaching teams formed by 'B' Squadron Westminster Dragoons flails and AVREs of 82 Assault Squadron RE under Major H.G.A. Elphinstone.

H-hour was 0730 hours and an 88 mm anti-tank gun in a concrete pill-box at the west end of Le Hamel soon caused trouble. The Sherwood Rangers Yeomanry D.D. tanks were launched close to the beach because of the rough seas. Five from 'C' Squadron on the left supporting the 1st Dorsets 'drowned' and so did three from 'B' Squadron supporting the 1st Hampshires. Trooper Philip Foster recalls:

> We slid off the ramps of the LCT into the sea only about half a mile from shore. The Germans from their surviving static defences greeted us by pounding the sea with their shells as we swam forward. A few of our tanks sank for one reason or another. We safely proceeded through the rain of shells right onto the beach as we had so often done in practice. I could see through my periscope over the dunes the little village of Le Hamel intact and seemingly deserted. We continued on and fired our first shell but then things went wrong for us.

An AP shell smashed into their Sherman killing or wounding the crew. 'Of our Squadron only four tanks reached their rendezvous. All the rest were casualties.' The Sherwood Rangers Yeomanry lost twelve tanks and suffered twenty-four casualties during the day.

Richard Bullock was the 2nd Troop Leader, 'A' Squadron, Westminster Dragoons and in his book *D-Day Remembered* has gathered together stories from nineteen veterans. Lance Corporal R.C. Eastwood of 'B' Squadron embarked on LCT No. 886 as a crew member in Lieutenant Townsend Green's troop. On board was No. 1 Assault Team of six AVRE or Crab tanks.

> About 100 yards from the water line, the ramp went down into 8–10 feet of water. The leading AVRE disappeared and drowned under the waves. Then all hell broke loose; the craft was hit numerous times on the bridge and in the engine room by shells from heavy calibre guns

on the beach. It was completely disabled and turned sideways on and started hitting beach obstacles and defences exploding mines and fused shells attached to them, causing a number of casualties on board. Through my periscope I saw the Hampshires assault infantry being cut down on the beach and numerous tanks ablaze.

Later that night four Crabs out of the original thirteen mustered in the village of Meauvaines. Patches of blue clay beach off Le Hamel claimed several 'bogged' victims, despite Bobbin Roly Polies.

Of the three lanes just east of Le Hamel, No. 1 and No. 3 were no good and all the D.D., gun tanks and Self-Propelled (SPs) had to use No. 2. Sergeant Bob Lindsay led his Crab in No. 2 Team, flailed through to the lateral and turned west towards Le Hamel, which was still strongly defended. Captain Brian Taylor's tank went up on a mine and Sergeant Lindsay charged towards the village, which was supposedly captured by the Hampshires but actually held by two platoons of German infantry. After many adventures in the village his tank was brewed up after flailing and firing alternately for a considerable time. Major H.J.A. Elphinstone, the officer commanding 82 Assault Squadron RE was killed by a sniper whilst commanding the first three breaching teams.

Corporal E. Lawrenson of 'B' Squadron recalls:

Under heavy fire we approached the dunes, engaged the flail and along with Sgt Lindsay's tank started flogging our way through the barbed wire and mines: the density of mines was unbelievable and the sound of exploding mines seemed continuous. My tank when about 15/20 yards from the lateral road was knocked out – there was a tremendous explosion, the tank reared up, then crashed down. We stopped in the minefield I saw our other tank legging it down the road to the second objective. We opened fire with our tank guns. My concern was the wireless which the explosion had damaged.

Captain Ben Taylor sent Lawrenson back to Major Elphinstone, who had been in charge of the Jig Green teams.

The infantry were taking heavy casualties on the beach and had only reached the dunes: lanes 1 and 2 did not exist. Major Elphinstone had been killed. I spotted Lt Col Nelson Smith of the Hampshires, who although wounded was trying to get his men off the beach ... some sappers appeared and with their help we cleared mines, repaired a damaged AVRE and re-opened part of the lane. The MG and small arms fire was slowing down and the Hampshires were now in Le Hamel, 4 hours late. Sgt Crockett arrived with the Squadron ARV and Lt Col Blair Oliphant [commanding officer of the Westminster Dragoons] who was determined to land on D-Day and had taken the place of a tank crew fitter.

No. 5 and 6 Teams half a mile to the east were more successful, but Lane 4 failed as the Crabs became bogged on the beach. A Bobbin of No. 6 Team laid its carpet down and then cleared obstacles up to the lateral road.

On his way to the shore Captain John Leytham of 82 Assault Squadron RE 'lost' the Roly Poly Bobbin from his AVRE. He now had an opportunity to fire a Petard for the first time. 'I let one go, it kept the chaps busy.' Captain Stannion of the Westminster Dragoons, who was in charge of Lane 5 had his Sherman brewed up so Leytham took command. 'I was somewhat bemused by now, nor did I know where I was, as I could recognise nothing up ahead.' The D.D. tanks were an hour late and the Royal Marine Centaur SP tanks had landed only four out of ten AFVs – all bar one were hit by 352 Infantry Division's shells. Leytham's own Lane 4 was blocked by blown-up or bogged AVREs. 'So for a time confusion reigned supreme.' Later that night Leytham saw a prisoner-of-war camp – 'a vast sea of grey uniforms' and 'my greatest shock was to see numerous French lassies embracing their German boyfriends in fond farewell'.

Lance Sergeant M. Scaife of 82 Assault Squadron RE had a remarkable day. Initially he laid his Roly Poly Bobbin mat successfully and then helped clear beach obstacles and pushed his way up to the lateral road east of Le Hamel. 'My AVRE was now on its own. My OC was out, my Tp leader Capt Wilford was wounded aboard the LCT when it was hit by shell fire. My Tp 2 i/c had his AVRE's track blown off by a mine missed by the flails and my following AVRE commander L/Sgt George was killed on the beach helping clear obstacles.' About midday some Hampshire infantry asked for help against defences in Le Hamel. Scaife's AVRE fired two Flying Dustbins against a fortified sanatorium on the clifftop and twenty prisoners were taken. Another Petard was fired into the 'back door' of a concrete pill-box whose 88 mm anti-tank gun was causing much trouble on the beaches. 'We then with Besa flushed out a sniper entrenched nearby.' After putting out a fire on the top

H-hour, D-Day Le Hamel, 6 June 1944. 82 Assault Squadron RE support
50th Northumbrian Division. 'D.D.' tanks swim for shore (Birkin Haward)

deck of the AVRE, Sergeant Scaife spent a busy afternoon destroying several MG nests along the coastal ledge of Le Hamel. Captain
Raymond Ellis, with three more AVREs, joined him at 4 p.m. and
jointly they rallied to Buhet in the evening. Scaife was awarded the
DCM and then commissioned in the field.

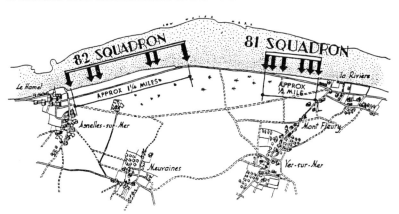

Fig. 4 Le Hamel and La Rivière

Lieutenant Raymond Ellis, who was in charge of No. 5 recalls:

> The skipper of LCT 2029 drove us on to the sand hard and the ramp lowered. I pushed out the 'Roly Poly' matting, went ashore without difficulty and blew off the waterproofing to the air inlet extensions and drove up the beach steering between the barbed wire, element 'C', Tetrahedra, wooden poles with mines facing out to sea. All the leading AVRES went roughly in line abreast. The shells were falling fast by the time we reached the top of the beach near the low sand-hills. I sent the first Crab to flail over the low sandhills into the mine-field; very many of the 1st Hampshires were killed and were lying blazing on fire near the sandhills, a rather horrifying sight. They were dead and the shrapnel had ignited the mortar ammunition they were carrying in packs on their backs. The noise of the shells landing was terrific. So many landed so close, many within 10 or 15 yards and made a Krunnnch not a bang.

Ahead lay the lateral road or track where there was an enormous crater 30 feet wide, 30 feet long and 10 feet deep, filled with water, which completely blocked the vital way towards Le Hamel. Ellis organized the delicate and difficult job of bringing up three AVRES with fascines and dropping them neatly in parallel, filling up the huge crater. 'By this time the gun tanks, D.D.s and others were queueing up nose to tail all the way back to the beach waiting to advance west to Le Hamel, Arromanches, and south to Asnelles and Meuvaines.' That night Captain Leytham took command of 82 Assault Squadron as a major, and Lieutenant Ellis became his second in command as a captain.

The eastern sector of Gold was King sector, where six breaching teams would tackle the sea defences just west of La Rivière. The 69th Brigade of the 50th Northumbrian Division with battalions of Green Howards and East Yorkshires were led in by the D.D. tanks of 4/7 Royal Dragoon Guards. The breaching teams were Crabs of the Westminster Dragoons and AVREs of 81 Assault Squadron RE. On the high ground inland of Mont Fleury and Ver-sur-Mer, batter-ies of 155 mm guns dominated the beaches. The supporting Royal Navy and RAF bombardment started at 6 a.m. with H-Hour set for 7.25. Rough sea presented a long-distance swim and LCTs landed 'C' Squadron (to support the 5th East Yorkshires) and 'B' Squadron (to support the 6th Green Howards), a couple of hundred yards from shore – a deep wade.

Trooper A.E. Baker of 'C' Squadron recalled:

An 88 mm knocked out two Churchill AVREs before we arrived, itself KO'd by a flail tank [Westminster Dragoons]. By now the beach was black with men and machines. Scores of LCTs were discharging their cargoes. Sea was rough, making things difficult. I saw several lorries overturn in the breakers. Our LCT went in, bows touched bottom, beach lined with metal spikes, some with Teller mines attached. Current swung craft around, backed out among infantry wading ashore, necks in water. Not so lucky. Terrific crash, LCT jerked back, hit one of the mines.

The three breaching teams on the right were commanded by Major S.P.M. Sutton of the Westminster Dragoons and the three on the left by Major R.E. Thompson of the Royal Engineers. No. 1 and No. 2 lanes were cleared, mainly by Lieutenant Pears, 'C' Squadron, Westminster Dragoons, whose team flogged up the shore, reached the lateral road, turned left towards the villa known as 'Lavatory Pan' and found a large crater, where an AVRE successfully laid its SBG bridge. Then Lieutenant Pears was joined by Major Sutton and their Crabs flailed a wide lane to allow the D.D. tanks of 'C' Squadron 4/7 Dragoon Guards to head for Ver-sur-Mer, a mile inland. The Crabs tackling No. 3 lane were bogged in the marshes, drew 88 mm fire and failed to clear a lane. Lieutenant B.M.S. Hoban, 1st Troop Leader, said, 'Two AVREs from our LCT charged ahead up the beach until in quick succession they simply exploded. Everything stopped of a sudden, then got going again in response to the resolute Canadian tones on the wireless of Major Tim Thompson RE, our breaching squadron commander, saying "Get on up that bloody beach, all of you."' Lieutenant Hoban and Sergeant Webb's Crabs exploded several mines but became bogged in the minefield.

Sapper Sidney Blaskett, an AVRE tank gunner, recalls: 'Our LCT arrived off La Rivière. AVRE commanded by Capt DS King was first off the LCT. Directly in front was our first objective a formidable heavy MG pill box. Our demolition NCO Corporal Bill Marsden then fired a petard.' The next was a dud and Blaskett had to get out of the AVRE to remove the round. The next mortar round destroyed the emplacement completely. 'We were 40 yards from the sea wall and Capt King ordered our driver to climb over the wall.' Through his periscope Blaskett saw fifteen or twenty German defenders running along the lateral road. 'I fired the Besa turret gun and the helmets disappeared. About 200 yards further along the road was a large 4 bedroomed detached house. We fired a dustbin round into the house and drove at high speed *into* the house.' They were tough old war horses, the AVRE Churchill tanks! The 69 Brigade infantry asked for help to clear a field full of defenders in trenches. 'We overran the trenches with our AVRE.'

Corporal Charles Baldwin of 'C' Squadron, Westminster Dragoons was part of No. 6 Breaching Team, which landed in King Red sector close to La Rivière. He saw 'the beach engineers who surged forward down the ramp only to be met by machine gun fire. They were thrown about like rag dolls and vanished under the water. Even the slightly wounded had little chance of surviving as they were carrying very heavy packs. Any further chance of their survival vanished with the passage of the four tanks over the top of them.' Later, 'our own flail tanks moved easily through the water to the sandy beach, stopped to blow the waterpoofing equipment off. I saw an AVRE pass us to the right and start climbing the slope ahead. Suddenly it stopped, three of its crew got out and were reaching down into the turret to get someone out. Suddenly the Churchill exploded and disintegrated. Our tank rocked with the force of the blast and we were struck very hard on the turret [hit by the gearbox of the destroyed AVRE].' The second AVRE also pushed up the beach to suffer the same fate.

Baldwin's Crab 'posted letters' from about 100 yards into the pill-box and destroyed the 88 mm anti-tank gun. Trooper Smith recalled 'an enormous cloud of black smoke and the two Churchills disappeared. We heard later they had been carrying Wade charges for blowing up the beach defences.'

No. 4 and No. 5 Teams failed to clear their lanes; Crabs bogged and an AVRE brewed while laying a Bobbin carpet. No. 6 Team, the furthest east, was successful but the lateral road was badly cratered and needed several fascines to be laid. Major Thompson and Captain J.M. Birkbeck later led 4/7 Royal Dragoons Guards D.D. tanks in their advance. La Rivière was captured by 9 a.m. after one and a half hours costly fighting on the Gold beaches. On the assault on the Mont Fleury battery of 155 mm guns Company Sergeant Major Stan Hollis of the Green Howards earned the VC, the only one won on D-Day.

Sapper Ralph Rayner of 149 Assault Squadron (armoured bulldozers) recalls:

We landed our waterproofed bulldozer on the left flank of 'Gold' beach just west of La Rivière. Our task was to clear the beach of all obstacles and we worked with the RM commandos. Their divers made safe the explosive charges attached to under water obstacles and secured the bulldozer winch rope so that we could tow the obstacles ashore. It took five days to clear the beach of all obstacles. On D+1 a padre requested our assistance in recovering a number of bodies which were floating just offshore. We recovered about 20 or 30 mostly from 42 RM Commando whose landing craft overturned during the approach to the beach. The highlight was when we recovered two crates, one with 5½ gallons of 100% rum, the other 2500 Players cigarettes.

Captain David Squirrell, Technical Adjutant of the Westminster Dragoons, traversed Gold beach from east to west on the evening of D-Day. In his scout car he made a note of eleven brewed up, ditched or bogged flails with a view to later recovery. On D+1 he collected a band of fitters and ARVs to return to the beaches to start recovery.

By the end of D-Day the two British beaches had seven successful breaching lanes, out of twelve attempted. Of the fifty Crabs deployed, twelve were destroyed and many more put out of action. And of 120 AVREs that landed, 22 were destroyed and again many more put out of action. The 5th Assault Regiment RE suffered 117 casualties, the 6th Assault Regiment RE 25, the 22nd Dragoons 20 and the Westminster Dragoons 7. On the beaches eight fascines, and ten SBG bridges had been dropped. Eight armoured bulldozers were deployed. The Bullshorn ploughs were used on Lion-sur-Mer beach and Porpoises carrying extra ammunition and stores were also used.

Hobart's 'Funnies' had had a magnificent first day in action.

9 The Bridgehead in June

In the House of Commons on the night of D-Day Winston Churchill paid tribute to Hobart's 'Funnies' when he told the packed house that the defences of 'Fortress Europe' had been badly surprised. Lodgements had been established, due in part to 'certain ingenious modifications' that had been made to British tanks. Brigadier N.W. Duncan, the officer commanding the 30th Armoured Brigade and Brigadier G.L. Watkinson of the 1st Assault Brigade RE had every reason to be proud of the success of their combined forces.

Churchill sent a message to Stalin on 7 June.

> We got across with small losses. We had expected to lose about 10,000 men. By tonight we hope to have the best part of a quarter of a million men ashore including a considerable quantity of armour and tanks all landed from special ships or swimming ashore by themselves. In this latter class of tanks there have been a good many casualties, especially on the American front owing to the waves overturning the swimming tanks.

In his book *Struggle for Europe*, Chester Wilmot notes General Eisenhower's opinion.

> Apart from the factor of tactical surprise, the comparatively light casualties which we sustained on all beaches except Omaha, were in large measure due to our success of the *novel mechanical continuances* which we employed and to the staggering morale and material effect of the mass of armour landed in the *leading* waves of the assault.

Wilmot then adds 'How many lives were saved on other sectors by the 79th Armoured Division nobody can tell but if it had not been for the specialised armour, the spearhead of the assault, progress on the British and Canadian beaches might have been almost as slow and expensive as it was on Omaha.'

General Hobart was ashore by the evening of 8 June to visit the beaches, inspect the many bogged or destroyed 'Funnies' and talk to his men. His tactical HQ had been refused shipping space but he more or less smuggled a skeleton staff and their vehicles in a large DUKW, an American amphibious truck. He found that his Crabs and AVREs were continuing to be used in the van of attack. Hobart states: 'The infantry are apt to claim that its mere presence [an AVRE with a Petard] has a moral effect on the enemy and therefore exposes AVREs to fire which cannot be returned.' And Crabs were being used to flail verges instead of minefields. Sergeant Frank Weightman of the 80th Assault Squadron RE remembered:

> Although no use as gun tanks we went in support of attacks at the caves in Fontaine Henri, to St Honorine Marcelet and Carpiquet Aerodrome. There we lost Bill Reed badly wounded and Duggie Moore, mortally so. One of the finest men I have known was tough little Duggie. As the desperate struggles for Caen went we saw action around Buron, Authie, Cussy, St Contest, Hill 112, Evrecy and survived very well. The lush rich countryside was devastated. Villages just heaps of ruins, roads of choking dust bringing down shell or mortar fire. The stench of death as summer came was utterly nauseating blended with cordite fumes. Thousands of unburied livestock – and men – knocked out and burned out tanks, some with dead crews inside being devoured by maggots. And bombs, mines and '*Achtung Minen*'; sunken roads with bocage hedges, ideal for tank traps.

Trooper Joe Minogue, a 20-year-old gunner in B Squadron, Westminster Dragoons, described a visit by Hobart.

> Major General Hobart fulfilled the promise he had made us at Lepe Point to visit us. He came unaccompanied [on D+2]. He walked among the crews with words of encouragement or sympathetic nods according to the stories they told him. When he heard that we and Sergeant Roberts had flailed successfully, he was delighted. But of course the Normandy landings were the big test for his beloved 'Funnies'. We were all convinced Sir Percy Hobart might be a Major General, but he was 'one of us', a tankman's tankman. We felt in spite of his high rank that he would have been happy sitting on an

upturned petrol tin chewing the fat with the crew enjoying our corny jokes and sharing a mug of tea with us. Like our own Colonel [Blair Oliphant] we felt Sir Percy was a wise old bird, who knew our fears and our hopes and thought quite a lot about us. But then there is a bond among tankmen.

For the next six weeks Hobart shuttled backwards and forwards from his Normandy Tactical (TAC) HQ to his Rear HQ in England. During that time there was rarely an operation when the 'Funnies' were handled 'correctly', in the manner he had originally envisaged.

The enormous build-up of men and material continued. Major Birt of the 22nd Dragoons described some of the amenities.

> Newspapers appeared practically on the day of their publication. A mobile bath unit settled a few hundred yards away in Plumetot and pumped out gratifying streams of hot water. A film unit established itself in Cresserons. Food was superb. The 'comp' boxes yielded up a different menu for each day of the week: tins rich in solid duffs and stews – a generous supply of chocolate, sweets and cigarettes. In the mined fields there were young potatoes and peas for the lifting. In the village bars of chocolate would buy a couple of dozen eggs; four cigarettes or a cake of soap, a fat rabbit, a thick piece of ham. If the beer was thin and the cider sour to an English thirst, a glass of calvados provided the drinker with one of the surprises of his life! Kilos of rich Normandy butter and baskets of Camembert cheese were obtainable.

'C' Squadron, Westminster Dragoons, had harboured on D+1 at Crepon, 2 miles inland from Asnelles. Suddenly they were attacked by an enemy gun firing over open sights from the far side of the next field, and within a few minutes there were six casualties. One of the survivors wrote, 'At this stage of the war we were all so raw that no one knew whether the explosions were bombs, mines or shells.' Lieutenant Hoban's flail tank then destroyed the enemy gun. Two Crocodiles from 'C' Squadron, 141 RAC, who had just landed, gave covering fire, led by Lieutenant Shearman, as the Dragoons retired to a more secluded spot. A counter-attack was quickly organized into the suspected enemy locality. A few squirts of flame and 75 mm rounds and this composite force captured four 75 mm guns, one 88 mm anti-tank gun and 100 prisoners. The rest of the Crocodiles of 141 RAC (Buffs) arrived in Normandy on 22–23 June. The third

Crab regiment, the 1st Lothians and Border Yeomanry, were not initially needed, arrived on 15 July and harboured at Crepon. The brigade of CDLs also arrived late in July.

In the constricted area of the bridgehead each formation of 'Funnies' had their harbour area from which, in dribs and drabs, they sallied forth to help the 50th Northumbrian, 51st Highland, 3rd British or any other division which needed flails, Crocodiles and to a lesser extent the AVREs. Juaye Mondaye, 5 miles south of Bayeux, was the Westminster Dragoons' base throughout June and July, a straggly row of houses, a church and a monastery.

The 3rd British Division launched a series of attacks on Cambes Woods and Lebisey a few miles inland from Lion-sur-Mer on D+2. By now (8 June) the whole area north of Caen was swarming with the enemy. The German 716 Division had been reinforced by 22 Panzer Regiment tanks and 1/192 Panzer Grenadiers with a whole series of defensive posts. The 26th Assault Squadron RE suffered heavily there on 9 June with twenty casualties including eleven ORs missing. It would be another four weeks of brutal fighting including Operation Mitten, before Caen was to be taken.

At Douvres-la-Delivrande west of Lion-sur-Mer, 200 Luftwaffe troops were putting up a superb defence of a radar station. With deep bunkers, concrete pill-boxes, minefields and wire, they had seen off an attack on the evening of D-Day when the 80th Assault Squadron RE lost three AVREs. On 12 June another attack supported by the 26th Assault Squadron RE also failed. The defenders had five 50 mm anti-tank guns and numerous Spandau and 20 mm guns. On 17 June 160 commandos of 46 Royal Marine Commando, supported by two Squadrons of the 22nd Dragoons' flails and seventeen AVREs of 26th Assault Squadron made a third determined attack. The 77th Assault Squadron made diversionary attacks from the west and south. RAF bombs had had little effect on the defensive bunkers, which were 300 feet deep. At 4.30 p.m. a huge barrage concentration came down on the radar station. 'C' Squadron 22nd Dragoons flailed hard losing five Crabs in the process. The AVREs petarded the two main strongpoints and behind smoke, Beehives – 70 lb explosive charges – were placed and fired. The commandos went in and in two hours winkled out over 200 prisoners. Seven AVREs were knocked out, with ten casualties. It was a small classic operation by the 'Funnies', Crabs and AVREs combining with the Commando storm troopers. But the Führer would have been proud of his Luftwaffe troops.

At the same time Westminster Dragoons flails supported the 2nd Hampshires towards La Senaudière. Lieutenants Hoban and Pears led their six flails in a successful advance of 1,000 yards before anti-tank guns knocked out both their Crabs, with nine casualties.

Westminster Dragoons flail crashing through Normandy hedgerow

Meanwhile General Montgomery was planning a series of attacks either to take Caen or outflank it. Operations 'Crust' and 'Cushion' had failed but still to come were 'Epsom', 'Mitten', 'Charnwood', 'Jupiter' and 'Goodwood'. Major Birt described the opposition.

The German troops fought with formidable tenacity, outgunned and searched out day and night by rocket firing aircraft that had the sky to themselves. The enemy dug themselves into the superb natural defences provided by the ditch-hedged 'bocage' country and did not yield until they were over-run or annihilated. Occasionally soft spots were found in their defences and prisoners were taken in quantity [usually Russians, Poles and other 'captive' nationalities] but for the most part advances were made into areas of cruel desolation where villages were pounded into total ruin and where the smell of death was heavy on the summer air. Wherever the attackers faced the fanatics of the SS divisions, prisoners came in only by twos and threes ... they were young [Hitler Youth troops] and they were malevolent, scowling at their captors with the air of supple small beasts of prey caged behind wire.

It was clear that the majority of the formations being supported were unaware of the strengths and weaknesses of the various 'Funnies'. A powerful Churchill AVRE tank could only fire its spigot bomb a distance of less than 100 yards. As Major Birt put it, it was 'a troublesome matter for a ['Funny'] detachment commander to decide whether to allow his unwieldy tanks to fight an infantry-tank role at the risk of severe losses, or to appear either *churlish* or *timorous* by explaining what tasks his machines were designed for and what were their limitations.... Trained [flail or AVRE] crews were very valuable.' The infantry always had mixed feelings when at dusk their armoured 'big friends' left them to trundle back to their harbour, a mile or two back. It looked bad but refuelling, replenishment of ammunition, basic repairs, food and sleep were essential if the 'big friends' were to reappear just after dawn to resume the battle. Some AVREs were now usefully employed petarding the typical bocage hedgerows to blast a gap for tracked and wheeled vehicles to pass through. The armoured bulldozers did the same and also dug huge holes in which to inter the poor bloated Normandy livestock.

On 15 and 16 June the 82nd Assault Squadron RE were involved in an attack on Lingeuvres and Verrières when 4/7 Royal Dragoon Guards had a field day bashing Panthers. And on the 19th it was Hottot, south-west of Tilly. Captain John Leytham remembered it well.

There are two places engraved on my memory with horror. One is Hottot and the other Fontenay. Looking at the map it seems incredible that two such small villages should become major obstacles but they were of strategic importance as they straddled the road for Villers Bocage. The battle for Tilly lasted nine days and it was eventually taken on 19 June with HMS Rodney shelling *Hottot* to help the 50th Northumbrian Division.

Leytham watched with enthusiasm as the RAF obliterated the two small towns of Villers Bocage and Aunay-sur-Odon. But Hottot was not taken until 19 July.

Lieutenant Ian Hammerton recalled vividly the events at Cresseron where the 22nd Dragoons had harboured before

'Operation Epsom', Montgomery's third attempt to take Caen. A 'bread basket' anti-personnel bomb had been dropped at night by the Luftwaffe. 'Sgt Jock Stirling and crew, Corporal Ferguson, Johnny Munden, Digger Butler and Dave Sawyer had all been wounded.' But now 'there was nearby a Field Hospital with *real* nurses and wonder of wonders a field bakery producing white bread and a shower unit which produced hot water from the nearest duck pond. Heaven!' Moreover, the BBC Home Service could be found on the radio and they could listen to the evening Promenade Concerts in London.

The 81st Assault Squadron RE had an unfortunate day towards the end of June. The crack Panzer LEHR Division was one of the three armoured divisions defending the outskirts of Caen. Tilly-sur-Seulles, 8 miles south-east of Bayeux, had been taken and retaken a dozen times. It was currently held by Panzer Grenadiers and was being attacked by the 2nd Essex, part of the 56th Infantry Brigade. Sapper Sidney Blaskett of the 1st Troop recalls:

> As we came near the crossroads in Tilly there was an explosion near the front of our AVRE. I immediately sprayed MG rounds at some bushes, where we thought they had fired at us. At the same time a German tank, possibly a Panther, came out of the road across our front. Captain Davies told us to fire a Dustbin at it, only 50 yards away. I traversed our turret slightly to the right, took aim and fired for its turret ring. [Blaskett's Petard hit a telegraph pole about 3 feet from the enemy tank.] When the smoke and dust cleared, the tank had stopped and did not move again. We agreed that the blast had put the tank and its occupants out of action.

Unfortunately George Murray reversed the AVRE which mounted some house rubble; it overturned on its side in a sunken lane and was subsequently captured by the Germans. On their return on foot, Major Thomson their OC was furious. He called the whole Squadron on parade and told them 'that now the Germans would find out all about their "secret" AVRE, its mortar, its explosive charges including the General Wade.'

'Operation Epsom' started on 25 June. The entire VIII Corps, the 15th Scottish, the 43rd Wessex and the 11th Armoured Divisions – all untried, but enthusiastic – were launched towards the River Odon between Rauray and Carpiquet. After a counter-attack which was repulsed on the 27th, Hobart's 'second' division, the 11th

Armoured gained the heights of Hill 112 across the Odon on the 29th. Because 'Enigma' (secret code-breakers at Bletchley Park) warned of a massive armoured counter-attack from the south by 2nd SS and 10th SS Panzer Divisions, however, the hill was abandoned. In the four-day battle VIII Corps incurred over 4,000 casualties. Major Birt wrote:

> On the approaches to the battle area once lovely villages with lovely names, Putot en Bessin, St Mauvieu, Bretteville l'Orgueilleuse were shattered by the weight of our bombardment and by the fighting that followed. As usual the enemy fought hard. Around Cheux 'B' Sqn 22 Dragoons advanced in open country in which the German and the British [mainly Scottish] dead lay tossed about the cornfields. There were scattered groups of mines – the tanks foundered on the first day.

Searching for mines in the waist-high cornfields was difficult. Dragoon crews had to dismount and search for them with bayonets. 'C' Squadron Westminster Dragoons, helped flail around St Mauvieu but no minefields were encountered. They supported the 9th Royal Tank Regiment as it moved up, in pouring rain until Carpiquet aerodrome, a mile to the east, was clearly visible. Three times a day at mealtimes they were fired on by a gun from the aerodrome. After watching 350 Lancasters bomb Caen the Dragoons returned to their base at Juaye Mondaye.

Crocodiles from the Buffs also took part in 'Epsom'. Major R.L. Cooper and Captain George Storrar led three troops of 'A' Squadron towards Cheux, and Captain G.H. Strachan two troops to St Mauvieu. On 27 June, Lieutenant Norman Harvey went into a courtyard to burn out some stubborn enemy when his tracks came off. He and his crew of four were captured and never heard of again. 'B' Squadron, later to be nicknamed 'the Playboys', were controlled by the buccaneering Major Sydney Spearpoint, Captain Nigel Ryle, with his trim moustache, Captain 'Bonko' Moss, a metallurgist by training, and wee witty Captain John Dean, the regimental LO, known as 'Nippy Chips'. Of the original nine officers, three were to be killed, five wounded and one left the Squadron shortly after landing on 22 June. Harry Bailey, their second in command, wrote in his history of the Playboys, 'Every day a bloody battle and "we must have flamethrowers". This was the universal cry.'

'Operation Mitten', the assault on le Landel and Chateau de la Londe by the 8th Brigade (3d British Division) began on 27 June.

Three miles north of Caen, this salient had been taken on the 22nd and promptly retaken by the Germans. The attack coincided with 'Epsom' a few miles to the south-west, part of General Montgomery's tactics of putting concentrated pressure on the German defences of Caen. The Playboys were to support the East Yorkshires, backed by two troops of the Staffordshire Yeomanry Shermans. Captain Harry Bailey wrote: 'It was an ill-fated party from the beginning. In those early days Crocodile tactics had still to be learned from the bitter experience of battle. The plan was hurried and instead of close support on to the objective from the supporting tanks these were to be given indirect support by acting on the flanks as anti-tank protection.' The strength of the enemy was seriously underestimated. Apart from a company of engineers, there were SPs, mortars, dug-in infantry positions and numerous enemy tanks on the flanks (with fourteen in the chateau area alone!). It was 'a blazing hot afternoon and in the FUP (Forming Up Point) the 'moaning minnies' [Nebelwerfer mortars] were coming down pretty thick and fast.' The Buffs' Crocodiles were late crossing the start line 'for technical reasons' and lost their infantry, who were held up halfway to their objective.

Lieutenant Raymond Brooke's 8th Troop was soon in trouble. Twenty yards away from the Chateau du Landel wall a MkIV destroyed his Churchill, killing Lieutenant Brooke and seriously wounding Trooper Woodcock and Corporal Marsden. Sergeant Burton's Crocodile suffered a jammed turret and the flame fuel trailer became wrapped around a tree. Only Corporal Hischier's survived.

AVREs of the 79th Assault Squadron tried to petard the Chateau. Lance Corporal Flint's Churchill was knocked out. 'We all baled out into a dry moat to discover the infantry had gone. We were left well behind the enemy lines feeling lonely and ill-used. There was concentrated shelling, mortaring and machine-gun fire.' The AVRE crew crossed a wheat field under fire until they met some Canadian soldiers in a Bren-gun carrier. Offered a tumbler full of transparent liquid, Flint swallowed it in one long gulp, believing it to be water. 'It was calvados. The effect was instantaneous. I had a befuddled memory of walking through an empty village firing a revolver in the air and shouting "Come out, you bastards".' Later at the Regimental Aid Post he was treated for shock and battle exhaustion until a suspicious orderly realised he was drunk! Ernest Kitson wrote, 'A number of 79th AVREs were sent towards Combes Wood where they encountered Tiger tanks. On rushing out of the wood they were met by the Royal Ulster Rifles (of the 3rd Division) who started to shoot them up. Nine men were killed, three wounded and five taken prisoner.'

Major Birt wrote:

> It was an appalling battle. The South Lancs managed to reach and hold La Londe but could not take the chateau around which the enemy had dug in more than 30 tanks supported by elements of 192 Panzer Grenadiers. The next morning [28 June] the Suffolks and East Yorks [with the 1st Troop, 'C' Squadron, 22nd Dragoons flails in support] were sent in behind a barrage of terrifying weight. But they were met by heavy shell and mortar fire which pinned them and their supporting tanks to the woods around Mathieu. During that long day, in which advances were measured in yards and infantry casualties were grievously heavy, tanks were engaged from the direction of Lebisey and accounted for eight enemy AFVs. Though Crocodile flame-throwers were brought up to burn the enemy out of their positions, it was obviously impossible to maintain the attack. Our flails were drawn back into harbour north of Gazelle where they were heavily shelled.

'Mitten' was called off and operations 'Abelour' and 'Ottawa' were cancelled.

During June the 82nd Assault Squadron RE were in action at Ryes, Tilly, La Belle Epine, Bernières-Bocage (where at night they acted as mobile pill-boxes in hull-down positions). At Lingeuvres they attacked the village firing Petard and Besa. Then they attacked Hottot on the 19th and a week later mounted three separate attacks.

'Operation Martlet' was another of General Montgomery's plans to seize commanding features in the area of Rauray and Fontenay-le-Pesnel, both south-east of Tilly. It was timed to start a day after 'Epsom' on 25 June with the 49th Polar Bear Division supported by the 8th Armoured Brigade. The 82nd Assault Squadron RE bombarded a strongpoint on the first morning, helped clear the village of Fontenay in the evening and took thirty prisoners on the second day whilst mopping up. Besa and Petard were used against spandau teams in houses and the AVREs helped in a final counter-attack after the village had been recaptured by the Germans.

Churchill AVREs support 49 Polar Bear Division in night attack on
Fontenay-le-Pesnil, 25 June 1944 (Birkin Haward)

Lieutenant Andrew Wilson and three other young subalterns
joined their regiment, 141 RAC, in Normandy. On arrival they
reported to the Adjutant as replacements for Harvey, Benzecry and
Davis, officers of 'C' Squadron who had been casualties since D+3.
Harvey and his crew had been lined up by SS troops against a farm-
house wall and shot. Benzecry's Crocodile was taken for a German
Panther tank one misty morning and was knocked out by a British
M-10 tank destroyer.

Captain Drysdale, the Buffs REME officer showed Andrew
Wilson round the battlefield near Tilly. At nearly every crossroads
were a group of charred buildings with bullet-spattered Dubonnet
and St Raphael signs. Upon the Tilly road were 10 or 12 Panthers
knocked out by RAF Typhoons. 'They looked enormous with their
long guns and thick sloping armour,' Wilson recalled. At La
Senaudière the wreck of a Panther faced the wreck of a Crocodile.
Lieutenant Davis and his Troop Sergeant, in their two Shermans,
had encountered the Panther, which fired point blank into the
Sergeant's tank; Davis's gunner fired back when the muzzles of the
two guns were almost touching; the whole action took about ten

seconds. Wilson recalled, 'When a Churchill, Crocodile or AVRE was hit it caught fire three times out of five and it could take up to ten seconds for the fire to sweep through the engine compartment to the turret. The American Sherman [Crabs] caught fire every time and the flames swept through them in about three seconds. The Germans called them "Tommy Cookers".'

Many small Normandy villages were fought over – taken, retaken and perhaps finally captured: Tilly-sur-Seulles, Cheux, Perriers, Mathieu, Brouay, Esquay and a score of others. Towards the end of June great storm clouds from the south-west burst over the battlefield with a furious drumming of rain and the yellow dust of the first hot sunny weeks became a slime of yellow mud. June came to an end after three bloody weeks of attritional battles, with the Germans – desperately and successfully – still holding Caen, the pivot to success.

10 The Bridgehead in July

Whilst the terrible battles were continuing in Normandy, to take Caen and draw forces away from the American sector, the Prime Minister was keenly directing the war. He was investigating the Army's psychiatric services, and the latest RAF night photography techniques, and congratulating the many people involved in designing and developing the Mulberry, Phoenix and Whale artificial harbours. These were partly destroyed in the great storms at the end of June, but were soon in action again. In July he was checking up on the slow process of jet-propelled RAF planes, requiring regular progress reports. The Navy was pressed to develop anti-U-boat lightweight nets 'which enwrapped the U-boat and towed a buoy on the surface'. The arrival of V-weapons and flying bombs over London and the south-eastern coast prompted many defensive decisions. 'Why is it that such a small weight in German robot bombs creates results which seem 8 to 10 times greater than equal quantities dropped on German cities by the RAF?' he asked. It was to be another two months before the launching sites for Hitler's terror weapons were to be captured.

Although the Crab Flails and Crocodiles were kept busy, there was not a great demand for AVREs during July and August. General Hobart, knowing that an eventual breakdown would require assaults on defended *water* obstacles on the way to the River Seine, organised water training near Blainville on the Orne Canal. The 26th, 77th and 79th Assault Squadrons remained until September, becoming proficient in close-support rafting, with a short introduction to the Class 50/60 raft (capable of taking a 50–60 ton load).

General Hobart had now established a system with General Montgomery whereby an adviser from the 79th Armoured Division was appointed for all major operations where the use of specialized armour would be of importance. Initially the two Brigadiers, Duncan and Watkinson put their divisional point of view at Corps

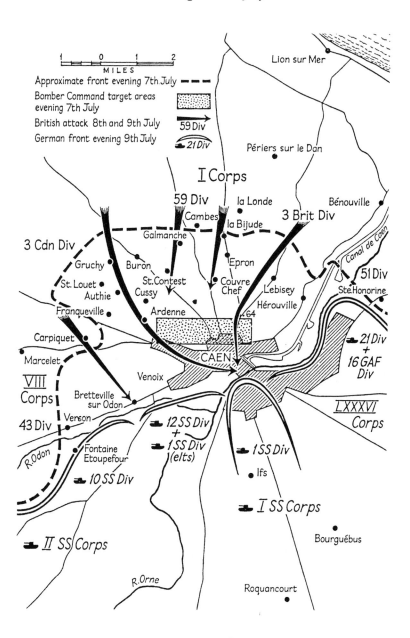

Fig. 5 Capture of Caen

level and once requirements were finalized, the allocation of 'Funnies' was made by the 79th Armoured Division HQ. Advisers or liaison officers were then responsible for planning joint operations at regimental or battalion level and then making sure that the 'Funnies' were duly returned to their base when the mission was accomplished. This was not always easy, as once a working relationship of AVREs, Crocodiles or flails was made at the 'sharp end', the hard-pressed infantry divisions preferred their new 'big friends' to stay with them.

The 22nd Dragoons were still based on Cresserons. For the attack to capture the village and airfield of Carpiquet, by the 3rd Canadian Division, fifteen flails of 'A' Squadron were allotted and assembled with Crocodiles and 80th Assault Squadron AVREs.

'Operation Ottawa' started on 4 July from Bretteville l'Orgueilleuse under the usual immense artillery barrage. The village was quickly taken but 12th SS Panzer Division tanks around the shattered aerodrome hangers held up the 27th Canadian Armoured Regiment. The 3rd Troop of 'A' Squadron flailed through a minefield, losing two tanks. Lieutenant Colonel Herbert Waddell, the commander of 141 RAC, came up to watch, and possibly to supervise his 'B' Squadron, the 'Playboys', as they carried out an amazing support action for the 7th Canadian Infantry Brigade. Captain Harry Bailey wrote:

> Carpiquet could only have been pulled off unscathed by the superb and uncanny luck of the Playboys – any other Sqn would probably have bought the issue, hook, line and sinker. Carpiquet cost the Canadian infantry, God knows what … All day long from 'dawn to dewy eve' the Sqn pranced around, hunting the horrid Hun in flat open country without the slightest vestige of cover, ground which presented to the Germans probably their best field of fire in Normandy (on the large airfield), and ended up completely unsupported mixing it with fanatical SS guys crawling all over them.

The 6th and 9th Troops were on the right, the 7th and 10th on the left. 'There is a ridge running NW from St Mauvieu, the perfect "school solution" for the hull-down [fire]. But the infantry wanted the Crocs closer. So in the bright sunshine, naked as new born babes, over the top they came. Fanned out in the flat cornfields and waited tensely – a rendezvous with death.' Nigel Ryle's 10th Troop got bogged and ditched over the railway. Peter Sander took his Troop to flame a bunker and then a hangar 500 yards to the south-west. Lieutenant

Beck led the 7th Troop towards and then into a quarry, flamed every-one in sight, got his Churchill stuck, caught fire and had to be rescued by Sergeant Brandi while Sergeant Maddock gave covering fire. Then Nigel Ryle suddenly discovered 'he was sitting in the middle of a well camouflaged [German SS] company position untouched by the advance. Literally dozens of Germans sprung out of concealment in the long grass. They stalked his tank, climbed on his tank, did every-thing except knock it out.' Everybody joined in the fight: Canadian Shermans and the CO's tank. The 6th Troop were sent over at the gallop. Besa fire accounted for twenty-five enemy and many more were flamed down. 'Very soon the party was well under control – later were found charred discarded equipment, burned bodies, bodies killed by Besa and HE and one that just died of fright.'

General Montgomery's next grand slam attack was 'Operation Charnwood' to assault Colonel Kurt Meyer's 12th SS Panzer on the outskirts of Caen. The day after the saturation RAF bombing of Caen, I Corps won through to the northern bank of the River Orne, which passes through the centre of the devastated city, in two days of desperate fighting. Once again Hobart's flails and Crocodiles were in demand. The 22nd Dragoons' 'C' Squadron supported Staffordshire Yeomanry tanks under the command of 185 Infantry Brigade (3rd British Division), two troops supported the East Riding Yeomanry under the command of 197 Infantry Brigade (59th Pithead Division), and a further two troops supported 13/18 Hussars under the command of 176 Infantry Brigade (59th Pithead Division). 'A' Squadron complete was allotted to the 9th Canadian Infantry Brigade in support of the 27th Canadian Armoured Regiment. During 'Charnwood' the Dragoons lost two Crabs with five casualties.

The Playboys' luck now ran out. They were detailed for 'Charnwood', but after Carpiquet they could only muster four troops to be parcelled out, as with the 22nd Dragoons, over two brigades of the 59th Division, a brigade of the 3rd Division and the 7th Canadian Brigade. It was an impossible situation, split up over four brigades on three divisional fronts. Captain John 'Nippy Chips' Dean and Lieutenant Rowland Beechey were both killed in action near Cambes on 8 July. The 8th Troop was in support of the South Staffordshires' and 13/18 Hussars' Shermans.

Harry Bailey describes the action:

The crack of the mortar teams, the chatter-chatter of the machine guns. The angry bang of the Shermans and the lovely brew up when they hit their mark. The battle was on and the bell was already tolling ... Jerry had Cambes absolutely taped and gave it everything he had. The South Staffs forming up took a colossal packet. There is a graveyard there now. And later as they buried those long, long rows of dead one of their comrades said, 'This isn't war – it's just sheer mass murder.'

Corporal Hischier's Crocodile was hit by a bazooka, then by a 75 mm shell which killed both driver and co-driver, and badly burned the three turret crew. Lieutenant Beechey's tank put out smoke to protect his corporal and a 75 mm shell hit his gearbox, setting his Churchill on fire. He evacuated the crew under fire, watched the flames go out, and climbed back in. The steering was gone and it was stuck in second gear so he moved in wide circles giving 75 mm and Besa support. Sydney Spearpoint brought up the 9th Troop to the same orchard to help and Peter Sander charged over the railway and 'went to town' with magnificent flaming. 'In this weird setting of dusk and burning flame the infantry came on, went in, passed through, surged on.' Now tragically, after the action was over, both officers on foot touched off 'S' mines and were killed. Both were later mentioned in despatches.

AVRE and flail support 3rd British Division attack on Hottot,
10 July 1944 (Birkin Haward)

At the same time 'A' Squadron was helping the Glasgow Highlanders (the 1st Highland Light Infantry) do battle at Gavrus, Evrecy and the peacefully named Le Bon Repos. Major A.J. Lewis, a company commander in the 4th Welsh Regiment, was ordered on 21 July to retake the notorious Le Bon Repos crossroads.

> The Crocs arrive and fire large squirts of flame at one of my platoons. The Germans and my own troops run away from those hellish flames. The Crocs then turn their attention to a house on the corner where some twenty Germans letting out agonising screams are sizzled to death. My lads appear to have dodged the flames, but God knows how. Our infantry continues to knock hell out of the enemy and they are soon on the run.

All went well but on the way back to harbour in Mouen, Captain Storrar's tank, in pitch darkness with a dense smoke screen, disappeared into a huge bomb crater. The indispensable ARV eventually hauled it out. Nicknamed 'the Seeker', the ARV was manned by Sergeants 'Rachmaninoff' Collins and Strong, and Troopers 'Taffy' Jenkins, 'General' Lee and 'Tom' Long. Their rest at Mouen was disturbed by enemy shelling, wounding Lieutenant Playford, Squadron Quartermaster Sergeant 'Bubbles' Wood and three troopers. Le Bon Repos was, like Hottot and Hill 112, taken and retaken, lost and won a dozen times. The 53rd Welsh Division had now just lost it and in half an hour 'A' Squadron Crocodiles recaptured it. General 'Bobby' Ross, the General Officer Commanding sent a message: 'The assistance of the Crocodiles was invaluable.' And after 'B' Squadron had helped the 51st Highland Division troops in clearing the notorious 'Triangle' south-east of Escoville, the I Corps Commander, General Crocker sent his personal thanks. Sergeant Pipkin's tank hit two Teller mines and was then brewed up by a bazooka. The crew of five were killed outright and of three of them no trace was ever seen again.

Captain Alastair Borthwick of the 5th Seaforths took part in an attack on the 'Triangle' south-east of Escoville.

> Crocs which were Churchill tanks with flame throwers were beyond doubt among the more hellish contrivances of war. I watched them operating on 'D' Coy's copse. The Spandaus were blazing away cheerfully enough and then one of these horrors came waddling up. It gave them a burst of MG fire and then quietly breathed on them. It was all very methodical and business like, just a thin jet of flame

which fanned out as it shot along, low to the ground, until it arrived on the target as a great blazing cloud. Bushes caught fire everywhere. There was a pause. Again the jet of flame, the spread, the billowing cloud. The Spandaus stopped. Men ran out burning.

But two Crocodiles were knocked out by 858th Panzer Grenadier Regiment.

The rest of the Westminster Dragoons arrived in Normandy on 14 July. With each squadron at full establishment of four flail troops and one roller troop, all was set fair for the next operation. But it was not to be. The establishment of a flail regiment was suddenly reduced to three flail troops per squadron.

'Operation Goodwood' was an all-armoured attack by VIII Corps on 17 and 18 July, south-east of Caen, to seize the high ground around Bourgebus, fanning out perhaps to Falaise. Despite a well co-ordinated attack after massive RAF and USAF saturation bombing, Rommel's concentric lines of defences in hamlets such as Cagny, Four, Solliers and Bras not only held out, but gave the 11th Armoured Division Shermans a terrible time. The 22nd Dragoon flails were in support and 'A' Squadron had a sharp action clearing the burning village of Le Mesnil Frementel losing a flail with all its crew killed or wounded. The CO, Lieutenant Colonel Grosvenor and Adjutant Captain Wien were wounded by shellfire from Cagny and Major Plowden, the second in command, took command.

The 1st Lothians and Border Yeomanry sailed from Gosport in LSTs piped on board by Pipe Major Mackay. On 15 July, safely assembled at Crepon, they were briefed for their first actions by Brigadier Duncan. Andrew Gardiner described the scene: 'The daylight had brought with it an amazing sight. The countryside seemed to sprout troops and vehicles, a military ant-heap warming and stirring in the early morning summer prior to moving off.' Their flails were soon in action around Esquay and Evrecy. On the way Trooper Gardiner's Sherman halted opposite a tank graveyard.

> There were rows and rows of burnt-out or 'brewed-up' Shermans with their turrets and guns at crazy angles or tracks missing, many with neat holes in the side where the solid shot from an 88 or 75 mm had penetrated with a bulge directly opposite where the same shot had failed to emerge. Apart from the skeletons of the gun breeches, the turrets were empty shells, the floors were carpeted in small pieces of broken metal: an amalgam of what had been wireless sets, periscopes, headsets, ammunition ... a sobering experience.

Sherman flail tank (Crab) crosses River Orne during 'Operation Goodwood'

'C' Squadron had a heavy first day and a sad one, with tank losses and casualties; but on 17 July they cleared a lane 2,000 yards long and 32 feet wide between Baron and Les Villains, under fire, with the loss of three tanks. The two troops involved covered each other with fire and smoke. Lieutenant W.J. Boreham of 'B' Squadron crossed the Orne–Carne canal to support the 3rd British Division around Escoville. He gives an excellent account of their day-long battle on 18 July.

> Our troops' task was to flail if required and watch the east flank about a mile from the enemy held villages of Touffreville, Sannerville and Bannerville-la Campagne. We were also to reduce the defences of Lirose. We brassed this area while a Stafford troop moved in. Then I knocked out a 75 mm A/Tk gun in a belt of wire east of the building. Two other guns which opened up were silenced by the Tp. Corp Dunbar hit a house suspected as being an OP [observation post]. To his surprise there was a terrific explosion as an ammunition dump was hit. One of my tanks was then knocked out at close range by a German PIAT and the crew baled out. Sgt Currie then shot up a house where there were two machine guns. Then I picked up the

baled-out crew, two were wounded. The remainder of the Tp were shooting in the infantry with both HE and small arms fire. In a short time all resistance ceased. We then rallied to Manneville.

Boreham then went on a reconnaissance and 'found a German officer and six Luftwaffe ORs whom I brought back'. At 8.30 p.m. his Troop was in action again. 'We fired super quick into the treetops giving an airburst effect. We put 100 shells and much Browning in and the Warwicks and Norfolks got in with little trouble, the enemy coming out with their hands up.' Out of shells, the Troop went back to laager at 11 p.m. 'By 0330 hrs we had replenished, and had one hour's sleep before we got up at 0430 hrs.'

'Operation Goodwood', 18 July 1944. Sherman tanks, Red Cross half-track in background. Crab flail in foreground

July ended with a bang for the Buffs. On the night of 26 July the Luftwaffe dropped sixty bombs onto an area 100 yards square, an orchard in which 'B' Squadron, the 'Playboys' were harbouring. Their echelon bore the brunt of the attack. Major Spearpoint and Sergeants Douse and Rowe were badly wounded. Captain Ryle then took command of 'B' Squadron.

The 82nd Assault Squadron RE had a typical AVRE month with

three actions – firing petards at houses and dug-in enemy positions at Grainville supporting the 50th Division. On 10–12 July there was another 'do' at Hottot and later on at Le Bon Repos, supporting the 43rd Wessex Wyverns.

The success of the 'Funnies' in Normandy had been relayed back to the Prime Minister. With tank and other supplies of AFVs building up in the bridgehead, he was anxious that General Alexander's forces in Italy should get help. 'He should receive a reasonable proportion of the latest type of equipment such as 17 pdr Shermans, heavy Churchill tanks, flame-throwers, special assault vehicles [AVREs] and sabbot ammunition.' The old warhorse had also been demanding a front-line visit, and on 21 July he visited the beachhead and 'watched LCTs disgorging tanks and DUKWs on the beaches swimming through the harbour, waddling ashore and then humping up the hill to the great dump'.

11 The Bridgehead in August – Breakout

The Americans had taken Cherbourg and General Patton's armour soon drove vigorously into Brittany. Meanwhile V-1 rockets continued to rain on London and south-east England, despite the RAF and AA's best efforts. General Montgomery's attritional battles to hold the bulk of the German forces, particularly their armour, around Caen were bloody but tactically successful. The Prime Minister wrote to him on 27 July.

> SHAEF [Supreme Headquarters Allied Expeditionary Force] announced last night that the British had sustained 'quite a serious setback'. ... Naturally this has created a good deal of talk here. For *my own most secret information*, I should like to know whether the attacks you spoke of to me, or variants of them are going to come off. It certainly seems very important for the British Army to strike hard and win through. ... As you know I have the fullest confidence in you and you may count on me.

The Canadian Corps had been forced back 1,000 yards from their furthest position gained and SHAEF had translated that into 'quite a serious setback by the British.' The Prime Minister visited Montgomery's HQ on 7 August.

Montgomery now unleashed two more major attacks southwards to produce unbearable pressure on the German escape route from Normandy. 'Operation Bluecoat' by British VIII Corps started on 31st July from Caumont towards the vital Mont Pincon and Vire, and a week later II Canadian Corps, in 'Operation Totalise', rolled towards Falaise. Hobart's 'Funnies' were involved in both these major assaults.

The balance of the 6th Assault Regiment RE, 87th and 284th

Squadrons, arrived together with the HQ 1st Assault Brigade RE and HQ 149th Assault Park Squadron. Brigade HQ was set up in St Gabriel, near Creully. Trooper John Smith of 'C' Squadron 141 RAC recalls:

> The main attraction [in Creully] was the Hotel St Martin which stood at one side of the square. A petrol pump riddled with bullet holes stood outside. The calvados there was the best I ever drank in Normandy. The farmhouses sold a terribly raw spirit but at the hotel the landlord said his stock was ten years old which I presume made it good. There was also Denise, the prettiest girl I ever saw in Normandy.

Trooper 'Smudger' Smith spent ten days on a flame course, a practical with a written test, and a refresher course on the wireless No. 19 set (a standards tank-radio) and morse. 'C' Squadron had flamed an MG position at St Germain d'Ecot which had held up several infantry attacks. Lieutenant Andrew Wilson's Churchill MK VIII tank, a replacement, followed the armoured drive in 'Bluecoat' through Villers-Bocage. 'There were no buildings and no streets – just a bulldozed canyon through a pile of rubble which stretched for half a mile, and over it all the bitter taste of dust and charred wood. Auray was the same, with sappers working their bulldozer with shaded headlamps.' Wilson found himself later at a crossroads two miles ahead of their infantry. Eventually he found 'C' Squadron at the foot of Mont Pincon.

> During 'Bluecoat' the Buffs flamethrowers motored behind the infantry for two or three miles. Then a wait for the engineers to put up a Bailey bridge or cleared some mines. Mostly they kept off roads and struck across country. Sometimes they'd come to a sleepy looking village and the enemy would open up with Spandaus. There'd be a little fight and the infantry would go in, take the village under cover of the tanks machine guns.

If the flame-throwers had a quiet time, the Crabs of the 22nd Dragoons met trouble on the way to Villers-Bocage, as Major Birt recounts.

> The roads and road verges were everywhere sown with anti-tank and anti-personnel mines. Deserted houses were death traps. Every road

crossing was the target for constant shell and mortar fire. The flails were at once brought up to the heads of the columns to sweep the roads clear. So thick were the mines and so long the beat upon the hard road surfaces that inevitably the chains began to go and tanks sooner or later foundered before they were through to their objectives. On the left, tanks commanded by Captain Gebbie, Lt Thwaites and Sgt Mackay were all blown up and some casualties were caused by shellfire. In the second column Sgt Swann and Sgt Johnson managed to get through to the first lateral of their advance before they too were wrecked by mines.

At nightfall the flail casualties had to be abandoned. Later they were found to have been efficiently looted by the Germans but not destroyed. The next day, 4 August, Lieutenant Martin Leake led the 3rd Troop down the main road into the flattened village of Villers-Bocage. There were mines everywhere, and two flails were quickly lost. So Leake dismounted his men and with other sappers cleared the road by hand. The deserted streets of Villers-Bocage were littered with abandoned German guns, tanks and half-tracks pounded by RAF bombardment. Also there were the Cromwells of the Desert Rats, who had been badly ambushed on 13 June. The dismounted Dragoons and sappers slowly cleared the roads through the village. An explosion burned Leake on hands and face, but he led his Troop through, eastwards, and took the high ground at Epinay-sur-Odon. He deserved his MC.

The Dragoon Squadron started with twenty-one tanks. At the end of the two-day action only nine were going, and only three could flail. The Westminster Dragoons joined the 7th Armoured Division at Torteval, then moved into shattered Caumont and Maisoncelles Pelvey. Lieutenant Richard Bullock flailed for the Desert Rats at Le Bauquet. During an attack by 'C' Squadron on Launay Ridge and St Germain d'Ecot Lieutenant Mackichan's Crab went up a track to engage a Spandau MG which was holding up a Tyne-Tees battalion. After 50 yards it struck a mine. He reversed and struck another mine. The enemy were 25 yards ahead, and his 'little friends' were 25 yards behind. Stuck in 'no mans land' for five and a half hours, he and his crew used their 75 mm gun and Besa before the enemy gave up and retreated.

'B' Squadron supported the 43rd Wessex Wyverns and 13/18 Hussars in their determined two-day battle on 5–7 August, which culminated in the scaling and capture of the 1,200-foot escarpment

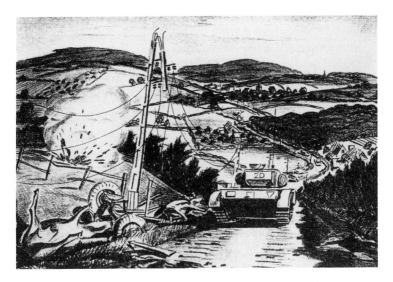

'Operation Bluecoat'; 'Funnies' support 43 Wessex Division south from Caumont in bocage country, 31 July 1944 (Birkin Haward)

of Mont Pincon. It was a crucial victory; from the top General Horrocks could deploy 350 guns to harass the enemy fleeing into the Falaise–Argentan corridor.

The Lothians and Border Yeomanry flailed mines in front of the 15th Scottish Division at Les Sept Vents, a village recently occupied by a German engineer unit which had left a maze of mines, shells and booby traps behind them. Lieutenant Carter led his troop of Crabs and exploded eight mines in 35 yards before being blown up. Sergeant Rawlinson then led and exploded two inter-connected mines, but the third knocked out his tank.

There were a great number of desperate actions during 'Bluecoat' and the 11th Armoured Division made deep inroads into the enemy defences around Vire.

'Operation Totalise' was a Canadian operation, launched towards Falaise. Lieutenant General Guy Simmonds of II Canadian Corps, with his speciality, seventy-six converted Priest SPs (prototype Kangaroos) to carry infantry, made a determined night attack at midnight on 7 August to seize the high ground around Bretteville-sur-Laize and Cramesnil. Four parallel armoured/infantry columns would race through the night towards Falaise, 18 miles due south, guided by Bofors guns firing tracer. The RAF bombarded the enemy lines ahead but 500 USAF Fortresses bombed wildly and caused 300 casualties – Canadians, British and Poles. Tilly-la-Campagne was superbly defended and held out, but on each side of the village a 6-mile gain was made. The 51st Highland Division was under Canadian command and supported by 22nd Dragoon flails and the 80th Assault Squadron RE.

Lieutenant Ian Hammerton of the 22nd Dragoons recalls: 'Tanks are almost blind at night and the enemy line was held by the Hitler Youth Division – all fanatical young fighters – in prepared positions. ... All we had to do was to follow our very brave navigating officer in a Honey tank, followed by a troop of AVREs.' A flail troop would follow them and then would come a long string of Churchill's with the Kangaroo infantry bringing up the rear. Major Birt wrote:

> In spite of the artificial moonlight, the night was still, an almost impenetrable barrier to the vision of drivers and commanders. They had no roads to guide them and the going was very broken. Shortly the tanks were tumbling into bomb craters and lurching against hidden obstacles. Worse, they ran into dense clouds of dust and smoke created by our air bombardment and the barrage. The columns crawled forward into the night in slow, convulsive jerks as of a wounded snake dragging itself painfully into cover.

Major Clifford's group of 'A' and 'B' Squadron flails supported the Northants Yeomanry on the left and Major Shuter with 'C' Squadron and Regimental Headquarters (RHQ) linked up with 144 RAC on the right flank. From Hubert-Folie the dense columns set off at 9.30 a.m. and for a time the intricately planned battle went well. The immediate objectives 2 miles south of the start line were reached by 3.15 and 5.40 in the morning. Three tanks then fell on top of each other in one bomb crater. A 3-foot high railway embankment north of Lorguichon foiled many others. By dawn the screen of German 88 mm guns were taking their toll, particularly of 144 RAC. The 22nd Dragoons rallied back to Bras with fourteen seriously damaged Crabs and two more destroyed. The Polish Armoured Division, in its first battle, passed through, and the depleted 22nd Dragoons supported them in the second phase, 'A' with the 2nd Polish Armoured and 'B' with the 1st Polish Armoured Regiments with 'C' in reserve with the 24th Polish

AVRE tank with menacing Spigot mortar bombard near Ondefontaine,
'Operation Bluecoat'

Lancers. Communication was difficult and interpreters were essential! The Polish Shermans were terribly mauled by the 88 mm anti-tank screen, but the struggle went on until 10 August when 'Totalise' was called off.

Sergeant L.A. Wells, an AVRE tank crew of 2 Fox took part by marking a clear path by tapes and minefield lamps. 'The troop was parked by a field in which cut grass intended for hay was lying. I took our mine detector from the AVRE and lifted 27 mines from the immediate vicinity. No. 3 troop arrived making their way across country. Bill Atkinson was in the lead who had to lift about 20 mines before he could extricate himself [from the minefield].' 'B' Squadron of the Buffs, under the eagle eye of their Scottish CO, Lieutenant Colonel Waddell, helped flame the Gordon Highlanders into Secqueville-la-Campagne at 4.30 p.m. on 8 August. The Playboys had just had their echelon bombed by Fortresses, causing several casualties. Sergeant Little earned the MM by driving away a burning fuel truck whilst Lance Corporal Knight got up behind and fought the fire out. George Storrar led the 10th Troop and Harry Barrow the 8th, flaming and laying about them to good effect. An isolated wood was shot up by the Shermans of 148 RAC, by the

Crocodiles and by *German* mortars. Harry Bailey wrote: 'Appalling carnage resulted. At the end of the day the wood was piled high with German dead.'

On the right flank of 'Operation Totalise' the 2nd Canadian Division was backed by Lothians and Border flails and AVREs of the 79th Assault Squadron RE plus a troop of the 80th Squadron. The latter were given the task of marking lanes with white tracing tape and lights for the gun tanks to follow. 'A' Squadron of the Buffs most unusually fought as a squadron, helping the battered Fusiliers Mount Royal Regiment into May-sur-Orne. Captain Storrar wrote:

> The dream of a whole squadron being used together materialised. No. 1 Tp led by Lt Griggs on the right of the main road running south and Nos. 3 and 4 Tps on the left – with nine 'flamers' up, the command Tanks providing smoke on the flanks. Everyone went in firing 75 mm and Besa at the village and as soon as flame range was reached, the target was enveloped in fire. The [Canadian] infantry came in behind the tanks very quickly and suffered no casualties – the attack was a huge success, over a hundred PoW being captured as well as the village.

The BBC reporter Howard Marshall watched the action, which was described on the nine o'clock news. Major Cooper was personally complimented and thanked by Major General Foulkes, the commander of the 2nd Canadian Division.

The Lothians deployed their flails with the four columns of armour attacking the fortress area of Fontenay-le-Marmion and Rocquancourt and the old aerodrome north-east of Cintheaux. In support of the 27th Canadian Armoured Regiment and the 8th Canadian Reconnaissance Regiment, were Major Watson, commanding the flank guard to the east, then Major Vigers, Major Pocock and Captain Henman. Very little mine flailing was needed but stalwart work as gun tanks was done by Lieutenants Burns and McDowall and Sergeants Wilson and Miller, who silenced a wide variety of enemy anti-tank guns.

For the next four days the Canadians and Poles kept up their pressure down the Falaise road. For the flail regiments in reserve, the heat, mosquitoes and horseflies were extremely unpleasant. Captain Westwell of 'A' Squadron the Buffs was so badly poisoned by mosquito bites that he had to leave the squadron.

Whilst 'Totalise' was coming to a close, the AVRE squadrons 81, 82 and 284 of the 6th Assault Regiment RE were concentrated near Courseulles-sur-Mer to prepare for rafting and bridging over rivers when the final breakout from Normandy came.

In the meantime, 'Operation Tallulah', part of 'Operation Tractable', was being prepared. It was the next major Canadian attack towards Falaise, and started on 14 August. The 2nd Canadian Corps was to attack on a two-division front: on the right the 3rd Canadian Infantry Division, on the left the 2nd Canadian Infantry Division. The main objective was Falaise but the German defences along the little River Laison were formidable. After an intense aerial bombardment (during which Canadian bombers of the RAF by mistake bombed their own troops causing 300 casualties), then a huge artillery barrage, the armoured attack started at midday, under cover of wide smoke screens. AVREs of the 80th Assault Squadron RE were loaded with fascines to be dropped in the river. The 26th Assault Squadron was in action, with the 77th Assault Squadron at Chenedollé and Veisseoix (predictably called 'Old Socks'), and both the flail regiments were needed, mainly in their gun-tank role.

The Lothians' 'C' Squadron was supporting the South Alberta Regiment but since the only bridge over the River Laison was covered by 88 mm guns they moved east. Andrew Gardiner described the scene. 'In an accompanying cloud of dust the mass of tanks moved off and the charge began. Not Hussars in gorgeous uniforms with flashing sabres and lunging neighing horses responding to a trumpet call, but their successors in dirty grey steel boxes on squealing tracks advancing on a radio signal and the wave of a hand.' Three guns, which had been lying undetected, knocked out three Lothian tanks, killing Sergeant Stiles and Troopers Jones and Purnell. Trooper George Wilkinson's tank was brewed and his Troop Leader, Lieutenant A.H. Rolland badly wounded. They were both captured; before interrogation Wilkinson ate his Crab maintenance book, along with an apple. Ten days later Wilkinson escaped and by devious routes rejoined the Lothians.

But 'A' Squadron on the right enjoyed a mad helter-skelter gallop of 4 miles to Rouvres, *en route* shooting up one 88 ton gun and two mortars, and taking about thirty prisoners. 'B' Squadron guarded the South Albertas successfully. Two of the leading Canadian tanks were knocked out, whereupon the Lothian officers opened up on likely gun positions with HE and claimed an 88 mm gun.

The 22nd Dragoons moved up to Estrée-la-Campagne in support

of the Fort Garry Horse and the 1st Canadian Hussars. 'B' Squadron stayed in reserve at Point 112, where they and the Polish echelons were bombed five times by RAF Lancasters. The approaches to the River Laison, in a steep valley, were patchy, with marsh and bogs, and there were urgent requests for 'scissors' bridges – double steel bridges carried on top of AVREs which, when unfolded, spanned a double length. But the Canadian objectives, the high ground west of Epancy only 4 miles from Falaise were duly reached. On 15 August the 22nd Dragoons were out of the battle, resting for ten days in harbour back near Louvigny and Fleury, where the greatest dangers were thousands of mosquitoes and dysentery from the polluted waters of the River Orne. Lieutenant Colonel W.A.C. Anderson took over command from Major Plowden, and almost his first order was to reduce to three troops, each of five flails, per squadron. Major General Hobart and Brigadier Duncan visited them. 'Hobo was his usual confident self and more than generous in his praise of our progress,' wrote Major Birt.

The Crocodiles of the Buffs had mixed fortunes during 'Tallulah'. 'B' Squadron supported the Regiment de la Chaudière to help clear Rouvres and its chateau, and this went to plan. But 'A' Squadron, supporting the 9th Canadian Brigade had a difficult day. Two hours after zero hour (midday) Lieutenant Brereton took his 4th Troop forward to flame some houses which were holding up the Canadians. A hidden 88 mm anti-tank gun hit the turrets of the troop five times: Lieutenant Brereton twice, Sergeant Roskilly twice and Corporal Fox once. All the turrets and guns were out of action but no shot penetrated; five men were mildly wounded and the troop withdrew! Later on Tiger tanks and 77 mm guns brewed up Lieutenant McCulloch's tank, killing Troopers Sheppard, Ashton and Froste. McCulloch and Trooper Shreeves were badly wounded and burned. Later on Corporal Harris's tank was knocked out; by 9 p.m. the Squadron withdrew back to harbour to be greeted by the news that the RAF had bombed the Squadron's transport, killing three, wounding four and destroying twelve vehicles. The Squadron moved via Cormelles to Le Marcelet and spent five glorious days resting by the sea at Lion-sur-Mer as guests of their Canadian allies.

'C' Squadron, after helping in the capture of Mount Pincon, helped clear Noron, capturing a company of Russian conscripts, and found themselves on the northern edge of the notorious 'Falaise Gap', which was remembered by Lieutenant Andrew Wilson as 'the village street turned into a narrow sunken road full of dead Germans, part of a column the Sqn had been pursuing, caught, jammed tight in a 25 pdr concentration'.

> Men and horses were mangled and crushed in the wreckage of guns and vehicles; some lay bloodily spread-eagled where the stampeding column had run over them. Beyond the shambles continued, the wood blocked with the burning wreckage of motor transport. All around the Falaise pocket the same scenes were being repeated. Bridges and narrow roads were straddled with bombs and artillery fire. Dead and dying Germans formed dams where they fell in the blood-tinted rivers. No one doubted that it was the end of the war in the West.

Major Duffy, who was in charge of 'C' Squadron, was persuaded to add a yellow Wehrmacht bus, an Opel and a Volkswagen to the temporary vehicle strength. Then Sergeant Pye and his fitters appeared, roaring with triumph, sitting on a Panther tank!

The 1st Tank Brigade, consisting of three battalions of CDL tanks, landed in Normandy on 8 August. The 11th RTR harboured up at Tilly-sur-Seulles, where further tactical training in CDL was carried out in daylight. Then they went to Meuvaines and Montilly and there the 11th, 42nd and 49th RTR stayed peacefully and sadly ignored by the Army generals. However, it was noted that new amphibious vehicles were becoming available to the Division. DUKWs, Terrapin and Buffaloes were the code names being bandied around.

It was ironical that 'Operation Totalise', a massive night attack of armour and infantry did not include the 1st Tank Brigade's CDLs, which undoubtedly would have played a very helpful role in causing confusion to the defenders.

On 17 August the third RE assault Regiment, the 42nd, arrived in Normandy with 16, 222 and 617 Assault Squadrons. They concentrated at Herouvilette on the east bank of the River Orne for training in rafting with the Class 50/60 rafts. Roland Ward was second in command of 617 Assault Squadron RE. 'The regiment embarked at Lee-on-Solent on 16 August and landed the next day near Arromanches – dry shod. It comprised HQ, Lt Col J.F.D. Savage the CO, 2 i/c Major R.W. Ewbank; 16 Assault Sqn under Major J.C. Woollett; 222 Assault Sqn under Major T. Woolfender and 617

Assault Sqn under Major J.O.M. Alexander.' Sapper Bill Woods recalls:

> We moved inland three miles and bivouaced in a field of smashed gliders. I inspected a burnt out German light tank, that to my horror still contained the charred remains of the driver and clouds of flies. The British dead had been buried where they fell. One, a Royal Scot, had a hand made cross inscribed 'in loving memory' ... We went to the Caen canal for rafting training, for the river Seine.

Major J.C. Woollett of the 16th Squadron said: 'We moved to Ste Honorine-la-Chardonnette. I overheard one sapper observing two little local boys chatting to each other say, "Cor, the kids are clever in this country, fancy being able to talk French at their age!" '

12 The Chase and the Recapture of the Channel Ports

All the allied armies (British, American, Canadian and Polish), with their air forces, created a stunning and terrible victory in the Falaise–Argentan corridor. Nevertheless, the Germans fought brilliant little rearguard actions all the way to the Seine, defending every river barrier with skill, tenacity and bravery.

There were few minefields and the Crabs of the three flail regiments were not needed, nor indeed were the Buffs required to flame. Their support was given to the 7th Armoured Division and the 51st Highland Division as they fought their way up to the barrier of the River Seine. Nor were the Class 50/60 rafts which had recently arrived in the theatre of war needed to help the 43rd Wessex Wyverns force a substantial bridgehead over the Seine at Vernon.

Captain Harry Bailey of 'B' Squadron, the Buffs, wrote:

> The advance along the whole front was now proceeding at a pace which made it impossible for the Crocs to keep up and be put into operation against any strongpoint before it was quickly reduced by normal arms alone. Eastwards and ever East, past the roadside havoc that had been a German Army. The dead horses by the road, the long lines packed tight with overturned and burnt out trucks, guns and tanks, the river valleys choc full of the German impediment of war.

At Bourg Achard near the Seine, 'B' Squadron 'liberally endowed itself with high powered German motor cars'. One old Chevrolet went on a trip to Brest and Brussels. 'A' Squadron had some short but sweet stays at Vimoutiers, Bernay and La Haye-Malherbe.

All the Buffs squadrons paid tribute to their commanding officer, Lieutenant Colonel Herbert Waddell, whose regiment never fought as a single unit. He joined every squadron action with a small TAC

HQ but never encroached on the squadron leaders' authority – a very rare gift.

The Westminster Dragoons supported 30 Corps in their advance via Gacé, Laigle and Rugles in perfect sunny weather, developing sunburn, blisters and cracked lips. On the way eggs, wine and fruits were showered on the troopers, cigarettes were given to pretty mesdemoiselles and chocolates and sweets to the children, and a few days were actually spent on training! With little else to do the local farmers were helped with transport and harvest parties. One embarrassing moment occurred as General Hobart was visiting the Dragoons. An elderly French farmer appeared and produced from a sack a huge goose followed by a shower of vegetables!

The Lothians also had an easy time, spending a week in the Louvigny area and ensuring that all their Crabs were roadworthy, before continuing to support the 51st Highland and 7th Armoured Divisions. Eventually 'A' Squadron, after driving about 25 miles a day for a week, crossed the River Seine at Elboeuf on 28 August.

The 22nd Dragoons also had ten days out of the line. All their tanks went to the 30th Armoured Brigade workshops for overhaul and engine replacement. At Fleury they bathed in the River Orne, inviting but polluted by the detritus of war, saw a film or two, and were visited by Brigadier Duncan and General Hobart, 'who was his usual confident self and more than generous in his praise of our progress', according to Major Birt.

Many units of the 79th Armoured Division now encountered the astonishing welcome given to their new liberators by the French population as Major Birt describes:

A triumphant progress among people whose whole being was seized with happiness and welcome. The flags were out and the bunting. We were waved through with greetings of flowers, salutes and kisses. At every stop the cars and tanks were swallowed up by a mass of people eager to shake us by the hand, to embrace us without qualification, to say over and over again, 'It was long coming.' 'Welcome.' The word greeted us in the shop windows, in banners strung across the roads and in the songs of carefree crowds who came out to see us pass. Gratitude showered about us in the shape of apples, pears, tomatoes, cucumbers and chickens. Biscuits and tins of bully were passed back in exchange. We soon heard the familiar chant of 'Chocolat? Bonbons? Cigarettes pour Papa?'

In Bolbec in particular the Dragoons had a delirious welcome. And the Benedictine liqueur made in the cathedral-like factory of the Fécamp monks was heady, smooth and delicious.

The armoured divisions raced through northern France and Belgium and into Holland. The 11th Armoured Division captured the city of Antwerp (but not all of the port), the 7th Armoured took Ghent and the fortunate Guards Armoured liberated Brussels, in a marvellous exhilarating series of 'cavalry' charges for mile after mile. The Americans cantered perhaps even faster into Brittany, Paris and far beyond. But the Channel ports, which were crucial for supplies of food, petrol, ammunition and mail were bypassed, and they were well defended.

The 79th Armoured Division was the ideal formation to breach them with all their 'Funny' elements – the AVREs with their bombards, bridges and fascines, deadly Crocodiles and brisk, plodding Crabs were now destined to make a vital contribution.

The garrison of Dieppe had surrendered and Dunkirk having little value as a port was simply ignored until their garrison surrendered at the end of the war. This left Le Havre, Boulogne and Calais to be attacked, and to everyone's surprise (as the Americans had previously declined the offers of Montgomery and Hobart to use their 'Funnies' in US operations), General Simpson also asked for a squadron of Crocodiles to help take the port of Brest.

Le Havre

'Operation Asconia', the capture of Le Havre, was the main responsibility of the 49th Polar Bear Division attacking from the south and south-west and the 51st Highland Division attacking simultaneously from the north and north-west. Colonel Eberhardt Wildermuth, the garrison commander with nearly 14,000 troops under his command, had rejected several ultimatums for surrender. His shore defences were more than adequate. The 11 miles of inland defences were interspersed with huge minefields (a million mines had been laid), barbed wire, the anti-tank ditches, which were 20 feet wide and 9 feet deep, and there were many substantial strongpoints which were impervious to RAF bombing.

Wildermuth had about 270 guns of various calibres and was quite confident that he could hold out for a considerable time. He also knew that the large resident French population presented the attacking forces with a moral and social problem: the Germans would fight mainly from their underground fortresses and the French civilians would suffer. So initially thousands of leaflets were dropped by aircraft or fired by gunners appealing to the German soldiers to surrender and for the French population to leave or take shelter. Front-line loud-speaker teams broadcast the same messages, but to little avail.

'Asconia' was to become a classic military operation. The Navy bombarded the shore defences. The RAF sent 900 Lancaster and Halifax bombers over and dropped 5,000 tons of bombs without loss in the air, nor on the ground to the 1 Corps assault teams.

Brigadier Duncan, with HQ 30th Armoured brigade, commanded the Crabs, Crocodiles and AVRE breaching teams. To support the Polar Bear assault were the 22nd Dragoon flails, 'A' Squadron of the Buffs' Crocodiles, and 222 and 617 Assault Squadrons RE. For 42 ARE this was the first engagement of the war, as they had just moved 160 miles up from the Caen canal in the previous week. Major Roland Ward, then second in command of 617 Assault Squadron RE has written an account of the Royal Engineers' role in 'Asconia'.

> The attack was to be in four stages – first the attack by the 56th Infantry Bde [Polar Bear Division] their objective being the Ardennes plateau which overlooks Le Havre from the north. On this front eight gaps were to be attempted but only the three middle ones were to cross the ditch which lay beyond the minefield. The second stage was to be a night attack further to the right by the 51st Highland Division. The third stage was an attack the following morning [11 September] through Harfleur by 146 Bde [Polar Bears]. The fourth stage would be penetration and exploitation into the heart of the city on the second and third days. The obstacles and defences at Le Havre were remarkably similar to those we had been practising on in Suffolk. A total of eleven gaps had to be made through the deep mine-fields, six of them to cross the wide A/Tank ditch.

Excellent overprinted maps and aerial photographs were provided. These had shown two places in the north-east near Montivilliers where the anti-tank ditch had not been completed. General Crocker, the Corps Commander decided to put the main attack on these gaps, which were both wide enough for a battalion to pass through. After a period of heavy rain D-Day – Sunday, 10 September – dawned fine and sunny. H-hour was 1815 hrs, after half an hour of saturation bombing and half an hour of a heavy Corps artillery programme.

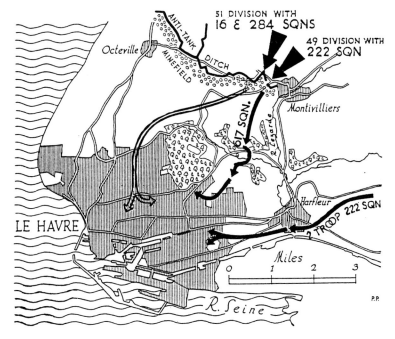

Fig. 6 Le Havre

The overweight Crabs had immense difficulty in getting up to the forming-up points, but Lieutenants Hammerton and Shaw sent their flails whirling to make the two-lane gap called Mary. No mines were encountered by Hammerton and within forty minutes the infantry were swarming through in carriers, rounding up many prisoners. Shaw's lane ran into trouble, however, with three tanks blown up or disabled. By 7 p.m. the 7th RTR, Crocodiles and infantry, had taken the key strongpoint beyond Mary. The central gap, Hazel, was abandoned as a failure after three flails were blown-up. So too were an AVRE with its long explosive Snake and the follow-up AVRE with a scissors bridge. On the right of the road, however, Lieutenant Thwaites, despite losing three flails, had cleared a lane, the AVRE bridge-layer dropped its precious cargo and the infantry went across in carriers. On the road itself an AVRE bridge-layer made a spectacular 'gallop' but was blown up yards short by Teller mines planted deep into the road. So 'B' Squadron had both gaps open, albeit with only two lanes cleared out of five.

'Operation Asconia', 'Polar Bear' attack on Le Havre. Flails and scissor-bridge supporting 'Funnies' in background

On the 146 Brigade front 'A' Squadron also tackled three lanes in the Laura gap, supported by the 7th RTR. Only one Dragoon Crab reached the start line: despite smoke an 88 mm anti-tank gun destroyed two, mines claimed two more but the one survivor had 'flogged' a 16-foot lane by 6.45 – a magnificent achievement. In the other two lanes Lieutenant Mundy lost two flails to mines but had cleared a 30-foot lane by 7 p.m. Sergeant Smyth's troop lost three flails to mines and AP but he had cleared a wide lane for follow-up troops by 7.30.

Of the total force of thirty-five flails and six Shermans engaged in the assault, twenty-nine flails and three Shermans were lost or seriously damaged and sixteen men were killed or wounded. Major Renton and Captain Barraclough were awarded the MC.

Major E.N.H. Bryants of 'A' Squadron, the Buffs, deployed three troops to help the South Wales Borderers and two (under Captain Hall) to support the Gloucesters. Six Crocodiles were put out of action altogether without any casualties and Position No. 5 was literally soaked in flame with 100 prisoners being taken. Strongpoints 1 and 2 were soon taken, No. 3 was flamed and went up in smoke. No. 4 was missed by the Crocodile but later captured and the Buffs then wiped out Nos. 9 and 10. General Hobart visited

'A' Sqn the next day at their harbour north of Montivilliers.

Two troops of 222 Assault Squadron RE under Captains MacDonald and Hamilton followed the 22nd Dragoons flails on lanes Hazel Red, Green and White. Sapper Monty Clay was the mortarman with Captain Hamilton's AVRE.

> We formed up to assault three lanes in the middle of a big minefield with one AVRE pushing a 'snake' and one with a small box girder bridge, to bridge a large anti-tank ditch on the far side of the mine-field. We were acting as a GP AVRE [providing machine-gun support] and I was giving covering fire with my Besa for the infantry. The minefield was a steep incline with a plateau at the top which concealed a large German encampment.

Two mines blew off the left-hand track of the Churchill AVRE and the crew bailed out. Using German bayonets they prodded and lifted six Teller mines on their way to a disabled flail. 'We proceeded to brew up and we sat there with our teas, content with the world.'

A rather different task forced 617 Assault Squadron RE – that of passing through the lanes, once opened, and supporting the Polar Bear infantry attacks on the cluster of enemy strongpoints. Major Ward wrote:

> No. 1 Tp (Capt Wilson) supported 2 SWB [South Wales Borderers] on the right (Laura) directed on Strongpoint 5, No. 3 TP (Capt Warde) supported 2 Glosters on the left (Mary). Both these troops carried fascines and towed sledges with sleepers and bundles in case of unforeseen obstacles. The OC Major Alexander with the two HQ AVREs and No. 2 TP (Capt Wylam) was in reserve with 2 Essex to go through to the Ardennes plateau and eventually to cross the Fontaine river in the valley beyond. They carried an assault bridge, a fascine, armoured sledges, ARMCO culverting and also two armoured bulldozers from 149 Assault Park Sqn.

Only two AVREs, one Crocodile and two tanks of the 7th RTR got through the lane Mary Green to reduce Strongpoint No. 1, which was finally taken by the 2nd Gloucesters. Two fortified houses were petarded and a Crocodile finished them off. Lance Sergeant Finan received the MM for working with his three-man AVRE crew dismounted, clearing mines and road blocks under mortar and small-arms fire.

The 51st Highland Division's assault towards Fontaine-la-Mallet in the north and north-west was supported by the Lothians' flails, 'A' Squadron of the Buffs' Crocodiles and 16 and 284 Assault Squadrons RE. Their attack started at 1 a.m. to make three lanes about 50 yards apart during the night, with Bofors tracer fire, coloured lights and white tape to guide the teams. Bomb craters made direction-keeping difficult. An AVRE led, then the flail troop commander and an AVRE with a Snake, an AVRE with a bridge and then the flail troop of 'B' Squadron Lothians.

On the way towards the anti-tank ditch a 16th Assault Squadron AVRE discovered it – by falling in! Then the 284 Assault Squadron Snake went off, knocking over Major J.C. Woollett. On top of that, the 16th Assault Squadron's Snake also went off and concussed Major J.R. Blomfield. But bridges and fascines were dropped successfully. The trouble started when the Lothian flails crossed and started into the minefield, and all were eventually blown up. Two lanes were eventually opened for the loss of fifteen flails, and Strongpoint 8 was captured. One Scottish battalion took No. 11, another seized a bridge near Fontaine-la-Mallet church and a third started to advance on Mount Trottins. 'C' Squadron the Buffs, had little to do, but 'C' Squadron, the Lothians, scrambled through their two hard-won lanes, obtained some good shots and forced their way through the Forêt de Montgeon.

On the Polar Bear front, on 11 September, resistance outside Harfleur came from two very deep and strong concrete pill-boxes called 'Oswald' and 'Oscar'. They caused the King's Own Yorkshire Light Infantry heavy casualties. Eventually Corporal Agnew of the 4th Troop, 22nd Dragoons, after flailing vigorously, 'posted' 75 mm shells point blank into 'Oscar'. By 8.30 it had surrendered, with 57 prisoners. Agnew was awarded the MM and later received a commission in the field for his fine leadership. After a further tussle, Lieutenant Martin Leake led his troop in front of 'Oswald' and had two flails blown up, but made two successful gaps. Captain Hall's Crocodiles then completed the action. The southern route into Le Havre was now open and the 22nd Dragoons helped the Lincolns enter the city, cutting through wire and sweeping a path through a thick belt of anti-personnel mines.

At midday on the 12 September Colonel Wildermuth surrendered with 12,000 troops and vast quantities of stores, guns and vehicles. The sad part of 'Asconia', in which military losses were amazingly low, was the death of nearly 5,000 civilians in the naval, air and land bombardments. Lieutenant General John Crocker, GOC I Corps, wrote to Major General Hobart: 'I wish to thank you for the splendid work done by all ranks of 79th Armoured Division in the assault on Le Havre.... The operation was well planned, all difficulties were surmounted.' The flails came as a complete surprise to the defenders; it seemed like madness to see the tanks entering their minefields and they were dismayed at the result. As for the Crocodiles, that was just unsporting!

Boulogne

The 3rd Canadian Division was given the responsibility for the capture of Boulogne with its 10,000-strong garrison under Lieutenant General Heim. Concrete forts and thick minefields were established in the hills on the east side of the town and strongpoints erected in the town and port. Mont Lambert was a key feature a mile to the east of the town. Lieutenant General Guy Simonds of 1 Canadian Corps launched the attack on 17 September with initial penetration by the infantry: the 8th Brigade to the north and the 9th Brigade to the south. Three armoured columns of 'Funnies' were then to pierce the outer defences and seize the bridges across the River Liane. Brigadier G.S. Knight commanded the 79th Armoured Division 'Funnies': 141 RAC, the Buffs' 'A' and 'C' Squadrons of Crocodiles; 'A' and 'C' Squadrons of the Lothians and the 81st and 87th Assault Squadrons RE. General Hobart did not know Brigadier Knight as well as Brigadier Duncan and so his part in the planning was significant. The 8th Brigade would attack in the north towards La Tresorie and Calonne and the 9th Brigade was to take Mont Lambert and La Cocherie to the east and south. The Canadian infantry were to be brought up in turretless Canadian Ram tanks (Kangaroos).

For the attack the three mixed armoured columns were A (Lieutenant Colonel Dallmeyer), B (Lieutenant Colonel Shepheard RE) and C (Lieutenant Colonel Waddell RAC, the Buffs). Each column comprised a troop of Lothian Crabs, a platoon of Canadian infantry in Kangaroos, two troops of Crocodiles and a half-troop of AVREs, and were led by conventional gun tanks. All three columns would advance from the eastern flank through the 9th Canadian Brigade's area around Mont Lambert.

Lieutenant General Simmonds's new tactic was for the infantry in Kangaroos to advance quickly up to the huge craters to be caused by the RAF bombing, dismount and then occupy the area. Bulldozers would then be brought up to clear lanes. Trooper John Smith of 'C' Squadron, the Buffs, wrote in *In at the Finish*:

> Overnight gun tanks and flails of the Lothians and AVREs of 87 Assault Sqn arrived on the other side of our field. Exhaustive briefings and rehearsals were a feature of our part of the cleaning of the Channel Ports. There was plenty of time for them. The men never expected the plans to work and maybe the officers did not either. There was a jumble of AVREs, Shermans, Flails, Crocodiles and Churchill gun tanks supposed to be divided into a 'Vanguard' and a 'Mainguard'. At the head marched an armoured bulldozer appropriately named 'The Sniper's Nightmare'.

The RAF plastered the town on the 17th with heavy bombing of the Mount Lambert and St Martin Boulogne areas.

On the northern front the 81st Assault Squadron, using fascines, and 'C' Squadron, the Lothians, flailed and cleared an 800-yard lane from Basse Cluse to Wicardine. Lieutenant Roberts took forty prisoners, although his flail tank was on its side in a ditch, and Lance Corporal Yates helped complete a three-width lane which was used

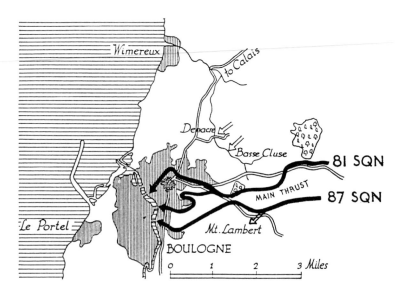

Fig. 7 Boulogne

by the evening as the 8th Brigade's axis of advance. Twenty mines were exploded but the Lothians had casualties to snipers, mortar fire and, of course, mines. Lieutenant Pelly took the 3rd Troop to L'Ermitage but the La Chaudière Regiment were held up at Rumpembert by mines (and cognac found in deserted houses). Pelly cleared a lane helped by an AVRE's dropped fascine; the first Canadian Sherman was hit by a mine over which Sergeant Beattie's tank had passed and the rest of the Canadian tanks cried off. Later Lieutenant Dales of the 81st Assault Squadron RE supported Canadian infantry into the dock area of the town and used Wade charges to force a gap.

On the south-eastern front the pill-boxes dug deep into Mount Lambert gave the Canadian 9th Brigade trouble. Captain Ritchie, in a bold drive using Petard and Besa, forced two positions to surrender and neutralized a third by long-range Petard fire. One AVRE of the 87th Assault Squadron was knocked out and its crew killed or wounded, and the sappers spent most of the night of the 17th uncomfortably under heavy fire.

On the 18th Captain Storrar of 'A' Squadron the Buffs, helped them out. He wrote:

> With Lt Andrews and his crocs we scrambled to the top of the hill to clear some pillboxes with some help from the AVREs of the 87th Assault Squadron. It was a very pleasant party with the AVREs blowing holes in the pillboxes and the Crocs shooting their flame into the holes. Many PoW and other oddments were picked up. After this strongpoint was cleared, the column commenced its mad hirouch into the town and it was given an excellent lead by Lieut Macksey and his tank. How Tp Brailsford, his driver managed to find his way through the bomb craters is almost incredible.'

Trooper John Smith completes the story. 'After his tank had been hit, and the crew had bailed out, the previous evening, he had crawled up a sewage pipe but had emerged when the Germans started to shoot it up. They had taken him to their HQ [in a big sugar factory near a bridge] where all their officers were arguing as to whether or not they should surrender.' When the factory was taken, Lieutenant Macksey appeared with forty prisoners and although badly burned and wounded, he was quite cheerful. Corporal Hams, his gunner, was also wounded and Troopers Brailsford and Lloyd were killed. For leading C column with such bravery Macksey was awarded the MC.

At 3.20 p.m. on the 17th, A column set off but were completely baulked by bomb craters and rubble, but B column managed to bypass them. In the indescribable confusion of mortar and shellfire, the gathering dark, damaged and knocked-out vehicles blocking the tracks, and the enormous craters into which vehicles slid and stuck, eight tanks got through to reach the Citadel in the town. The Germans had of course blown all three river bridges but on the morning of the 18th A column blasted down the gates of the Citadel and white flags were promptly raised. B column, in their laager by the docks, combed out the enemy around the waterfront, taking nearly 300 prisoners. C column had not moved on the 17th but on the evening of the next day they met B column withdrawing from the town – head on in one of the Mont Lambert minefields!

In the north the 8th Brigade were engaging two forts in Wimereux. The noise of the flails and the sight of cubic feet of mud and stones churned and hurled into the air made such an impression that one fort discharged 200 prisoners. But desultory fighting and clearing up of isolated pockets including the Ondia factory continued. Wimille in the north held out until the Buffs flamed it on the 20th, and Wimereux was only taken on the 21st. There was hard fighting in the docks and factory area over the river. On the 21st, after five days of fighting, the enemy in the Le Portal forts on the west bank of the Boulogne surrendered. A member of the *Forces Francais d'Interieur* (FFI), Louis Bertin, travelled in a leading Vanguard tank and, being a taxi driver, he gave good advice on how to get the bulky Churchills and Shermans through the network of streets. Another Channel port had fallen to the Canadians and their 'Funny' friends.

Calais and Gris Nez

More or less the same team that had taken Boulogne moved a few miles north to capture three more important targets: not only the important port of Calais but also two key long-range artillery batteries that for four years had bombarded Channel shipping and, on occasions, Dover. A thousand yards inland from Cap Gris Nez (halfway to Calais), at Framzelle, was a battery of four 15-inch guns. A mile south at Haring-Zelles was a second battery of four 11-inch guns. Another battery was in position between Sangatte and Escalles west of Calais.

The 3rd Canadian Division now sent their 7th Brigade up to invest Calais, the 8th Brigade onto the Escalles-Sangatte feature and later the 9th Brigade to take out the batteries around Cap Gris Nez. The battle was initiated in an unusual way. Major D.R.R. Pocock, the officer commanding 'A' Squadron the Lothians, had stopped on their way to the five-day battle of Boulogne on 13 September for their own private party. The Onglevert strongpoint, with two 75 mm guns, was 2 miles north-west and inland of Audresselles and guarded an approach road to the Cap Gris Nez batteries. In ten minutes 'A' Squadron fired 500 rounds of HE indirectly at a range of 5,000 yards into the concrete gun position. The guns, several MGs and an ammunition dump were destroyed and the Canadians collected 25 prisoners.

The 'Funny' team to assault Calais consisted of 'C' Squadron 22 Dragoons and 'B' Squadron, the Lothians, backed by 'A' Squadron, the Buffs, with Crocodiles and the 81st Assault Squadron RE, whose equipment included Congers – long, dangerous mine-clearance tubes.

The 8th Brigade were to attack the nearby Sangatte-Escalles targets on the same day, H-Hour being 1000 hrs on 25 September. Their support team was 'C' Squadron, the Lothians, two troops of 'C' Squadron, the Buffs, and a troop of AVREs from 284 Assault Squadron.

The RAF saturated the defences on the high ground west of Calais at 8.30 and three hours later 'B' Squadron, the Lothians, flailed away towards the key objective of Chateau Pigache, which was taken at midday, but found no mines. On their left the Canadian infantry attacked Belle Vue. 'C' Squadron 22nd Dragoons spent a miserable time in poor weather and heavy shelling from the enemy's heavy guns as they supported the Regina Rifles at Peuplingue. 'A' Squadron, the Buffs, who had harboured at Leubringhen were well briefed. The Army at this stage was so efficient that pre-attack conferences proliferated and Major Bryant and Captain Bristow commented – not particularly favourably – on the mass of maps, defence overprints and aerial photographs showered on them. All they proved was that the German defenders were in an impregnable position!

During the morning the Crocodiles fired HE continuously at the Belle Vue defences of dug-in 88 mm guns and mortars and in the afternoon Lieutenant Saunders led four Crocodiles into a point-blank flame attack. Two hundred prisoners emerged. 'It was a grand sight watching the Crocs weaving in and out of the hillocks spouting flame at all and sundry. How they managed to get out of the maze of precipes, bomb holes and pillboxes is a mystery that will never be explained', Major Storrar, the 'A' Squadron historian wrote. The 8th Canadian Brigade found a strongpoint at Noires Mottes to be a formidable task with its four 16-inch guns ensconced in concrete behind minefields and an anti-tank ditch. On the extreme left of the attack 'C' Squadron, the Lothians, supported the North Shires Regiment. Despite many large bomb craters, they cleared a fairly wide lane through the minefields. Captain March led the 3rd Troop 284 Assault Squadron RE in the attack on Sangatte and fired a Conger into the minefield, which was successfully blown, but continuing down a steep slope his AVRE fell over the edge of a German blockhouse! Lieutenant Robertson's troop of Lothian Crabs made another lane further west and exploded thirty-seven mines, cutting down two double apron wire fences to boot. The Lothian HQ was in a farmhouse on the brow of a hill overlooking Calais. General Hobart turned up to watch the battle in a foul mood, as he had been forced to scramble through fences, hedges and soggy ditches.

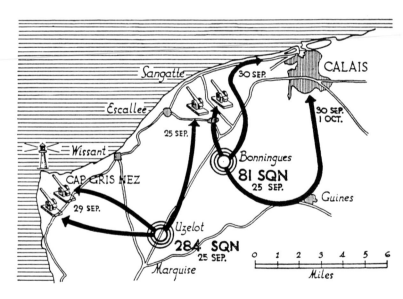

Fig. 8 Calais and Cap Gris Nez

Trooper John Smith's Troop Leader was Lieutenant Sutherland Sheriff (known as Sherry), and the Crocodiles were named Sandgate, Sandling, Sandwich and Sidcup. 'C' Squadron were helping the 8th Brigade.

> Before us grassland sloped down and then steeply upward to the top of Noires Mottes. The flails were beating a track diagonally across the opposite slope, a minefield, dragging great tangles of barbed wire in their wakes. On the other side of the hill, columns of smoke rose and the rumble of exploding bombs was audible above the roar of our engine. The infantry walked by the side of the track hopping gingerly on to the verges as we drew level. We could see more khaki tin-hatted figures dodging about among the mounds and bushes on the summit. The leading flail heaved itself over the brow. There was a crash, a ball of black smoke and the whole whirling contraption was flung violently upwards. The tank hesitated, seemed to shake itself like a dog coming out of the water and then ploughed on with determination. Its mates spread out behind and the explosions came sharply and quickly.

During the day John Smith's tank was hit fifteen times by HE or mortars; nine bogies were out of action and a shot had pierced the track and damaged the off idler. In turn his Crocodile had fired all their HE and most of their AP at targets which were out of range for flaming. Two days later, at the end of the battle, he stood on the top of the hill in front to gaze at Dover cliffs, clear and white over a rippling blue sea.

On the 16th, Captain J.L. Hall of 'A' Squadron, the Buffs, supported the Canadian infantry along the coast road towards Calais. He and his gallant party of Crocodiles poured flame and derision on one pill-box and strongpoint after another. Over two days they helped take Ferme Tournant, Ferme Oyez, Ferme Trouille and then Fort Lapin. They found their way through a maze of naval shells along Sandgate promenade. 'Hall got out of his tank with 250 mm shells raining down, guiding the column on foot through minefields, in between craters, prodding, searching, ducking and signalling to his driver regardless of the risk of his tank hitting a mine and blowing him to Kingdom come,' wrote Storrar. On the 28th the Canadians completed the capture of Calais.

For the capture of the two Gris Nez coastal batteries, the 9th Canadian Brigade had as support 'B' and 'C' Squadrons, the

Lothians, two troops of 'C' Squadron, the Buffs, and 284 Assault Squadron RE. The plan was that the Highland Light Infantry (HLI) of Canada with 'B' Squadron, the Lothians, would attack the Framzelle area a mile from Cap Gris Nez itself. The Nova Scotia Regiment with the Lothians' 'C' Squadron, a troop of Crocodiles and a troop of AVREs, would attack Haringzelles and the command post of Cran-aux-Oeufs some 3 miles to the south. The concrete forts housing the huge calibre guns had easily survived RAF bombing attacks. Moreover the battery on the ridge east of Haringzelles had all-round traverse. Surrounded by wire and numerous minefields the two main forts were formidable objectives. Additionally the concentrated bombing had produced deep cratering, making it difficult for Crabs, Crocodiles and AVREs to operate. The meandering River Noirde and two streams were, moreover, effective anti-tank ditches.

At 6.45 a.m. on the 28th the attack on Framzelle began, preceded by fire from eighteen regiments of artillery and another RAF bomb drop. The 284 Assault Squadron RE AVREs failed to get through the right-hand minefield, but the Buffs' Crocodiles took a chance that bombs had exploded most of the mines and plunged down a hill to deal with the casements in the forts and pill-boxes. Lieutenant Andrew Wilson in his book *Flamethrower* describes his action with the 14th Troop. 'C' Squadron.

> The machine guns started firing. At the bottom of the valley the column stopped. The infantry had suddenly gone to ground. A pill-box on the far slope was firing and everyone had their guns trained on it. The armour started moving again firing at the pillbox. Still no mines but a flail nosed into a small stream and got stuck. An AVRE with a fascine lumbered up. The bundle of brushwood failed to spread out but eventually flails and Crocs went over the stream, a section of infantry crept up to the pillbox with sticky bombs and grenades. There was a lot of mortaring and a couple of explosions.

Wilson saw three disabled Sherman tanks and an AVRE driver 'racing and backing a Conger, to get out of a deep rut. The liquid nitro-glycerine needed only one hard knock to explode it. The Crocs gave the Conger a wide berth.'

Suddenly Wilson's tank 'reared up over a bank of clay: in front was a vast wall of steel and concrete with an enormous gun-barrel hanging over him – the battery. Over to the left were the other guns, grey, square and motionless.' Wilson and his wireless operator dismounted and with pistols scrambled up the concrete platform and opened a narrow door in the cupola. 'In the dim shaft-of-daylight was the gun mechanism, open breech, a great shell lying in a cradle, a platform of steel plates and a heavy smell of oil.' Many scared prisoners appeared, including a corporal who gave him his Iron Cross. The infantry then arrived and Captain Pattenden's sappers began fixing a Beehive explosive charge to a closed concrete blockhouse. Lieutenant Derek Barber came up in his support tank and said 'Everything stops for lunch with the Canadians.' So the Buffs crews cooked tins of steak and kidney pudding looking across at the fire-control station which they were going to take in the afternoon.

On the left section 'C' Squadron, the Lothians, was ordered to flail two lanes into the Haringzelles fort and then another one towards a promontory called Cran-aux-Oeufs, while the Nova Scotias, AVREs and Crocodiles would follow. The stream held up the attack until fascines were laid and the Lothian Crabs flailed two lanes 1,000 yards long and 24 feet across right into the forts themselves. One stronghold gave up and the Crocodiles following up persuaded the others to do likewise. Enemy opposition had been relatively feeble; prisoners reported that, seeing tanks pass through supposedly impenetrable minefields, they gave up hope.

The final attack took place 'after lunch'. The HLI went forward with a troop of Lothians. On the left 'C' Squadron started flailing a lane the whole way from the fort to the German HQ on Cran-aux-Oeufs. In the deep minefields ten out of eleven flails were blown up but the eleventh won through. Trooper Andrew Gardiner wrote:

Alastair Burn's tank led off and we followed. The ground unfortunately had been heavily bombed and our flails were making little impression as one tank after another had its tracks blown off as they ran over the mines. 'Saladin' seemed to bear a charmed life until we had almost reached the inner edge of the minefield, past the disabled Alastair Burn.

Gardiner's tank, 'Saladin' was blown up, set on fire and burned out. Unperturbed, 'we left "Saladin" to burn and joined the infantry who had induced the troops manning the fort to surrender. The day was bright and the White Cliffs of Dover were clearly visible: so near and yet so far.'

Lieutenant Wilson took his Crocodiles down into another valley on the way to the German HQ, a fire-control station, a concrete structure like a ship's bridge surrounded by blockhouses and trenches. They followed the road, firing 75 mm into every target, and air-burst over the 'ship's bridge'. About a hundred Germans then surrendered to the Buffs troop including a naval Kapitan-Leutnant, a 50-year-old, whose batman produced a tray with two glasses and a bottle of Benedictine. In the gloom of the smoke-filled bunker they solemnly drank each other's health. Then the infantry arrived and it started to rain – a cold fine sea rain.

By nightfall on the 25th all the objectives had been taken on both fronts, with a good haul of prisoners. The German defenders had flooded the ground west of Calais and the Lothian flails were not needed. Crocodiles flamed a fort east of les Barraques. The combination of Sherman Fireflies firing their 17-pounder guns and a Crocodile flame was too much. AVREs cleared the road and dropped a Class 40 bridge on the way into Calais, which finally fell to the Canadians on 30 September.

Brest

In addition to helping clear the Channel ports, 'Funnies' were in action in the capture of Brest, a formidably defended submarine base on the western edge of Brittany, which was of possible use to the Americans. So General Omar Bradley asked for some Crocodiles to help reduce Fort Montbarey and its 250-strong garrison. A moat and anti-tank ditch plus casemented fortress walls, many guns, three lines of defences and a minefield full of large naval shells combined to make an assault very difficult. The fort was the key to the capture of Brest.

Major Nigel Ryle's 'B' Squadron, the Buffs, the Playboys, were selected to be loaned to General C.H. Gerhardt's investing forces. The first problem was logistical, that of covering the 400 miles via Bernay, Alençon, Domfront, Mayenne, Fougères, Rennes, St Brieuc to Le Folgeat on huge Diamond T tank transporters. By late afternoon on 8 September, however, they reached Bourblanc. After a reconnaissance a plan was hatched to attack a huge fortress at Lambezelec, 2,000 yards north of the main harbour. After two days of firing with heavy guns the American artillery were unable to breach the walls for a Crocodile flame attack so the operation was called off. On 12 September 'B' Squadron moved 50 miles in a wide detour to Locmaria west of Brest, linking up with the 29th US Infantry Division attacking Recouvrances and Fort Montbarey, which barred the way into the giant submarine pens and harbour.

Again Major Ryle and Captain Harry Cobden made a detailed reconnaissance. The main problem was how to get the Crocodiles to the flaming distance of 80 yards, first through the colossal naval shell minefield (with no flails available) and then across the wide anti-tank ditch (with no AVREs to lay bridges). The fort itself was hedged in by sunken roads surrounded by a moat 40 feet wide and 20 feet deep, with loopholed walls so that the garrison could fire into the moat from their side. The Americans, led by Texan Major Dallas, started their attack on the night of 13 September. Casualties were high but by midday they had penetrated to within 200 yards from the fortress. There they were halted and pinned down. Two hours later Lieutenant Tony Ward (who subsequently won an American Silver Star) led the 8th Troop through the minefield, but Sergeant 'Jake' Morley's Crocodile hit a 30 lb shell, which killed the driver and badly wounded the crew. This explosion blocked the column behind but Ward alone continued indomitably in and out of craters, somehow crossed the anti-tank ditch and got up to the sunken road on the north side flaming every possible target. He destroyed two 50 mm anti-tank guns and the US infantry were soon taking prisoners. After the Crocodile had exhausted its fuel, every round of 75 mm ammunition and twenty belts of Besa, Ward headed back; but his Churchill fell into a 10-foot tank trap. Soon he was surrounded by German troops with white flags, who then contemplated capturing Ward's crew. Using a Bren gun he persuaded thirty-nine Germans to surrender and doubled the column back. But Captain Harry Cobden had launched a rescue attack with US engineers fighting as infantry.

Corporal Briggs's gun tank fell into a deep cesspool, Captain Cobden's shed a track and Lieutenant Hare got stuck in a crater! Somehow they escaped and headed for home with many prisoners; on the way a naval shell destroyed Lieutenant Hare's tank killing or wounding the crew. But Fort Montbarey still held out. The next day, battle was rejoined whilst the minefield gap was completely cleared and the approaches to the fortress bulldozed. On the 16th all three troops – the 9th, 10th and 6th were in action as Captain Harry Bailey describes:

163

Terry Conway came in with 10 Tp and used up the whole of his HE and flame in one mad outburst, quickly replaced by Cliff Shone, with 6 Tp who piled in just as heavy. At the same time all available fire-power, infantry mortars, phosphorous shells and heavy weapons crashed down. Two 105 mm close support Hows lined up into action against the gate itself, Roy Moss pounding away with them. The outhouses were now a blazing inferno and a truly Walt Disney night-mare of flame, smoke, flying metal, sound and fury. A task force of infantry jumped into the moat and placed charges against the walls. ... Straightway into the hole charged the infantry covered by an absolute crescendo of flame, 75s, Besa and smoke.

Eighty-three prisoners surrendered and many defenders were killed in the inferno. Further battle plans were made to tackle Brest itself but on the 18th the whole garrison of 30,000 surrendered. Praises were heaped on the Squadron and in addition to Tony Ward's Silver Star, twelve Bronze Stars were awarded. They were featured on the BBC and in *Life* magazine. Generals Simpson, Sands and Gerhardt all wrote commendations.

Back at Le Folgeat the Playboys made merry in Morlaix. The FFI fêted them. They were trounced 12–1 in a football match against Lesneven. Then came a move after ten days of bliss to St Michel on 28 September and two LSTs set sail on the 30th for Ostend via several days of unofficial UK leave – which they thoroughly deserved.

13 Autumn Operations

Although the 11th Armoured Division, the Black Bulls, had taken the City of Antwerp in a four-day battle ending on 5 September, the approaches to the vital harbour and docks through the estuary of the River Scheldt remained in German hands. Dunkirk had been bypassed and Ostend seized, but General Gustav von Zangen, the German commander of the defence forces around Antwerp, told his troops: 'We must hold the Scheldt fortifications to the end. The German people are watching us.'

Major Raymond Birt of the 22nd Dragoons described the battle-fields which Hobart's 'Funnies' would have to fight over to clear the estuary.

> The Germans did not hold the Scheldt fortifications 'to the end' as ordered by General Von Zangen. When all was over thousands more German prisoners moved out of Hitler's war. But they fought their delaying action with such tenacity that the whole of 21st AG reserves had finally to be employed in the 'Breskens island' on the NE approaches to Antwerp, and in the assaults on Walcheren and Beveland. It was of course a country perfectly made for imposing delay; its low-lying fields were impassable in this season of heavy rain to tanks and lorries and much of it was flooded. All advances had painfully to be made upon banked roads which in this featureless land exposed soldiers and their machines as nakedly as if they rode along the crest of a hill. It was cold and bitter fighting. The infantryman stood in slit trenches into which water seeped knee-deep while the rain beat down upon his protecting gas cape. Tank crews huddled into what shelter they could find around the peasant farms waiting through the long and empty hours for movement while the infantry slogged forward and the engineers brought up their bridge.

There has been much controversy over the delay in clearing the Scheldt estuary to open up Antwerp. Montgomery, now a Field Marshal, had committed himself to the complicated 'Operation Market Garden', a bold assault to seize Arnhem and the vital Rhine river crossings. To have cancelled this operation would have resulted in a huge loss of face with the British and American armies. The clearance of the Scheldt would have been a long, difficult, brutal operation with no clear kudos to Montgomery, who hoped supplies for the invasion of Germany would appear from the recently freed channel ports.

Three major areas of German resistance had to be overcome: the pocket on the south bank of the Scheldt centred on Breskens, and the islands of South Beveland and Walcheren on the north bank. The operations were codenamed 'Switchback', 'Vitality' and 'Infatuate' respectively.

'Operation Switchback'

On 2 October the 2nd Canadian Infantry Division began its advance north of Antwerp with the British 49th Polar Bear Division on its right flank. R.W. Thompson's *The 85 Days* describes the savage and brutal battles to clear the Scheldt. The 3rd Canadian Infantry Division were responsible for clearing a 5-mile area of the West Scheldt (25 miles west of Antwerp) between Terneuzen and Hoofdplaat. In between was the wide channel, the Savoyaards Plaat. Hobart's 'Zoo' was now joined by two new amphibious 'beasts' which would have gladdened Churchill's heart. The first was the Buffalo. The 5th Assault Regiment RE had secretly been equipped with these tracked landing vehicles in August, which the US Army had used with success in beach landings in the Pacific theatre of war. These amphibious armoured troop carriers were to become vital members of the 'Funnies' club. Major General Sir Percy Hobart personally briefed the 11th RTR, the senior of the three unfortunate CDL regiments at Rupelmonde in Belgium, on their new role. He told them about the American tracked landing craft, which could travel at about 4 knots in the water and could climb out of a river. It could hold a platoon of infantry (thirty men) and the MK IV version had a movable ramp at the stern and could carry small vehicles such as scout cars, carriers, jeeps or small guns. At first it seemed to the 11th RTR to be an unwieldy and awkward giant, but once on the move, it proved a workmanlike vehicle. Twenty-three days later they were to take part in an assault landing with ninety-six of them. In the darkness they looked like small tanks without turrets and carried a

Browning or Lewis gun fired by a gunner from the body of the craft. The Buffalo commander was an NCO, and with him in the cargo space were two gunners. Forward were the driver on the left and a 19 set wireless operator on the right. Each squadron of thirty craft was organized into five troops of six and a Squadron HQ of two.

The other 'beast' was the Terrapin. The 82nd Assault Squadron RE now detached from the 6th ARE, manned forty of these, the British equivalent of the ubiquitous DUKW, manufactured by Morris. They had six or eight wheels, were equipped with two engines, twin propellers and rudders for water warfare. They had twice the load capacity (3 tons) of a DUKW, but their mechanical unreliability and lack of tractive effort trying to climb steep banks out of water caused many problems in the months ahead. Five hundred were ordered.

In 'Operation Switchback' the five AVRE assault squadrons' main task was to put the North Nova Scotia Highlanders and HLI of Canada ashore on two beaches, 'Green' and 'Amber', 5 miles west of Terneuzen. In the treacherous mud and silt of the Scheldt were mines, boobytraps and 'Element C'. Backwards and forwards went

Terrapins carrying supplies to Savojaardplaat, 10 October 1944
(Birkin Haward)

the Buffaloes with troops and the Terrapins with stores. The Canadians had a very tough time indeed. The heavy guns from Flushing and the Beveland, Cadzand and Breskens batteries ranged over every yard of the Breskens pocket. General Eberding commanded a division of veterans from the Russian front and they fought fiercely. 'Switchback' lasted from 8 to 15 October, with Terrapins carrying 800 tons of ammunition, petrol and supplies and Buffaloes making 880 loads, including 680 vehicles and guns.

The 3rd Canadian Division now were tasked with the clearing of the Breskens pocket, an area 12 miles to the west of Terneuzen and immediately south of Flushing. By 17 October, the 9th Canadian Infantry Brigade had established themselves on the line from Hoofdplaat, Ijzzendyke, St Kruis and Ede. The 'Funnies' included AVREs of 617 Assault Squadron RE, Crocodiles of 'B' Squadron, the Buffs (the Playboys) and the Crabs of 'B' Squadron, 22nd Dragoons.

On the 21st, the RAF bombers and Typhoons battered the defences of Breskens and tried to neutralize the enemy fire from Flushing. The day before, 284 Assault Squadron RE moved up to support the Canadians. Near a farm at Ijzzendyke a terrible disaster took place. As the sappers and Canadian Royal Army Service Corps (RASC) were unloading three tons of 822 nitro-liquid explosive for use in Congers, the lorry exploded, possibly from a 'rogue' mine. Twenty-three men of 284 Squadron were killed and forty-four wounded. The Canadian RASC lost ten men killed and fifty-one wounded. Eleven AVREs with their fascines and bridging were destroyed, together with the squadron stores and supplies. Lance Sergeant Martin Reagan commanded 3 Fox AVRE in the 3rd Troop was there and has written a detailed account of the tragedy. At short notice 617 Assault Squadron were sent into the Breskens pocket, moving up 200 miles from Overloon by transporters.

'B' Squadron 22nd Dragoons had three weeks of dismal fighting during 'Switchback' but were not asked to flail. Breskens fell on 22 October, and a few dazed enemy soldiers tottered up out of the cellars like rats; the rest had gone. For four days General Eberding's men fought to hold Groede, which was covered by the Flushing and Fort Hendrik guns. The roads were impassable and it was a duel of heavy artillery as 25-pounders had little effect in polder country. The veteran German 64th Division was now crammed into the last pocket. Oostburg fell on the 26th and AVREs of 617 Assault Squadron firing their Petards and dropping fascines supported many local attacks near Zuidzande. The 22nd Dragoons flailed here in order to get Crocodiles within reach of pill-boxes. Major Birt called these operations 'nurse-maiding under the heavy rain and intermittent storms of mortars and shells'.

The Playboys of the Buffs helped the Canadians into Breskens, flaming pill-boxes along the mole. Harry Barrow and Sergeant Brandi squirted flame at blockhouses, Spandaus and snipers, encouraging fifty prisoners to come in. A crafty combined operation to take the fort, 800 yards from Breskens, was foiled on the 23rd when the defenders gave in. For the next five days Crocodiles, Crabs and AVREs fired at every possible target westwards towards Knokke, using 75s, Besas, flame and Petards when required. It was heady stuff. Captain Harry Bailey wrote:

> On 29th all spare crews were sent up to help the Canadians march back the amazing column of some 3,000 PoWs that now came down the road. It was a motley crowd – old men, young men, Mongols, Russians, Germans, Poles, French, the long and the short and the tall … including a ravishing girl in riding breeches and white blouse, flowing hair and proud face. Yes, mighty cute.

'Switchback', at long last and painfully, was over; Knocke, Zoute, Sluis, Heyst and finally Zeebrugge fell.

'Operation Vitality II'

This assault was intended to clear the enemy from South Beveland island, 12 miles west to east and 10 miles north to south, across the River Scheldt from Terneuzen. The 2nd Canadian Division were fighting yard by yard westwards on the mainland north of the Scheldt and 156 Brigade of the 52nd Lowland Division (trained, of course, for mountain warfare) would be blooded in their first action. An amphibious assault was launched from Terneuzen, 9 miles north-east across the river onto Amber and Green beaches.

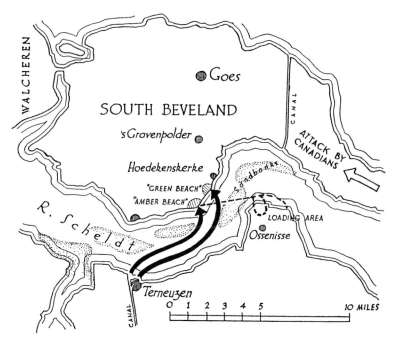

Fig. 9 'Operation Vitality'

The three flotillas of Buffaloes were 'A' (seventy-eight from the 5th Assault Regiment RE), 'B' (fifty-nine from two squadrons of the 11th RTR), and 'C' (thirty-seven from a squadron of the 11th RTR), backed up by eighteen D.D. swimming tanks of 'B' Squadron Staffordshire Yeomanry. The night assault on 25 October was successful, although the Green beach defenders caused casualties. Only four D.D. tanks operated inland because the mud claimed a dozen. In ten hours from the first landings the forces from the two beaches linked up and Baarland was captured. By the end of the operation on the 29th the 11th RTR had made 393 loads at the rate of twelve every two hours, taking back British wounded, civilian refugees and 600 German prisoners. Two Lowland brigades were ashore and 'Vitality' was over with nominal casualties to the ferrying teams. The enemy had withdrawn 3,000 troops into the Walcheren fortress but the 500 who fled across the Zandkreek into North Beveland almost immediately surrendered.

Buffaloes night assault from Terneuzen across River Scheldt, 8 October 1944 (Birkin Haward)

'Operations Infatuate I and II'

The island of Walcheren is a shallow saucer or bowl surrounded by sand dunes rising to heights of 30 to 70 feet above the Scheldt. It is 9 miles wide and 9 miles long and the farms, villages and rich polder are well below sea level, protected by dunes and dykes. Middelburg, 3 miles north of Flushing, is the commercial centre of the island. The 10,000 German defenders of the 70th Division had turned Flushing and Westkapelle on the western rim of the saucer into formidable fortresses, with many concrete strongpoints. The RAF had bombed four gaps in the dykes around the island. As a result most of the polder was under water, except for the town of Middelburg and the coastal belt of dunes. Underwater and beach obstacles were similar to those encountered on D-Day.

During the assaults 'Element C', Hedgehogs, ramps and posts were encountered on the beaches and minefields in the dunes. It was a combined forces operation. The RAF bombers had played the initial role and now the Typhoons and Spitfires flew over 800 sorties against radar installations, AA gun sites and gun positions. The Royal Navy, commando units and 52nd Lowland Division were to be key formations in the assault. 'Infatuate I' was the code name for the direct attack on Flushing, and 'Uncle' was the code name for a beach, which was used as a rubbish dump west of the main harbour and which was the landing objective.

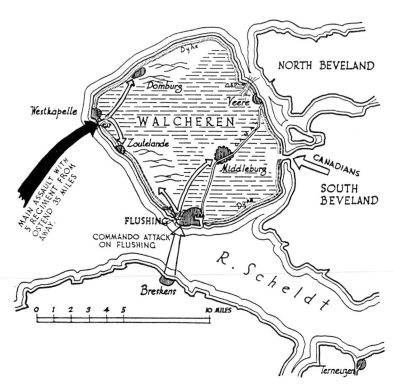

Fig. 10 'Operation Infatuate'

The main German defence unit was nicknamed 'the Stomach' (as in 'ulcer'), or 'White Bread' or 'Dyspeptic', as they were garrison troops of mature age and delicate constitution. But they were experienced, and were backed by a fortress battalion, AA artillery, coastal defence artillery and Luftwaffe manning the radar installations.

'Operation Vitality' Buffaloes lift 52 Lowland Division infantry across Scheldt in South Beveland attack (Birkin Haward)

The plan was that 155 Scottish Brigade would be responsible for the capture of Flushing led by 4th Commando and some Dutch troops who would sail in twenty landing craft artillery (LCA). Early in the morning of 1 November they would seize a bridgehead on Uncle and clear a half-mile sector in Flushing. In all, forty LCAs, twenty Buffaloes of 'A' Squadron 11th RTR and twenty-six Weasels (small tracked amphibious Jeeps) were assembled in Breskens harbour. A supporting barrage of 284 guns pounded across the Scheldt but weather conditions were not suitable for the Lancasters of Bomber Command.

The initial landings went according to plan and by 8 a.m. a terrible battle was raging ½ mile deep into Flushing. The defenders then rained down such intensive mortar fire on the approaches to Uncle that some follow-up 'flight serials' (waves of attacking amphibious 'Funnies') were postponed. Typhoons flew 150 sorties to try to take out the defence's batteries. By midday on 2 November the whole of 155 Brigade was ensconced in Flushing, where many of the streets were 3 feet deep in sea water. It took four days of furious close-quarter fighting before Colonel Reinhardt and his men surrendered.

And for four days and nights the 11th RTR's Buffaloes plied backwards and forwards across the 3,000 yards of the Scheldt led by Major Newton Dunn, Captain Hatch and Lieutenant Berry.

'Infatuate II' was the larger and more complicated assault on Westkapelle by the 4th Special Service Brigade of Commandos, and who were transported by four LCTs manned by the Royal Navy. These were codenamed 'Cherry', 'Damson', 'Bramble' and 'Apple', and each carried five Buffaloes crammed with troops.

The 'Funnies' deployed at Westkapelle were under the command of Lieutenant Colonel Dallmeyer, commanding officer of the Lothians, Major Pocock of the Lothians commanded a team of ten flails, two Lothian Shermans, eight AVREs of the 87th Assault Squadron RE, and four bulldozers of 149 Assault Park Squadron. In addition 104 Buffaloes of the 5th Assault Regiment RE plus the 82nd Assault Squadron (and eighteen craft from the 11th RTR) would land the Commandos from the LCTs.

The combined expedition sailed from Ostend at about 1 a.m. on 1 November and soon after HMS *Warspite* and the monitors *Lord Roberts* and *Erebus* bombarded the Domburg and Westkapelle batteries. For the assault the beaches were named Red and White to the north of the roaring torrent of the RAF-breached dyke, and Green to the south. Red beach was to be used by the tank force only. At 9 a.m. the LCT Damson, ahead by two lengths of Cherry, ran into heavy fire 600 yards from shore. A shell collapsed the bridge carried by the AVRE which fell on a flail. A fascine was set alight by another and vehicles were damaged, and the vessel was making water and was on fire, so it was ordered back to Ostend.

Cherry was hit several times; 20 yards off Red beach it was hit again and ordered offshore. It was hit again and started to run in on White beach. As with Damson, the bridge on the AVRE collapsed on the flail in front but somehow two AVREs, a flail, a Sherman and a bulldozer got off on the beach alongside Bramble, which was already unloading. Again the bridge on the AVRE was hit; it collapsed and jammed the Churchill. As it was coming off Apple touched down on White beach, but a soft patch bogged down all the vehicles that landed and blocked others trying to get ashore. The two tanks were drowned by the tide.

The objectives of the battered 'Funny' task force were to breach obstacles on the Westkapelle dyke and get into fire positions on the dyke; then to give fire support to the Commandos attacking Westkapelle itself.

82 Assault Squadron RE support 48 Royal Marine Commando on Westkapelle, island of Walcheren, 1 November 1944 (Birkin Haward)

The 82nd Assault Squadron had eight craft sunk, with nineteen people killed or wounded, during 'Infatuate II'. Captain Michael Wilford was one of them, wounded in the leg by a shell.

The first wave of LCTs carried Paul Bennett's 3 Buffaloes with a commando Tp aboard, the second myself with 4 Buffaloes, another commando Tp plus their mortars. The OC Tony Poynder next with 4 Buffaloes and Commando HQ. The second wave had Jim Skelly with 5, and Bill Green with 4 Buffaloes. Soon the shore batteries concentrated their fire on the LCGs [landing craft guns] in the Support Squadron. They were very hard pressed, taking hits from heavy calibre weapons. Once our ramp was let down all hell was let loose with a mixture of shells, mortar bombs and small arms.

Lance Sergeant L.A. Wells of the 80th Assault Squadron RE had a troop of 46 Royal Marine Commando perched on top of the ammunition carried in the second wave of LCTs. They were due to land at 11 a.m. at Westkapelle and then move towards Vlissengen.

Captain Oxtoby's Buffalo was in the stern and mine was immediately behind it. I told Les Amos my driver to follow closely (i.e. six inches!) behind him. The scene ashore was one of absolute devastation. The sea was flooding through the gap in the dyke. The church and most of the village were on fire.

Sergeant Ferguson of the Lothians had fired eleven rounds of 75 mm at the church spire, which was used as a German OP: it burst into flames and the Germans came running out.

Shells were bursting everywhere, tanks were coming to grief. An RTR Buffalo, abandoned by its crew was on fire, floating inland. Its cargo of ammunition was on fire and popping off in all directions, a mobile firework display. Weasels were being swamped by the current. The artillery wireless link to the other side of the Scheldt was in a Weasel that was lost.

Sergeant Wells later moved towards Zooteland and the following day guarded 200 German prisoners. By 6 p.m. 41 Commando had secured half the village of Domburg 3 miles north-east of the beaches. By nightfall a 6-mile strip of coast from Zoutelande through Westkapelle to Domburg had been captured. The next day, the 2nd, a very high tide had flooded three Lothian flails and the armoured force ashore was reduced to two Shermans, two AVREs and one bulldozer. Lieutenant Colonel Dallmeyer reported this to Brigadier Leicester who was pleased that he had *any* armour to support him! Major Pocock then led his survivors north to help 10 Commando in Domburg.

For the next two days the 26th Assault Squadron RE, with their Buffaloes, assisted 40 and 41 Commandos; the 77th Assault Squadron RE were with Commando Brigade HQ; the 80th and 82nd Assault Squadrons were with 47 and 48 Commandos respectively, whilst the 79th Assault Squadron RE assisted medical units ashore. On the 3rd, white flags were seen over the village of Zoutelande. The two Shermans shot up Domburg and in mid-afternoon it surrendered, with 200 prisoners. The two Shermans eventually fired 1,400 rounds of 75 mm rounds and 30 boxes of Browning MG. The two Churchill AVREs found and made tracks just passable for the Shermans. Captain McDowell the RA Forward Observation Officer (FOO) was seen often leading the charge with a rifle in one hand, a sten in the other and uttering berserk Highland cries.

Captain Scarrow, the Lothians' medical officer, took about a hundred wounded (plus 500 German prisoners) by LCT back to Ostend. It was appallingly rough and the voyage, normally a four-hour trip, took twelve. Every minute seas broke over the LCT and the tarpaulins covering the wounded were swept overboard. The weather was so bad that the Navy was unable to land supplies. Food and ammunition was dropped to one commando from the air.

Major Newton Dunn led eleven Buffaloes of the 11th RTR into Middelburg on the afternoon of the 6th, guided in by a Dutch civilian. On the way mines claimed three Buffaloes but Lieutenant V.R. Lowe took up position in the main square. Lieutenant General Daser, the German commander, was then persuaded to surrender, but only to a 'senior' officer. Major Johnson of the 7/9th Royal Scots, the infantry OC, promoted himself to Lieutenant Colonel on the spot. Honour was satisfied and the General and 2,030 defenders surrendered. It was a proud moment for the 11th RTR and Major General Hobart visited them and told them so.

By midday on the 8th all resistance on Walcheren had ceased. The heavily defended pill-boxes and defences fell, with 150 prisoners, although a quarter of the armour (i.e. one AVRE) was blown up, killing three of the crew. The Lothians only lost one man in 'Infatuate II' but in the 5th ARE twenty-seven Buffaloes failed to return; of sixty-three casualties, fourteen were killed. Major Pocock's 1st Lothians' reward was an MC; SQMS Evans and Sergeant Hickson were awarded MMs, but the commandos and the infantry of the 52nd Lowland Division suffered badly. In all 8,000 German prisoners were taken.

One accolade came from Brigadier B.N. Leicester, the commander of the 4th Commando Brigade.

I want to let you know how very well your chaps did. The few tanks we got ashore were worth their weight in gold. There is no shadow of doubt that the tanks were of the greatest assistance tactically to us, quite apart from their moral value and the example of their officers and men. It was thoroughly bad going but the tanks somehow got there and played a most important role as close support artillery where no other was available.

General Foulkes, the commander of 2nd Canadian Corps paid a great tribute to the 1st Assault Brigade (with the 11th RTR) and their amphibious Buffaloes.

On the morning of the 4th three minesweepers started to sail up the Scheldt to Antwerp, sweeping for mines, and for the first time unchallenged by enemy gunfire. On 1 December the first 10,000 tons of cargo were unloaded.

'Operation Aintree'

The 3rd British Division was tasked with the capture of Overloon and then Venraij by attacking south-east from Oploo to clear large German pockets of resistance west of the Maas. This was 'Operation Aintree'. The German 180 Infantry Division was boosted by battle groups Paul, Hoffman, Kerutt and Walter, which had given the unfortunate American 7th Armoured Division a bloody nose. Their defence lines included the Molen Beek stream and deep minefields. AVREs from the 42nd ARE and flails of the Westminster Dragoons were in support, together with 'A' Squadron, the Buffs. There were thick woods, open muddy countryside much cut up by dykes making tracked warfare very difficult indeed.

On 12 October 'A' and 'C' Squadrons, Westminster Dragoons, flailed lanes north and east of Overloon for the tanks of the 6th Guards Brigade to follow through. Lieutenant Sutton's Crab was blown up and Lieutenant Hall engaged a Panther tank. Two days later a Tiger tank knocked out seven of the Guards tanks. The infantry of the 3rd Division slowly, and tenaciously fought their way into Overloon. Bridging over the Molen Beek was difficult, but the attack on Venraij started on the 16th and lasted for three days. In every field and track bogged Churchill, Sherman and AVRE tanks could be seen. By the end of 'Aintree' the 3rd British had suffered 1,400 casualties. Venraij became a battle honour for the Westminster Dragoons, who received congratulations from the Corps Commander, Lieutenant General Richard O'Connor.

'A' Squadron the Buffs supported a Coldstream Guards tank battalion but no flaming was required. Their commander, Major Bryant, was wounded by a mortar. Their historian Major Storrar wrote, 'Nothing but the most unpleasant memories remain of this period – rain, mud and heavy mortar fire.' 'A' Squadron said good-bye to their commanding officer: 'hero of Scottish rugby crowds, Lt Col Herbert Waddell will always be for Croc veterans remembering grimmer fields, a hero too and something of a legend.' An officer, William Douglas Home, had refused to go into action at Le Havre

3rd Division sappers and flail tank advance through Overloon

for humanitarian reasons, and Waddell had delayed putting him under arrest. Hobart therefore relieved him and sent him back to the UK.

Sapper Bill Wood of 617 Assault Squadron RE kept a diary of 'Aintree'. The 2nd Troop was sent to an equipment building site to assemble and mount a Conger for use in a minefield which was giving 4th Coldstream Guards' Churchills problems. On the way mortar bombs mortally wounded Tommy Hopkinson with shrapnel in the gut and two others. 'Filling congers was a hazardous job, being a liquid explosive 822. We were only allowed to fill it in turns, a jerry can at a time, needing a steady hand and risk of fumes.' The next day, the 13th, the 2nd Troop used the armoured bulldozer to clear debris on the outskirts of Overloon. And on the 14th the Sappers spent thirteen hours in their AVREs (verified in the CO's diary) in a jam of armour, with the carriers trying to get through Overloon being shelled and mortared most of the time.

A reconnaissance on the 15th showed that assault bridges and fascines would be needed to cross the Molen Beek. The AVRE 2 Fox with a Jumbo assault bridge waddled 2 miles up to the stream on the 16th. Bill Wood described the scene thus: 'Star wars, tracer in both directions, gun flashes and 88 mm firing the deadly black puffs of air bursts and the whole unreal scene lit by artificial moonlight, playing off the lowering clouds, softening the horror and menace of that bleak countryside. A final touch of desolation was the relentless rain. The SBG bridge was then placed in exactly the right position at the abutments of the bridge which had been blown by the Germans, but the electric cable had been shot away and the release mechanism would not work. Sapper Jack Stringer then stood on Sergeant Finan's shoulders to release the bridge bomb release by hand. It was a perfect drop, but under cover of AVRE smoke Sapper Bill Wood, the driver, spun 2 Fox into a neutral turn and slid by mistake into a very deep ditch. Sergeant Finan earned a bar to the MM which he had won at Le Havre, and Captain Ellis Shaw won the MC. Corporal Woolf, instead of jumping off his AVRE into new, safe tank tracks on the ground, dropped onto an anti-tank mine and was blown apart. Captain Wilson had his leg broken in the traffic jam in Overloon and Lieutenant Henderson was killed by a mortar bomb fragment.

Two troops of 617 Assault Squadron fought in 'Aintree'. 'It cost us 3 killed, 13 wounded, 1 officer injured plus 3 AVREs out of 12, quite a price,' wrote Bill Wood. AVREs then laid fascines near Beck but two bulldozers trying to ramp them over were both bogged. Fighting took place near Volen south of Venraij and Lieutenant D.C. Bright of the Westminster Dragoons took out a 75 mm gun and brought in sixty prisoners.

'Operation Colin'

The Division was now spread across most of Holland supporting every British and Canadian Division. Major Birt of the 22nd Dragoons described the devastated countryside.

> The Germans at once reacted as they were to do throughout the battles of the next ten days by laying down heavy harassing fire on the towns from which they had pulled back and which soon began to burn and to tumble into the familiar ruin of broken tiles, dragging telephone wires and glass that glittered about the streets. It was the sort of delaying action that inflicts dreadful punishment on a country tight with small farms and villages which go first under the barrages of the attackers and then under the counter-fire of those who are in retreat. And the ruin of these places – these farms and solid small houses of the Belgian–Dutch frontier – was in some ways more shocking than the destruction in Normandy. For all were as neat and bright as the models of a toy shop display whose breaking seemed the malice of fools or madmen.

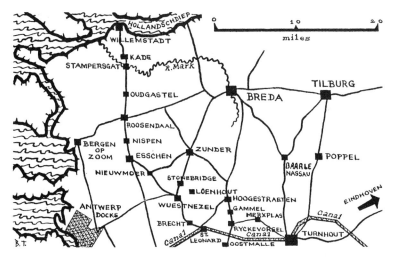

Fig. 11 South Holland

Highland Division Seaforths in a Kangaroo advancing near
's-Hertogenbosh in 'Operation Colin'

One curious episode concerned the Polar Bears of the 49th Infantry
Division and the 22nd Dragoons' flails. On 21 October Major
General 'Bubbles' Barker had sited his Divisional HQ on a road
junction near Wuestwezel, well ahead of his infantry and very close

181

to his forward troops. His right flank was wide open to an attack from the north and enemy SPs and tanks rudely disturbed the caravanserai. 'C' Squadron, with their flails and echelons, arrived to protect it. Drivers, cooks and batmen dug in, astonished to find themselves with a front-line task. Early on the 22nd Divisional HQ was briskly shelled and SPs fired at the General's caravan. Sergeant Wilkins knocked out an SP but he was killed by another. A deadly game of hide and seek went on for some time. Captain Wheway led a counter-attack, cleared the Wolfsheuval wood, attacked a farm and rescued several captured Polar Bears. The Timberwolves (the US 104th Division) arrived in some haste to take over the defence of the flank. They were counter-attacked on a lively night on the 25th.

At the end of October the 51st Highland Division, the 53rd Welsh Division and the 7th Armoured Division were tasked with a major drive to clear the Maas pocket and capture the province of Brabant, including the town of 's-Hertogenbosch. 'C' Squadron, the Buffs, provided twelve Crocodiles to help clear the town, which was being defended by the German 59 and 256 Divisions and then, in 'Operation Guy Fawkes' to help the Highlanders clear a final pocket west and north west of 's-Hertogenbosch.

Trooper J.G. Smith of the 13th Troop, 'C' Squadron, described the scene:

> The Normandy smell, the sickening odour of burnt and decaying flesh, the bitter stench from the blackened shells of buildings. Dead cattle littered the fields. A grey-clad figure looked out of a foxhole clasping the twisted wreck of a machine gun. A Sherman at the roadside, hatches gaping, gun cocked enquiringly, a neat hole pierced in the front of the turret. German rifles, Spandaus, tin hats, gas masks and other equipment, littering the verges and piled in the ditches. A rough wooden cross, the broken stump of a rifle, with a tin hat and the name printed in indelible pencil marked the graves. All this bordered the country lanes leading towards 's-Hertogenbosch supposed to be the pivot of the German defences.

However Tubby Faulkner, a squadron clerk, brought up the mail, Paddy Scallan, the Squadron Sergeant Major, came up in a scout car to distribute the NAAFI ration and Ted Currie of the 10th Troop had killed a Dutch pig which the fitters had cut up and were distributing.

From Heesch along the Rijksweg into the town, the Buffs were kept busy using HE and Besa. Lieutenant Andrew Wilson, in Rosmalen, saw in the distance a row of haystacks. He had been warned that German SP guns disguised themselves in this way. He wrote:

> Co-ax-stop. Seventy five, load AP, traverse right, steady ... on ... haystack eight hundred. Fire. The gun breech running back on recoil: a haze of flame and heat above the muzzle; the shot with its single red trace, spinning towards the target. As it struck there was a violent flash. The haystack burst into flame and poured out smoke – the thick black smoke which comes from fuel oil.

Later, 'I was elated. I'd led in the infantry, flamed an antitank gun, burned down half a dozen buildings, switched tanks (one had over-turned into a cottage) knocked out a Mark IV in a haystack and seen a Tiger tank long enough to fire at it.'

> It took two days to get into the city. A troop would be sent forward to flame something and as it came back for more fuel it would pass another Croc pressurising up for the next day. Every now and then there was a heavy explosion as the Germans blew up another bridge. The Buffs troop flamed across canals. The Spandaus kept firing. You couldn't locate them in the houses on the far bank.

Wilson got his Sergeant's and Corporal's tanks up beside him and together they 'pumped in the flame methodically, left and right, as far as the guns could reach. Presently there was no need to go on.'

Major R.N. Deane of 'A' Company, the 2nd Monmouths, wrote:

> In the battle of 's-Hertogenbosch, a new element was added to the atmosphere of modern war – Flame. The successful three day set-piece attack on the dykeland village of Bruggen was due to the Crocodiles in close support of our infantry. During a dusty dull day we took a remarkable number of prisoners, related to the frighten-ing power of flame as a weapon. The work of the flame-thrower tanks became more obvious and more spectacular as night fell. It was out of the slits in the dyke-roads and out of the hide-outs in the peasants' cottages and little farmyards that the enemy were burned. About every two hundred yards in any direction over an area of a

square mile, there appeared flame – a burning house, barn or haystack. Each of these made its own vicious crackling during lulls in the gunfire.

Trooper John Smith wrote:

> I experienced the feeling of walking through Hell. Two more days were spent in 's-Hertogenbosch but the fighting was over. We had a church service and a booze up. And we were busy selling cigarettes, a guilder for ten. Haricot Oxtail and concentrated soup sold well too. For the bath we had to go to Oss, a journey of about 15 Kms.

'C' Squadron then helped the Highlanders in 'Guy Fawkes' before moving east to Meijel to support the 6th Guards Armoured Brigade.

When the 16th Assault Squadron RE harboured in a village north of Helmond, the AVREs had to be checked and cleaned up. Each crew was assisted by Dutch children, whose small hands were suitable for cleaning the twenty-two bogey wheels and springs on which the Churchill tracks ran. Major John Woollett of the 16th Assault Squadron recalls:

> The problem on 24 October was to secure a bridgehead over the river Dommell at St Michaels Gastel for 7th Armoured Division. We towed up Bailey bridging in sledges for some ten miles behind the AVREs building a 60 foot bridge SW of the village. This enabled a squadron of Shermans to get across so that Divisional engineers could construct an all-purpose Bailey.

But the River Beerge at Esch was too difficult. 'The bridge abutments were so damaged that a much larger bridge was needed. A working party of 12 Sappers began to prepare the site but heavy shelling caused heavy casualties wounding Capt Weston. The fire came from an SP moving from site to site.' The CRE 7th Armoured Division told Major Woollett that another site at Voorburg was going well so Esch was abandoned.

Major Woollett supported the 15th Scottish Division, attacking from the south on Tilburg. 'Three miles of road into the town from Hilvarenbeet was cratered and two bridges destroyed. The gaps were all within the capability of our assault bridges so we built and mounted three of them.' The first AVRE bridge was dropped on 28 October.

Our AVREs began to move faster and faster to keep up with the advancing infantry. The assault bridge placed a heavy load on the front bogies which overheated and caught fire. The second AVRE completed its task and two crew members ran beside it squirting the bogies with fire extinguishers. When the third AVRE bridged the gap at the entrance to the town a loud cheer went up from the local people. It took half an hour to clear the streets and the German forces got clean away.

Captain David Squirrell of the Westminster Dragoons led five flails from south-west of Boxtel to help the 4th Coldstream Guards' tanks into Tilburg. There was no call for flailing. 'We stayed there for three days [27–30 October] in supreme comfort fighting off hospitality from the local population who would give us anything including vast quantities of drink. Our liberation of Tilburg was then over.'

Before the attack on Meijel, from 3 to 5 November, Lieutenant Andrew Wilson of 'C' Squadron, the Buffs, saw the road to Helmond littered with burned-out British transport, twenty to thirty RASC 3-tonners and the wreck of a German MKIV tank destroyed by PIAT. The Crocodiles were not to be used until Phase 4 in the attack, the assault on Meijel itself.

> It was a long wait and all the time the enemy 105s made the most of their opportunity. The tanks stood nose to tail on a road with my troop behind them. The infantry were trying to dig in on the forward edge of the high ground where the enemy could see every movement. Soon there was a regular procession of ambulance jeeps racing back with loaded stretchers.

It was a disaster. The best part of three troops of the 6th Guards Brigade went up on mines.

> It was all confusion now. The Guards tanks were firing from the ridge. From beyond came the slam of the [88 mm] A/Tk guns. On the minefield crews of the 'diversion' Sqn were baling out and trying to get back to the infantry lines. The smoke [fired by Lieutenant Wilson] built up in a big white cloud. Then the firing of the 88s changed its tone and direction.

Two tanks then brewed up. 'Then the 105s struck. Suddenly there was a deafening crash and everything went red.' Driver Stone was hit and put into an ambulance and Trooper Randall took over the controls. The attack was delayed. 'C' Squadron, Westminster Dragoons, arrived and their Crabs beat a lane. The attack resumed. A few days later Wilson and his OC Major Duffy from Zomeren went into Eindhoven, 'cinemas with the latest English and American films, a NAAFI tea shop – shops with lighted windows; bars which glowed softly with their bottles of Geneva and Cherry Bols'. A few days later Meijel fell. Wilson was sent on a foot reconnaissance and was wounded by a hand grenade. Later in hospital, twenty-five fragments were extracted. The Westminster Dragoons gained another battle honour, that of Meijel. Major General Barber GOC 15th Scottish Division sent them a note of thanks – and of condolences for their losses on 3–5 November clearing minefields south of Schelm. 'C' Squadron lost more than half their flail tanks. The 3rd Troop lost its troop officer, troop sergeant and half the men, with four tanks destroyed and the fifth damaged. The enemy opposition had been so heavy that only two platoons of infantry reached the start line and the Grenadier Guards lost twenty-three tanks in one hour.

14 Winter in Holland and Belgium

The 79th Armoured Division was now very widely dispersed. Divisional HQ was in Antwerp under daily bombardment by flying bombs. Major Woollett of the 16th Assault Squadron recalls:

> Instructions were received throughout the winter to report to a Divisional HQ where one met the CRE and was given an outline of the plan. I was then taken to meet the Divisional Commander and was able to tell him of the contribution that Assault RE could make to the operation, as [our] capabilities were not widely known at that time. Then the equipment was ordered via 42 Assault Regt RE HQ and was usually delivered with great speed and efficiency.

Once in Germany the CRE of the 42nd ARE, Lieutenant Colonel Ewbank sent a message to Brigade HQ: 'Henceforward Petarding will be indulged in with added zest and vigour.'

The 6th Regiment ARE were based around Bergen-op-Zoom, with the 77th Squadron on the flooded island of Walcheren, and established the 'Golden Cock Club' for various amusements whilst repairing their Buffaloes after the Scheldt clearance battles. Refit, rest and recreation lasted into the New Year. The 6th Regiment ARE were widely spread across Holland between Tilburg, 's-Hertogenbosch and Venraij.

The 42nd Regiment ARE were sent down to the Maastricht and Sittard area, where Geilenkirchen was to become a major battle for Hobart's 'Funnies'. The number of assault squadrons in each regiment was now reduced to three. After participation in 'Guy Fawkes', helping the 51st Highland Division assault crossing of the Aftwatering Canal, and 'Mallard', ferrying the 53rd Welsh Division over the Wessem Canal on 14 November, the 11th RTR then wintered in Belgium around Wetteren, Waalre and Stamproij. Later they concentrated near the Meuse-Escault canal, ideal for training. Football was played against local clubs and Eindhoven was popular for theatre, ENSA shows and NAAFI.

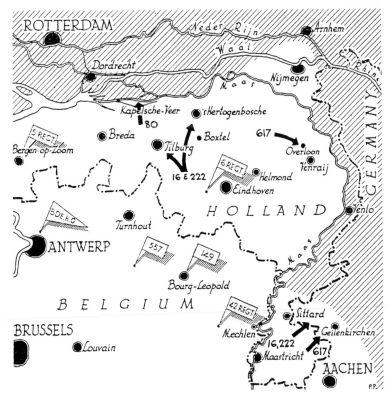

Fig. 12 Winter Operations

'Operation Clipper'

'Operation Clipper' was a major attack planned for the 84th US Division (known as the Railsplitters) to capture Geilenkirchen, an important industrial town and part of the Siegfried Line. 'Drewforce' was the code name for Lieutenant H.D. Drew's mixed force of 'Funnies' to support the American attack, plus Sherman tanks of the 8th Armoured Brigade. The 43rd Wessex Wyverns were tackling the northern sector villages of Bauchem and Tripsrath.

The American armies had already penetrated the Siegfried Line in the south; 'Operation Clipper' was directed along Hitler's Westerwall, and was not a frontal attack on the town of Geilenkirchen itself, which lies in the valley of the River Wurm. 'B' Squadron Crabs of the Lothians, 'B' Squadron, 141 RAC (under Major Stratton) and 617 Assault Squadron RE (Major Alexander) were allocated to support the 'green' Railsplitters in their right flank attack. 'C' Squadron Crabs of the Lothians would support the 43rd Wessex Wyverns on the left (northern) flank. Lectures and sand-table models were prepared to explain to the Americans, in their first action, the advantages and shortcomings of Crabs, Crocodiles and the various AVREs.

The attack began on 18 November in pouring rain, with 'B' Squadron flaming two lanes through the orchards and woods round Briel, across an open field to a railway line ¾ mile south-east of Geilenkirchen. Despite soft ground which bogged many flails, the lanes were open by 7.15 a.m.

The 3rd Troop, 617 Assault Squadron RE brought up two bridges and fascines on their AVREs. Lance Sergeant Bob Harvey dropped his bridge in the railway cutting and his AVRE was hit by a Panzerfaust, a hand-held anti-tank weapon. 'A piece of white hot metal came off the inside of the turret and roared round with a

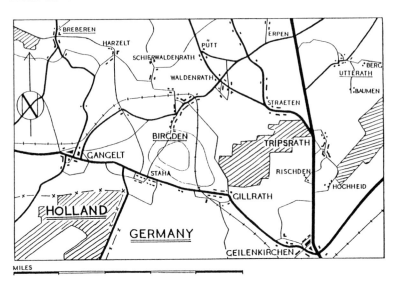

Fig. 13 Siegfried line battleground

189

brilliant golden light hitting no one, a miraculous escape.' Lieutenant Harry Warde was wounded by a mortar splinter and cared for by the US medics. Lieutenant Peter Glibbery brought up the second bridge and with fascines filled the gap. The American infantry and Sherwood Ranger tanks then went through.

On the northern flank 'C' Squadron, the Lothians, had an 'easy' day since the ground was impossible for flailing, and reached Neiderheide and Bauchem on the outskirts of Geilenkirchen. The next day, the 19th a new column of 'Funnies' under Major Stratton came into action on the southern flank. Two AVREs of 617 Assault Squadron RE carrying fascines lost their way to the start line and entered the town of Geilenkirchen – by mistake. Sapper Bill Wood wrote: 'We entered a large village into a large square. Through my visor it seemed undamaged, no one to be seen, not a sound. It was eerie. Then we heard [Sergeant Finan] over the radio, "We've made it lads, we are now in Germany and I think we have come too far." ' So they trundled out again! Later in the day the 2nd Troop under Lieutenant Ellis Shaw reduced two pill-boxes with Petards and took nine prisoners.

Major Alexander became ill with dysentery and Captain Roland Ward took over, went to all the conferences and at Palenburg gave out the orders each evening. When Lieutenant 'Diamond Jim' Stacey's troop of Buffs assaulted various pill-boxes with revolvers and grenades, one yielded three prisoners, one gramophone and one accordion. Later the American infantry were badly mauled near Suggerath. Lieutenant Stacey carried back twelve wounded GIs, one at a time and Sergeant Wheatcroft came to the rescue and flamed several houses.

On the 20th the Buffs' Crocodiles were busy in and around Suggerath and Prummern 'cleaning up' the numerous pill-boxes in the area. One Crocodile was knocked out but towed back, as indeed was Captain Bristow's which received two direct hits from an 88 mm anti-tank gun. Lieutenant Ellis Shaw took the 2nd Troop of AVREs under a railway tunnel with an American lieutenant in his turret pointing out five pill-boxes as targets. Besa fire killed about twenty Germans and nine were taken prisoner. Sapper Bill Wood reported: 'We were in a column when I saw a flash against the bogie of 2 Charlie, Ted Knight's AVRE, it was a Panzerfaust. We at once turned line abreast. As we advanced a platoon of German infantry rose from a fold in the ground and took off at a rate of knots but still kept their arms and discipline.' Wood 'had a pop with my pistol through the port. Jack Hersey's Besa jammed and 2 Fox hit a pillbox with a Petard. The faces of the GIs were truly scared.' At night the Americans fed the sapper team. 'They yarned with us and loved our tales of derring-do, after all, we were battle-hardened veterans with all of 3 months under fire in this campaign.'

For 'A' Squadron, the Buffs, 21 November was a black day. Captain John Hall went into action against pill-boxes north-east of Prummern with his gun tank and the only two Crocodiles that were battleworthy. Moving across open ground, both were knocked out. Corporal Fox and Trooper Clarke were the only two not killed or seriously wounded. Eleven were killed including a US Liaison Officer (LO). A very sad company moved back to Palenburg in the evening. The Lothians lost Sergeant Mackie's flail on an uncharted minefield, killing or wounding all the crew.

On the 22nd the Buffs got their revenge. The only three Crocodiles available in 'A' Squadron did a magnificent job flaming one pill-box after another. When two Crocodiles got bogged the gun tanks went round behind the pill-boxes and fired HE and smoke through the slits. After the battle Major Stratton and Lieutenant Griggs who led his troop throughout the whole battle, were awarded the MC, and Sergeant Jock Ross and Trooper Dave Simpson the MM. Before they left the battlefield two jettisoned trailers were recovered and the secret flame equipment in Captain Hall's brewed up Crocodile was destroyed by Lieutenant Stacey on a dawn patrol into 'no man's land'. The Lothians fired 600 rounds of HE on Prummern and on the 23rd another 400 rounds, and were warmly thanked by the commander of the Sherwood Rangers Yeomanry. On the 24th the Lothians' and Buffs and the AVREs moved back to Geleen for a restful week of maintenance and rest. 'Operation Clipper' was over. The Americans awarded medals to Lieutenant Ellis Shaw and Corporal Ollenshaw of 141 RAC.

The Fife and Forfars Arrive

Crocodile flame-throwers had proved to be in so much demand that a second regiment, the 1st Fife and Forfar Yeomanry, were converted to their violent and destructive use. Their commanding officer, Lieutenant Colonel W.G.N. Walker took his three squadron commanders out to Normandy to see Lieutenant Colonel Herbert Waddell's 141 RAC in action, and thus acquire first-hand technical knowledge. Major Barlow, the second in command, carried on the drive for the new Mark VII Churchills to be supplied. Early in October the Fife and Forfar landed at Ostend and Le Treport and were soon visited and inspected by Major General Hobart. The regiment harboured at Bornhem, near Antwerp. Soon 'C' Squadron were helping the 2nd Essex Regiment, Polar Bear Division near Stapelheide and Leonhout. They flamed vigorously for two days with five casualties, Troop Sergeant Major (TSM) Warner captured one officer and 10 ORs. 'A' Squadron supported the Canadian Algonquin and Lincoln and Welland Regiments at Nispen. The recovery vehicle was kept busy towing out bogged tanks and repairing others damaged by mines and bazookas. 'A' Squadron suffered seven casualties including their commander, Major Sheppard. On the 28th both squadrons were in action near Bergen-op-Zoom and Roosendaal.

Major Harvey Miller and 'C' Squadron supported the 1st Polish Armoured Division assaulting the village of Mode on 4 November. The Polish commander was impatient and their infantry received 'a very bloody nose' before their Crocodile 'friends' arrived. Mode was very heavily defended, every house being stubbornly occupied. So the two 95 mm mortar guns on the HQ tanks pumped shells in the general direction of some troublesome mortars, and silenced them. 'To everyone's surprise, "a blooming miracle" was Corporal Sudding, the gunner's remark. The volatile Poles were now all smiles and ready to attack again.' A plan was laid. 'As No 1 Tp, Lt Owens, flamed the front of the first houses, the German infantry rushed out the back to be caught by Nos 2 and 4 Tps.' Lieutenant Owens charged ahead and on being checked on the wireless by his CO answered, 'But, please we're killing masses of Germans.' They were too. The village was soon captured and the Poles took many prisoners.

After this success the Poles, indeed most of the 21st Army Group, were inclined to ask Crocodiles to do the impossible. In mid-November 'A' Squadron was allocated to the 51st Highland Division in the Bocholt area, 'C' near Schoor, whilst 'B' and RHQ were with American forces near Heelen. 'A' Squadron put thirteen Crocodiles on one side of the Nederweet Canal on the 14th and during darkness flamed across it. Despite the 90-yard width the operation was very successful and was later repeated at the canal near Kraan and also at the Uit canal. The Highlanders were delighted and the Gordons' CO sent them a testimonial. Captain Gordon was awarded the MC for these three actions.

'B' Squadron, working with the US 2nd Armoured Division, had total success at Geronsweiler and on 22 November, total failure at Meerzenhausen. Deadly 88 mm anti-tank guns destroyed or knocked out five Crocodiles with eleven casualties. Later a conference was held with certain US commanders to try to explain the limitations of the Crocodile. So 'B' Squadron gave two demonstrations to a great crowd of American spectators, including Lieutenant General Simpson, GOC 9th US Army.

Operations 'Mallard', 'Ascot' and 'Guildford'

A series of operations were mounted by 12 Corps to eliminate enemy bridgeheads and pockets west of the River Maas, an area defended by the lines of the Wessem, Noorer and Deurne Canals. Behind this line were the few roads capable of bearing heavy traffic converging on Venlo. Snow had fallen on 9 November, but it rained heavily throughout the month. Major Birt of the 22nd Dragoons commented: 'Once committed to these operations to the Meurse [Maas] troops abandoned all hope of keeping dry. In this sixth winter of the war, their element was mud, their enemy mud and their horizon mud. It was a bleak postscript to the victories we had left behind.' Ironically the winter issue of heavily zipped heavy tank suits arrived the day the rains ceased!

'Operation Mallard' was the Corps plan, and 'Ascot' the 51st Highland Division section. From 14 November the 22nd Dragoons flailed, or tried to flail, in squalid fighting through mud: 'A' Squadron to Baexem, 'C' to Zelen and Helden, with 'B' helping the Polar Bears towards Blerick. Major Birt reported:

> On the roads we were a nuisance, and off them we were helpless. We did what was to be done in this desolate country smeared with the filth and destruction of the war. The Germans had done their part with the viciousness of gangsters on the run. Printed and chalked across the walls one read 'We shall return! The fight goes on! We shall win!'

By the 24th Blerick on the west bank opposite Venlo still resisted. 'Guildford' was the code name for a set-piece attack by the 15th Scottish Division, backed by the 'Funnies'. The defenders had dug an anti-tank ditch, guarded by wire, minefields, many slit trenches, Spandaus and anti-tank guns with heavier batteries firing from around Venlo on the east bank. Brigadier Knight of the 31st Tank Brigade had two assault teams to breach the defences:

'Andersonforce' and 'Shepheardforce' of 22nd Dragoons' flails and AVREs of the 81st Assault Squadron RE, carrying four SBG bridges and two fascines. Each gapping team was tasked with clearing three lanes to the ditch, make crossings, and extend the lanes into Blerick for the Scottish infantry to follow up in Kangaroos. In bitter rain at 7.45 a.m. on 3 December, behind the usual solid barrage, the flails and AVREs set off in terrible going. One whole troop of flails sank so deep into the mud, 100 yards from the start line, that a reserve troop had to take their place. Sergeant Swann won the DCM for leading a furious attack. Lieutenant Beal and Lieutenant Martin Leake dismounted under heavy fire and 'recovered' and towed out tanks bogged down in the anti-tank ditch. Eventually, at 11 a.m. after the AVREs had laid six SBG bridges, the infantry and Kangaroos of the 49th Armoured Personnel Carriers (APC) Regiment (a 'Funny' Unit) passed through and took Blerick. 'Guildford' was a classic success: artillery, gun tanks, flails, AVREs and Kangaroo-borne infantry all combined perfectly.

Lieutenant Ian Hammerton of 'B' Squadron returned from forty-eight hours' leave in Brussels, and 'B' Squadron moved along the canal to Nederweert and into Pannington. The Dragoon tank crews were highly pleased with their new 'zoot' suits. No one knows, except a tank man how wet and cold one gets in a tank, especially moving through the rain. But by the end of 'Guildford' all of Hammerton's tanks had been disabled.

> Mines of several different kinds were everywhere. A half dozen or so would be hidden across every sandy track, or at a corner of each of the many little copses, hedgerows or woods. Anti-tank Teller mines, anti-personnel SCHU-mines and some new non-metallic mines which could not be detected by a mine detector.... Gradually one after another my tanks succumbed to mines owing to the soft going.

Captains Lawson and Huw-Williams, authors of the history of the Westminster Dragoons, described the desolate Dutch landscape of the Peel country over which most formations of the 21st Army Group fought and suffered that dreary winter of 1944/5.

> The country was completely flat and waterlogged. There was hardly a tree to be seen, few houses and no roads worthy of the name. Mud tracks were the main means of communication and these were often impassable to wheeled vehicles due to huge lakes of rainwater which

turned them into a sea of mud. Shell holes filled with muddy water, a German gun upside down in a ditch, a shattered farmhouse surrounded by white tape and notices 'Danger – Booby traps'. Half a dozen box mines lying uncovered by the side of the road, a Bailey bridge spanning a small stream and beside it a shattered stone bridge blown by the Germans, perhaps a knocked out Sherman tank and nearby three or four white crosses to mark the graves of its crew who died for England in this dreary waste.

The Dragoons helped flail minefields east of Deurne in support of the 23rd Hussars, who lost several tanks to SP guns and mines. Lieutenant Sutton won the MC for flailing under fire, his Crab being hit twice, and for rescuing a badly wounded Hussar under heavy fire. In the very heavy mud the flails were not fully effective and the Dragoons lost several Crabs in the minefields.

The village of Broekhuizen on the west bank of the Maas and its Kasteel harboured a veteran company of the 20th Parachute Regiment. Supplies came over at night from the east bank and gun batteries there had decimated a platoon of the 9th Cameron Highlanders. On 30 November, the 3rd Monmouthshires of the 11th Armoured Division, backed by two troops of Westminster Dragoon flails and a squadron of 15/19 Hussar Shermans made a set-piece attack on the fortified castle and Broekhuizen village. Despite successful flailing of lanes up to both objectives the 'Mons' suffered 110 casualties during the day. Eventually the 15/19 Hussars poured shells into the defences until the parachute troops died or surrendered.

On the same day, the 30th, Field Marshal Montgomery was inspecting the Lothians and Border Yeomanry. 'B' Squadron produced 'Canongate II' flail for his inspection and apparently even Hobart admitted it was the cleanest flail he had ever seen. So Corporal Imrie, Lance Corporal Main and Troopers Wilson, Reece and Fraser passed the test of all those very senior officers' eyes! Montgomery went to look at 141 RAC's Crocodiles at Geleen together with Corps Commander Lieutenant General Horrocks. This time it was Sergeant Roskilly and his crew who did the Buffs proud. The two VIPs visited 617 Assault Squadron RE at Geleen where Major Anderson's AVRE was inspected. Zero Able's crew under Lance Sergeant Ron Smith had their Churchill tank in spot-less condition. Anderson, Captain Roland Ward and Sergeant Finan were presented to them and for some reason Montgomery gave

Finan one of his old pullovers and a pair of old gloves as a keepsake!

Early in December 557 Assault Training Regiment arrived from England under Major P. Ronaldson and was established at Gheel in Belgium. It was reorganized by General Hobart as the Assault Training and Experimental Establishment RE. New ideas and methods of dealing with sapper problems were needed, such as detecting and clearing the horrible German Schu-mines, improved ways of firing smoke shells from a multi-barrelled smoke discharger and more sophisticated tank bridges. 82 and 284 Assault Squadrons did a great deal of this experimental work, which was handed over at the end of December to 'F' Wing under Colonel H.D. Drew with a mixed staff of RAC, RE and REME. Trials were conducted with several different kinds of equipment: indestructible Canadian rollers pushed in front of the tanks; a tapeworm anti-mine device (a development of the earlier Conger); a Crocodile used to scorch and burn mined areas; a Weasel mine-clearer, for use against Schu-mines; folding SBG bridges; Arks; log and other carpets; and a tank-dozer (a bulldozer device mounted on a tank).

Few of Hobart's 'Funnies' were called on to help 30 Corps act as northern longstop in the unexpected Ardennes counter-offensive 'Operation Griffin' under Army Group B. The 49th APC supported the 6th Airborne Division in icy weather and the 11th RTR sent a troop to assist the 53rd Welsh Division. 'B' Squadron, Fife and Forfar, Crocodiles went to Ciney, still under American Army control. 'A' Squadron, the Buffs, had a very hurried Christmas dinner and moved to Phillipville near Namur also in support of the 53rd Welsh Division, finding good billets in a nunnery. The Mother Superior and her team were overjoyed to see their first British troops since the liberation. 'B' Squadron, the Buffs (the Playboys), moved on 23 December to the cold Belgian barracks of Hasselt in support of the 43rd Wessex Wyverns. Their commander, Major General 'Butch' Thomas, sent them a message that Christmas *would* be celebrated: so Corporal Gough and his cooks produced a sumptuous repast, with beer, rum and a bottle of cognac. On New Year's Eve they returned to *their* nunnery in Berjeik, south-east of Eindhoven.

'Operation Blackcock'

Originally planned to take place in December, but delayed by icy weather, 'Operation Blackcock', involving 12 Corps, aimed to clear a triangle of Dutch–German borderland. The 7th Armoured Division (the Desert Rats), the 43rd Wessex Wyverns, 52nd Lowland Division, two armoured brigades and assorted 'Funnies' would tackle 176 and 183 German Infantry Divisions. They held a line between Maesyk and Sittard, 12 miles in a north-easterly direction, between the rivers Roer, Wurm and Maas.

AVRE support would come from 16 and 222 Assault Squadrons, with Lothians' and Westminster Dragoons' flails, 'B' Squadron, Fife and Forfars, 'B' Squadron, the Buffs (with the 52 Lowland Division) and 'A' Squadron, the Buffs (with 7th Armoured Division). Captain Harry Bailey described how 'the Crocs were tricked out in their cute snow camouflage whitewash on the hull and little frocks from parachutes draped round their darling little turrets. Now they looked really chic and distingué.' Lieutenant Colonel Dallmeyer, the commander of the Lothians was appointed the 'Funny' adviser to the 7th Armoured Division; 'A' Squadron went to the 8th Armoured Brigade, 'B' to the Queen's Infantry Brigade (the Desert Rats) and 'C' Squadron to the 52 Lowland Division. Bakenhoven was to be the startpoint of 'Blackcock', and was duly taken on 12 January.

Crocodile north of Schilberg. 'Operation Blackcock'

Corporal Imrie's smart 'Canongate II' flail was cut off by a collapsed bridge, and when a very energetic counter-attack came on the night of the 13th, he helped the Queen's Infantry defend the village, and received an immediate award of the MM. At H-hour on the 16th the Lothians flailed up to the Floed Beek stream under stiff opposition. AVREs of 222 Assault Squadron laid a scissors bridge, which later collapsed, leaving Corporal Bradford's flail stranded on the far side with the Queen's Infantry. Bulldozers improved the approaches, and Bradford received an immediate award of the DCM for holding off the enemy and feeding back reports of bridging progress. Bryan de Grineau, the official war artist, commemorated this feat in the *Illustrated London News*.

'A' Squadron, the Buffs, were supporting the Queen's Infantry brigade on the west side of Dieteren to Echt and Schilberg. At a crossroads, Lieutenant Stacey's Crocodile was hit by a bazooka, and then destroyed by an SP. Corporal Emberson's was hit three times at point-blank range and three troopers were killed. Captain Storrar was wounded in the face as German counter-attacks continued all day and all night. Six out of seven of the 1st RTR's Cromwells were also knocked out and the Devons of the Queen's Brigade suffered heavily. Sittard was the Buffs' base and on the night of the 17th it was heavily shelled causing more casualties.

'B' Squadron Westminster Dragoons, spent a week from 20 to 26 January supporting the 43rd Wessex Wyvern attacks on Breberen, Schierwaldenrath, Pütt and Schiefendahl. Several hundred mines were destroyed but seven flails were blown up.

The 43rd Divisional plan was to attack all the many village strongpoints from the rear. Tanks and infantry would set off at 3 a.m. from the assembly area, moving across country to arrive at the back door of the objective by first light. The ground was frozen solid and the temperature below freezing point. The hot evening meal came with a tot of rum, sleep for four or possibly five hours and then back into the attack again.

Two troops of AVREs of the 16th Assault Squadron RE arrived at the Saeffelen Beek stream with SBGs and fascines, but a sudden thaw prevented one crossing from being made and another bridge was captured intact. Later an 80-foot skid Bailey bridge was slid, unbelievably, for 4½ miles along an icebound road, eventually across a bomb crater near Heinsberg. The 'B' Squadron, the Buffs, ARV spent a day and a half recovering bogged flails, AVREs and Shermans; Sergeant Potts and Trooper Wear rescued many ditched AFVs.

Two villages north-east of Saeffelen were giving trouble. The main reconnaissance party received a colossal mortar barrage which wounded the infantry senior officers. Lieutenant Cliff Shone then took command. 'Look here,' he said, 'I'm going to flame the western edge and the southern approach, then you go in. I'll meet you in there and see if there's any more trouble.' Later, he recalls: 'the whole village was on fire and the troop had used up all its fuel but still had plenty of ammunition left.' After helping clear three more villages by flame and fire during 'Blackcock', Shone earned a deserved MC.

On the 21st Barkelaer and Eiland were taken and 'B' Squadron Westminster Dragoons flailed between Birgden and Waldenrath. On the following day, according to Trooper John Smith of 'C' Squadron, the Buffs, 'The 43rd Wessex Division had taken Breberen and was fighting in Schierwaldenrath. We had two objectives. Firstly the villages of Pütt and Waldenrath. Pütt was to be burnt to the ground, Waldenrath only singed unless the infantry wanted us to do more.' On the icy roads up to the start line 'our tracks beat furiously on the icy surface unable to grip, clanging and jangling at twice the speed. George, Len and Jinx jumped down to drag bales of straw from a nearby barn and litter the road.' It took them five hours and twenty minutes to reach the start line, 4 km from their billets. Their Crocodile was soon bogged. They were bombed by a Typhoon, rescued an Australian war correspondent who was bogged in a bomb crater, watched the flails setting off mines and were mortared. Eventually Sergeant George Ive persuaded a Guard's tank to pull their Crocodile out, up and over a bank.

Andrew Gardiner of 'C' Squadron, the Lothians, wearing a new tank suit and with his flail painted white, took part in flailing across soft open fields near Heinsberg. The Troop Leader, Alastair Burn's flail got bogged, as did Lance Sergeant Sammy Ballantyne's. Giving covering fire for the infantry Gardiner let fly with the Browning, which soon jammed, so Les Harris, the gunner, used the 75 mm gun, firing HE at the target of several houses 'until the infantry officer thanked us, adding that his chaps could now advance'. On their return to their old billets in Geleen the tank crew were greeted with open arms by their Dutch hosts.

Meanwhile 'A' Squadron, the Buffs, with their fifth commander, Major John Hoare, flamed St Joost on the 20th, but the next day fanatical German paratroops destroyed four Crocodiles of Captain Bristow's half-squadron, causing eight casualties. Three Buffs were taken prisoner and spent four months in Stalag IIB near Fallingbostel. Captain Storrar took his half-squadron to Schilberg, flaming many houses and trenches, and capturing prisoners as the infantry took the village. It was bitterly cold weather so each night the rum ration was distributed in 'Smoky Joe's' by the Schilberg crossroads.

The Playboys, 'B' Squadron, continued to advance, with fierce, costly battles each day, in Aphoven and in Heinsberg, where an OP saw five Tiger tanks and seven SPs. An 88 mm went through Corporal Phillips's Churchill turret, and brewed it up. Trooper Emm leaped out, dropped head first on the ground and discovered he had two broken legs, a dozen pieces of metal in his arms and the same number in his back. Carried back to the RAP by Trooper Brooks, Emm sang 'Donkey Serenade', and cheered on his mount. He later received the MM. Lieutenant Terry Conway gave a demonstration flame shoot on the road into Heinsberg to 'his' infantry, who had not seen flame in action. From the houses all around emerged some fifty Germans, which cheered up the infantry no end. Lieutenant Peter Sander was killed by mortar fire and was later buried in Bruges. Major Nigel Ryle was awarded the MC for the magnificent support the Playboys gave to the 7th Armoured Division during 'Blackcock'.

The Lothians' Crabs at various stages during 'Blackcock' supported the 52nd Lowland Division, the 8th Armoured Brigade, the 6th Guards Tank Brigade and the 7th Armoured Division. 'A' Squadron flailed or shot in Overhoven and Susteren, 'B' Squadron in Geleen and Broek Sittard, 'C' Squadron in Soeffelen and Aphoven. Here Lieutenant Robertson and Sergeant Hunter were ordered with their tanks to bring in a number of prisoners. Both tanks were suddenly ambushed and hit by shells at close range and both crews were killed, wounded or taken prisoner. Lieutenant Robertson recalls:

After our tanks were hit, I managed though wounded in the chest to get out of my burning tank, getting my face and hands burnt. A machine gun opened upon us killing Tpr Nicholas. Tpr Naylor and I tried to make our way back but were rounded up as we were unarmed. The others were also taken PoW except Tpr Lawler who had been killed in his tank. Sgt Hunter and others were made to carry me to a house where I was placed in a cellar.

Two days later, as he was being marched along a road under British artillery fire, Robertson managed to escape and was rescued by troops of the 52nd Lowland Division.

The Lothians also took a leading role in the three-day battle to take Heinsberg, supporting the 52nd Lowland Division in three battle groups, and 222 Assault Squadron RE had a troop of AVREs with each of the three divisions involved in 'Blackcock'. Two bridges were laid which led to the capture of Susteren and in an action near Sittard, Captain Bayton Evans was awarded the MC. At the end of the operation 222 officers' mess was installed in the house of the Burgomaster, who had seven daughters!

Lieutenant General Ritchie, GOC 12 Corps, wrote to Major General Hobart: 'We all appreciated the extraordinary fine co-operation carried out by all elements of your Division throughout 'Blackcock'.... Nothing is ever too much trouble for them, nor any task too difficult.'

'Operation Elephant'

The small lozenge-shaped island of Kapelsche Veer on the lower Maas, north-west of Tilburg, was completely bare of cover but had dykes and drainage ditches. It had proved difficult to capture and attacks by both Poles and British commandos had failed, since the German paratroops there were resourceful and aggressive.

The Kangaroos of the 80th Assault Squadron RE under Captain P.C. Grant supported the 4th Canadian Division troops in 'Operation Elephant' to capture it on 26 January, carrying them and a Wasp flame-thrower in Buffaloes. Lance Sergeant Wells reports:

> The attack was in two parts, from the east with No 1 Tp, the other from the west with No 2 Tp. The temperature was sub-zero with heavy overcast sky and the ground covered with snow. Both the ground and river were frozen solid. The Canadians wore snow suits and our Buffaloes were painted white. Capt. Oxtoby in the lead carried a pair of metal trackways to bridge a small stream for the Wasp.

Wells made an improvized bridge from kapok floats and wooden trackways. From Waspik the 80th Assault Squadron shuttled troops and supplies back and forth. In close quarter fighting, Canadians on one side of a dyke were exchanging hand grenades with Germans on the other side. Eventually one Sherman tank was rafted across the river, a path having been swept to keep the ice broken up. Once across, 'Operation Elephant' was soon over. Two hundred and twenty Germans were killed, and thirty-eight prisoners taken, but the Canadian losses were also heavy. The 80th Assault Squadron was then broken up and re-employed with the 87th, 79th and 77th Assault Squadrons.

15 'Operation Veritable' – the Battle for the Rhineland

The Russian armies had launched a tremendous offensive on the Eastern Front that had carried them through Poland, into East Prussia and the Oder by the end of January. Hundreds of thousands of Germans (and their captive '*Frei*' forces) had died defending the Reich. But the formidable main defences of the Siegfried Line still held firm between the Maas and west of the Rhine.

'Operation Veritable' was a huge, ambitious plan for the 1st Canadian Army with 30 Corps under command, to wipe out and capture all the German forces west of the Rhine from Nijmegen to Julich. The 9th US Army would strike northwards from the line of the River Roer (which was secure after 'Blackcock') to take the defenders of the Siegfried Line from the rear. The Germans then flooded the Roer valley and delayed the American attack for over a week. Hobart's 'Funnies' were now deployed to support five infantry divisions advancing in line: from north to south 3rd Canadian, 2nd Canadian, 15th Scottish, 53rd Welsh and 51st Highland Divisions. Lieutenant General Horrocks had 200,000 men under his command.

The 3rd Canadian Division had Buffaloes from most of the 11th RTR and the 5th Assault Regiment RE, 'C' Squadron the Lothians, Crabs and troops of 617 Assault Squadron RE. The 2nd Canadian Division had a troop of 'C' Squadron Lothians, Crabs and AVREs from 617 Assault Squadron RE. The 15th Scottish had the 22nd Dragoons (as a regiment), 'B' and 'C' Squadrons, the Buffs, and 81 and 284 Assault Squadrons RE, and were carried in Buffaloes of the 49th and 1st Canadian Armoured Carrier Regiment. The 53rd Welsh Division had 'B' and 'C' Squadrons, Westminster Dragoons, 'A' Squadrons, the Buffs, and the 82nd Assault Squadron RE. The 51st Highland Division had 'B' Squadron, the Lothians, 'A' Squadron Fife and Forfars, Crocodiles and 222 Assault Squadron RE. In the second stages of 'Veritable', called 'Blockbuster', five more divisions would push through to the Rhine: the Guards, the 11th Armoured Division, the 4th Canadian Armoured Division and the infantry of the 43rd Wessex and 52nd Lowland Divisions.

The battleground was shaped like a bottle. The 84th German Division, with 100 guns, held the 'cork' to the north-west in the Groesbeek area. Then there was a key plain east to Nutterden, the huge sinister Reichswald forest and the forest of Cleve. Next came two major defence areas of the towns of Cleve and Goch, and southeast of them the fortified towns of Weeze, Kevelaer, Uden and Kervenheim. The original Siegfried Line defences, in great depth, were now the last major barrier into Germany, apart from the River Rhine. In reserve were three German infantry and two panzer divisions. Hitler had made sure that his Westerwall on the German–Dutch frontier was a formidable defensive barrier.

'Veritable' and 'Blockbuster' required 35,000 vehicles almost nose to tail bringing up men and supplies. Five special bridges had been constructed over the River Maas and 100 miles of roads had been made or improved. The 79th Armoured Division had deployed 560 tracked vehicles converging around Nijmegen, under the command of Brigadier N.W. Duncan. The REME and APC workshops had in two weeks overhauled and repaired all the Crabs, Crocodiles, AVREs, and Buffaloes, and over 250 Kangaroos. Originally the operations had been planned for midwinter, with hard frosty ground but days of rain had since waterlogged the terrain. 'Veritable' and 'Blockbuster' were destined to take almost exactly a month of non-stop fighting before the west banks of the Rhine were cleared. In that time Hobo's 'Funnies' fought several hundred actions. H-hour was 1000 hrs (after a five-hour barrage) on 8 February.

The 22nd Dragoons

The 15th Scottish Division axis of advance lay to the north of the Reichswald forest along the Kranenburg–Cleve road. They would breach the Siegfried Line north of the forest, take the Materborn feature, capture Cleve and push towards Emmerich.

'Veritable' was launched by a thunderous barrage of 1,034 guns, including Pepperpots – massive short-range bombardments of enemy positions with every possible weapon for only 3–5 minutes,

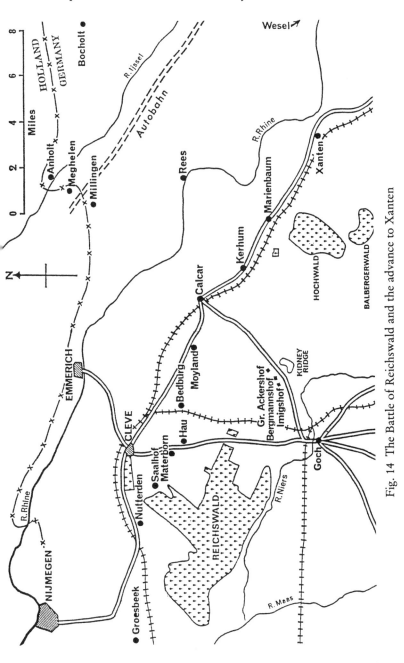

Fig. 14 The Battle of Reichswald and the advance to Xanten

an ineffective waste of ammunition, but a boost to morale. Nonetheless, the first few days were frustrating for the Dragoons. They started from Nijmegen, now a dingy, mud-spattered town, with their inhabitants for four months under threat of a German counter-attack. The flails of 'C' Squadron were all pulled down into the mud in the atrocious going. 'A' Squadron were in reserve, but 'B' failed on two lanes; only Lieutenant Ian Hammerton's 1st Troop got through to the first road.

Major Birt wrote:

In this flat borderland of forest tracks the going was appalling: tracked vehicles sank into mud every few yards and had to be hauled forward by tow ropes and by the long labour of crews who shovelled the rubble of smashed houses into the deep morasses that lay before them. Wheeled vehicles were as helpless. It began once more pitilessly to rain – a rain that rarely ceased during the next fortnight. To the left of the main road the country was already a vast inland sea whose islands were farms and copses, the floodwater began to rise. . . . 'B' Squadron pursued its weary way, bogged at Frasselt, sank on the Materborn ridge, ditched in a hamlet ironically called Esperance and reached Cleve railway station on 13 February. The RAF had pulverised the town, acres of cratered rubble, a vast rubbish heap as bulldozers tore slimy roads through the piled bricks. Floodwater crept up into the lower part of the town.

And on the night of the 15th 'B' Squadron were forced to seek higher, drier ground. For the next eleven days frustrating, aborted attacks were planned in support of the 6th Guards Tank Brigade in Churchill tanks. The Dragoons' second in command Major P.S. Plowden, left to command the 2nd Armoured Reinforcement unit, and the commanding officer, Lieutenant Colonel Anderson to take command of 3/4 County of London Yeomanry (CLY), on 28 February. 'Operation Blockbuster' started on 26 February with a drive through the Hochwald forest to Xanten, and in its twelve days, the frustration continued. 'All flails bogged' was the familiar report. The Dragoons lost three men wounded when the RAF bombed 'C' Squadron's harbour. On 3 March Lieutenant Colonel J.M. Sidey took command and by 14 March the Dragoons were assembled in the captured town of Weeze.

The Westminster Dragoons

Supporting the 53rd Welsh Division sweeping the Reichswald forest, 'B' and 'C' Squadrons were quickly bogged and after four days ARV crews hauled most of them back to the start point at Malden, where Captain McMillan was killed by a chance shell. 'B' Squadron then stayed in Laden for a week and moved back to Belgium to practise crossing rivers on rafts. On the 16th and 17th 'C' Squadron supported the 52nd Lowland Division as gun tanks from Gennep towards Afferden, and despite heavy and accurate mortaring their objectives were taken. The crews slept in their tanks that night. On 25 February 2 officers and 30 ORs of 'C' Squadron reported to the 82nd Assault Squadron RE near Goch to help make assault bridges and fascines under regular shelling. The Squadron then joined in a mobile force with the 1st Oxfordshire and Buckinghamshire and 4/7 Royal Dragoon Guards (RDG) south of Weeze. Enormous craters blocked the road, with mines laid in fields on both sides of the craters. Each time the 3rd Troop tried to flail round the craters they were bogged in thick mud. Kevelaer was cleared on 3 March. The 2nd Troop, with the Sherwood Rangers Yeomanry advanced east towards Issum, and when 'Blockbuster' was over went back to Nijmegen on tank transporters. At Dommelen they unloaded and marched to Riethoven to a touching Dutch welcome.

The 1st Lothians and Border Yeomanry

'B' Squadron's flails were under the command of 107 RAC (King's Own), and with 222 Assault Squadron RE were to make three lanes on 8 February for the 51st Highland Division attack – called 'Wordsworth', 'Tennyson' and 'Shelley'. The many hazards included *American* mines, 107 RAC's tanks which were bogged and blocking routes, a 20-foot anti-tank ditch, burned-out German vehicles across the tracks and a bazooka team that killed Sergeant Cox. 'Shelley' was, for Lieutenant Stewart's Troop, a story of 'bog, de-bog and re-bog'.

'C' Squadron, supporting the 3rd Canadian Division, assembled at Beek and Corporal Keenan was the hero of the day. The only flail that was needed, he cleared a road along the top of a dyke into Zyfflich and led the Regina Rifles into the village, exploding Teller and Schu-mines as he went. A hundred Germans came out and surrendered to him, and he received the MM for that morning's work.

The area was by now so flooded that neither squadron was needed until ten days later, when they moved south to help the 51st Highland Division which was making slow but steady progress through the west of the Reichswald. 'A' Squadron, which was involved in refitting and rafting training at Mechelen, was called up to help the US 743 Tank Battalion at Laurensberg, a long way away, near Aachen. One attack from Neiderzein was successful, but on the night of the 26th, during an attack on Kich and Troisdorf in poor visibility, half of the 2nd Troop were destroyed by friendly fire by American tanks. The 1st Troop passed by and were horrified to see the devastation. 'A' Squadron stayed in the Kairath area until 3 March, then returned to Laurensberg.

'C' Squadron were attached to the 102nd US Division on 23 February and crossed the River Roer on 26 February. From Hottorf they advanced with the Americans to Krefeld until the end of 'Blockbuster'.

141 RAC The Buffs

For 'Veritable' Captain Storrar commanded 'A' Squadron in support of the 53rd Welsh Division entering the Reichswald forest. One by one the Crocodiles became bogged down, and Lieutenant Simkins went up on a British mine. In the end magnificent driving by Troopers Wells and McCormick steered their Churchills all the way through the pinewoods. The Squadron ARV did Trojan work pulling out tanks. 'A' Squadron returned to Groesbeek and to its old billets at Droge until the 52nd Lowland Division requested their help clearing Afferden and the woods nearby. Major Hoare returned from leave and took command. The only shell to land in the harbour area killed Corporal Cross and seriously wounded Trooper Tohill.

From 25 to 27 February they were lent to 51st Highland Division and then returned to the 53rd Welsh for an attack on Weeze. The Welsh brigadier needed flame support over a large anti-tank ditch to the west of the town. The ditch and houses were drenched in flame, but one Crocodile was in a ditch and another had shed a track. On the way back, Lieutenant Jim Stacey's Crocodile was hit by two AP shells, killing him and Trooper Risk and wounding Corporal Leach.

For this action Captain Strachan received the MC, Sergeant Scott the MM, and Trooper Syd Morphew was mentioned in despatches. After a few days' rest in Goch they returned to the 52nd Lowland Division through Weeze to Kevelaer, Geldern and Issum. Their final action was to clear villages just short of the Rhine bridge at Wesel; then go back to Weeze to help clear some woods.

'B' Squadron, the Playboys, were attached to the 15th Scottish Division. Captain Harry Bailey wrote: 'It was night and raining steadily. Monty's moonlight cast its half light over the desolate landscape. All through the night the column crawled along. As day broke on the mud and rain, it was still west of the Frasselt–Kranenburg line.' During the late afternoon of the 9th the armour headed over the rough tracks, passing the ominously bogged mass of 'C' Squadron Crocodiles up to their turrets, through the floods of Kranenburg, over the minefields, the anti-tank ditch, the trenches and bunkers of the Siegfried Line extension to Nutterden. Captain Roy Moss was asked by a Scottish Borderers (KOSB) company commander to flame a house west of Cleve near a lookout tower.

> It was a lovely sight as Terry's [Lieutenant Terry Conway's] troop came up with no time for lengthy orders, poured flame into every house in turn twisting and manoeuvring to get through the trees. The houses burned like tinder and the Germans fled. From the low ground of Nutterden the rest of the Playboys were giving silent applause as they watched in sympathy the impressive party. The long feathers, orange red, soaring through the darkness.

Two frustrating days followed in and around the ruined Cleve, where two British divisions were fighting each other and the Germans in the midst of a monumental traffic jam. Half the Squadron advanced on Rosendaal and Bedburg and the other half on Moyland, but half the attacks planned were cancelled or deferred. Then on a Canadian attack towards Calcar on the 26th, out of a column of over twenty Crocodiles, Kangaroos and Shermans, only two command tanks survived the mud.

Slowly and inexorably, however, the British and Canadians were squeezing the fanatical German paratroops into the bitter Xanten pocket. On 7 March the remains of 1 German Parachute Corps were holding the town with SP guns and artillery support from the far side of the Rhine. The 43rd Wessex Wyverns had two objectives, the

Marienbaum–Xanten road and Luttingen. The 4th Somersets, with the 81st Assault Squadron RE putting down a Jumbo 70-foot skid Bailey bridge plus fascines, were heading down the main Marienbaum–Xanten road. Dougie Peacock, Terry Conway, Rex Lowe and others belted out 75 mm HE and Besa fire and destroyed two 75s, and finally Sergeant Maddock charged up a village street flaming alternate sides. Captain Roy Moss, just returned from UK leave, fired 95 mm and Besa from his command tank. Altogether 150 paratroopers were taken prisoner, and even more were killed. The difficult and irascible Major General Thomas personally congratulated Captain Moss.

On the left flank, starting from Wardt, the 5th Wiltshires were trying to take Luttingen. By 7.15 a.m. on 9 March, with the Rhine only 400 yards away, Lieutenant Rex Lowe, who was borrowed from 'A' Squadron, flamed into the village. The day before they had received a bloody nose, with many casualties and prisoners taken. Now they were happier, having captured twenty-one paratroopers and recaptured many of their own men. Captain Harry Barrow and Lieutenant Geoff Crowe, with the 8th and 9th Troops were lent to the 4th Canadian Brigade to attack Xanten from the west. In very fierce fighting into the suburbs under intense mortaring, 200 prisoners were taken. Many Crocodiles were bogged or disabled, and later Lieutenant Crowe was awarded the MC.

'C' Squadron, the Buffs, were supporting the 15th Scottish and the 6th Guards Tank Brigade, flaming Kranenburg on the Nijmegen–Cleve road and railway. Trooper John (Smudger) Smith

saw 14 Tp crossing our front and waved. Heavy tanks wallowed in the mud, Honeys [light, American-built reconnaissance tanks] lurched about trying to find a way out of the tangle. Valentine 17 pdr SPs sped up a very steep bank. An AVRE loaded with a Bailey Bridge reached the top in safety. Two of our tanks [Churchill Crocodiles] were bogged at the top and a bulldozer stuck when it tried to pull them out. There were glider wrecks everywhere. Tattered fabric flapped in the wind. A Panther tank stood beneath a hedge. The hatches were open and a still form lay beside the track. A lorry was half out of a copse, its bonnet riddled with bullet holes, the windshield shattered. Among the gliders but thickest near a [knocked-out] half track lay German soldiers, green and black flesh rotting and smouldering ... The going was increasingly difficult. There were bogged tanks all the way from Nijmegen to the Siegfried line.

After its third bogging, Trooper Smith's tank needed three armoured recovery vehicles (ARVs) to haul it out of a crater as a German jet fighter flew low overhead.

In Frasselt the Squadron eventually assembled and moved into Donsbruggen, where they were visited by a Church of Scotland canteen van. A large cage of German prisoners nearby 'excited our greed, loud complaints at the way MPs were making money [looting watches etc.] while others did the dirty work'. Sergeant Steve O'Neill's Crocodile was the only one in 'C' Squadron to flame in Cleve. The 13th Troop under Lieutenant Dunkley was ordered into Goch to flame out a nest of snipers out of a church. Then they returned to Pfalzdorf.

Trooper John Smith had been transferred to Sergeant O'Neill's Churchill Crocodile.

> Turret cleanliness was one of my fads and it was heartbreaking work in wet weather. We had a lot of spare kit and, owing to the abundance of fresh food [German chickens, ducks and geese], a large surplus of compo rations. Every nook and cranny in the driving and fighting compartments was utilised. Tins of M&V steak and kidney and bully beef were beneath the turret floor, thermos flasks were secured in place between the air cleaners and the carbon dioxide bottles, plates were jammed between the wireless set and the turret roof, biscuits stacked neatly behind the bins beneath. A small library was stowed away beneath the smoke bomb box – *Teach Yourself Dutch*, *Vanity Fair*, *Pickwick Papers*. Tattered, dog-eared, soaked and bleached. Storage was a continual compromise between fighting efficiency, safety and comfort.... Sherry [Lieutenant Sutherland-Sheriff] had the troop tank (Sandgate), Reg Webb 13 Able (Sandling), Steve 13 Baker (Sandwich) and Sgt Jackman 13 Charlie (Sidcup).

On his return from hospital Lieutenant Andrew Wilson was given the 14th Troop with 'Superb', 'Sublime' and 'Supreme'. Captain Carroll was killed outside Kervenheim. Lieutenant Bottomley's Crocodile was hit by a bazooka. The crew sheltered under the trailer and were rescued by Carrol's HQ tank, which with ten occupants was itself hit by a bazooka. At the end of 'Blockbuster' 'C' Squadron moved back to Marienbaum. Trooper John Smith found a pair of German jackboots which fitted well and reported that the food was good – a new arrival had been a butcher in civilian life and knew exactly what to do with captured German pigs!

The Fife and Forfars

Known as the 'Knife and Forkers', the Fife and Forfars' 'A' Squadron was in support of 152 Brigade of the 15th Scottish Division. On the 10th the 5th Seaforths had suffered heavy losses trying to take Hekkens, which stood on an important crossroads. A branch of the Siegfried Line ran throughout the village, with pill-boxes and an anti-tank ditch. Lieutenant D.J. Dudley's troop flamed and cleared a wood for 300 yards and seventy-six prisoners were taken. The Highlanders then had a clear advance of 1,000 yards. The 5th Black Watch were supported into Gennep on the 12th. The 1st and 3rd Troops under Captain Thomas flamed over twenty houses, twelve being completely gutted. However, the infantry did not realize it was safe to attack the instant the Crocodile Troop Leader gave his signal, and a delay of several minutes allowed many Germans to escape.

Hassum was the next flame victim, on the 17th; the village was set well alight, the railway station obliterated and the 1st Black Watch took prisoners. Pill-boxes around Goch were treated to flame but Besas in the slits proved effective. It needed 222 Assault Squadron's AVRE to pound one huge concrete fortress with twelve Petard bombs before eighty-seven prisoners were winkled out on the 19th.

Crocodile support for Rifle Brigade tps of Desert Rats; attack on St Joost, 20 January 1945

Whilst 'A' Squadron were in the thick of the battle, 'B' were prac-tising rafting exercises at Vucht on the River Maas and 'C' were instructing the new flame regiment, the 7th RTR. On 23 February whilst 'A' Squadron were reserve at Asperden, Field Marshal Montgomery and the GOC 30 Corps, Lieutenant General Horrocks, visited them. Lance Corporal Imrie bet the Field Marshal five shillings that the war would not be over in 1945 – he lost.

From Habbenshof 'A' Squadron helped two Canadian battal-ions, who were being held up by bitter and tenacious opposition, into Follingshof. Corporal Burrow was killed when his Crocodile was hit by an 88 mm anti-tank gun as ammunition and the oil trailer exploded. On 9 March, the 4th Troop supported the Algonquin Regiment near Xanten and flamed enemy-held houses. They had two more actions that evening. The first yielded thirty-three prisoners from the Austrian army, and the second over 200, despite a military mix-up caused by the French Canadian language.

Two heavy actions had taken place in fourteen hours; refuelling the oil trailer after battle was hard work, since 4 tons of liquid had to be manhandled by the crew of five, or four if the tank comman-der was called away to a conference. Eight-gallon containers were often carried 200 yards or more from the refuelling track, plus 'bottles', petrol, gun and Besa ammunition.

Although most infantry commanders welcomed flame support, and could be persuaded that the target should be within 100 yards, the infantry often had mixed feelings. Outside Goch the flame-throwers always attracted heavy mortar fire, and if the infantry were not well dug in, they would suffer casualties.

The Assault Squadron Sappers

The 81st and 284 Assault Squadrons were allocated to 15th Scottish Division, the 82nd to the 53rd Welsh, 222 to the 51st Highland and 617 to the two Canadian divisions. In addition Buffaloes of the 77th and 79th Assault Squadrons were allotted to the 3rd Canadian Division.

Brigadier Gerry Watkinson, who had commanded the 1st ARE Brigade since its inception in 1943, was posted to become Chief Engineer of Lieutenant General Horrocks's 30 Corps. Brigadier P.B. Sydenham then took over command.

AVRE supports 53rd Welsh Division night attack in Reichswald Forest,
9 February 1945 (Birkin Haward)

The 82nd Assault Squadron's actions were typical of the assault
sappers' role in 'Veritable'. Supporting the 53rd Welsh Division on
8 February, they forced a crossing of an anti-tank ditch with bridge-
layers and fascines and supported infantry through the Reichswald.
In Afferden from the 17th to the 19th, they helped the 52nd
Lowland Division in an attack south-east of the village; next, in
Hulm, the 51st Highland Division were supported in a night attack
south-west of Goch. Three assault bridges and four fascines were
laid to open up three main exit roads. In the critical battle for Weeze
from 28 February to 1 March, in a night attack, the 82nd Assault
Squadron made two crossings of the anti-tank ditch by assault
bridge and one by skid Bailey. Finally they filled in craters with
fascines at Kevelaer, Geldern and Issum.

In the Reichswald 222 Squadron laid Somerfeld track timber
(pre-assembled artificial road track), log roads and filled craters
despite Schu-mines to keep traffic moving eastwards. They crossed
the River Niers, helped take Heijen, bridged a crater, destroyed a
road block then moved on to Gennep, Kessel, Aphoven and Goch
(where an AVRE was brewed up by friendly bombing). At the end
of February they moved back to Nijmegen to watch demonstrations

214

of the class 50/60 raft by 617 Assault Squadron. Sapper Monty Clay was gunner/mortarman in AVRE 1A. Reluctantly he

> ... was loaned to 1 Baker which was carrying a small box girder bridge to an anti-tank ditch in the Reichswald, which was under heavy fire from mortars and MG fire. We approached the gap and the L/Sgt positioned the AVRE and the bridge in place. He and the demolition NCO on the bottom of the turret took the wire ends to connect them up to the Ellison lamp to fire the guncotton charge between the blow plates to cut the small box girder (SBG) to drop the bridge.

Nothing happened. Clay was ordered out of the turret onto the engine cover to winch the bridge down by hand. As he started to do so the Lance Sergeant finally connected the leads, and the bridge fell neatly into position. Clay was knocked off the tank and concussed. 'I was never loaned out again.' In Hervost, twenty-four Petards persuaded the garrison to come out and in the attack on Goch on 19 February, 222 Assault Squadron fired eighteen Flying Dustbins to finish off the main pill-box, with sixty prisoners taken.

82 Assault Squadron RE AVREs with assault bridges, fascines – Night attack, 'Operation Supercharge', near Goch (Birkin Haward)

The Buffaloes

When the German defenders blew the Quer Dam, the key dyke running out of the Wyler Meer north of the main road to Cleve, both the 2nd and 3rd Canadian Divisions lost their main supply routes. All work, supply and attack, now had to be carried out using Buffaloes. The 11th RTR, training at Meers, a loop of the River Maas near Roermond, were suddenly brought into action at very short notice. Supporting the 9th Canadian Infantry Brigade, the fifty-one Buffaloes of 'A' and 'B' Squadrons not only did yeoman service ferrying the Canadian infantry but, under cover of smoke cannisters, helped them attack strongpoints from the rear, literally swimming to the back door of supposedly impregnable positions. Dummy windmills were discovered, strongly fortified and housing large-calibre guns, and dummy haystacks also concealed guns or SPs. Radio communications had failed and practically all landmarks had disappeared. The heavily flooded area was subject to strong currents of extremely fast-flowing water, so the standard military P8 compass was vital. The 6th Parachute Brigade defended each flooded strongpoint and the isolated villages of Doffelwaard and Donsbruggen. The minimum 'swimming' time for the round trip of 18 miles was six hours, if possible skirting barbed wire fences (which wrapped themselves round driving sprockets), sunken mines and anti-tank ditches. On the 14th, six 11th RTR craft were sent off to the southern flank to carry for the 51st Highland Division.

The 7th Canadian Reconnaissance Regiment at Millingen and Groenland were in danger of being entirely swamped by the floods and they were evacuated out on the 14th and 15th. Some of the flood water was released by blowing a hole in the bund along the Rhine under cover of a smokescreen. It was so successful that Captain Robertson of 'B' Squadron was bundled by the flood water down a 12-foot drop into the Rhine and his Buffalo was swept down to Nijmegen bridge! Then the 8th Canadian Reconnaissance Regiment had to be rescued from swamping on the 18th. The next day three Buffaloes were blown up by mines, with casualties, on the Cleve–Emmerich road. Gradually the floods receded and Buffaloes were slowly released to Eysden by 7 March – the end of 'Blockbuster'. The activity was akin to Noah's Ark. One craft returned to base, lowered its ramp door, and out came pigs, dogs, sheep, chickens, ducks, geese and a calf. And the next Buffalo in was full of German parachute prisoners of war and a dazzling blonde lady.

The 5th Assault Regiment supplied the 77th and 79th Assault Squadrons for 'Veritable' as part of the 'Buffalo brigade' supporting the 3rd Canadian Division. On the night of 9 February, Niel was the Canadian objective. In the attack Captain T.W. Fairlie of the 77nd Squadron, the infantry CO and the crew were killed or wounded when their Buffalo was hit by two panzerfausts. Lieutenant J.K. Tarling took command and with the artillery FOO brought down gunfire on Niel, which was taken at dawn. Other actions took place at the River Niers crossing and at Afferden. The 79th Assault Squadron was in support of the 8th Canadian Brigade and carried them to Zanpol. By mischance, Captain R.C.A. Cunningham found himself in charge of a Canadian infantry company and led them successfully into Leuth, taking 200 prisoners. Two days later the Regimental Medical Officer, Captain Harbinson, was badly wounded and two men were killed when a Buffalo was blown up. Ferrying continued into Millingen and Gennep and on the night of the 13th/14th, they lifted two 51st Highland companies across the River Niers between Hekkens and Zelderheide.

Skid Bailey Bridge being launched in night attack on Weeze by 82 Assault Squadron RE, 28 February–1 March 1945 (Birkin Haward)

Lieutenant General Horrocks wrote:

> During the course of this horrible battle nine British and Canadian
> divisions supported by a vast array of artillery had been under
> command of 30 Corps. We had smashed our way through carefully
> prepared enemy defensive positions under the most unpleasant
> conditions possible. No one in his senses would wish to fight a winter
> campaign in the flood plains of north-western Europe, but there was
> no alternative. We had encountered and defeated three panzer, four
> parachute and four German infantry divisions.

Allied losses in the four weeks of brutal fighting were 15,634. But
Operations 'Veritable' and 'Blockbuster' should best be remembered as a bitter infantrymen's battle against well-trained enemy
divisions, fighting with the utmost tenacity on their 'home ground',
the Siegfried Line, in appalling weather conditions. In the
Reichswald forest the infantry often fought at close quarters in the
dreary, dangerous pinewoods.

16 'Operation Plunder' – Across the Rhine

By the end of 'Blockbuster', the 79th Armoured Division had grown into the only all-armoured formation in the British Army and, with 21,430 all ranks had also become the single largest formation in any Army in north-west Europe. The seventeen regiments under command now mustered 1,566 tracked armoured fighting vehicles.

There were three flame-thrower regiments – 141 RAC (The Buffs), the 1st Fife and Forfar Yeomanry and now the 7th RTR; three flail regiments – the 22nd Dragoons, the 1st Lothians and Border Yeomanry and the Westminster Dragoons; and the 1st Assault Brigade RE, with the 5th, 6th and 42nd Assault Regiments. Newcomers included for the crossing of the Rhine were two D.D. units (the Staffordshire Yeomanry and the 44th RTR), and a Buffalo Brigade, the 33rd (under Brigadier H.B. Scott), with the East Riding Yeomanry, the 1st Northants Yeomanry and 144 RAC (to become in March 1945, the 4th RTR), plus two Kangaroo Regiments, the 49th APC and the 1st Canadian Armoured Carrier Regiment (CAC). 'B' Squadron, the 49th APC, one of the original CDL searchlight/tank regiments, was on call for night attacks.

Major General Hobart, anxious as ever to find practical solutions to problems in the field, had formed four Experiment Wings: F (mainly for mine clearance) at Gheel in Belgium, G (assault river-crossing devices) near Maastricht, H (rafting camp) near Nijmegen and J (navigation techniques) near H at Waal. By the end of March, 16, 79, 81, 222, 284, 617 Squadrons had been trained to use the heavy Class 50/60 raft. One major problem was that the banks of the Rhine were steep, and muddy, and often sown with Schu-mines. Another was that darkness and smoke created a need for reliable navigational aids. The gyro-compass was the most reliable but an RAF-type radio beam with a flickering needle quite often worked.

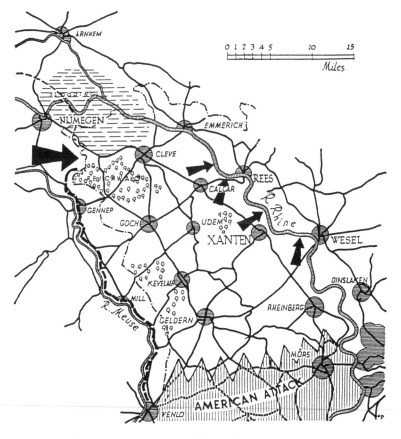

Fig. 15 Operations 'Veritable', 'Blockbuster', 'Plunder'

The GOC now appointed Colonel Alan Brown to be his Chief of Staff for the huge group of 'Funnies'. The British 2nd Army planned to cross the River Rhine during the night of 23/24 March on a two-corps front between Wesel, Rees and Emmerich, a distance of 18 miles. On the left, near Xanten, was 12 Corps, with 30 Corps on the left near Rees. Field Marshal Montgomery chose the two Scottish 15th and 51st Divisions to make the initial break-in. The Buffaloes, D.D. Sherman tank regiments, and eight Class 50/60 rafts would lead the way, with flails, Crocodiles, Kangaroos and AVREs amongst the follow-up formations. Further south the 9th US Army would attack at the same time. Two airborne divisions, the 6th British and the 17th US would drop in front of 12 Corps. The enemy were known to have the 8th Parachute Division round Rees, with the 6th and 7th Parachute Divisions on its flanks. In reserve were the 15th Panzer Grenadier and 116th Panzer Divisions, equipped with at least 150 guns on each corps front. The British artillery, with 1,700 guns and a massive medium bomber RAF and USAF force would soften up the enemy defences. A special attack by No. 1 Commando Brigade called 'Operation Widgeon', was to be launched on Wesel. They would be carried across the Rhine by the 77th Assault Squadron in fifteen Buffaloes.

Supplies of equipment, guns, ammunition and smoke shells to shield the crossing poured into the west bank of the Rhine. Sappers had built three Class 70 and nine Class 40 bridges, together with railway bridges at Ravenstein and Mook, to allow the convoys of material to deploy. A railhead and store depot was opened near Goch. In all 118,000 tons were needed, including 30,000 tons of engineering stores and bridging.

Major Tony Younger, the officer commanding the 26th Assault Squadron RE, was told by his CO Lieutenant Colonel Ernest Hall to take command of the 77nd Assault Squadron for the Rhine crossing as their OC was on leave in the UK. The 77th Squadron, equipped with Buffaloes was tasked with carrying 46 Royal Marine Commando first, then 6 Commando, then 45 Royal Marine Commando and lastly 3 Commando in their immediate assault on Wesel. The Squadron had four troops, each with six Buffaloes, plus two more in Squadron HQ. Each would hold twenty men with equipment for an attack and thirty men for the follow-up. Younger met his new command in Gennep on the banks of the Maas and 'the first night exercise with a simulated assault across the Maas was an utter failure. Everything went wrong, Buffaloes turned up in the wrong order, got tangled up with each other, missed the designated exits from the river or just got lost.' The third night exercise was more successful! The bund on the river banks, 15 feet high with 45-degree slopes, was a major obstacle. From Ginderich Younger took his twenty-six Buffaloes forward to Perrich, their forming-up point.

A Tp commander came up to tell me that 'Hobo' had arrived and was talking to some of his men. My heart sank because Major General Sir Percy Hobart, our GOC was a very strong personality who could reduce strong men to tears with his persistent, probing questions. I saw his black beret in the middle of a group of our men. I walked over quickly determined to persuade him to leave. I could not afford to have men going into enemy fire with their morale at rock bottom after 'Hobo' had given them the rough edge of his tongue. I need not have worried, he knew far too much about war to do what I had feared. He saw me and beckoned me over 'Have you had your rum, Tony?' In high good humour he moved down the line transmitting his enthusiasm to all those he met. As H-hour approached he shook my hand warmly, wished us well and saying how pleased he was with all he had seen.

At 9.57 exactly, the 77th Squadron set off, climbed the steep bank of the bund, teetered a bit on the top, dropped down the other side, across some grass into the river, turning upstream to counter the strong current. The enemy were jamming radio waves and Younger's code word 'splash' was not received. Nevertheless the four-minute sail went according to plan and the four waves of Buffaloes landed the 1st Commando Brigade safely, except for one Buffalo in the first wave which was hit by friendly fire.

The four Buffalo regiments made 3,842 craft trips. Of the 425 operating, only nine were destroyed and fifty-five damaged, and casualties were forty. On the 12 Corps front the 42nd Assault Regiment RE with 16, 222 and 81 Assault Squadrons had the task of constructing and operating four rafts at Ardath and Abdullah crossings, north-west of Bislich. The 44th RTR had two crossing points for their D.D. tanks, and the Buffaloes of the 11th RTR and East Riding Yeomanry had two crossing points each. On the 30 Corps front, the 5th Assault Regiment RE with 79, 617 and 82 Assault Squadrons under command would also operate four rafts, at Tilbury and Gravesend crossings. The Staffordshire Yeomanry D.D. tanks and the Buffaloes of the 4th RTR and the 1st Northants Yeomanry had four crossing points in their sector.

Under an intense smoke screen and heavy artillery barrage, with H-hour at 2200 hrs on the night of 23/24 March 'Operation Plunder' started under a clear full moon, first with the commando operation, then 51st Highland Division crossing either side of Rees and the following morning the 15th Scottish Division crossing at Xanten.

Captain Angus Stewart, Adjutant of the 7th Battalion Argyll and Sutherland Highlanders, 51st Highland Division described being carried across the Rhine by the 1st Northants Yeomanry.

At 0800 we got into our buffaloes, ponderous great clumsy creatures looking very much like the original tanks of 1916. They stand about eight feet high on dry land and are driven both on land and water by great tracks which travel round the whole perimeter of the vehicle, instead of on bogies as on a modern tank. These machines can carry a platoon of men or a small vehicle like a jeep or a carrier.

At 0815 we started up, and there was a great din of engines revving and guns firing. The 25 pounders make a sharp crack, while the big heavy guns made a resonant dong! Like the G string of a cello being plucked. What an orchestra! I thought back to Medenine, Mareth, Enfidaville, Sicily and remembered all those other times I had experienced this same experience. This time it was rather different, though, more complicated, more hazardous, and just as vital. This time our division assaulted alone; the next division on our flank didn't cross till three in the morning, others not till ten, while the airborne Divs were also landing about ten. We were playing the good old game of trying to draw his reserves onto us again, like Akele out hunting with pack.

At nine o'clock the first buffaloes entered the water and chugged across to the other side, none failed, none sank, all landed our men where we wanted them. They were good, those crews. I followed about half an hour later with the 2 i/c and a carrier with a wireless set. Without difficulty we climbed out onto the West bank of the Rhine after a fine crossing. I hardly knew when we were in the water. We tilted our noses right up as we climbed over a bund and then see-sawed on top with our noses right down. There was the water beneath us, and we waddled unceremoniously into it. We looked quite graceful in the water, low and manoeuvrable, though not at all fast. We had about six inches freeboard and shipped nothing. When we came out on the far bank we found a slight fire burning, so we put it out, let down our back and spewed out the carrier. The companies by now were all on their objectives, the track was being swept for mines and we started our job of fielding the vehicles as they came in and disposing of them. So far, no enemy reply, and not a vehicle had been lost; a remarkable feat.

The D.D. tanks of the Staffordshire Yeomanry also supported the 51st Highland Division. Trooper Bernard Cuttiford was a Sherman driver in the 2nd Troop, 'C' Squadron, under Major P.B. Griffin. After a substantial NAAFI liquor issue

> ... we were ready for anything. Round about midnight we started moving by squadron to the Inflation area between Cleve and Calcar. There the screens were inflated which would transform our Shermans

into boats (I never wanted to be a sailor). The Recce party under Lts Kennedy and Pead followed the Highland Division in Buffaloes to prepare our exits on the far bank. 'C' Sqn was to lead the assault. We were being shelled heavily while we were getting prepared, Jerry knew what was happening and laid down a heavy bombardment during which our canvas screens were holed several times. . . .

The river was about ¾ mile wide at the point where we crossed. Suddenly a yell from the co-driver told us water was pouring into his lap. The Commander shouted on the intercom 'For God's sake, keep going . . . we are only half way over.'

The D.D. Sherman sank, luckily on a sandbank. The crew of five stood on the turret treading water until eventually a friendly Buffalo returning to the west bank rescued them. 'C' Squadron lost three D.D.s to shellfire, six were stuck on mud and eight got ashore.

On the 12 Corps front a brigade of the 15th Scottish Division were carried across by the Buffaloes of the 11th RTR. Just before embarkation they were visited by Chester Wilmot and Winford Vaughan Thomas of the BBC. It was a warm spring day. 'B' Squadron's route was north-east of Luttingen, and 'C' Squadron's

Operation Plunder, Rhine crossing, 24 March 1945. AVRE with fascine being ferried across, supporting 15th Scottish Division (Birkin Haward)

south-east. Two troops of the CDL squadron, the 49th RTR, were under command, deployed on each flank of the 44th Lowland Brigade front. They helped the 6th Royal Scots Fusiliers and engaged 'beam' targets to illuminate their respective flanks from H–2 to H-hour. At 2 a.m. thirty-six Buffaloes took to the river with all craft firing their Polsten and Browning guns at the enemy-held bank. Vaughan Thomas travelled in Captain Segar's craft and made a recording for the BBC as he went across. A piper of the Royal Scots Fusiliers piped the leading infantry company ashore. By 2.16 the first craft was back in the collecting area where 'C' Squadron had fifteen minutes of brisk shelling. By 8 a.m., 'C' Squadron had ferried forty-two carriers, four anti-tank guns, two jeeps and three Weasels across. By 2 p.m. on 24 March 'B' Squadron had lifted 165 vehicles and 'C' Squadron 119 vehicles. At the final count the 11th RTR had made 1,360 loads and, besides the infantry brigade, had carried 1,167 vehicles. On average it took fifty-five minutes to carry a battalion across the Rhine.

'H' wing had devised a Chespale carpet 14 feet wide and 75 feet long to help D.D. tanks get out quickly from river crossings. Captain J.G. Firth took a Buffalo-laying troop across the Rhine to lay two overlapping carpets.

The D.D. tanks of the 44th RTR crossed at 6.30 a.m. and fifty-five got across safely but five bogged down on the far bank. Their commanding officer, Lieutenant Colonel Hopkinson recalls: 'Soon the river was full of tanks looking rather like floating hip-baths drifting down stream. One tank was hit as it left the shore and sank like a stone. The crew abandoned ship rather quickly.' Soon the 44th RTR captured the villages of Bislich, Vissel, Jockern and Vah.

The four Class 50/60 rafts at Gravesend, Tilbury, Abdullah and Ardath played an important role in getting heavy equipment across the river. The first two were the responsibility of 79, 284 and 617 Assault Squadrons, the second two were the responsibility of 16, 81 and 222 Assault Squadrons. Each ferry unit required a detachment of 149 Assault Park Squadron bulldozers and also a detachment of RAF balloon winch men. Captain R.H. Stafford was reconnaissance officer for Tilbury ferry. He crossed from Honopel with the 1st Black Watch in their Buffalo to reconnoitre two suitable sites on the far bank and then pass the map reference back by radio. This he and his troop sergeant did despite Schu-mines, friendly tracer fire and enemy snipers. Then came the ferrying of cable (3-inch steel wire rope), which was wound on a drum, mounted on a sledge and towed by an AVRE, acting as anchorage. The two RAF balloon winches were mounted on a landing vehicle tracked (LVT) with wire paid out over the stern. The LVT swam across whilst the winch operators paid out. The junction point was then wound back to the home bank, ferrying cable was attached, then wound across to the far bank and anchored. The pontoons were towed down on their trailers by AVRE, backed into the river and launched, and the rafts were constructed. Two rafts were destroyed by gunfire and many more damaged. Tilbury and Gravesend carried 390 AFVs and 51 other vehicles across, and Ardath and Abdullah over 250 tanks.

Churchill aboard Daimler armoured car Xanten/Calcar, before Rhine crossing, 25 March 1945

On 26 March, the day after the river operation ended, four Buffaloes of the 11th RTR carried some illustrious passengers. Near Bislich, Captain Andrews, the Adjutant, met Winston Churchill, the CIGS, Field Marshal Alan Brooke, the C-in-C 21 Army Group, Field Marshal Montgomery, the Commander 2nd Army, Lieutenant General Miles Dempsey, the GOC 12 Corps, Lieutenant General Ritchie, a senior naval officer and of course Major General Hobart. They were engaged in a tour of inspection of the Rhineland battle-front. Most of the VIPs crossed the River Rhine in 'Satan' Buffalo,

Major Slator's craft. Churchill said, 'I congratulate you and your Buffaloes on a splendid job of work. We are now over the Rhine. Under your splendid leader forward we go, driving a beaten army back to that dire sink of iniquity, Berlin.'

Churchill in a Buffalo of 'B' Squadron, 11 Royal Tanks crossing the Rhine

17 'Cracking About in Germany'

Once beachheads had been well and truly established across the Rhine, 'Operation Plunder' really got under way. The three armoured divisions, the 7th (Desert Rats), the 11th (Black Bull) and the Guards together with the 4th (Black Rat) and 8th (Red Fox) Armoured Brigades, fairly tore into Germany. There were of course hundreds of relatively small engagements and a few real battles (the Ibbenburen Ridge defenders held up the best of the British Army for nearly a week). But the surge forward was irresistible and only one German city on the British/Canadian front put up a determined resistance.

The casualties of the last nine months, together with two leave schemes ('Python', which allowed all ranks with five or more years overseas to return to Britain almost immediately; and 'Lilop', which was leave in the UK in lieu of Python), had produced a serious shortage of young leaders particularly in the infantry divisions; the replacements were young and inexperienced. Many came from lines of communication units or from units such as AA regiments where there was now little call for their services. However, Major Birt of the 22nd Dragoons wrote:

> Our state was administratively tidy and well provided. Our morale was high, our confidence as firm as ever it had been. We were all of us by this time battle-wise soldiers whose edge of recklessness had long ago been worn away but who had instead the shrewd caution and 'know how' which is in the end the quality that wins wars and this without the loss of dash which is also necessary to force success in an engagement.

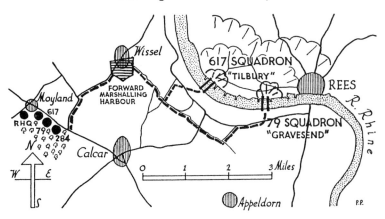

Fig. 16 Rees – 42 Regiment ARE

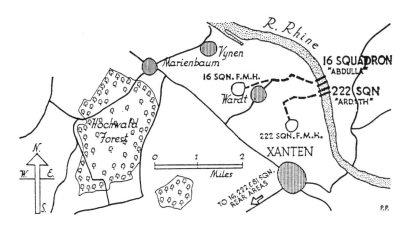

Fig. 17 Xanten – 42 Regiment ARE

The British 2nd Army pushed rapidly east and north with 30 Corps on the left, 12 Corps in the centre and 8 Corps on the right flank next to the US 9th Army. In the final six weeks of the campaign the AVREs had a key role. Petards were the best weapons to destroy the hundreds of quite amateurish road blocks. Fascines and SBGs were frequently needed to fill bomb craters and replace river bridges, which were inevitably blown. The flame-throwers from the three regiments were always in demand as being the quickest way to end the defence of a pill-box or defended house. The flail regiments encountered very few substantial minefields. Quite soon

229

– mid April – the 22nd Dragoons, to their delight, were to be 'translated' into their usual role as gun tanks. The Kangaroo regiments were on call all the time (including now the 49th APC Regiment) for carrying leading infantry rapidly up the centre lines. The Buffaloes of the 4th RTR were in the 2nd Army Reserve but those of the 11th RTR did yeoman service with the 1st Canadian Army clearing up in Holland.

The Flail Regiments

After 'Veritable' the Shermans of the 22nd Dragoons were a mess. Their guns were filthy, their turrets loaded with mud, their tracks slack, their flailing gear shaky. Broken sprockets were repaired, unwanted links were struck out. In the midst of ruined Weeze and Uden the Dragoons swept up the litter of war and burned or buried it. Ready once again for battle, they were to spend the next six weeks supporting the 3rd British and 51st Highland Divisions. On 28 March 'B' and 'C' Squadrons crossed the Rhine over 'London Bridge' to support 'Monty's Ironsides' in clearing Haldern, and again back into Holland on 1 April. Major Birt wrote:

> On the one side empty windows, silence and the white flags out on every house; on the other a delirium of joy and the orange and red-white-blue banners making the streets riotous with colour. It was Easter Sunday and for the people along the road to Groenlo and Enscheide a festival or rebirth and liberation indeed.

Then they went back into Germany, to Nordhorn, Bentheim, and Schuttorf with the 51st Highland Division. Plans changed daily, often hourly but in Dotlingen, the 5/7th Gordons and the 5th Black Watch met a battle group of SS officer cadets, and young fanatical parachutists. The Dragoons had six Crabs knocked out and others damaged by mines and SP guns. Lieutenant Martin Leake was killed by a mine splinter – 'one of the bravest troop leaders and most loveable men', according to Major Birt. Lieutenant Eaton's Sherman took four AP hits through the steering gear. On 17 April Ippener and Horstedt were occupied but on the outskirts of Delmenhorst, Corporal Ferguson had a duel with an 88 mm which he destroyed, winning the MM. Trooper Smith (again in the words of Major Birt), 'footballer, wit, jester and best of comrades' was killed by a panzerfaust. By the 22nd 'C' Squadron were in the handsome barracks, and

'B' Squadron esconced in the comfortable houses and inns of Delmenhorst. The 51st Highland Division regarded the 22nd Dragoons as 'their tanks'.

The 1st Lothian and Border Yeomanry had enjoyed two weeks' rest near Veldhoven in Holland with football and a Burns Club dinner (the haggis was too late, and too ripe, and was buried at Mook). 'B' Squadron crossed the Rhine and spent a peaceful week with 701 US Tank Battalion near Hardinghausen. But on 6 April, while with the 75th US Division near Recklinghausen, Lieutenant Melville and Sergeant Currie in a bitter fight to help some US MPs whose jeeps were smashed by a 75 mm gun, were both shot up.

'A' Squadron moved back across the Nijmegen bridge to help the 49th Polar Bear Division in the clearance of the Arnhem area. One hundred and twenty-five rounds of HE per gun were fired at 6,000–8,000 yards onto the Haaldered, Gent and Doornenburg area. Major Pocock used Bemmel church tower as the OP and Lieutenant Newman's 2nd Troop led the Polar Bear infantry from Zand to Rikerswaard. Under mortar fire two Crabs blew up on mines, and the third was reversed onto a mine. The three Shermans had to be abandoned.

'C' Squadron crossed the Rhine on 4 April to support Canadian forces near Zutphen. Captain Henman used a church tower as an OP in an action near Greisbeck, when 1,000 rounds of HE were fired. And the same thing happened next day, except that Henman was aloft in Dreimpt church tower and 1,000 HE rounds landed on Doesberg. 'C' Squadron moved to Arnhem on the 14th and 'A' Squadron, split between two task forces of flails, AVREs and South Wales Borderers, crossed the Ijssel for the two-day battle to take Arnhem. The 1st and 3rd Troops flailed, and then shot in a mad hell-for-leather dash through the streets. Sergeant Hopkins earned the MM flailing well and shooting up the gasworks. On the 17th Velp and Renkum were liberated.

'C' Squadron also helped the 5th Canadian Division up to the Zuider Zee at Harderwijk, using their guns to good effect. Andrew Gardiner in Lance Sergeant Sammy Ballantyne's Crab supported the British Columbia Dragoons. The Sherman sported

> ... a handsome Scottish Standard flying from the wireless aerial. In Arnhem a passing Canadian officer called up from his vehicle. 'Have

you people got the King on board?' The Canadians were dressed very smartly. So smartly that the Lothians' Sqn Sergeant-Major told Sammy Ballantyne 'for heavens sake, Sammy, get your blokes to smarten up a bit. We look like a bunch of buccaneers alongside this crowd' . . . But after all we were a typical unorthodox Yeomanry regiment.

Still each day had its perils. On the 17th Sergeant Leishman's tank was blown up near Heelsum on a mine, burnt out with four men wounded. And the next day Corporal Edwards's tank was blown up on a heavy mine near Zetten with four casualties. The regiment now earned a rest in liberated Holland.

The BBC announced a few hours prematurely that the Westminster Dragoons was across the Rhine. At first light on 26 March, Major Wallace led 'A' and 'B' Squadrons and RHQ over by pontoon bridge at Xanten. Although Rees still held out and a panzer counter-attack had been halted, the link-up with the airborne forces was made on D+2. A strange fate befell 'A' Squadron in corps reserve. After moving in leaps of 50 miles a day, past German prisoners, sad, pathetic hordes of displaced persons and the detritus of war, they arrived in Celle. The tanks were parked in a large granary, as garrison to this picturesque Lower Saxony town with its thirteenth-century castle and palace of Bohme. And there they stayed!

Quite soon 'B' Squadron moved in 21 Army Group reserve to Winterswyk in Holland. 'C' Squadron were rushed to Rheine where 12 Corps HQ might be attacked, but it was a false alarm. There followed another urgent move on 12 April to defend Wildeshausen – a huge distance of 120 miles in a day. The fitters under Sergeant Wiswell worked all night on tanks scattered along the road for 60 miles. For three days and nights 'C' Squadron helped a battalion of Royal Scots Fusiliers defend the town from SPs, shelling, sniping, Spandau and panzerfaust, and from a bombing sortie by the RAF. Sergeants Bingham, Whybrow and Wright helped render excellent tank co-operation. On the 15th 'C' Squadron joined 'A' and RHQ at Warpe, west of the River Wesel.

The Flame-Throwers

'A' Squadron, the Buffs, had a peaceful time, moving across 'London Bridge' and through battered Rees, backing up the 3rd British

Division to Haldern and Werth. Then they crossed over the frontier for the joys of liberation in Aalten, Lichtenvoorde, Groenlo and Enschede, then back again into Germany into a real battle at Lingen where the Guards Armoured Division was held up, as all bridges across the Dortmund–Ems canal were blown. A midnight attack supporting the Lincolns was a success: both streets attacked were burned down and over 100 prisoners taken. Sergeant Joe Sykes accidentally covered Lieutenant Russell's Crocodile in flaming fuel. Lance Corporal Armitage won the MM by beating out the flames, keeping the guns in action and directing the disabled tank. Captain Storrar, who was responsible for the Lingen battle, was awarded the MC. Three troopers were wounded in the action, and Trooper Parker's Crocodile had a gun duel with a battery of light AA guns at about 10 yards' range at Mundersum, which they lost. Captain Storrar took a half-squadron eastwards through Furstenau and Badbergen, liberating an egg-packing warehouse where Major Hoare was cooked eight eggs for supper. Then they went on to Dinklage, Lohne and Vehchta where Sergeant Sykes flamed a 'hostile' farm. One night attack saw Lieutenant Tunbridge's tank hit by a bazooka, before they moved on to Wildenhausen.

Captain Strachan took the other 'A' half-squadron with the Guards Armoured Division to Ohrte where Lance Corporal Spain 'liberated' a goods train crammed with bags of sugar. Then they moved to Loningen, Lastrup, Essen and Bevern where they stayed for three days collecting eggs and resting. A reunited 'A' Squadron then arrived at Ahlen, where the Polish Armoured Division had been held up on the Kusten Canal for three days. Despite linguistic problems an attack on the canal defenders on the 19th was most successful. Typhoons deluged the far side of the canal with accurate bombing, 'A' Squadron Crocodiles deluged them with flame and the Poles swarmed across, taking seventy prisoners and establishing a bridgehead. Then they went back to Papenburg for two days of major maintenance on the Crocodiles: new tracks, new bogies, new final drives, even new engines and gearboxes for some. Parties were held and Sergeant White organized a concert party.

Initially 'B' Squadron, the Playboys, were in 30 Corps reserve and attacks were planned on Dinxperlo and Anholt, but no flame was needed. The HE and smoke fired at Anholt was the last shot fired in anger on German soil. On 15 April the Crocodiles chugged mile after mile to Wilp, south-west of Deventer, back across the Rhine, via Hockleton – 150 miles in two days – good going. The 2nd

Canadian Division were held up at Appeldoorn, but the defenders left in the night. Captain Roy Moss led the Playboys in their final action, bowling along in his scout car, 10 miles west of Appeldoorn along a forest road. An anti-tank gun opened up and soon the Canadian infantry were pinned down. Roy Moss organized four Crocodiles with Sergeant Jackman flaming on the left and Jack Huxtable on the right. The woods burned furiously and so did the wretched defenders. The Hastings regiment counted a hundred dead and took twenty-five prisoners.

Trooper John Smith recalls that in the 'C' Squadron assembly point in Myland Wood (part of Weeze forest) there were neat tracks, roads, log cabins and dugouts, and all the 'streets' had names tacked to the pine trees: Wilhelmstrasse, Adolf Hitler Strasse, Friedrichstrasse, Dr Goebels Strasse. The two films in the camp cinema were *Going My Way* and *Winter Time*. Perhaps surprisingly the Luftwaffe were active each night.

Smith's Crocodile took twenty minutes to cross the Rhine on a raft. They then went to Empel for a few days, where loot included an Iron Cross ribbon, a wallet from a dead German and a shaving mirror. Next was Ijsselburg and the wrecked AFVs around the auto-bahn. Lieutenant Andrew Wilson took his troop of Crocodiles into the battle of the Autobahn, supporting a night attack with Kangaroos carrying infantry. At zero hour, 9 p.m. 'there was an outburst of noise, sudden confusion of messages. Every station was shouting "Bazookas", Kangaroos were being hit one after another. A Sherman was alight. From out of the darkness came a clash of Brens, Brownings and Spandaus. All through the night the Crocodiles stayed on guard because of the danger of a counter-attack.' The following day Wilson led the 14th Troop towards a village. Two were bogged in lush green fields, so Wilson took over Corporal Milner's Crocodile. He made three runs through the village, flaming barns, cottages, all the buildings, back and forth. He was seized by 'the same unfeeling madness as at Rosmalen [where he earned the MC]. 'It was all over. By the barn a group of grey clad Germans appeared without helmets or weapons waving a sheet on a pole.' Wilson stopped firing and opened the hatches. There were thirty or forty prisoners.

Trooper John Smith wrote: 'In Bienen the narrow lanes were littered with German weapons and equipment, Spandaus, Bazookas and vehicles, cars, carts, trailers, a field kitchen. On one corner a boot lay in the middle of the road. I gave it a kick and there was a foot in it.' They moved on to Emmerich over the new pontoon bridge, to Calcar, Goch and Uden and back to the original log cabins. For two weeks 'C' Squadron stayed in Weeze forest, with parades: a parade for the Colonel, a parade for General Hobart, a church parade. Then there was an advance on Arnhem via Zevenaar and Westervoort, with red tulips, storks' nests, fat cattle in the fields, orchards, girls waving from bedroom windows, fields fresh and green in the spring sunlight. 'C' Squadron passed through Oosterbeek, with all the sad litter of the airborne battle: red, green and white parachutes, scattered containers with mines, mortar bombs and anti-tank ammunition lying among the brambles, burnt out jeeps, a tattered Red Cross flag and a solitary grave marked 'Unknown British Soldier'. In Heelsum they found a brewed-up flail tank with two of the crew dead on a triple-mine. Then came Renkum, Wageningen, Zutphen, followed by a journey by tank transporter back to the German border again – Nordhern, Lingen and Route 70 to Meppen – a very long, boring Cooks tour, with no fighting and no flaming.

The 'B' Squadron Crocodiles of the Fife and Forfars took thirty minutes to cross Nan pontoon bridge on 27 March on their way to Mollen. For six months they had supported units of the American Army and they flamed vigorously at Koster on behalf of 320 US Regiment. Major W.B. Sheppard praised their efficiency, gallantry and quick sense of improvization. The American code name for 'B' Squadron was 'Alligator'. Emmerich was strongly held and the Canadian 7th Brigade in the factory area had been brought to a halt by heavy fire. So 'C' Squadron helped the Regina rifles in with 75s, Besa and later with flame. But an SP ambushed and killed Lieutenant Walford, wounding two of his crew. Nearby Groendhal and Hahnenkamp were defended by large roadblocks which held up the Fife's Crocodiles. Emmerich was destined to become the terminus for the 'Pluto' oil pipeline, which started at the River Mersey, then ran under the Channel and on to central Germany.

On 1 April Lieutenant Colonel W.G.N. Walker of the Fife and Forfars had under command units of the 1st Northants Yeomanry (Buffaloes), the Lothians (flails), the 7th RTR (Crocodiles), the 1st Canadian Armoured Car Regiment (CARC) (Kangaroos) and the 26th and 79th Assault Squadrons RE (AVREs) – a complete cross-section of Major General Hobart's 'Zoo'!

'B' Squadron spent the first two weeks of April with their American friends, mainly in the area of Bochum, a great steel city in the Ruhr. Lieutenants Bruce and Britten deployed their 'dragon breath' with success against snipers, machine guns and bazooka teams. On the 20th 'B' Squadron returned to the British 8 Corps control at Celle, on the River Aller. At the end of the month the Elbe bridges would not support the 50-ton weight of a Crocodile, so they were halted.

Arnhem was a key objective and the main attack on it was from the east across the River Ijssel at Westervoort and Gorsel. Buffaloes carried three battalions of Polar Bear infantry across and on 13 April the 'Zoo' poured across a new sapper-made bridge. 'A' Squadron, the Fifes, supported the 2nd Essex with a new partnership. Each Crocodile was closely followed by a Wasp (a Bren-gun carrier) flame-thrower to flame small targets which might have been missed by 'big brother'. The attack took two days and 'A' Squadron fired an immense amount of HE and Besa and a great deal of flaming. Next came Velp, where Major H.C. Walker led half the squadron in the south and Captain L. Thomas the other half in the north. Suddenly they were whisked off 109 miles over the German border into East Friesland to help to subdue the seaport of Emden. The 8th Canadian Infantry Brigade had Fife Crocodile support for two weeks until 4 May, clearing many road blocks, despite the many enormous road craters encountered in country totally unsuitable for tank work.

The Canadians also heavily relied on 'C' Squadron Crocodiles. From Dornick in the Rhine bridgehead they had a brisk flaming action on 4 April at Leesten against dug-in Hitler Youth troops. Both attacks took place in early evening and the flame effect was terrifying. Zutphen was their next action, but by the 15th they were being fêted by Dutch civilians in Leeuwarden. Ten days later, with new Crocodiles, they were on the outskirts of Bremen. Their last action with flame was to help the 43rd Wessex Wyverns take Tarmstedt near Bremerhaven.

A newcomer to the flame-thrower regiments, and part of the 79th Armoured Division, were the 7th Battalion RTR, who had landed in Normandy with their Churchill tanks as part of the 31st Tank Brigade. Later they took part in 'Asconia' at Le Havre and besieged Dunkirk. Perhaps to their surprise, in early February 1945 they found themselves at Waterscheideil, Belgium, a long way from the front line under the command of Lieutenant Colonel R.B.P. Wood. There the Fife and Forfars took them in hand and converted them to the rather different business of flame-throwing. The 7th RTR bestowed a silver salver on the officers of 'C' Squadron as thanks for their tuition. All three squadrons were involved in 'Plunder'. Captain Pearson of 'A' Squadron supported the Royal Scots Fusiliers on 26 March.

> The company commander pointed out the troublesome area, a house in the woods. We decided to blast the house with HE. The 95 mm and 75 mm of HQ Tp closed in. The enemy obliged by firing Spandau at the 95, whose driver Tp Bell cleverly spotted the exact position. The first round brought the house down; a second round and it was blazing nicely. Tpr Longford finished it off with a spray from his Besa. The company commander was happy and asked us to deal with one more house.

'A' Squadron supported the 15th Scottish Division and then helped the Canadians clear Holland with several opposed canal crossings. Deventer was liberated on 19 April, then came a 160-mile scurry in three days to Bremen.

At Delmenhorst Lieutenant De Groot and Corporal Ingall were part of Captain Pearson's half-squadron. '2 Tp led the attack at 2000 and flamed foxholes, dugouts and houses along the lateral road. They almost reached the crossroads when 3 Tp took over. By 2200 beautiful fires were burning along its entire length lighting the night.' The infantry commander asked them to clear some farm buildings 600 yards away, where they were lucky to escape bazookas fired at them.

'B' Squadron advanced on Bocholt with the 53rd Welsh; just to be on the safe side most of the town was brewed up. Then it was on to Alstatte, Gronau and Neuenkirchen. Ibbenburen was probably the toughest area of German resistance to the British 2nd Army. In bitter fighting with the officer cadets 'B' Squadron destroyed parts of the town with flame. Then with the 52nd Lowland and 7th Armoured Divisions they moved on to Hopsten, Recke, Bersenbruck and Diepholz. The River Weser was crossed at Nienburg and then there was an assault on Soltau. Pearson wrote: 'The lads had a real lust for burning down buildings at this time.' Then they moved to the outskirts of Bremen.

7 RTR Crocodile, belching flame, clearing fouled ground, Belsen
Concentration Camp, 16 April 1945

'C' Squadron had a frustrating two weeks moving from division
to division, corps to corps, with orders received and cancelled,
standing to and standing down. The speed of the advance was gener-
ally so fast that many set-piece attacks were cancelled. Nevertheless
on 10 April, linked with the 53rd Welsh, they had plenty of action
clearing the west bank of the River Aller and then crossing it. They
too arrived at Bremen with the 52nd Lowland Division via Walle,
Usen, Achim and Hastedt.

The Buffaloes

'Operation Anger' was the code name for the assault on Arnhem by
the 49th Polar Bear Division, with help from the 'Funnies'. For
months the German defenders on their heights north of the Neder
Rijn dominated the low-lying 'island' to the south. The 11th RTR
were to ferry the attack in from the east flank. The first task was to
get across the River Ijssel from Westervoort a few miles south-east
of Arnhem. The assault started at 11 p.m. on 12 April. The high
'bund' had not been breached to allow Buffaloes through into the

river; the Polar Bear sappers tried to blow three gaps but failed. Even when the Buffaloes were unloaded, only two of the dozen succeeded in getting up and over, then reloading with the infantry of the 56th Brigade. Captain Dunne of the 11th RTR was killed desperately trying to force an alternative route. Bulldozers tried to breach the bund, but failed. At 11.20 the 11th RTR struggled to get their Buffaloes away one by one. Another route was made at 12.40 a.m. soon after a Class 40 bridge was floated down the Neder Rijn and by 11.20, after 260 loads, the 56th Brigade were across. Captains E.R. Allan and J.J. Pollock distinguished themselves. Crabs and Crocodiles crossed, followed by the Polar Bears' second Brigade. It took two more days to clear Arnhem, with the whole of the 49th Division and the Lothians' Crabs, the Fife and Forfars' Crocodiles and the AVREs of 617 Assault Squadron in full cry.

Two weeks later, in 'Operation Enterprise', the 11th RTR Buffaloes, with the 77nd Assault Squadron RE, ferried the 44th Brigade of the 15th Scottish Division across the River Elbe, the last great water barrier. The 11th RTR travelled some 300 miles by slow transporters up winding roads, which took three days and nights.

'Flying Dustbin' Spigot mortar bomb fired by AVRE to demolish road block in Bocholt, 29 March 1945 (Birkin Haward).

239

There were two crossing points, Hohnstorf on the right opposite Lauenburg and Artlenburg to the left. 'B' Squadron, the 11th RTR and the 77th Assault Squadron RE, were to lift the 1st Commando Brigade, and 'A' and 'C' Squadrons would lift the 8th Royal Scots and the 6th Royal Scots Fusiliers respectively. The preplanning for the Commando Brigade was haphazard and for the Scottish Brigade first class. From Scharnesbeck Forest the Buffaloes moved out in a long single line to the marshalling area. The artillery barrage came down and all the crossings were made successfully with minimum opposition. At this late stage the Luftwaffe inflicted casualties (eight including Captain Jock Barclay who was killed) but the Polsten 20 mm, .3 and .5 Brownings of the Buffaloes put up tremendous AA fire, claiming a Focke-Wulfe 190. At 11 a.m. on 30 April the RE opened a Class 40 bridge for the author's Comets of 11th Armoured Division to cross on their way to Kiel and the Danish borders. The Buffaloes of 11th RTR and 77th Assault Squadron RE made 1,139 lifts during 'Enterprise' of infantry, carriers, jeeps, scout cars, Weasels, anti-tank guns and trailers.

The 4th RTR, formerly 144 RAC, joined the 79th Armoured Division and changed their Shermans for Buffaloes in time for 'Plunder'. They carried the 5th Black Watch, the 1st Gordons and 5/7 Gordons fairly safely across the Rhine on their way to help take Rees. Their next major crossing was to swim the 1st Canadian Division across the River Ijssel at Gorssel, north of Zutphen.

It was a classic crossing, using smokescreens and artillery fire for cover. By 13 April the RE had built a bridge for the last of nine battalions to cross. In three days the 4th RTR had ferried the rest across. Lieutenant A.S. King of the 4th RTR and Lieutenant J.H. Wilson of the 79th Assault Squadron RE distinguished themselves during 'Enterprise'.

Then on 25 April the 4th RTR provided the Buffaloes to help the 3rd British Division take Arsten (a suburb of Bremen) over heavily flooded and boggy ground. Captain Harris commanded the fleet of forty-seven Buffaloes, and they made 115 trips before ferrying ceased. The CO of the bewildered defenders thought it most unfair of the *schwimpanzers* to launch the 2nd Royal Ulster Rifles (RUR) across 3 feet of flood water!

Their last action was for 'A' Squadron to ferry stores, casualties, vehicles and captured Germans for 505 US Infantry Regiment and Lieutenant General Ridgeway sent them a nice letter of thanks.

The Kangaroos

In December the 49th RTR (and the 1st Canadian Armoured Carrier Regiment) came under the command of the 79th Armoured Division with their Kangaroo fleet, turretless tanks converted to carry eight infantrymen in reasonable security. The Canadian-built Rams, which were similar to Shermans, had been used by the Canadians with considerable success earlier in Operation 'Totalise'. They helped the 15th Scottish Division at Blerick and later carried them during Operation 'Veritable'. Two hundred and fifty vehicles were overhauled in two weeks by REME workshops. Seven were knocked out in the Calcar action. The Goch, Bucholt, Kervenheim, Winnenken and Donck actions all needed Kangaroos. 'B' Squadron used their CDL tactics with effect at the Rhine crossing. Over the Rhine, 'F' Squadron north of Rhede carried the 53rd Welsh Division and lost eight Kangaroos.

On 1 April 'A' Squadron carried the Queen's Brigade infantry of the 7th Armoured Division from Ahaus to Metelen. 'C' carried the 43rd Wessex Wyverns into Borne and 'F', the 53rd Welsh, near Rheine. All the squadrons 'empouched' their infantry with considerable dash.

'F' Squadron carried 52nd Lowland troops east of Hopsten, and late in April 'A' Squadron continued to carry the Desert Rats infantry to Walsrode and then went up to Liebingen with the 79th US Division infantry. 'C' continued with the Wessex Wyverns and 'F' with the Welsh from the River Aller to Walsrode and Holtum. Both 'C' and 'A' were involved in the capture of Bremen, with actions near Mahndorf, Hastedt and Bassen, while 'F' continued to support the Desert Rats to Neundorf and Sieversen. The 49th APC carried the 51st Highlanders into Bremervorde, and the 7th Armoured Division infantry into the mined city of Hamburg on 2 May.

An accolade to the 49th APC came from Brigadier Carver, officer commanding the 4th Armoured Brigade, who had enjoyed two weeks' profitable partnership with the 53rd Welsh in the River Aller battles.

This was a powerful, flexible and effective organisation. It was proved that a normal infantry battalion from an infantry division which had *never* fought in 'Kangaroos', had never undertaken a similar operation before, had only 'married up' with their armoured regiment on the day on which the operation started, could very quickly adapt itself and could function efficiently in this new role. . . . Together we did a great deal of damage to the enemy.

AVREs advance: armoured dozer leads, then scissor bridge on
Churchill AVRE. On left AVRE with fascine

The AVRES

After the Rhine crossing, the 82nd Assault Squadron supported the
53rd Welsh Division whilst the 81st and 284 were put into 12 Corps
reserve. The 26th Assault Squadron had two troops with the 51st
Highland Division, another with the 43rd Wessex Wyverns. The
16th Assault Squadron RE were with the 3rd British Division, as
were 617 Assault Squadron. Both 222 and 79 were in reserve with 30
Corps and the 2nd Canadian Army.

With fast-moving battles on a wide front there were scores of
engagements where petarding of blockhouses or pill-boxes were
needed, SBG bridges had to be dropped and craters filled with
fascines. For instance in a seventeen-day period in April, the 16th
Assault Squadron dropped two assault bridges, built a Jumbo 160-
foot bridge of folding boats and had street-fighting actions with
Besa and Petards in the course of their 130-mile advance. Captain
Wilton's troop helped capture Cloppenburg, and another launched
a skid Bailey bridge west of Bocholt over the River Aa. The 22nd
Assault Squadron also built two skid Bailey bridges, and the 82nd

dropped assault bridges near Rethem and later near Bremervorde. The 49th Polar Bears were helped by 617 Assault Regiment on the flooded Nijmegen–Arnhem 'island', dropping fascines and an assault bridge, crossing the River Ijssel on rafts and destroying road-blocks in Arnhem with Wade charges or Petard fire.

On 17 April Captain Warde earned a bar to his MC in an attack on Otterlo, near Barneveld.

> We moved up the road, petards were cocked and Besas loaded. About 500 yards on we ran into a platoon of enemy coming down the road and through the woods on either side. We opened fire with our Besas and advanced towards them. They tried to give up but we had no infantry with us and were unable to take PoW. Those that were not killed by Besa fire were killed by .36 grenades thrown from the tanks as we passed them and by AVRE commanders firing their pistols. 800 yards further up the road on the outskirts of Otterlo we gave the enemy who were fairly thick on the ground the same treatment. In the village we used our Petards against enemy occupied houses and large groups of enemy in the open.

Warde's tank later received four direct hits from 75 mm HE fire from guns in a wood to the right. 'My crew baled out and set to with spanners to remove the twisted metal sandshields jamming the turret.' In front was a battery of Canadian 25-pounders which had been overrun. 'On the edge of the wood the five AVREs halted and two salvoes of Petards were fired at maximum elevation into the wood after which the infantry went in.'

About fifty to a hundred Germans were killed or wounded, a 75 mm gun received a direct hit, and the battery of 25-pounders was recovered.

The 87th Assault Squadron had had their AVREs swapped in January for Centaur-dozers, with which they trained in Belgium. They were kept busy thereafter and helped clear the Bremen dock areas at the end of April. Later still the 16th and 82nd Assault Squadron cleared up on the way to Hamburg. A few days before the ceasefire at 8 a.m. on 4 May, the 82nd Assault Squadron had four casualties dropping an assault bridge at Bremervorde. On V-E Day the 1st Assault Engineer Brigade had a strength of 158 officers and 3,611 other ranks, and their vehicles included 186 AVREs, 9 AVRs, 12 armoured bulldozers, 25 Buffaloes and 36 Centaur-dozers.

Tank dozer pushes enemy tank off the Bremervorde road, 1 May 1945
(Birkin Haward)

The Last Battle – The Capture of Bremen

Four British divisions had closed in on Bremen but Adolf Hitler had
determined that the defence would be made in the small towns to
the west, south-west and south. Units of 'Funnies' supported the
7th Armoured, 3rd British, 43rd Wessex Wyverns and 52nd
Lowland Divisions.

For the capture of Bremen the 22nd Dragoons supported the 3rd
British Division, two squadrons with the 2nd Lincolns and the 1st
KOSB. The battle began on the night of 24/25 April with heavy
fighting around Kattenturm. Corporal Tremeer won the MM
destroying a rather vigorous 88 mm anti-tank gun, and the airfield
and ruins of the Focke-Wulfe factory were occupied. Then came a
sudden call to join the 51st Highland Division and help take
Bremervorde. In Glinde 'A' Squadron lost Captain 'Pat' Sadler to
shellfire which severely wounded Lieutenant Hickey, who died on
14 May. Major Birt described Sadler as 'one of those happy spirits –
a leader in a battle who showed the same combination of shrewdness
and caution, with reckless disregard for his own safety. As a friend

he was steel-true and much loved.' 'B' Squadron suffered too. Sergeant Stirling knocked out an SP at short range, but its companion had its revenge, killing Stirling and Trooper Taylor. Stirling had been with the 22nd Dragoons for five years of loyal service.

The flail regiments were mainly used as gun tanks but the Crocodiles of the 7th RTR had flame actions in Uphusen, Mahndorf and Hastedt. They flamed the 3rd Division into Dreye, Arsten and Harlenhausen on the 25th whilst 'B' Squadron helped the 52nd Lowland Division take 800 prisoners on the 25th and 26th. The Centaur-dozers of the 87th Assault Squadron RE were in great demand clearing the RAF-bomb-damaged roads and dock area. The 16th, 82nd and 222 Assault Squadrons RE petarded their way into Bremen, clearing roadblocks, laying a skid Bailey bridge and dropping fascines. By the 28th Bremen was clear. The 'Funnies' had been in at the death of this huge, battered city.

Assault bridge laid by 82 Assault Squadron RE in final action at
Bremevorde, 2 May 1945 (Birkin Haward)

Envoi

V-E Day was celebrated by the British Army in a variety of ways. The Fife and Forfar Yeomanry staged a great firework display; 'B' Squadron cut a great 'V' in the earth, filled it with flame-throwing fuel; when ignited it was a spectacular sight.

Lieutenant Ian Hammerton mourned the loss of Sergeant Stirling and Trooper Taylor at Gline. 'Our joy at learning that there was no more fighting was enormous but our joy greatly dampened by the loss of two great friends and comrades.' On 15 May the 22nd Dragoons held an open-air thanksgiving service, and a memorial service on 19 June. Major Birt wrote:

> Meanwhile the darkening sky above Bremervorde and Glinde was filled with a firework display that in variety if not in weight outdid the best that 21st Army Group's gunners ever managed – Smoke, Tracer, Very Lights, Star Shells, Bofors tracer – all were flung up into the sky – winking, flashing, joyous signals of a victory unparalleled.

After six very enjoyable weeks in Holland the Westminster Dragoons returned to Germany. On 19 June Major General Hobart addressed the regiment standing on a jeep, with the red, gold and purple of the regimental flag in the background.

> Many of you will soon once again become civilians. Some of you may go to the Far East and Japan where there is still a war to finish. You will forget many of the things that happened in this last year. The hard times and the unpleasant moments. None of you will ever forget the memory of the spirit of comradeship, the spirit of the Westminster Dragoons.

But to many there was a strange sense of anti-climax. Trooper John Smith of 'C' Squadron, the Buffs, commented: 'Canadians of the Toronto Scottish were parading for drill every morning with scrubbed belts and polished brasses. German prisoners streamed in by the thousands without guards, driving their own trucks and singing 'Tipperary'. It was all crazy and there was a sudden feeling of emptiness and pointlessness about everything we were now doing.' Even the brave dashing Playboys of 'B' Squadron had the same cafard. Captain Harry Bailey wrote:

> The war was fizzling out for the Playboys, fizzling out in the rain and mud of that miserable forest near Meppen in deadly boredom in the leaking bivouacs, listening only to the rumours and counter-rumours of the endless news bulletins. And when the final news did come out, it was all too prosaic. It was typical of this fantastic campaign that the greatest moment of all should fall so flat – it had been too long expected. But somehow that evening the memory of those that had died seemed stronger. There was a nostalgia – some of us had woken at last from a bad dream, but some of it remained so irrevocably real and true.

In their eleven months of continuous fighting Hobart's 'Funnies' suffered nearly 1,600 casualties including 286 killed in action. Hobart sent the 79th Armoured Division the following farewell message:

> Owing to the requirements of the Far East, orders have now been received for the disbandment of the 79th Armoured Division.
>
> This Division was formed as a normal armoured division in October 1942. In April 1943 it was changed to its present role. It was given a completely novel task which had no parallel in the British, or any other Army.
>
> The 79th Armoured Division was unique in many respects. No other Division was 'all armoured'. No other Division achieved a size of over 1,500 tanks. No other Division had the great responsibility of introducing and proving the value of so many new and important weapons. These weapons had never been tried in war, and there was scepticism as to their value. Had they been less skilfully and gallantly handled their importance might never have been recognised, and the Army would have been deprived of weapons which made success swifter and less costly, and which in some cases were decisive.
>
> On 'D' Day, 6 June 1944, we were the first to land on the Normandy beaches. The success of those landings was decisive. The

small cost at which they were achieved was in no small part due to specialised armour. From then onwards, troops of the 79th Armoured Division have fought with distinction on every battlefield in FRANCE, BELGIUM, HOLLAND and GERMANY; taken a leading part in the crossings of the SCHELDT, RHINE and ELBE; and supported almost every Division of the British Second and Canadian First Armies in action. They have also fought in support of many formations of the United States Army. Owing to the needs of secrecy, our units have received little publicity but wherever they have fought they have received praise and distinction. Many of these tributes from Senior Commanders of British, Canadian and American formations have been repeated in orders. It is sufficient here to republish the words of our Commander-in-Chief, Field-Marshal Sir Bernard Montgomery: 'The record of the Division is unique and its contribution to the winning of the Campaign in NW Europe incalculable.'

This success was achieved by you all. You who fought the Armoured Vehicles with such skill and courage; you of the Services who worked so untiringly behind the front; and you of Headquarters Staffs and Signals whose long hours of equally vital work are not always appreciated as they should be.

It has been achieved by team work; that is mutual trust, devotion to duty, and an unflagging spirit. It is what has made and sustained our nation through the centuries.

I have had the honour and happiness of having commanded 79th Armoured Division since its formation.

We can look back on it with pride and satisfaction. The spirit of the 79th Armoured Division will live on in the similar Specialised Armour Formation which the Commander-in-Chief has recommended be included in all future Expeditionary Forces.

We have fought our fight.
Goodbye, and thank you.

	PCS HOBART
20 August 1945	Major-General
Germany	Commanding 79 Armoured Division

Captain Harry Bailey wrote:

The story ends, but the melody will for ever linger on. No more, no less than millions of others, the Playboys in the world's crucial hour of suffering and tribulation gave of their best, to the supreme sacrifice. Tough, noble, generous, laughing at the odds. I pay tribute to the greatest bunch of guys I ever knew. John Dean, Roland Beechey, Peter Sander, Freddie Roberts, Ginger Deverson, Tom Vernon – the long, long line of heroes and the far-off echo of the blazing guns.

Winston Churchill would have been proud of his huge armoured force, Hobart's 'Funnies', who with their fearful weapons – many inspired, possibly created, by him – helped destroy the Third Reich.

Bibliography

Books

Bailey, Harry, *The Playboys* (141 RAC)
Birt, W.R., *XXII Dragoons 1760–1945*
Borthwick, Alastair, *Sans Peur*
Bryant, Arthur, *Turn of the Tide* (Alan Brooke diaries)
Churchill, Winston, *The Second World War*
Hammerton, Ian, *Achtung Minen* (22 Dragoons)
Lawson/Huy-Williams, *Westminster Dragoons 1901–67*
Macksey, Kenneth, *Armoured Crusader*
Macrae, Stuart, *Winston Churchill's Toyshop*
Miller, C.H., *13/18 Royal Hussars 1922–47*
Smith, J.G., *In at the Finish* (141 RAC)
Stirling, John, *4/7 Royal Dragoons Guards*
Thompson, R.W., *The 85 Days* (Walcheren Campaign)
Wilson, Andrew, *Flamethrower* (141 RAC)

Journals/Articles

Bullock, Richard, 'D-Day Remembered' (Westminster Dragoons)
Dewing, Geoff, 'Aldeburgh 1939–45'
Ellis, Raymond, 82 Assault Sqn RE
Gardiner, Andrew, 'A Romantic with the Yeomanry (Lothians & Borders Yeomanry)
Leytham, John, 82 Assault Sqn RE
Mee, Ken, 'Before and During the 2nd Front' (70 Assault Sqn RE)
Reagan, Martin, 284 Assault Sqn RE
Squirrell, Lt Col David, 'Tactical handling & usage of specialised armour'
Ward, Major Roland, 617 Assault Sqn RE

Bibliography

Wells, L.A., 'Projectors to Petards' (80 Assault Sqn RE)
Wilford, Michael, 82 Assault Sqn RE
Wood, T.W., 'On Tracks' (617 Assault Sqn RE)
Woollett, Major General John, articles in the *Sapper*
Younger, Major General A.E., articles in the *Sapper*

Letters

Charles Baldwin
John R. Bull
Monty Clay
Bernard Cuttiford
Tom Davis
Alan Duncan
Geoffrey Flint
Brian Hutchison
Ian Isley
E. (Doc) Kitson
John M. Leytham
J. Robinson
Syd Sadler
Charles Salt

Index